THE
LAW
OF
MOSES

AMY HARMON

FOR MARY SUTORIUS,
MY NANA,
WHO WOULD HAVE LOVED
THAT I TURNED OUT TO BE A WRITER

PROLOGUE

THE FIRST FEW WORDS of every story are always the hardest to write. It's almost as if pulling them out, putting them on paper, commits you to seeing it all through. As if once you start, you are required to finish. And how do you finish when some things never end? This is the story of love with no end . . . though it took me a while to get there.

If I tell you right up front, right in the beginning that I lost him, it will be easier for you to bear. You will know it's coming, and it will hurt. It will still make your chest ache and your stomach flip with dread. But you'll know, and you'll be able to prepare. And that's my gift to you. I wasn't given that same courtesy. I wasn't prepared.

And after he was gone? It got worse, not better. The days grew harder, not easier. The regret was just as intense, the sorrow just as cutting, the endless stretch of days before me, days spent without him, just as hard. In truth—since I've decided that's all I have—I would gladly submit myself to anything else. Anything but that. But that is what was given to me. And I wasn't prepared.

I can't tell you how it felt. How it still feels. I can't. Words feel cheap and ring hollow and turn everything I say, everything I feel, into a tawdry romance novel full of flowery phrases designed to illicit sympathetic tears and an immediate response. A response that has nothing to do with reality and everything to do with easy emotion that you can set aside when you close the cover. Emotion that has you wiping your eyes and chirping a happy hiccup, appreciating the fact that it was all just a story. And best of all, not your story. But this isn't like that.

Because it is my story. And I wasn't prepared.

PART 1
BEFORE

I

GEORGIA

THEY FOUND MOSES in a laundry basket at the Quick Wash, wrapped in a towel, a few hours old and close to death. A woman heard him cry and picked him up, putting him against her skin and wrapping them both in her coat until she could get help. She didn't know who his mother was or if she was coming back, she only knew that he wasn't wanted, that he was dying, and that if she didn't get him to a hospital soon, it would be too late.

They called him a crack baby. My mom told me crack babies are what they call babies who are born addicted to cocaine because their mothers do drugs while they are pregnant. Crack babies are usually smaller than other babies because most of them are born too early to unhealthy moms. The cocaine alters their brain chemistry and they suffer from things like ADHD and impulse control. Sometimes they suffer from seizures and mental disorders. Sometimes they suffer from hallucinations and hyper sensitivity. It was believed that Moses would suffer from some of these things, maybe all of these things.

They shared his story on the ten o'clock news. It was a great story, a human interest piece—a little baby left in a basket at a dingy laundromat in a bad neighborhood in West Valley City. My mom says she remembers the story well, the pathetic shots of the baby in the hospital, hanging onto life, a feeding tube in his stomach and a little blue hat on his tiny head. They found the mother three days later, not that anyone wanted to hand the baby over. But they didn't have to. She was dead. The woman who had abandoned her baby in a laundromat was pronounced dead on arrival from an apparent overdose at the very same hospital where her baby lay struggling for life, several floors above her. Somebody had found her too, though not in a laundromat.

The roommate, arrested that same evening for prostitution and possession, told the police what she knew about the woman and her abandoned baby in hopes of getting a little leniency. An autopsy of the woman's body showed she had, indeed, given birth very recently. And later, DNA testing proved that the baby was hers. What a lucky little guy.

He was "the baby in the basket" in news reports, and the hospital staff dubbed him baby Moses. But baby Moses wasn't found by the daughter of the Pharaoh like the biblical Moses. He wasn't raised in a palace. He didn't have a sister watching from the reeds, making sure his basket was pulled from the Nile. But he did have some family—Mom said the whole town was a buzz when it was discovered that baby Moses's deceased mother was sort of a local girl, a girl named Jennifer Wright who had spent summers with her grandmother, who lived just down the street from our house. The grandmother was still in the area, Jennifer's parents lived in a neighboring town, and a couple of her siblings, who had moved away, were still well-known by many as well. So little Moses had some family after all, not that any of them wanted a sick baby who was predicted to have all sorts of problems. Jennifer Wright had broken their hearts and left her family tired and shattered. Mom told me drugs do that. So the fact that she left them with a crack baby didn't seem especially surprising. My mom said she'd just been a regular girl when she was younger. Pretty, nice, smart, even. But not smart enough to stay away from meth, cocaine, and whatever else she became a slave to. I imagined the crack baby, Moses, having a giant crack that ran down his body, like he'd been broken at birth. I knew that wasn't what the term meant. But the image stuck in my mind. Maybe the fact that he was

12

broken drew me to him from the start.

My mom said the whole town followed the story of baby Moses Wright when it happened, watching the reports, pretending like they had the inside scoop, and making up what they didn't know, just to feel important. But I never knew baby Moses, because baby Moses grew up to be just plain Moses, juggled between Jennifer Wright's family members, passed around when he became too much to take, transferred to another sibling or parent who then put up with him for a while before making someone else step in and take their turn. It all happened before I was born, and by the time I met him and my mom told me about him in an effort to help me "understand him and be kind," the story was old news and nobody wanted anything to do with him. People love babies, even sick babies. Even crack babies. But babies grow up to be kids. Nobody really wants messed up kids.

And Moses was messed up.

I knew all about messed up kids by the time I met Moses. My parents were foster parents to lots of messed up kids. They'd been taking in kids all my life. I had two older sisters and an older brother who were out of the house by the time I was six. I'd been kind of an oops, and I ended up being raised with kids who weren't my siblings and who came in and out of my life in stages and revolving doors. Maybe that was why my parents and Kathleen Wright, Jennifer Wright's grandma and Moses's great-grandma, had several conversations about Moses sitting at our kitchen table. I heard a lot of things I probably had no business knowing. Especially that summer.

The old lady was taking Moses in for good. He would be eighteen in a month and everyone else was ready to wash their hands of him. He'd spent time with her every summer since he was little, and she was confident they would do well together if everyone would just butt out and let her do her thing. She didn't seem concerned about the fact that the month Moses turned eighteen she would turn eighty.

I knew who he was and remembered him from summer to summer, though I'd never spent any time with him. It was a small town and kids notice each other. Kathleen Wright would bring him to church for the few Sundays he was in town. He was in my Sunday school class, and we all enjoyed staring at him while the teacher tried to coax him into participating. He never did. He just sat in his little metal folding chair like he'd been heavily bribed to do so, his oddly-colored eyes roving here and there, his hands twisting in his lap. And when it was over he would race for the door and out into the sunshine, heading straight for home without waiting for his great-grandma. I would try to race him, but he always managed to get out of his seat and out the door faster than I could. Even then I was chasing him.

Sometimes, Moses and his grandma would go for bike rides and walks, and she would haul him into the pool in Nephi almost every day, which had always made me so jealous. I was lucky if I got to go to the pool more than a few times all summer. When I was desperate for a swim, I'd ride my bike to a fishing hole up Chicken Creek canyon. My parents had forbidden me to swim there because it was so cold and deep and murky—dangerous even. But drowning was preferable to never swimming at all, and I'd managed not to drown so far.

As Moses got older, there were some summers when he didn't come to Levan at all. It had been two years since he'd been back, though Kathleen had been pushing for him to come stay with her permanently for a long time. The family told her he would be too much for her to handle. They told her he was "too emotional, too explosive, too temperamental." But apparently, they were all exhausted and they gave in. So Moses moved to Levan.

We were both entering our senior year, though I was young for my grade and he was a full year older. We both had summer birthdays— Moses turned eighteen July 2nd and I turned seventeen August 28th. But Moses didn't look eighteen. In the two years since I'd seen him last, he'd grown into his feet and his eyes. He was tall with broad shoulders and clearly-defined, ropy muscles that covered his lean frame, and his light eyes, strong cheekbones, and angled jaw made him look more like an Egyptian prince than a gang banger, which rumors claimed he was.

Moses struggled with his school work and had difficulty concentrating and holding still. His family even claimed he had seizures and hallucinations, which they attempted to control with various medications. I heard his grandma telling my mom that he could be moody and irritable, that he had difficulty sleeping, and that he zoned out a lot. She said he was extremely intelligent, brilliant even, and he could paint like nothing and no one she'd ever seen before. But all the medication they had him on to help him focus and sit still in school made him slow and sluggish and made his art dark and frightening. Kathleen Wright told my mother she was taking him off all the pills.

"They turn him into a zombie," I heard her say. "I'm willing to take my chances with a kid who can't hold still and can't stop painting. In my day, that wasn't a bad thing."

I thought a zombie sounded a little safer. For all his beauty, Moses Wright was scary looking. With his tapered body covered in bronze skin, and those funky-colored, light eyes, he reminded me of a jungle cat. Sleek, dangerous, silent. At least a zombie moves slowly. Jungle cats pounce. Being around Moses Wright was like befriending a panther, and I admired the old lady for taking him on. In fact, she had more courage than anyone I knew.

Being one of only three girls my age in the whole town made me a loner more often than I liked, especially considering neither of the other girls liked horses and rodeo the way I did. We were friendly enough to say hello and sit by each other in church, but not friendly enough to spend time together or pass the boring summer days in each other's company.

It was an especially hot summer. I remember that well. We'd had the driest spring ever recorded, which led to summer wildfires popping up all over the west. Farmers were praying for rain and the sizzling nerves and sky-rocketing temperatures made tempers short and self-control shorter. There'd also been a rash of disappearances throughout the clustered counties of central Utah. A couple of girls had gone missing in two different counties, though one was thought to have run away with her boyfriend and the other was almost eighteen and her home life was bad. People assumed they were okay, but there had been a few similar disappearances in the last ten or fifteen years that had never been resolved, and it made parents edgy and a little more watchful, and my parents were no exception.

I'd grown restless and resentful, itchy in my own skin, eager to be done with school and on with life. I was a barrel racer and I wanted to hitch the horse trailer to my truck and follow the rodeo circuit, seeking freedom with only my horses, my projected rodeo winnings, and the open road. I wanted that so badly. But at seventeen, with disappearing females in the forefront of their minds, my parents wouldn't let me go on my own, and they weren't in any position to take me. They promised me we'd figure something out when I graduated and turned eighteen. But graduation was so far away, and summer stretched out in front of me like a dry, empty desert. I was so thirsty for something else. Maybe that was it. Maybe that was the reason I waded in too far, the reason I got in way over my head.

Whatever it was, when Moses came to Levan, he was like water—cold, deep, unpredictable, and, like the pond up the canyon, dangerous, because you could never see what was beneath the surface. And just like I'd done all my life, I jumped in head first, even though I'd been forbidden. But this time, I drowned.

"WHAT ARE YOU LOOKIN' AT?" I said sharply, finally giving Moses what I assumed he wanted, which was my attention. All the kids my parents took in soaked up attention like it was as necessary as air and they were all gasping to breathe. I hated it. Not the fact that they needed it from my parents, but that they also seemed to need it from me. I liked nothing better than being alone with the horses. Horses weren't needy, and everybody else was so needy I thought I was going to lose my mind. Now Moses was here, in the barn, watching me, invading my time with Sackett and Lucky, my horses, sucking all the oxygen out of the room the way all the foster kids did.

Kathleen Wright had asked my parents if Moses could work out some of his new, un-medicated energy on our little farm. She said he would muck stalls, weed the garden, mow the lawn, feed the chickens, whatever they had available if they would help keep him busy that summer and into the school year if it all worked out. Those were all my chores, and I was happy to have him help if it meant I wouldn't have to do any of them. But my dad found other things for Moses to do and Moses worked hard—so hard that my dad was running out of jobs. It would be impossible to keep him busy all summer.

Apparently, my dad had included cleaning the barn on the list and Moses had been stacking hay bales, sweeping, shoveling, and organizing tack like a mad man all morning. I didn't know whether or not I wanted him there. Especially when he stopped suddenly and just stood, hands at his sides, staring. But Moses wasn't looking at me. He was staring over my shoulder and his yellowish-green animal eyes were huge. He was holding perfectly still, which I'd never seen him do, not even once since he arrived. Moses didn't respond to my question but his fingers moved, flexing and closing like he was trying to improve his circulation. It was what I did while waiting for the bus when I forgot my gloves. But it was June, unseasonably hot, and I doubted his fingers were cold.

"MOSES!" I barked, trying to snap him out of it. The next thing I knew he would be writhing on the floor, twitching, and I would have to do mouth to mouth or something. The thought of putting my lips on his lips made my stomach feel strange. I wondered if I could press my mouth to Moses's, even if it was just to force air into him. He wasn't ugly. I felt that funny swoosh once more, a slipping in my gut that wasn't exactly unpleasant. Moses wasn't ugly at all. He was strangely beautiful—different looking, especially those weird wolf eyes, and I had to admit to myself, on Moses, different looked good. It looked cool. Too bad he was cracked.

My parents used horses for therapy with the foster kids. In fact, theirs was a world-renowned program, all non-verbal kind of stuff, you know, because horses can't talk. That was something my parents said in their sales pitch to make people laugh and put them at ease. Horses can't talk, but sometimes, kids can't talk either, and equine therapy—a fancy term for bonding with a horse and figuring things out about themselves by watching the horse —was how my parents made a living. That, and my dad was a vet, which was what I wanted to be when I grew up. Our horses were well-trained and used to kids. They knew to stand still when a kid approached, when a child was near. They were unfailingly patient.

They would allow a stranger to slip a bridle on, even curling their lips to allow the bit. And children responded to them in ways that had the grown-ups using words like "miracle" and "break-through" whenever the troubled kids my parents took in returned to their families or moved on from ours.

Moses had been hanging around for the last two weeks, working, weeding, eating—holy crap could he eat—and generally getting on my nerves because he was so unsettling. He didn't do anything wrong, ex-actly. He just made me jittery. He didn't talk to me, which I convinced myself was his only redeeming quality. That and his cool eyes. And his muscles. I flinched, slightly repulsed at myself. He was weird. What was I thinking?

"Have you ever ridden a horse?" I asked, trying to distract myself.

Moses seemed to tear himself away from the daydream that had him standing and staring off at nothing.

His eyes re-focused on me briefly but he didn't respond. So I re-peated myself.

He shook his head.

"No? Have you ever been close to one?"

He shook his head once more.

"Come on. Come closer," I said, nodding toward the horse. I was thinking maybe I could help Moses with some equine therapy, just like Mom and Dad. I'd seen them work. I thought maybe I could do what they did. Maybe I could fix his cracked brain.

Moses stepped back like he was afraid. In the weeks he'd been working on the farm he'd never gotten close to the animals. Ever. He just watched them. He watched me. And he never talked.

"Go ahead. Sackett's the best horse ever. At least give him a pat."

"I'll scare him," Moses responded. I was startled once more. It was the first time I'd heard him speak and his voice wasn't two-toned like my foster brother Bobbie's and so many other boys, as if it was hover-ing between the steps that would eventually take him to the basement, squeaking and shifting, before finally sinking into position. Moses's voice was deep and warm and so soft it tickled my heart a little as it settled on me.

"No you won't. Sackett doesn't get excited about anything. Nothing scares him or makes him nervous or anything. He would sit here all day and let you hug him if you wanted to. Now, Lucky, on the other hand, might bite off your hand and kick you in the face. But not Sackett."

Lucky was a horse I'd been wooing for months, a horse someone had given my dad as payment for services they couldn't afford. My dad didn't have time for Lucky's attitude, and he had turned him over to me and said, "Be careful."

I had laughed. I wasn't ever careful.

He laughed too, but then warned, "I'm serious, George. This guy is named Lucky for a reason. You'll be lucky if he ever lets you ride him."

"Animals don't like me." Moses's voice was so faint I wasn't sure I heard him right. I shook off thoughts of Lucky and patted my faithful companion, the horse that had been mine for as long as I had been able to ride.

"Sackett loves everyone."

"He won't like me. Or maybe it's not me. Maybe it's them."

I looked around in confusion. There was no one in the barn but Sackett, Moses, and me. "Them who?" I asked. "It's just us, dude."

Moses didn't answer.

So I stared at him, waiting, raising my eyebrows in challenge. I stroked Sackett's nose and down the side of his neck. Sackett didn't move a muscle.

"See? He's like a statue. He just soaks up the love. Come on."

Moses took a step forward and raised his hand tentatively, reaching toward Sackett. Sackett whinnied nervously.

Moses dropped his hand immediately and stepped back.

I laughed. "What the hell?"

Maybe I should have listened to Moses about animals not liking him. But I didn't. I guess I didn't believe him. Wouldn't be the last time.

"You're not going to wimp out are you?" I taunted. "Touch him. He won't hurt you."

Moses leveled his golden-green eyes at me, considered what I had said, and then reached forward once more, taking another step as he stretched out his fingers.

And just like that, Sackett reared up on his hind legs like he'd been hanging around Lucky too long. It was completely out of character for the horse I'd known all my life, the horse who hadn't bucked once in all the years I'd loved him. I didn't have a chance to scream or shout or even reach for his halter. Instead, I got a hooved foot in my forehead, and I went down like a sack of flour.

Blood stung my eyes when I opened them and stared up into the rafters of the old barn. I was laying on my back and my head hurt like I'd been kicked by a horse—I realized suddenly that I *had* been kicked by a horse. By Sackett. The shock was almost greater than the pain.

"Georgia?"

I focused blearily on the face that suddenly loomed above me, cutting off my view of crisscrossing beams and dust motes dancing in the streaky sunlight peeking through the cracks along the walls.

Moses held my head in his lap, pressing his T-shirt to my forehead. Even in my dazed state, I still noticed the naked shoulders and chest and felt the smooth skin of his abdomen against my cheek.

"I need to get help, okay?" He shifted, moving my head to the floor, still holding his shirt to my bloody forehead. I tried not to look at the amount of blood on that shirt.

"No! Wait! Where's Sackett?" I said, trying to sit up. Moses pushed me back down and looked at the door as if he had no idea what to do.

"He . . . bolted," he answered slowly.

I remembered that Sackett hadn't been tied off. I'd never needed to restrain him before. I couldn't imagine what had gotten into my horse to make him rear up and then go tearing out of the barn. My eyes found Moses again.

"How bad is it?" I tried to sound like Clint Eastwood or someone who could handle a devastating head wound and still not lose his cool. But my voice wobbled a little.

Moses swallowed sympathetically, his Adam's apple bobbing up and down in his brown throat. His hands were shaking too. He was as upset as I was. It was easy to see.

"I don't know. It isn't wide. But it's bleeding a lot."

"Animals really don't like you, do they?" I whispered.

Moses didn't pretend not to understand. He shook his head. "I make them nervous. All animals. Not just Sackett."

He made *me* nervous too. But nervous in a good way. Nervous in a way that fascinated me. And even though my head was pounding and there was blood in my eyes, I wanted him to stay. And I wanted him to tell me all his secrets.

As if he felt the shift in me and didn't welcome it, Moses was up and running, leaving me with his T-shirt pressed to my head and a sudden insatiable interest in the new kid in town. It wasn't long before he returned, my mom trotting behind him, Moses's grandma bringing up the distant rear. Alarm was stamped across her face as well as my mom's, and seeing their concern made me wonder if the wound was worse than I thought. I experienced a flash of female vanity, a new experience for me. Would I have a big scar running down my forehead? A week ago I might have thought that was cool. Suddenly, I didn't want a scar. I wanted Moses to think I was beautiful.

He stood back, way back, letting the adults fuss and swarm. When it was determined that I could probably get by without an expensive trip to the ER and a couple butterfly bandages were applied to hold the gash together, Moses slipped away. Equine therapy wasn't going to heal the cracks in Moses Wright, but I promised myself that I would worm my way into those cracks and corners if it was the last thing I did. Summer had just become a rainforest.

II

GEORGIA

ABOUT A WEEK AFTER MOSES spooked my horse and I got kicked in the head, Dad and I discovered a mural on the side of our barn. Sometime during the night, someone had painted a stunningly realistic depiction of the sun setting over the western hills of Levan. Against the rosy-hued backdrop, a horse that looked like Sackett stood with his head cocked, a rider sitting comfortably in the saddle. The rider was in profile and the fading sun left him in shadows, but he looked familiar. My dad stared at the picture for a long time with a wistful look on his face. I thought he would be mad because someone had used the side of our barn as a canvas . . . kind of like what I imagined gangs did in big cities. But these weren't geometric gang signs or bubble letters in bold colors. This was kind of cool. This was something you would pay for. Something you would pay a lot for.

"It looks like my dad," my father whispered.

"It looks like Sackett, too," I added, not able to tear my eyes away.

"Grandpa Shepherd had a horse named Hondo, Sackett's great-grandpa. Do you remember?"

"No."

"Yeah. You were too little I guess. Hondo was a good horse. Grand-pa loved him as much as you love Sackett."

"Did you show him a picture?" I asked.

"Who?" Dad turned toward me, puzzled.

"Moses. Didn't he do this? I heard Mrs. Wright telling mom that Moses was sent to juvie for vandalism or destruction of property or something. He likes to paint stuff, apparently. Mrs. Wright said it's com-pulsive. Whatever that means. I just thought you decided to put him to work."

"Huh. No. I didn't ask him to paint the barn. But I like it."

"Me too," I agreed wholeheartedly.

"If he did this, and I don't know who else it could be, he's got se-rious talent. Still, Moses can't go painting wherever and whatever he feels like. The next thing you know the house will have an Elvis mural on the garage."

"Mom would love that."

My dad laughed at my sarcasm, but he hadn't been kidding around. That evening he announced that he was heading over to visit with Mo-ses and Kathleen Wright, and I begged to go along.

"I want to talk to Moses," I said.

"I don't want to embarrass him, George. And having you there while I get after him will definitely embarrass him. This conversation doesn't need an audience. I just want him to know he can't be doing stuff like that, no matter how talented he is."

"I want Moses to paint something on my bedroom wall. I've got some money saved up and I'll pay him. So you tell him he can't paint wherever he wants and then I'll give him a place where he can. Would that be all right?"

"What are you going to have him paint?"

"Remember that story you used to tell me when I was little? The one about the blind man who turned into a horse every night when the sun went down and turned back into a man when the sun rose?"

"Yeah. That's an old story my dad used to tell me."

"I keep thinking about it. I want the story on my wall—or at least the white horse running into the clouds."

"Ask your mom. If it's okay with her, it's okay with me."

I sighed heavily. Mom would be a harder sell. "It's just paint," I grumbled.

Surprisingly enough, Mom was fine with the paint, but she was a little worried about Moses in my room.

"He's intense, Georgie. He scares me a little. I don't know how I feel about you two being friends, honestly. I know that's not very generous of me. But you're my daughter, and you have always been drawn to danger like a moth to a flame."

"He'll be painting, Mom. And I won't be in there in a lace negligee while he does. I think I'll be safe." I winked.

My mom swatted my butt and gave in with a laugh. But truthfully, Mom was wise to warn me away. She was right. I was absolutely fascinated by him, and I didn't see the fascination dying anytime soon.

And so Dad and I were off, knocking on Kathleen Wright's back door a little after sundown. Moses was at the kitchen table eating the biggest bowl of Cornflakes I'd ever seen, and his grandmother sat across from him, peeling an apple in one long, curling red ribbon. I wondered suddenly how many apples she'd practiced on in her eighty years to hone the skill.

"I won't ever paint on your property again," Moses said sincerely after my dad gently told him that painting on our property without permission wasn't acceptable. Kathleen seemed a little upset until my dad reassured her that the painting was beautiful and he didn't want Moses to cover it up. She relaxed after that, and I seemed to be the only one who noticed that Moses hadn't promised not to paint on someone else's property ever again. Just ours.

"You captured a good likeness of my father," my dad added, almost as an afterthought. "He would have liked your painting."

"I was trying to draw you," Moses said, his eyes not quite meeting my dad's. For some reason I was sure he was lying, but didn't know why he would. It made a whole lot more sense that he had used my dad as an inspiration. He certainly hadn't known my grandpa.

"Actually, Moses," I inserted myself into the conversation, "I wondered if you could paint a mural on my bedroom wall. I'd pay you.

Probably not as much as you're worth, but it's something."

He looked at me and looked away. "I don't know if I can."

His grandma, my dad and I stared at him, dumbfounded. Proof that he definitely could was plastered all over the side of our barn.

"I have to . . . to . . . be . . . inspired," he finished weakly, throwing up his hands, almost as if he were trying to push me away. "I can't just paint anything. It doesn't work that way."

"Moses would love to, Georgia," Kathleen interrupted firmly and leveled a warning gaze at her great-grandson. "He'll come by tomorrow afternoon to see what you want done."

He pushed his empty bowl away and stood up abruptly. "I can't do it, Grandma." Then he addressed my dad. "No more paint on your property, I promise." And with that, he left the room.

IT WAS TWO WEEKS BEFORE Moses and I ran into each other again, though the circumstances were even more unpleasant than the first time. The Ute Stampede in Juab County is bigger than Christmas for most of the people who live here. Three days and three nights of parades, the carnival, and, of course, the rodeo. I counted down the days each year; it was always the second weekend in July, and it was the highlight of the summer. To top it off, this year I had qualified to compete in the barrel racing. My parents said I had to wait until after high school to join the circuit, but they told me I could do all the statewide events I qualified for. I'd won Thursday night which had gotten me back into the Saturday night Championship round. I'd won that too. First night as a professional cowgirl, and I'd won it all.

Afterwards, I'd decided to hang around at the carnival to celebrate the night. But my friend Haylee who lived in Nephi, about fifteen minutes north of Levan, was with her boyfriend Terrence, who I didn't especially like. He was always pulling mean pranks and instead of a cowboy hat, he wore one of those trucker caps perched way too high on his head.

"You wear it like that because it's the only way you're taller than the girls," I told him.

"Tall girls aren't my type," he replied, and gave me a little shove.

"Well, then. I've never been more thankful that I was a tall girl."

"You and me both," he said.

"I couldn't go out with you anyway, Terrence. Everyone would think you were my little brother," I teased, tossing his stupid hat into a nearby trashcan and patting him on his sweaty head.

After that, he kept throwing nasty comments my way, and I could tell Haylee was wishing we would stop fighting. I was bored anyway, so I took off by myself, pleading hunger and the need for taller men. I found myself wandering away from the carnival toward the chutes and the nearby corrals that housed the animals during the three consecutive days of the stampede.

It was dark and there was no one else around, but I wanted to get a better look at the bulls. I'd always wanted to ride one and I was sure I could. I climbed the first rungs of the fence and braced myself against it once I was high enough to look down into the stalls separating man from beast. The arena was still lit and although the corrals were in shadows, I could easily make out the heavily muscled back of the bull Cordell Meecham had ridden just hours before. It had been a 90 point ride. He'd won the night and it had been a picture-perfect performance—knees high, heels digging, back bowed, right arm pointed to the heavens as if reaching for the stars would make him one. And it had made him one tonight. The crowd had screamed. I had screamed. And when the bull named Satan's Alias finally threw Cordell free, the buzzer had already sounded and the bull had been bested. I smiled at the memory and imagined it was me.

Barrel racing was the only thing cowgirls did, and I loved it. I loved flying down the arena on the home stretch, head low, hands fisted in Sackett's hair, like I'd caught the current and was letting it take me back to shore. But I wondered sometimes how it would feel to ride an earthquake instead of a wave. Up and down, side to side, bucking, shaking, riding an earthquake.

Satan's Alias wasn't interested in me. Neither were the other bulls crowded in the enclosure. The manure was fresh and so was the straw. I breathed in, not minding the smell that had others wrinkling their noses as they passed the livestock. I stayed a moment longer, watching the animals, before I stepped down from my perch on the fence. It was late. I needed to find Haylee and get my butt home. It rankled that I had a curfew at all, and my thoughts were immediately filled with the future when I wouldn't have to answer to anyone but myself.

When the shadowy figure separated himself from the darkness, I wasn't scared. Not at all. I'd never had reason to be afraid of a cowboy. Cowboys were the best people in the world. Go to any rodeo, anywhere in America, and you'd get the sense that the men and women who attend them could single-handedly save the universe. Not because they are the smartest, the richest, or the most beautiful people in the world. But because they are good. They love each other. They love their country. They love their families. They sing the anthem and they mean it. They take off their hats when the flag is raised. They live and love with devotion. So, no. I wasn't nervous. I wasn't nervous until I was pushed face first into the dirt, freshly churned by the hooves and heels of both men and beasts.

I was stunned for a moment, long enough for my hands to be lashed behind my back like a rodeo calf. The man knew how to wrap and release. I arched and tried to scream. I sucked in a mouth full of manure-flavored muck and knew I was in deep shit. My mind recognized the pun even as I felt hands on the waistband of my jeans. And that's when I got well and truly pissed, the shock shifting to outrage the moment I felt his hands where they had no place being. I reared up and found his face with the back of my head. He swore and shoved my nose back into the mud, hog-tying my heels to my hands before he turned me over. It was an impossible position, my legs and arms bent beneath me, all my weight on my head and neck, my quadriceps screaming as he pushed mud into my eyes and held his hands over my face as my blinded, grit-filled eyes went wild. My nose was filled with mud and with his hands over my mouth I couldn't breathe. I gasped and bucked and tried to bite his fingers. The pain in my lungs was worse than my fear, and I thought I was going to die. With a grunt, he tossed me up over his shoulder and turned, as if to run. Then he froze, caught in indecision as a car door slammed close by and somebody called my name.

He dropped me. Just like that. And he was gone. I thought I heard him curse as he ran, the sound of his boots smacking the ground as he bolted. I didn't recognize his voice. From the moment he stepped out of the shadows to the moment he stepped back in, maybe sixty seconds had passed. Surely another rodeo record.

The rope around my wrists and feet hadn't loosened when he tossed me, but falling so abruptly and hitting the ground without being able to break my fall had knocked the air out of me. I gasped and choked and rolled to my side so that I could spit out the filth in my mouth. I could feel my belt buckle digging into my hip. He'd pulled at my Wranglers and my belt had come loose. I couldn't stand up. I couldn't even wipe my eyes. I lay like a rodeo calf, helpless and hog-tied. I tried to wipe my face against my shoulder, just to remove some of the grit from my eyes so at least I could see. I had to be able to see so that if he came back I would be able to identify him, so I would be able to protect myself. So I would be able to attack. I don't know how long I laid there. It could have been an hour. It could have been ten minutes. But it felt like years.

I swore I had heard someone call my name. Wasn't that why he ran? And then, like I'd conjured him, he was back. Adrenaline coursed through me once more, and I rocked and lurched, trying to move away an inch at a time. I screamed, only to cough desperately. I'd drawn some of the grit still coating my mouth into my lungs. He stopped as if he hadn't expected me to still be there.

"Georgia?"

It wasn't him. It wasn't the same guy.

He came toward me quickly, closing the space. I squeezed my eyes shut like a child trying to make herself invisible by closing her eyes. Oh, no, no, no, no. I knew that voice. Not Moses. Not Moses. Why did it have to be Moses?

"Should I call someone? Should I call an ambulance?" I could feel him beside me. He wiped at my face as if to see me better. I felt a tugging on the ropes around my wrists and ankles, and suddenly I could straighten my legs. Blood rushed back toward my feet with an enthusiastic ache, and I started crying. The tears felt good, and I blinked desperately, trying to clear my vision as I felt Moses pulling away the rope that was looped around my hands. And then my hands were loose too, and I moaned at the dead weight of my arms and the searing pain in my shoulders.

"Who did this? Who tied you up?"

I looked everywhere but directly at him. I could see he wore a black T-shirt tucked into cargo pants along with a pair of army boots that no self-respecting cowboy would wear at the Ute Stampede. My attacker had worn western wear. He'd worn a button-down shirt. With snaps. Cowboy attire. I'd felt the snaps against my back. I started to shake, and I knew I was going to be sick.

"I'm okay," I lied, gasping, wanting desperately for Moses to turn away so I wouldn't have to throw up in front of him. I wasn't okay. Not at all. I mopped at my cheeks and I looked up at him, my eyes darting to his face to gauge whether or not he believed me. I looked away immediately.

He asked me if I could stand and then tried to help me to my feet. With his help I managed, teetering like a newborn foal.

"You can go. I'm fine," I lied again desperately. But he didn't leave.

I turned around, walked several steps on shaking legs, and threw up against the fence. Mud, manure, and my rodeo hamburger burst forth in a gush of Pepsi broth, and my knees buckled beneath me. I clung to the corral so I wouldn't fall as I heaved and purged, but Moses didn't leave. The snort and stamp of the bulls on the other side of the wooden rails reminded me where I was. Satan's Alias and his minions were nearby, and I had no trouble believing I'd fallen through a rabbit hole straight into the bowels of hell.

"You're covered in mud and your belt is hanging off." The statement was flat, accusing almost, and I could tell Moses didn't believe I was okay at all. Imagine that. I kept my back turned to him, pulled my big shiny belt buckle into place with stiff fingers, and shoved the end of my belt through my belt loops, ignoring the fact that my button had come undone too and my zipper was down. My T-shirt now hung over my waistband so maybe he hadn't noticed that. And I wasn't going to draw attention to it. The belt would keep my pants in place. I shuddered.

"Someone tied you up."

"I think someone was playing a joke," I stuttered, still coughing and wheezing at the irritation in my throat. "I think it was Terrence. He was pissed at me earlier, and maybe he thought I would laugh or squeal instead of fight. I fought hard. Maybe it wasn't supposed to be scary. Maybe he was just supposed to tie me up so they could come find me and laugh at me all trussed up . . . I'm totally fine." I wasn't sure I believed anything I said. But I wanted to.

Weird how Moses was the one who had cut me loose. Ironic. A cowboy had hurt me and a troublemaker had come to my rescue. My mom thought Moses was the one who was dangerous. It had been Moses she warned me about. And he had saved me.

"I'm okay," I insisted and pushed myself completely upright, still mopping at my eyes and at my trembling lips, humiliated by what Moses had seen, devastated by what could have happened. What almost happened. And most of all, destroyed that it had happened at all. If it really was a prank gone wrong, then it had gone terribly wrong. Because Georgia Shepherd was now afraid. And I didn't do afraid very well. I wanted to go home. I didn't know where Haylee was, and I didn't want to go looking, especially if she was in on whatever that was.

"Can you take me home, Moses? Please?" My voice sounded strange, and I winced at the child-like tone.

"Someone needs to pay."

"What?"

"Someone needs to pay for this, Georgia." It was weird hearing him say my name as if he knew me so well. He didn't know me at all. And suddenly, I barely knew myself. Same town, same street. Same world. But it didn't feel like the same world at all. And definitely not the same girl. I wondered for a moment if I was in shock. Nothing had really happened. I was okay. I would be okay, at least. I just needed to go home.

"I need to go home. I'm okay," I insisted. "Please?" I was pleading now. Begging. And the tears were streaming down my cheeks again.

He looked around almost desperately, like he wanted to call for help, like he needed to get advice on how to handle the situation. *I* was the situation. He didn't know how to handle *me*. Taking me home was the easiest solution, but he obviously didn't think that was good enough.

"Please?" I urged. I wiped my face on the sleeve of my T-shirt, the tears and the dirt leaving wet streaks on the new top I'd bought especially for this night. I always got new outfits for the stampede. New Wranglers, new shirts, sometimes even new boots. New duds for the big event.

I could see the Ferris wheel turning in the distance, visible above the row of dark outbuildings that separated the animals and the arena from the fairgrounds beyond. A soft breeze lifted the hair from my damp cheeks and brought with it the carnival cologne of cotton candy and popcorn before it merged with the smell of vomit and manure and lost its sweetness.

I teetered slightly and felt the horror of the last few minutes start to sink in. Sinking, sinking, sinking. I needed to go home.

Moses must have felt me slowly plummeting into the abyss, because without another word, he reached out his hand and loosely took my arm, offering support. I loved him at that moment, more than I thought I could. Way more than our brief encounters warranted. The troublemaker, the delinquent, the crack baby. He was now my hero.

He walked beside me slowly, letting me lean on him. And when we reached his Jeep, I stood, staring blankly at it, a Jeep I'd seen day in and day out since he moved to Levan six weeks before. I had been jealous of his cool wheels when I only had an old farm truck to drive, a truck that didn't go above forty miles per hour. I'd been jealous before, but now I was so grateful for it I wanted to fall to my knees and give thanks. Moses gently urged me up into the passenger seat and buckled me in. The buckles were more like harnesses and I welcomed the relative safety, even as I worried about the fact that the jeep had no roof and no doors.

"Moses, Jeeps, seatbelts, home, Moses," I listed, not even aware I was speaking out loud, and not caring that I'd repeated Moses twice. He'd earned two spots tonight.

"What?" Moses leaned in and lifted my chin, his eyes worried.

"Nothing. Habit. When I'm . . . stressed, I list the things I'm grateful for."

He didn't say anything, but he kept looking at me as he climbed in and started the Jeep. I felt him watching me as he maneuvered his way across the gravel, around the corrals and horse trailers, through the parking lot and out onto the road.

The wind roared into our faces, tangled in my hair, and pushed against my body as we sped down the highway, leaving the fairgrounds, the glittering Ferris wheel, and the happy sounds that had given me such a false sense of security behind us. Those sounds had lulled me and lured me in all my life. Now I wondered how I would ever go back.

III

MOSES

I HAD GONE TO THE RODEO for Georgia. Not because I had some premonition that she needed me, or even some hope that she wanted me to be there. Definitely not because I expected to find her tied up, covered in mud, crying because someone had tried to hurt her or scare her. Or take her. She said it was probably a prank. I wondered what kind of friends pulled pranks like that. I wouldn't know. I didn't have any friends.

My grandma had presented me with an extra, general admission ticket that afternoon and informed me that Georgia was "competing in the barrel races and you don't want to miss it." I had the sudden image of Georgia atop a barrel, balancing as she made it roll, her feet flying, trying desperately not to fall off as she tried to cross the finish line ahead of all the other barrel racers.

I had never been to a rodeo before. I had no idea how crazy white people could be. Considering I had been abandoned by a white, crack addict mother, I should have known.

But I actually enjoyed myself. There was a wholesomeness about the entertainment—lots of families and flag waving and music that made me wish I'd worn a cowboy hat, no matter how stupid I would have looked in it. I ate six rodeo burgers, which may have been the best thing I'd ever eaten in my life. Grandma hooted like she'd just been called down on The Price is Right and stomped her feet and generally acted like she was eighteen instead of eighty, which I also enjoyed. Roping, riding, cowboys being flung like rag dolls from bucking horses and twisting bulls, and girls like Georgia, riding like they'd been born in a saddle. I was pretty sure Georgia had. I'd seen her ride plenty of times when she thought I wasn't watching.

I'd avoided Georgia since the incident in the barn. I didn't know what to do with her. She was a wild card. She was a small town girl with a simple way of speaking and thinking, a frank way of being that turned me on and turned me off at the same time. I wanted to run from her. But at the same time, I spent all my time thinking about her.

I watched Georgia fly into the arena on her pale horse, dust swirling, hair streaming out behind her, hugging the strategically placed barrels with a grin so huge I knew she was enjoying her flirtation with death. I knew horses were to her what painting was to me, and as I watched her fly, I desperately wanted to paint her. Just like that, full of life and motion, completely unbound. I usually painted when the images in my head became too much to contain and then spilled out in furious frustration. I had rarely painted pictures just for the joy of it, just for the pleasure of painting something that appealed to me. And Georgia, in front of a screaming crowd, hurtling around a dusty arena, had somehow become something that appealed to me.

I left before it was all over, Grandma assuring me she was riding with the Stephensons and didn't need me to stay. I drove around aimlessly, with no desire to brush up against people at the carnival, ride the Ferris wheel, or watch Georgia with her friends, celebrating her winning ride. I was sure she had friends. And I was sure I was nothing like them.

I drove and drove and then I felt it coming on, the warning that rose in my veins and made my neck and ears throb with heat. I turned up the radio, trying to use sound to drown out sight. It didn't work very well. Within a few seconds I saw a man by the side of the road. He just stood, looking at me. I shouldn't have been able to see him. It was dark. And it was a country road, lit only by moonlight and the headlights of my Jeep. But he stood illuminated, as if he'd borrowed light from the moon and wrapped himself in it.

I recognized him almost immediately. And the images started to flood my brain. They were all of Georgia: Georgia with her horse, Georgia leaping fences, Georgia falling to the ground in the barn when I'd spooked her horse.

The image kept repeating—Georgia falling, Georgia falling, Georgia falling. It didn't scare me. I'd seen her fall. It was in the past. And she was fine. But then I wondered if maybe she wasn't. I wondered if this man—the man on the side of the road, the same man I'd seen in Georgia's barn when Sackett reared up and kicked Georgia, the man I'd painted on the side of that same barn because he kept coming back—I wondered if he was trying to tell me something. Not about his life, but about Georgia's.

And so I turned the Jeep around and went to the fairgrounds. I didn't park in the lot, but crept around from the side, weaving around the outbuildings and the horse trailers as if I had any idea where I was going. I thought I caught another glimpse of the shadowy man—or was it just a flash of light, a cowboy needing a smoke? I came to a stop, stepped out of my Jeep, and called Georgia's name. I felt ridiculous, and I stayed still for a minute, unsure, unwilling to join the masses that moved beneath the colorful carnival lights a hundred yards away. I was more comfortable watching from the dark.

Someone ran into me from behind, making me lurch forward and stumble, careening into me and then away from me, disappearing into the night without apology and without giving me a chance to push back. Drunk cowboy. But after that there was silence, peppered only with the stomp and snort of the animals penned and quartered nearby. I didn't want to go any closer to the animals; I might cause a stampede of my own.

I headed toward the carnival and walked the perimeter, searching for Georgia from the sidelines. And then I saw the man again. Georgia's grandfather. He was standing by the darkened entrance to the arena. He didn't call to me. They never did. They just filled my head with their memories. But no images came. He just stood in a swath of pearly moonlight. And I walked toward him until I was back to where I'd started. He disappeared as I approached, but something gleamed at my left, disappearing around the chutes, beneath the grandstands, closer to the animals. And that's when I found Georgia.

GEORGIA

I TOLD MY PARENTS what happened at the stampede. I had to. I also told them that I thought it might be Terrence who had tied me up. Moses came inside with me and stood anxiously by the door, not making eye contact with anyone in the room, his eyes glued to the floor. My parents urged him to sit, but he refused and they finally let him be, ignoring him as studiously as he ignored them.

What was already a late night became much later as my parents reacted with alarm, unending questions, and finally a phone call to the sheriff, who fortunately lived on the outskirts of Levan and not on the other side of the county.

My parents called Moses's grandma and told her he would need to stick around to tell the sheriff what he saw. She ended up coming right over, bustling in the back door like it was ten am instead of two am. She patted Moses's cheek and gave him a squeeze before she moved to me and wrapped me up in her arms. Her head only came to my shoulder, and her grey curls tickled my chin, but I immediately felt safer. Better. She sat down at the table and I went and showered the dirt from my skin and hair while we waited for the sheriff to arrive. I was sore and bruised and there were rope burns on my wrists and a wide scrape on my left cheek. The back of my head ached and even my lips felt tender from where my face had been shoved into the ground. But worse than all of that was the sick fear in my belly and the sense that I'd escaped something truly awful.

When I walked into the kitchen with my head in a towel and my body swathed in polka-dotted pajamas, Sheriff Dawson was sitting at the kitchen table, a Pepsi at the ready and a slice of pie in front of him, thanks to Mom, the unfailing hostess. Sheriff Dawson was lean and fit in his brown sheriff's uniform, his blonde hair parted and neatly combed, his blue eyes bright in a tanned face that revealed his preference for the outdoors. He was in his late thirties or early forties and had recently been re-elected sheriff. People liked him and he liked horses. That was a pretty good resume for the people in our county. I didn't see him losing his job any time soon. He and my dad were talking about breaking Lucky when I settled down at the table next to Mrs. Wright. Moses was seated across from the sheriff, and the sheriff started asking him questions right away. Moses was quiet and guarded and he kept looking at the door like he couldn't wait to bolt. It reminded me of Sunday school, and the thought almost made me smile. The interview didn't take long; Moses gave the briefest answers ever recorded.

He went to the rodeo with his grandmother. His grandma nodded helpfully. He came to see me ride. Mrs. Wright nodded again.

He did? The thought made me squirm and feel all warm inside. He continued in a quiet tone, giving the barest of details.

He was parked near the animal pens, standing next to his Jeep, trying to decide whether to go to the carnival for a couple corndogs and a caramel apple or to just head home. Someone had bumped into him from behind. He didn't see who it was. A cowboy, he thought. Not especially helpful, I thought. But I couldn't add anything to that description either. He thought he heard someone call out, scream even. And he found me. He untied me, he brought me home. The end.

Then Moses stared at the sheriff and repeated the same answers when Sheriff Dawson pressed him a little harder. Sheriff Dawson asked why he was parked by the pens instead of in the parking lot.

Moses answered that he didn't want to walk.

The sheriff wanted to know why he couldn't give a more detailed description of the man he'd seen running away, the man who'd run right into him?

Moses said his back was turned, and it was dark.

The sheriff seemed uneasy and suspicious, but I wasn't. Moses wasn't the one who had tied me up. He was the one who freed me. And that's the only part I cared about.

Then it was my turn. I told my story too, my small audience hanging on every word. I told Sheriff Dawson that I thought it might be Terrence Anderson who had been pulling a prank, which was highly uncomfortable, considering Sheriff Dawson was Terrence's uncle. But to his credit, the sheriff didn't bat an eye or argue with me, and he promised to look into it. The sheriff took down everything I said and even took some pictures of the rope burns on my wrists and the scrapes on my face.

"What's this? Is that something we need to document?" The sheriff pointed to the place Sackett's hoof had connected with my forehead. It was three weeks old and mostly healed, but having my head ground into the dirt and gravel had irritated the scar, and it was now red and raw looking.

"Sackett got excited," I said, shrugging, not wanting to rehash the incident. I knew the sheriff knew who Sackett was.

The sheriff grinned a little and pointed to a knot on his own forehead. "I wonder if Tonga was excited about the same thing. She got me good, damn horse. You can never get too comfortable around animals. Just when you think you've got 'em figured out, they'll do something completely unexpected."

"Yeah. People are like that too." I said, without thought.

And it was true. Tonight, more than ever. I felt the fear flood my mouth immediately and wondered how in the world I would be able to sleep tonight . . . or ever again. The sheriff nodded sympathetically and stood to go, but he reached out and patted my shoulder.

"I'm sorry, Georgia. I am. Whether it was a prank or something a lot scarier, I'm just grateful you're okay. We'll follow up with Terrence Anderson and Haylee Blevins and see if they know anything about it. We've got your statement and the pictures too. And of course, Mr. Wright's statement as well." The sheriff looked at Moses nervously, and I almost rolled my eyes. Everyone was afraid of Moses. I was pretty sure if I hadn't been absolutely adamant it wasn't Moses who tied me up before he untied me, he would be the number one suspect. He just *looked* wicked.

The sheriff stepped toward the kitchen door.

"I'm glad it's the last night of the stampede. People get a little crazy. Hopefully, life will settle down a little around town and we'll figure out what happened. We'll be in touch."

With that, Sheriff Dawson let himself out into the early morning darkness and we all sat, staring at the table, deep in our own thoughts, too tired to move just yet.

"Well." Kathleen Wright sighed. "Sheriff Dawson is a nice boy." He was almost forty, but that was apparently boyish to an eighty-year-old. "Moses, he and your mother used to be sweethearts. He was so in love with her. I thought maybe she would come back to Levan and marry him. He tried. Went after her over and over again. Lord knows he did. But she was too far gone, I guess." Mrs. Wright patted Moses's cheek again and stood up from the table. His face was tight at the mention of his mother, and I wondered how often anyone talked about her. I had the feeling Moses never did.

My parents stood as well, but Moses, surprisingly, looked at me. We were the only two still sitting, and for a minute, the adults weren't watching.

"You wanted me to paint your room. I'm here. I might as well have a look."

My mom tuned in right away.

"It's almost three a.m.," she protested.

Moses lifted his eyes to hers. "It will be hard for Georgia to sleep tonight."

That's all he said, and everyone fell silent. But my heart sounded like a drum. I stood and led him down the hall. No one objected, and I heard Mrs. Wright leave and my parents move to their bedroom down the hall.

"It's summertime, Mauna," I heard my dad murmur. "It's fine. We're here, just a few doors down. Let it be."

And they did. They let us be.

"Tell me the story," Moses demanded after I told him what I wanted

41

painted in my room. He stared at the blank white wall I had cleared two weeks ago in hopes he would agree to do the mural. My tastes were basic, plain even, and I prided myself on the lack of frills and the rows of books that lined the shelves, all westerns except for *Where the Red Fern Grows*, *Summer of the Monkeys,* and another long row by Dean Koontz. After Louis L'Amour, he was my favorite.

"Do you like to read?" I asked, pointing at my little shelf.

Moses eyed my books. "Yes."

His answer surprised me. Maybe it was his reputation as a gang banging delinquent. Maybe it was because of the way he looked. But he didn't seem like the type who enjoyed sitting quietly with a book.

"What's your favorite book?" I sounded suspicious and his eyes tightened.

"I like *Catcher in the Rye. The Outsiders*, *1984*, *Of Mice and Men*, *Dune*, *Starship Troopers*, *Lord of the Rings*. Anything by Tom Clancy or JK Rowling."

He said JK Rowling quickly, like he didn't want to admit to being a Potter fan. But I was stunned.

"You've really read all those books?" I'd read *The Outsiders* and liked it, but hadn't read any of the others. I wondered if he was lying to me.

"No Stephen King or Dean Koontz?" I added, trying to find something we had in common.

"*Green Mile* and *The Girl Who Loved Tom Gordon*. But nothing else by Stephen King. And Dean Koontz knows too much."

"What do you mean?"

Moses shook his head, not explaining.

"I can't imagine you holding still long enough to read."

"I can hold still when my mind is occupied. TV makes me crazy. Usually, music does too. But I like stories." His eyes found mine again. "You were going to tell me yours."

"Oh. Yeah. The story. It's a story that my grandpa used to tell my dad when he was a boy, and my dad then told me. I don't know where it comes from, actually. But it always felt real to me."

"Your grandpa. The one your dad mentioned the other night? The one he thought I painted?"

"Yes."

Moses looked strangely relieved. I stared at him for several long seconds, trying to decipher his expression.

"Go on," he said.

"There was a blind man who lived in a small western town. He hadn't been blind all his life. An illness had taken his eyesight when he was a little boy. Along with his eyesight, he'd lost his freedom. He had to have someone lead him around if he went outside, he had to have someone do most of his cooking and cleaning. And worst of all, he wasn't able to see his horses or the hills around his home. One night he had a dream that he was running in the mountains. When he stopped to drink from a cool stream, he saw his reflection in the water. He wasn't a man anymore, but a beautiful white horse that could run for miles without tiring. When the man woke in the morning, the woman who came and helped him each day noticed his hands and the bottom of his feet were filthy even though he'd taken a bath the night before.

"He dreamed the same dream the next night, and in the dream the horse caught his foreleg on a branch as he leaped over a log. It was just a scratch on the horse's leg, but in the morning when the man awoke he realized he had a long scratch on his leg exactly where he, the horse, had been wounded in the dream." The words came as easily to me as reciting the pledge of allegiance. I'd been told the story so many times as a child that I was probably using the very same words, the same descriptions that had been used then.

"Then people started seeing the white horse at night, and as the rumors reached the blind man, he realized that he wasn't dreaming. He was actually turning into a horse at night, running and leaping, seeing all the things he hadn't seen for so long, but through the eyes of this beautiful animal.

"He didn't dare tell anyone, because he knew how crazy it was. But crazy or not, it was the truth. Night after night, he continued to turn into a horse, and night after night the sightings continued, until a few men in the town made plans to capture the beautiful, white horse.

"The men did as they planned and between the three of them, they cornered the horse. But just when they thought for sure they had it, the horse leaped the fence and ran straight into the clouds, disappearing forever.

"The next day when the woman went to the blind man's house to make him his breakfast, he was gone. And he never came back home. No one ever knew what had happened to him, but the woman always suspected the truth, because the bare footprints leading down his front walk became hoof prints in the soft mud of the yard."

Moses had been staring at my face as I talked, but his eyes had grown distant and unfocused, as if he wasn't really looking at me at all.

"Can I take up more than one wall?" he asked.

"Uh, sure." I scrambled up and started pulling down pictures and yanking out thumbtacks. Before long, my furniture was in the middle of the room and Moses was wildly sketching with what he called a grease pencil. He pulled a few of them out of his pockets as if he carried them wherever he went.

I watched in fascination as Moses became lost in the story I'd shared with him. He rarely stepped back to see what he'd sketched, and his hands flew. He was using both hands interchangeably, and before long, he had a pencil clasped in each and was drawing frantically with both hands at once. It was mind-boggling to behold. I could barely write with my left hand, not to mention draw, and draw while my other hand was doing something else. Moses didn't speak to me, and the one time I interrupted him, when it was close to dawn and my eyes were growing heavy, he looked at me blankly like he'd forgotten I was there.

"Let's stop. I can't stay awake," I yawned. "And I don't want to miss anything. You're a genius. You know that, right? Maybe you'll be famous one day and they'll turn my room into a Moses Wright museum." He started shaking his head immediately.

"I don't want to stop," he said, and his eyes pled with me. "I can't stop yet. If I do, I might not be able to finish."

"Okay," I agreed immediately. "But you better be gone before my parents wake up. You can come back every day until it's done. You just have to promise that you'll let me watch."

I fought the battle with sleep as long as I could, desperate not to miss the magic. But as brilliant as the images unfolding across my walls were, it was Moses himself who kept me spellbound. And when my eyes would no longer focus and my lids slid closed one last time, it was Moses who danced in my dreams, arms flying, eyes glowing, color and curved lines flowing from his fingertips.

I didn't open my eyes again until well past noon. And when I did, it was because someone was making a racket outside my bedroom windows.

"What are you doing?" I asked Moses, dumbfounded, stumbling out of bed and rubbing the sleep from my face.

"Putting screens on your windows. If I'm going to paint in there, we need some ventilation. Without screens, I'll have bugs biting me, swarming around the light, and getting stuck in my paint. And you and I will get high from the fumes. My brain is already scrambled enough.""Cracked," I said, not thinking.

"Yeah." Moses scowled.

"Well, it's working for you." I turned and looked at my walls. "Cracks and all. In fact, if your brain wasn't cracked, none of the brilliance could spill out. Do you realize that?" And it was brilliant. He hadn't used any paint yet. But with a grease pencil and a cracked brain, Moses had filled two walls with the beginning scenes of a blind man who found his sight and a horse who came alive only at night. It was already beyond anything I could have imagined.

"Have you even slept?" I turned back to him with a yawn.

"Nah. But I'll go crash for a while now. I'll be back after dinner."

After dinner was too far away and I had hours to kill until then. After I took care of my chickens, mowed the front lawn, and helped mom for an hour with the two foster kids we'd taken in for a few days, I retreated to the corral. My horses were happy to see me, and I felt bad that I'd made them wait for my attention. The meadow was still grassy and they had water, so it wasn't as if they were starving, but I rarely missed a morning with them. I made it up to them by spending the rest of the long afternoon until dark trying to make Lucky fall in love with me.

Lucky was a horse with a black coat and an even darker mane. He was the most beautiful horse I'd ever seen, but he knew he was beautiful, and he had a temper. He didn't want to be touched or ridden or coaxed into standing still. He wanted me to leave him alone. Dad had a client that hadn't been able to pay his vet bills, so they'd worked out a trade. It wasn't a great trade, because Dad needed horses he and Mom could train to be around kids. But the horse had a pedigree Dad liked, and he thought maybe he could get some stud fees out of him.

Lucky reminded me of Moses—powerful and perfectly formed, muscles sinuous and defined just below the sleek surface, and the way he held his head and ignored me was almost spot-on Moses. But then Lucky would look at me and I knew he was well aware of my presence. He hadn't forgotten me for a moment, and he wanted me to chase him. Call me crazy, but I was pretty sure what worked with the horse could work with the boy.

Moses came back that night. And again the next night. And the next. I watched him in wonder as he added color to the lines and a dream-like quality to the story that made me feel like I'd stepped inside the blind man's head and was seeing it all through his eyes—seeing the world for the very first time.

Moses didn't stop with my walls. On the third night the story continued on my ceiling, and he rigged up some scaffolding so he could paint the Sistine Chapel right on my ten by twelve bedroom ceiling. I had to admit, I didn't know about the Sistine Chapel until Moses told me all about Michelangelo as he assembled the platform he intended to lie on while he painted. He said some day he would see it in person. He wanted to travel all over the world and see all the great art. That was his dream. I stayed very quiet while he talked, only contributing when I thought he was losing steam and might stop talking. I needed him to keep talking. I wanted to know everything about him. I wanted inside, and little by little, especially when he was painting, he was giving me glimpses, brief moments with him that I treasured up like a child collecting fragile shells and shiny pebbles. And when he wasn't with me, I took out those treasures and turned them over and over in my mind, studying them from every angle, learning him.

My parents didn't know what to think about my room. Nobody did. It was too much, almost, for such a small space. When you stood in the center with the story cocooning you in color, it was easy to get dizzy and grow lightheaded from the sheer magnitude of the detail and the depth of the work. But I loved it. I left my furniture arranged like a little island in the center of my room so nothing covered the walls, and I strung golden twinkle lights around the edges so that when I turned off my bedroom lamp to sleep, the little lights would cast the blind man's dream in a soft, warm glow. It was magical.

I felt like an idiot when I handed Moses a hundred dollars the night he finished. I was pretty sure it would barely cover his paint and supplies. But it was all I had, and I'd had no idea what I was getting into when I asked him to paint a mural on my wall.

He actually seemed pleased by the money, like he'd forgotten he'd been commissioned, and thanked me sincerely, folding the bills inside a soft leather wallet and shoving it into the pocket of his jeans.

IV

GEORGIA

DAD SAID HORSES REFLECT the energy of the people around them. If you're scared the horse will shy away from you. If you doubt yourself he'll take advantage of you. If you don't trust yourself, neither will he. They are truth detectors. It isn't rocket science. It isn't voodoo. There's a reason you give a horse his head if you're lost. He'll always take you home.

It hadn't escaped me that the horses were afraid of Moses. And if Dad's theory was correct, it was because Moses was afraid, and the horses were simply mirroring a very powerful emotion. Horses scare some people. They're so big and powerful, and if it's you against a horse, well, the horse will kick your ass.

But I didn't think Moses was afraid of the horses. Not exactly. I was pretty sure Moses was just afraid in general. Anxious, desperate, manic. Whatever. And our horses knew it.

"You know how Sackett kicked me?" I asked my dad one morning as we were getting ready for a counseling session.

"Yeah," my dad grunted.

"He was just mirroring Moses, wasn't he?"

My dad looked up sharply, not liking the suggestion that Moses wanted to kick me in the head.

"Moses is afraid, Dad. I think he paints because it releases a lot of nervous energy. But I was thinking maybe we could get him around the horses, maybe help him that way too."

"First rule of therapy, George," my dad said.

"What's that?"

"You can lead a horse to water . . ."

". . . but you can't make him drink," I sighed, finishing the old maxim.

"That's right. You might be right about Moses. And I'm sure we could help him, when and if he wants our help. Kids, married couples, people with addictions, people who are depressed, everybody and almost anybody can be helped by equine therapy. I've never known a man who couldn't be helped by spending time with a horse. But it's really up to Moses. You're pretty headstrong, George, but you've met your match with that boy."

I was convinced I had. Met my match, that is. Maybe that kick to the head or the brush with violence at the stampede had permanently altered me, maybe it was his role as savior, or maybe I had just fallen in love with the artist who brought a white horse to life on my bedroom walls, but I couldn't get Moses out of my thoughts. I found myself looking for him from the moment I stepped outside in the mornings until the moment I gave up in the evening and went home. His grandma was calling in favors right and left, and once Moses finished doing odd jobs for my dad, he started repairing fence for Gene Powell, which would probably take him the rest of the summer, considering how many acres Gene Powell had. On top of that, he'd been hired to do some demolition inside the old mill west of town that had shut down twenty years before.

I could make up reasons to be riding along the fence line, but the old mill was a different matter entirely. I figured I would cross that bridge when I got to it, but I was already plotting. I didn't let myself think about my infatuation, because then I would have to acknowledge it. And I wasn't the kind of girl to be infatuated or to get caught up in crushes, the kind of girl who checked her lips or fluffed her hair when boys were around.

Yet, I found myself doing just that, loosening my braid and running my hands through my unbound hair as I approached the edge of Gene Powell's property on my horse in late July. I had Moses's lunch. I'd made sure to intercept Kathleen on her way out and had casually mentioned that Sackett and I were headed this way. She smiled at me like she wasn't fooled, and I felt pretty stupid. Kathleen Wright might be eighty years old, but I was sure she didn't miss much. Especially since I'd just happened to stop by three days in a row, just in time to bring Moses his lunch.

When Moses saw me coming he didn't look pleased, and I wondered for the umpteenth time what I'd done to piss him off.

"Where's Gigi?" he asked.

"Who's Gigi?"

"My grandma. She's my great-grandma—two G's in a row. GG."

"I seen her heading this way, and I thought as long as I was out riding, I may as well bring your lunch."

"You *saw* her heading this way." He looked up at me with disgust. "Not seen. And it's 'we were' not 'we was.' You say that wrong too."

It didn't sound wrong to me, but I made note of it. I didn't want Moses to think I was stupid.

"Everyone in this town says it wrong. My grandma says it wrong! It drives me crazy," Moses grumbled. He was in rare form today. But I didn't mind that he was complaining as long as he was talking to me.

"Okay. I'll fix my grammar. You want to tell me what else you don't like about me? 'Cause I'm thinking that isn't all," I said.

He sighed but ignored my question, asking a few of his own. "Why are you here, Georgia? Does your dad know you're here?"

"I'm bringing you your lunch, Einstein. And no to the second question. Why should he? I don't check in every time I ride my horse."

"Does he know how you're out here jumping fences?"

I shrugged. "I've been riding since I could walk. It's not a big deal."

He let it drop, but after a few bites of his sandwich he was picking on me again.

"Georgie Porgie puddin' and pie. Kissed the boys and made them cry. What kind of name is Georgia?"

"My great-great grandma was Georgia. The first Georgia Shepherd. My dad calls me George."

"Yeah. I've heard him. That's just nasty."

I felt my temper rise in my cheeks, and I really wanted to spit on him from where I sat atop my horse, looking down on his neatly shorn, well-shaped head. He glanced up at me and his lips twitched, making me even angrier.

"Don't look at me like that. I'm not trying to be mean. But George is a terrible name for a girl. Hell, for anyone who isn't the King of England."

"I think it suits me," I huffed.

"Oh, yeah? George is the name for a man with a stuffy, British accent or a man in a white, powdered wig. You better hope it doesn't suit you."

"Well, I don't exactly need a sexy name, do I? I've never been a sexy girl." I gave Sackett a hard nudge in her flanks and pulled the reins sharply, more than ready to leave. I swore to myself that I wouldn't be bringing Moses his lunch again. He was a jerk, and I was sick of it.

But as I rode away I thought I heard him call after me, "Just keep telling yourself that, Georgie Porgie. I'll keep telling myself that too."

I brought his lunch again the next day.

MOSES

"SHE LIKES YOU, YOU KNOW." Gigi smiled at me, teasing.

I just grunted.

"Georgia likes you, Moses. And she's such a good girl. A nice girl. Pretty too. Why don't you give her some attention? That's all she wants, you know." Gigi winked at me, and I felt the heat that I had so prided myself on controlling start to spread through my chest and down my abdomen.

Georgia may only want attention now. But that wouldn't last. If I gave her attention, she would want to spend more time with me. And if I spent time with her, she might want me to be her boyfriend. And if I was her boyfriend, she would want me to be normal. She would want me to be normal because she was normal. And normal was so lost to me that I didn't even know where to look for it.

Still . . .

I thought about the way she looked when she fell asleep the night I painted the ceiling in her room. I'd looked down through the slats on the scaffolding, and she was directly below me, curled around a pillow she'd pulled off her bed. It was as if I floated over her, my body hovering six feet above hers. Her hair was loose around her shoulders, the same color as the wheat in the fields around the small town where we lived. But her hair wasn't coarse and wispy. It was silky and thick and wavy from the braid she'd worn all day. She was tall, not as tall as I was, but long and lean, with golden skin and deep brown eyes that were a sharp contrast with her fair hair. My opposite. I had light eyes and dark hair. Maybe if you put us together, our physical oddities would even out. My belly tightened at the thought. No one would put us together. Especially not me.

I found myself watching her sleep, the painting temporarily forgotten. The man in the corner of the room who shared his thoughts, who shared Georgia's story in pictures that poured into my head and out my hands, had disappeared. I wondered if I could call him back. I wasn't finished yet.

But I didn't try to call him back. Instead, I stared down at Georgia for a long, long time, watching the girl who was easily as persistent as the ghosts in my head. And for once, my mind was full of pictures of my own making, filled with dreams only I had conjured. And for the first time ever, I fell asleep with Georgia beneath me and peace inside of me.

GEORGIA

LUCKY HADN'T BEEN WORKED with at all before he came to us. Dad didn't have much time to train him, but I had nothing but time. I had a knack, everyone said I did. So I spent a few hours with him every morning getting him used to me, making sure I was the one who fed him, I was the one who he saw, day in and day out. He would run when I drew near, deliver a skittish two-step when I cut off his desired direction, and generally get very irritated with me. The day I got a rope around his head and he let me lead him around was a month in the making. It took me another two weeks before we were in a bridle and he let me draw his head back toward me as I stood at his side.

"That's it, baby. You gonna let me have your head?" I smiled as I talked, trying not to gloat. You train a horse with pressure. Not pain. Pressure. A horse doesn't want to get in the trailer? You don't force him. You just run him in circles, round and round the trailer until he's breathing hard. Then you try to take him up the ramp again. He doesn't want to go? You keep running him. Eventually, he'll figure out that the pressure lets up when he's in the trailer. He gets to rest in the trailer. So he'll climb that ramp eagerly every time.

I got a little impatient. My dad always said when you're working with people or with animals, impatience is the worst mistake you can make. But I'd grown a little cocky. He was giving me his head, and I wanted the rest of him. I fisted my hands in his mane and drew my body up so that my belly brushed his side. He went still, quivering, and I felt that quiver echo in my stomach, anticipation zinging down my legs and arms, making me stupid.

"We're friends aren't we, Lucky?" I whispered. "Let's go for a little run. Just an easy little run."

He didn't pull away, and I took the hesitation for consent. In one quick move I hoisted myself up and over, and as my butt hit his back we were off, and I knew with a terrible twist in my gut that he wasn't ready. But it was too damn late. I was on his back, hands in his hair, committed. I would have been fine if he'd just decided to shake me loose. I knew how to fall. But he bolted instead, flying across the field with me clinging to his back. We cleared the fence separating our property from Gene Powell's and I did my best to meld my body with his, but it's incredibly hard to stay on a horse without a saddle. They are smooth, slick, and powerful, and my thighs were screaming with the effort to keep him between them. We cleared another fence and I stayed seated, but my arms were trembling, and I was terrified that Lucky was going to hurt himself. Horses break their legs and it's not just an easy trip to the ER and a big cast and crutches. It's over. I wasn't thinking about myself. I was thinking of my mistake in judgment, how I'd pushed him too far. And I didn't know how to fix it.

On the third fence, Lucky landed hard and I started to slide to the side. I cursed a streak of the bluest words I'd ever said, yanking with all my might on Lucky's mane, and trying to right myself. But there was no stopping my descent, and I hit the ground hard, my shoulder and hip getting the worst of it as I rolled and found myself staring up at a sky that was far too blue for dying.

If I hadn't been trying to pull air back into my lungs and life back into my limbs, I might have noticed where I was, but it wasn't until Moses squatted down beside me and peered into my face that I realized where Lucky had thrown me.

He didn't ask if I was okay. He didn't say anything for a moment. We just stared at each other, and I saw that his breaths were as labored as my own. It pleased me to think he'd run to make sure I wasn't mortally wounded.

"Well, shit." I sighed, trying to sit up.

Moses sat back and watched as I brushed the dirt from my right side, wincing as I swept my hand over my shoulder. I had a long scrape that stretched almost to my elbow, but other than that, I was fine. I would hurt like hell tomorrow, but nothing was broken. I was on my feet brushing off my rear end and scanning the horizon without any help from Moses.

"Did you see which way he went?" I asked, casting my eyes across the field.

"No," he answered finally. "I was too busy watching you fall."

"I rode for a while before that," I answered defensively. "We cleared two fences."

"Is that normal for you?"

"What?"

"Riding without a saddle, full out, on a horse that obviously doesn't want to be ridden?"

"He gave me his head . . . I thought he was ready. I was wrong."

"He gave you his head?"

"Yeah . . . never mind. It's horse speak. When a horse lets you control his head, pull it all the way back along his body, move it this way and that, he's yours. But Lucky's never been ridden. I needed to court him a little more."

Moses's lips were pursed and his eyebrows quirked and I thought for a minute he was going to laugh. I seemed to have that effect on him.

"Shut up," I said.

He laughed, just as I predicted. "I didn't say anything!"

"But you're thinking it."

"What am I thinking?"

"Something dirty. I can see it all over your face."

"Nah. That's not dirt. I'm just black."

"Har, har."

"You've never been thrown, huh?" He rose to his feet beside me.

"I've been thrown plenty," I clipped, turning away. I started to walk in the direction I'd come. No use wandering around looking for Lucky. I'd go back for the truck and drive around until I found him.

"So is that what you're trying to do with me? You want me to give you my head, just like the horse?" he called after me.

I stopped. Moses never gave me much. I'd been pushing him day after day, week after week, since he'd painted my room, just like I'd been pushing Lucky. Lucky had come around. But Moses hadn't.

"I don't want a damn thing from you," I lied.

"That's why you bring me my lunch every day and spy on me and

56

drop by my grandma's house every night."

I felt like I'd fallen all over again, and this time it wasn't my shoulder that hurt. My heart ached like I'd taken one of Lucky's feet to my chest.

"I don't want your head, Moses. I just thought you might need a friend."

"I won't let you in my head, Georgia. You don't want to see what's in my head.""Okay. Fine. Then I'll give you mine," I said, turning on him. I don't know where my pride was. I should spit on him and tell him to go to hell. Instead I was bowing at his feet.

"I'm kind of thinking there isn't anything in your head. I've seen you get kicked and thrown, and I'm guessing you'll be right back at it as soon as you find your horse."

"Screw you, Moses."

"That's the first thing you've said that appeals to me."

I gasped and he laughed. Again. I knew he was just trying to irritate me and make me run away crying. But I wasn't the crying kind. He was right about one thing. I got kicked and thrown, and I came back for more.

So I did something I had never done. I turned and walked back to him, took his face between my hands, and I kissed him hard. It was probably the worst kiss ever delivered in the history of angry kisses. It was a terrible kiss. I had never kissed anyone before, and my lips were pressed into a hard, little line, my eyes squeezed shut, my hands gripping his face like they'd gripped Lucky's mane.

He pulled away, but not far, and his breath was harsh across my mouth. "Careful, Georgia. You're about to get thrown."

"You son of a—"

And then his lips were back, swallowing my angry words, and I forgot almost immediately what a jerk he was. He wasn't impatient or pushy or rough—not like I had been. He took his time and he showed me how to take mine. One hand held my head, cradling it, while the other found the curve of my waist and curled around my belt. And when I tried to take charge he bit down on my lip.

"Stop it," he hissed. "Let me lead."

So I did.

And he led me round and round, up and down, until my legs turned to jelly and my eyes rolled back in my head, until I was leaning against him because I was too turned on to stand.

And when he lifted his head and laughed, just a soft little chuckle, I struggled to open my heavy eyelids and drift back down to earth.

"Well, whaddaya know?"

I shook out the fog and turned my head, finding the spot where Moses's eyes were trained.

Lucky was sauntering across the field like he hadn't just freaked out and taken me for the ride of my life.

"See? The moment you quit chasing him, that's when he wants you. He looks jealous. He thinks he's been replaced."

Our eyes clashed and I peeled myself off him, trying to play like I'd been kissed a hundred times by a hundred different boys.

Moses's eyes drifted down to my mouth, and I shoved my hands into my pockets so I wouldn't be tempted to reach for him again and prove that I could lead as well as he could.

As if he read my mind, Moses nodded toward the horse.

"Go on. You've learned your lesson. He doesn't want to be ridden."

I flipped around, immediately cured from any desire to kiss him again. I gritted my teeth as I walked back to my horse, my stride long, my hands clenched.

Lucky watched me come. He didn't shy away or flinch as I drew near, and without allowing myself to hesitate, I grabbed his mane and swung myself immediately back up onto his bare back. He reared up once, spun a little, dancing and prancing, but I was ready for him and I held on.

And he gave in.

As I urged him back toward home, I couldn't help looking back. Moses stood frozen to the spot, a look of absolute amazement on his face. And it was my turn to laugh.

V

MOSES

I SLEPT ON THE SECOND FLOOR, across the hall from Gi. The old house had no air conditioning, and by the end of the day, the upper rooms were stifling. Gi never seemed to mind, she was always cold, but each night I would open my window, soak my T-shirt with water before putting it on, and then turn the little oscillating fan in the corner on full blast so it blew directly on me, just so I could sleep without drowning in a pool of my own sweat.

Utah had experienced record-breaking temperatures all summer, but the first week of August was unbearable. For the fourth night in a row, I was laying in my bed at midnight, so miserable I considered taking another shower just to cool down, when I heard someone say my name.

I sat up in bed, listening.

"Moses!"

I turned off my fan and waited.

"Moses!"

I ran to the window and looked down to see Georgia in shorts and a tank top, a towel wrapped around her neck and a big, striped pool bag on her shoulder, standing below my window.

She waved merrily, as if her being there in beach wear made total sense.

"I was going to sneak into your house and up the stairs to your room, but I thought maybe you slept naked and I might embarrass you."

I stared down at her, dumbfounded. She didn't try to whisper or disguise her voice in any way. I looked toward Gi's room. The hallway between our rooms was dark and there was no light beneath her door. Still, I put my finger over my lips and shook my head. I had no idea how she even knew which room was mine.

"I'm going to the water tower. Come with me. It's too damn hot to sleep," she said, not softening her voice at all.

"Quiet!" I hissed down at her. Georgia just smiled and shook her head.

"The sooner you get down here in some shorts with the keys to your Jeep, the sooner we can go, and the sooner I'll shut up. We can't take Myrtle. She'd wake the neighborhood."

A laugh escaped my nose in an unattractive snort, and Georgia smirked, obviously well aware that if anyone was in danger of waking the neighborhood, or at least my grandma, it was her.

"What the hell. It is too hot to sleep," I sighed, and her smile widened considerably.

"Meet you out front," she whispered. Oh, now she was being quiet. Now that she got her way.

I'd never been to the water tower, but Georgia directed me to a little paved road, south of town, that wound its way through the fields and crossed a set of railroad tracks before running past a large metal silo with a ladder running up the side. A sign warned that trespassers would be prosecuted, and a chain link fence with a lock on the gate further discouraged what we were about to do, but Georgia wasn't the slightest bit fazed.

"It's easy to climb the fence. I've done it a bunch of times. The water tower beats the pond up the canyon, where I usually swim when I'm desperate, but I can't swim here during the day because I'll get caught and prosecuted to the 'full extent of the law,'" Georgia mocked the sign, "but last summer I came here once a week—always around this time, and nobody ever knew. It's like my own private pool."

The thought of Georgia coming to a dark water tower late at night, all alone, nobody the wiser, made the gooseflesh rise on my arms. I just shook my head and followed her out of the Jeep, glad I'd worn my sneakers if I was climbing chain link. She handed me her pool bag and scrambled up the gate and over as if she truly had done it a hundred times. I slung the bag over my shoulder and was up and over without a hitch. She didn't slow, but climbed the silo ladder with confidence, babbling all the way, filling the darkness with cheerful conversation.

A little door opened inward onto a narrow ledge that circled the inside of the water tower. Georgia slid inside and I followed, leaving the door wide open behind us. Thoughts of being locked in the water tower for days had me propping it with my shoes and testing the knob repeatedly.

"It locks from the outside, silly. And the lock is broken, which is why we have this all to ourselves." Georgia pulled a big LED lantern out of her striped pool bag that still hung over my shoulder, and turned it on, illuminating the interior of the water tower, making it feel like a cavern, complete with hidden pools.

"Now shut the door so no one sees the light."

I obeyed immediately.

"Cool, huh?"

It was kind of cool, I had to admit. The light threw our shadows across the wall, and Georgia danced in front of it for a second, making us both laugh.

"You're gonna fall," I warned as she broke into a segment of Michael Jackson's "Thriller" choreography, the part everyone knows with the zombie arms and the side toe taps. The ledge was not wide enough for dancing, but Georgia apparently didn't agree. I yanked my shirt over my head, set it on our towels, and stared down at the black, glass-smooth surface, waiting for further instruction. I wasn't jumping in first.

Georgia pulled off her T-shirt and tossed her shorts to the side, baring everything but the little that was covered by a baby blue bikini, and I forgot about the water or the fact that there was probably a creature living beneath the surface who liked dark meat. Georgia could save me. I would gladly let Georgia save me if she wore that suit. Her body was long and lean, with surprising curves and swells where a girl should curve and swell. But the best part was the way she seemed unconcerned and unbothered by it all, as if she was absolutely fine with the way her body looked and had no need to strut or pose or seek my approval.

She reached for my hand, and I jerked away, not wanting her to pull me in before I was good and ready.

"We'll go together. The first jump is always the best. The water feels amazing, you'll see." I didn't yield, and she kept her hand out-stretched, waiting.

"Come on, Moses. I'll let you lead," she said, her voice bouncing silkily off the metal walls, the sound more alluring than any singer on any mic in any nightclub across the country. Suddenly, I needed to get in the water or I was going to embarrass myself in my thin shorts. I grabbed her hand and without warning, plunged us both into the inky depths. Georgia's squeal was muffled as the water covered my head, and I released her hand so I could fight my way to the surface.

We both came up sputtering, me from fear, Georgia from laughter, and it didn't take me long until I had abandoned the fear and was laugh-ing with her. She spurred me on, splashing and talking and playing in the flickering shadows that danced on the walls. We swam for a long time, unconcerned with the lateness of the hour, unafraid of discovery, strangely at ease with one another.

It wasn't until I braced my arms on the ledge, my legs kicking out behind me in the water, resting momentarily, that I noticed the light bouncing off the water gave the wall in front of me an iridescent sheen. I reached my hand out to touch it, tracing the watery reflection with my finger, wondering how I could recreate the sheen with paint. Georgia moved to my side, holding onto the ledge, watching my finger as it painted invisible lines.

"When you paint . . . do you know what you're going to paint be-fore you start . . . or do you just let your heart take over?" she asked softly. It was a good question—a sweet question—and her sweetness unlocked something in me that I kept guarded most of the time. Still,

I chose my words carefully, not wanting her to know everything about me, not wanting to ruin the moment with ugly truths, yet not wanting to lie and ruin the memory when the moment had passed.

"There are so many things that I see . . . that I don't want to see. Images that come into my mind that I would rather not think about. Hallucinations, visions, or maybe just an overly vivid imagination. My brain might be cracked, but it's not just my brain. The sky is cracked too, and I can sometimes see what's on the other side."

I sneaked a look at Georgia, wondering if I'd scared her with that last confession. But she didn't look scared. She looked intrigued, fascinated. Beautiful. So I kept talking, encouraged.

"When I was younger I was scared a lot. When I would visit Gi, she would try to tell me stories to calm me down. Bible stories. She even told me about a baby named Moses. A baby found in a basket just like me. That's how I got my name, you know."

Georgia nodded. She knew. Everybody did.

"Gigi would tell me the stories to fill my head with better things. But it wasn't until she started showing me artwork that things started to change. She had a book with religious art in it. Someone had donated it to the church and Gi brought it home so that nobody at church would see all those paintings of naked white people and get offended. She colored all the naked parts in with a black Sharpie."

Georgia laughed, and I felt the air lodge in my throat. Her laugh was throaty and soft, and it made my heart swell like a balloon in my chest, fuller and fuller until I had to sneak breaths around its increased size.

"So you liked the pictures?" Georgia prodded after I stayed frozen and silent too long.

"Yes." Georgia laughed again.

"Not the naked people." I felt ridiculous and actually felt my face get hot. "I liked the beauty. The color. The anguish."

"The anguish?" Georgia's voice rose in question.

"It was an anguish that had nothing to do with me. An anguish everyone could see. Not just me. And I wasn't expected to make it all go away."

Georgia's gaze touched on my face like a whisper and drifted away almost immediately, drawn to my tracing fingers.

"Have you ever seen the face of the Pieta?" I wanted her eyes on me again and I got what I wanted.

"What's the Pieta?" she asked.

"It's a sculpture by Michelangelo. A sculpture of Mary holding Jesus. Her son. After he died," I paused, wondering why I was telling her this. I seriously doubted she cared. But I found myself continuing anyway.

"Her face, Mary's face . . . it's so beautiful. So peaceful. I don't like the rest of the sculpture as much. But Mary's face is exquisite. When I can't take the stuff in my head, I think about her face. And I fill my mind with other things too. I think about the color and light of a Manet, the details of a Vermeer—Vermeer includes the tiniest things in his paintings, little cracks in the walls, a stain on a collar, a single nail, and there is such beauty in those little things, in the perfect ordinariness of them. I think about those things and I push out the images I can't control, the things I don't want to see, but am forced to see . . . all the time." I stopped talking. I was almost panting. My mouth felt strange, numb, like I'd surpassed my daily word limit, and my lips and tongue were weak from overuse. I didn't remember the last time I'd talked so much all at once.

"The perfect ordinariness . . ." Georgia breathed, and she lifted her hand and followed the wet path my finger made, as if she, too, could paint. Then she looked at me solemnly.

"I'm a very ordinary girl, Moses. I know that I am. And I always will be. I can't paint. I don't know who Vermeer is, or Manet for that matter. But if you think ordinary can be beautiful, that gives me hope. And maybe sometime you'll think about me when you need an escape from the hurt in your head."

Her brown eyes looked black in the shadowed light, the same color as the water we were immersed in, and I reached blindly for something to hold onto, something to keep me from falling into them. Georgia's right hand was still pressed to the wall beside mine, and I found myself tracing her fingers, like a child traces their hand with a crayon, up and

64

down and around until I paused at the base of her thumb. And then I continued on, letting my fingers dance up her arm, feather light, until I reached her shoulder. I traced the fine bones at her collar as my fingers glided to the opposite side and back down her other arm. When I found her fingers, I slid mine in-between, interlocking them tightly. I waited for her to lean in, to press her mouth to mine, to lead, as she was prone to do. But she stayed still, holding my hand beneath the surface of the water, watching me. And I gave in. Anxiously.

Her lips were wet and cool against mine, and I imagine mine felt the same. But the heat inside her mouth welcomed me like a warm embrace, and I sank into the softness with a sigh that would have embarrassed me had she not matched it with one of her own.

GEORGIA

MOSES AND I WATCHED as my parents conducted a therapy session with a small group of addicts from a rehab center in Richfield, about an hour south of Levan. Every other week, the van would pull up and the young people would pile out—kids ranging from my age to their early twenties—and for two hours, my parents would bring them out to the round corral and let them interact with the horses in a series of activities designed to help the kids make connections to their own lives.

I helped with the sessions with autistic kids and the kids who rode horses for physical rehab, but when the clients were my age or older, my parents didn't like me involved in the counseling, even if it was just to work with the horses. So I'd wandered over to Kathleen's, knowing Moses should be done with work, and coaxed him to the backyard with a couple of Cokes and two pieces of lemon meringue pie Kathleen had been happy to part with. She liked me, and I knew it, and she was incredibly helpful in maneuvering Moses when he pretended to not want my company or lemon meringue pie when we both knew darn well he wanted both.

Moses and I couldn't hear what was being said from where we sat, stretched out on Kathleen's back lawn, but we had a decent view, and I knew we weren't close enough to attract the attention of my parents, even though we could still see the class being conducted. Being my normal nosy self, I was trying to make out which kids were still hanging around and which ones had either graduated from the ninety day program or been released. I made a mental catalogue of the ones who looked like they were miserable and the ones who were making progress.

"What do you call them . . . the different colors? Aren't there different names?" Moses asked suddenly, his eyes trained on the horses milling about the enclosure. He held a paint brush in his hands as if he'd grabbed it out of habit, and he wove it between his fingers like a drummer of a rock band twirls his drumsticks.

"There are so many colors and kinds. I mean, they're all horses, obviously, but each color combination has a different name." I pointed to a reddish horse in the corner. "That red one there? Merle? He's a Sorrel, and Sackett is a Palomino. Dolly is a Bay, and Lucky is a Black."

"A Black?"

"Yes. He's solid black," I answered easily.

"Well, that one's easy enough." Moses laughed a little.

"Yep. There are greys, blacks, browns, whites. Reba's an Appaloosa, the greyish one with spots on her rump. We don't like to label them by their colors in equine therapy though. And we don't call the horses by their names. We don't even tell the clients if the horses are male or female."

"Why? Not politically correct?" Moses quipped. He laughed again, and I poked at him, liking that he seemed interested, even relaxed. Now if I could only get him inside the corral.

"Because you want the client to identify with the horse. You want the client to put their own labels on the horse. If a horse is exhibiting a certain behavior that you want the client to identify with, you don't want the client to have any preconceived ideas about who or what that horse is. That horse needs to be whoever the client needs it to be." I sounded just like my mother, and mentally patted myself on my back for being able to explain something that I'd grown up hearing but never had to put into words until now.

"That doesn't really make any sense."

"Okay. For instance, let's say you have mother issues."

Moses shot me a look that said, "Don't go there!" So of course I did.

"Let's say you are in a therapy session where you are discussing your feelings about your mother. And the horse starts exhibiting certain behaviors that suddenly clarify your behavior . . . or your mother's behavior. If we've already labeled that horse as Gordie and said he's a boy, you might not be able to identify your mother with that horse. In a therapy session, the only labels the horses get are the ones the client gives them."

"So you wouldn't want me to notice that the Palomino horse, the one with the white mane and the tan body, looks like you and that she's always making a nuisance of herself?"

"Sackett?" I was outraged on Sackett's behalf more than my own. "Sackett isn't annoying! And Sackett's a *he*, which just proves my point about pre-conceived ideas. If you knew he was a he and not a she, you wouldn't be able to label him as Georgia and say mean things. Sackett is wise! Whenever things get really deep, you can always count on Sackett being right in the thick of things." I heard the affront in my voice and I glowered at Moses for a moment before launching my own attack.

"And Lucky is just like you!" I said.

Moses just stared at me blandly, but I could tell he was enjoying himself. "Because he's black?"

"No, stupid. Because he's in love with me, and he tries to pretend every day like he doesn't want to have anything to do with me," I shot back.

Moses choked, and I punched him hard in the stomach, making him gasp and grab for my hands.

"So you want the clients to not pay any attention to the color of the horse. That's not even human nature, you know." Moses pinned my hands over my head and stared down into my flushed face. When he could see I wasn't going to continue punching he relaxed his hold, but he looked back toward the horses and continued talking.

"Everyone always talks about being color blind. And I get that. I do. But maybe instead of being color blind, we should celebrate color, in all its shades. It kind of bugs me that we're supposed to ignore our differences like we don't see them, when seeing them doesn't have to be a negative."

I could only stare. I didn't want to look anywhere but at him. He was so beautiful, and I loved it when he talked to me, when he suddenly became philosophical like this. I loved it so much I didn't want to say anything. I just wanted to wait to see if he would say more. After several long minutes of silence he looked down at me and found me staring at him.

"I like your skin. I love the color of your eyes. Am I supposed to just ignore that?" he whispered, and my heart galloped to the round corral, cleared the fence, and raced back to me in giddy delight.

"You like my skin?" I breathed, stupefied.

"Yes. I do," he admitted, and looked back at the horses. It was by far the nicest thing he'd ever said to me. And I just laid there in happy silence.

"If you had to paint me, what colors would you use?" I had to know.

"Brown, white, gold, pink, peach," he sighed. "I'd have to experiment."

"Will you paint me?" It was something I desperately wanted.

"No." He sighed again.

"Why?" I tried not to be hurt.

"It's easier to paint the things in my head than the things I see with my eyes."

"So . . . paint me from memory." I sat up and placed my hands over his eyes. "Here. Close your eyes. Now picture me. There. See me? I'm the Palomino filly up in your grill all the time."

His lips twisted and I knew he wanted to laugh, but I kept my hands over his eyes. "Now keep them closed. You're holding a paint brush in your hand already. And here's the canvas." I brought the hand holding the brush to my face. "Now paint."

He dropped his hand back to his lap, holding the brush, debating. I dropped my hand from his eyes, but he kept them closed. Then he lifted his hand once more and slid the dry brush softly against my face.

"What was that?"

"My forehead."

"What part?"

"The left side.

"And here?"

"My cheek."

"Here?"

"My chin." It tickled, but I didn't let myself move. Moses traced the tip of my chin, followed it down and around, making a straight line to my neck. I swallowed as the brush slid down my throat and whispered down my chest to the opening of my T-shirt. My T-shirt made a neat V above my breasts, and Moses paused, holding the brush pressed against my skin, directly over my heart. But he kept his eyes closed.

"If I were to paint you, I would use every color," he said suddenly, almost wistfully, as if he was sure he couldn't paint me . . . but he wanted to. "You would have crimson lips and peach skin and ebony eyes with purple shadows. You would have hair streaked with gold and white and blue and skin tinted with caramel and cream, swirled with pink and shaded with cinnamon."

As he talked, he moved the brush this way and that, as if he were actually painting with the colors in his head. And then he stopped and opened his eyes. My breath was stuck somewhere between my heart and my head, and I concentrated on letting it out without giving myself away. But he knew. He knew what effect he had on me. He threw the brush and stood up, breaking the spell he'd woven with gentle strokes and soft words. He headed back into the house and I could have sworn I heard him mutter to himself as he left me lying on the grass, "I can't paint you Georgia . . . you're alive."

VI

MOSES

GEORGIA WOULDN'T STAY AWAY. I did my best to make her go. I didn't need her tying me up and tying me down. I was leaving as soon as I could, and she was not part of my plans. I treated her like shit most of the time. And she just shrugged it off and handed it right back. It didn't faze her and it definitely didn't make her go away. The problem was, I liked kissing her. I liked the way her hair felt in my hands and the way her body felt when she crowded me and got in my space, demanding attention and getting it, every damn time.

And she made me laugh. I was not the laughing kind. I swore more than I smiled. Life just wasn't that funny. But Georgia was extremely funny. And laughing and kissing does not make it easy to convince someone you want them to go away. And she just wouldn't go away.

I thought after that night at the rodeo, tied up and terrorized, Georgia would lose some of her sass. Terrence Anderson, who had nothing but insults for Georgia, had definitely lost his sass when I cornered him a few nights after the stampede and made sure he knew that little boys who liked rope got sliced up by men who liked knives. The truth was, I was good with knives—I could throw them and hit the target dead center at twenty paces—and I made sure Terrence knew that. I showed him a nice big one I'd taken from Gigi's kitchen drawer, and I gave him a little knick on his cheek, marking him up in the same place where Georgia's cheek had bled.

He said he hadn't done it. But his eyes shifted around like maybe he had. Even if he hadn't done it, he was an asshole, so I didn't feel bad that I made him bleed. The only thing I felt bad about was that I had been compelled to scare him off at all. Georgia's problems were not my problems. Georgia was my problem. Like right now, when she was determined to help me repair fence, talking and making me laugh and then making me angry because she was making me laugh.

"I can't get any work done when you're around. And it's gonna rain, and I'm not gonna finish. This section of fence has been a bitch, and you aren't helping."

"Whine, whine, whine," Georgia sighed. "You and I both know I rock at repairing fence."

I laughed. Again. "You suck at repairing fence! And you didn't bring gloves, so I had to give you mine, and now my hands look like porcupines from all the damn splinters. You are not helping."

"That's it, Moses. Give me five greats." Georgia said, like she was demanding push-ups, a drill sergeant barking out a command.

"Five greats?"

"Five things that are great about today. About life. Go."

I just stared at her sullenly.

"Okay. I'll go first. It's easy. Right off the top of my head, five things I'm grateful for. Bacon, wet wipes, Tim McGraw, mascara, and rosemary," she said.

"That's kind of a strange assortment," I said.

"What did you tell me about finding beauty in little things? What was that painter's name? Vermeer?"

"Vermeer was an artist, not a painter," I objected, scowling.

"An artist who painted nails and stains and cracks in the wall, right?"

I was impressed that she remembered.

"The five greats game is kind of like that. Finding beauty in ordinary things. And the only rule is gratitude. My mom and dad use it all the time. Grumbling isn't really allowed around my house. Foster kids learn that real quick. Any time you start feeling sorry for yourself or you go into a rant about how bad life sucks, you immediately have to name five greats."

"I can name five grates. Five things that are grating on my nerves." I smiled sarcastically, pleased at my play on words. "And the fact that you're wearing my gloves is at the top. Followed by your annoying lists and the fact that you just called Vermeer a painter."

"You gave me your gloves! And yeah, it's annoying, but there's something to it. It changes your focus, even if it's just for a minute. And it shuts down the whining. I had one little foster sister who named the same five things every time. Toilet paper, SpaghettiOs, shoelaces, light bulbs, and the sound of her mother snoring. She had a pair of flip flops when she came to us, and nothing more. The first time we bought her shoes, we got her a pair with fluorescent green laces with pink hearts on them. She would walk, staring down at those laces.

"The sound of her mother snoring?"

"It meant she was still alive."

I felt a little sick. Kids all over the world put up with too much from people who should know better. And then those kids turned into adults that repeated the cycle. I would probably do the same if I ever had kids. All the more reason not to. Georgia continued on while I considered how much people truly sucked.

"My mom lets the kids tell her five things that are bothering them, things they needed to express. They count them off on their fingers." Georgia grabbed my hand and ticked the items off on my fingers to demonstrate. "Like, I'm tired. I miss my mom. I don't want to be here. I don't want to go to school. I'm scared. Whatever. Then they make a fist with the fingers they just used to express their problems. And then they throw the things away, they toss them." Georgia illustrated the motion with my hand, wrapping my fingers around my palm, making a fist so I could throw away the imaginary ball of wadded up complaints. "Then she makes them name five greats. It helps them to refocus and it reminds them that even when life is pretty bad, it isn't all bad, ever." She looked at me, still holding my hand, waiting. I stared back.

"So give it to me, Moses. Five greats. Go."

"I can't," I said immediately.

"You sure as hell can. I can name five things for you, but that doesn't work as well. Gratitude works best when you're the one feeling it."

"Fine. You do it then—you name five greats for me," I fired back and pulled my hand from hers. "You think you know me?" I said it mildly, but there was a prickling under my skin, an irritation that I couldn't quite tamp down. Georgia thought she had it all figured out, but Georgia Shepherd hadn't suffered enough to know shit about life.

Georgia grabbed my hand back stubbornly, and lifting it up, she gently placed a kiss on each fingertip for each item on the list. "Georgia's eyes. Georgia's hair. Georgia's smile. Georgia's personality. Georgia's kisses." She batted her eyes. "See? Definitely five greats for Moses."

I really couldn't argue with that. All of those things were pretty great.

"Feeling pretty good about yourself, aren't you?" I said, shaking my head, grinning in spite of myself. My fingers tingled where her lips had been. I wanted her to do it again. And somehow, she knew it. She pulled my hand back to her mouth. "And these are mine." She kissed my smallest finger. "Moses's eyes." She moved to my ring finger. "Moses's smile." Another kiss on the tallest tip. "Moses's laugh." Her lips were so soft. "Moses's art." She rounded to my thumb and placed her mouth gently against the pad. "Moses's kisses." Then she moved her lips from my fingertips and pressed her mouth to my palm.

"Those are my five greats for Georgia today. Those were my five greats yesterday and they will be tomorrow and the next day, until your kisses get old. Then I'll have to think of something else."

GEORGIA

WE ALL STARED. Even though it was only the second week of the new school year and he was a new student, everybody knew Moses. Or of him. He wasn't white, for starters, in a small school of mostly white kids, so that made him stand out. Plus, he was beautiful. But that's not why we were staring. Moses was in my English Lit classroom, drawing on the board, and he wasn't even enrolled in the class. We'd come back from lunch to find him there, the two huge boards filled with a drawing that was beyond anything any of the students had ever seen. Except for me. I knew what he was capable of.

Moses had halted abruptly, as if torn between finishing his masterpiece and running from the room. And then Ms. Murray was there, and running was no longer an option. There was a black smudge on his brown cheek and the sides of his hands were stained as well, as if he'd used them as tools to blend and create the erotic image behind him. He shifted uncomfortably from one foot to the other and his eyes were restless and wide, their golden color making him look like a cornered animal. And he was definitely cornered. Ms. Murray stood in the doorway, her eyes trained on the chalkboard. When I looked at her to see whether or not Moses was going to get yelled at, or worse, kicked out of school, I noticed that there were tears streaming down her face and her hands were pressed to her lips. It was kind of a weird response.

Ms. Murray wasn't really a crier. She was usually pretty serious and stiff. She was a good teacher and she didn't yell or get all emotional when kids messed up or were disrespectful, which I frankly appreciated. High school was crazy enough without teachers adding to the drama. When Ms. Murray wasn't happy, she usually just stared you down and started heaping on the homework. She didn't cry.

This wasn't good. Apparently Moses recognized that fact, because he dropped the marker clutched in his hand and stepped away, looking from side to side like he was planning his escape.

"What is that, anyway?" Charlie Morgan spoke up, never one to hold still or hold his tongue. I usually hated that he could never shut up. But I didn't hate it now. Now, I was glad. I was glad because I wanted to know too. Charlie pointed at the board. "Is that a waterfall?

When Moses didn't respond Charlie continued. "Behind the waterfall—those are people, right?" Charlie laughed. "They're making out! And it doesn't look like they're wearing any clothes."

A few of my classmates laughed, but we all stared, our eyes drawn to the way the water spilled down from the cliffs surrounding the two people who were almost hidden in the silvery fall. If I squinted, blurring the reality of the black lines and the unromantic whiteboard, I could almost imagine the picture was real, that the people behind the water were living and breathing, that they were truly kissing and we were peering through the spray, watching the intimate encounter unfold. And they were definitely naked. I felt my cheeks get hot and I pulled my eyes away. Looking at what Moses had drawn made my skin feel too tight and my body ache with a need that had become an ever-present thing where Moses was concerned. It made me think of the night at the water tower, and the kisses we had shared and the heat that had remained in my belly long after we parted.

"Did you draw that?" Another kid spoke up from behind me. It sounded like Kirsten, but I didn't turn my head to see for sure. "It's so good. You're an amazing artist."

"Students!" Ms. Murray had found her voice, though it shook and wavered like she was still crying. "I need you to head out to the commons area. Take your things. Use the time to work on the paper due Friday. Moses, please stay."

Working on my paper didn't sound half as interesting as seeing Ms. Murray crying over a whiteboard drawing of naked people, drawn by none other than Moses Wright—my Moses—who also happened to be the strangest person I'd ever met. But free-time was way better than instruction, and I didn't have any choice in the matter, so we all reluctantly rose and filed out the door. I was the last to leave, and I caught Moses's eye as I let the door shut behind me. He looked as if he wanted to call me back, as if he wanted to explain. But then the door swung closed, and I stood on the other side. Still, I thought I heard Mrs. Murray ask Moses the weirdest question.

"How did you know?" she asked. "How did you know about Ray?"

GEORGIA

MOSES WAS SUSPENDED. Apparently, Ms. Murray didn't like him drawing naked people kissing under a waterfall on her whiteboards. I was actually a little surprised. It hadn't seemed malicious. But I guess it was a little erotic for the classroom. I felt hot all over again and wondered what Moses had been thinking. What had compelled him to do something so stupid? Was it the attention? It was only the beginning of the school year, May was a long way off, and from what I'd been able to coax out of a reluctant Moses, he couldn't afford to miss anything. He was a senior but didn't have enough credits to graduate unless he worked his butt off. And getting suspended was pretty counter-productive.

I thought for sure his grandma would be able to twist some arms and smooth things over to get him right back, but over the next two months it was one thing after another, and Moses couldn't stay out of trouble. He painted another barn in town with blacks and silvers and streaks of gold so vivid it looked as if the entire north side had been swallowed by a black hole that left a violent storm in its wake. I didn't find out until later that that barn had been struck by lightning thirty years before and burned to the ground, killing a man in the process. The man had been trying to get his horses out and was engulfed in flames. The painting wasn't quite as beautiful when I knew the story behind it.

The barn had eventually been rebuilt and his wife had remarried, but Charlotte Butters, his widow, wasn't especially impressed by Moses's artistic ability and made sure everyone in town knew what a cruel joke she thought it was, though I doubted it was anything but a coincidence. It would be a shame to paint over something so awe-inspiring, but Charlotte Butters was fuming, and Moses's grandma had smoothed her feathers by promising that Moses would fix it, plus paint the rest of the barn to make amends. No swirls of color or Sistine chapel this time.

Just plain barn red and long hours on a ladder. I was, of course, keeping him company even though he was trying to convince me to leave. As usual.

It was October, but although there was a nip in the air and the light warmed the earth at a different angle, we were having a string of unseasonably warm days, warm enough to make painting a barn after school not completely unappealing, especially if it meant I could see Moses... whether or not he wanted to see me. He and I had the strangest relationship. One minute he was telling me to scram and the next he was kissing me like he would never let me go.

To say I was rattled and confused would be putting it mildly. When I showed up in a pair of worn Wranglers and a tank top that had withstood a thousand washes and offered to help him, he took one look at me and started down a list of do's and don'ts that were a little extreme, considering we were only painting a barn. After the exhaustive list of instructions and parameters, I sighed loudly and picked up my brush, only to have him watch me critically for a few minutes then take the brush from my hand and go back over what I'd just done.

When I protested, he interrupted.

"My job site, my rules."

"So those are your rules. Your laws?"

"Yeah. The Law of Moses." He smirked.

"I thought the Law of Moses was the Ten Commandments."

"I don't know if I have that many."

"Well, this is the state of Georgia, and in Georgia we have a different set of laws. So when you're in the state of Georgia—"

"When I'm in the state of Georgia?" he asked, so softly I almost missed it.

I blushed, realizing that there were sexual connotations to what I'd said. But never one to back down, I blustered on. "Ha. You wish." I tried to resume painting, but he pushed me away from the paint can.

"You're just hanging around me because you love breaking the rules—and don't think I don't know your parents have some rules when it comes to us. You being with me makes them crazy. Especially your mom. She's afraid of me."

Well, that was true. And he wasn't stupid. It was definitely part of the attraction. But when he lost himself, painting like a demon, painting incredible things that came from somewhere behind those amber-green eyes, I couldn't get close enough. And I wanted him to paint me. I wanted to stand in front of him and let him cover me in color, let me be one of his creations. I wanted to be part of his world. I wanted to fit in. It was ironic, for the first time in my life, if blending in meant being absorbed into his thoughts, sucked into his head, then I wanted to blend in. Maybe it was being seventeen, maybe it was first love, or first lust. Maybe it was just hot. But I wanted him with a desperation that consumed me. I had never wanted anything so much in my life. And I couldn't imagine wanting something so much ever again.

"Why do you like me, Moses?" I huffed, hands on my hips. I was tired of being pushed and pulled, never knowing what he really wanted.

"Who says I do?" he answered softly. But he turned his eyes on me. And his eyes kept me hopeful when his words would have crushed me. His eyes said he did.

"Is that one of your laws? Thou shall not like Georgia?

"Nah. It's thou shall not get strung up."

His words made me sick. "Strung up? Like lynched? That's just sick Moses. We may sound like hicks. I may say seen when I should say saw. I may say was when I should say were. We may be small town people with small town ways. But you being black, or whatever color you are, doesn't matter to anyone here. This isn't the sixties, and it sure as hell ain't the Deep South."

"But it's Georgia," he answered softly, playing games with my name the way I had done. "And you're a sweet Georgia peach with fuzzy pink skin, and I'm not biting."

I shrugged. But he *was* biting . . . and that was the problem. His words made me want to lean over and sink my teeth into his well-muscled left shoulder, and bite him too. I wanted to bite him hard enough to express my frustration, yet sweetly enough that he'd let me do it again.

"So what else? What are your other laws?"

"Thou shall paint."

"All right. Looks like you're obeying that one. What else?"

"Thou shall stay away from blondes."

He was always trying to sting me. Always trying to get under my skin. "Not just Georgia, but all blondes? Why?"

"I don't like blondes. My mother was a blonde."

"And your dad was black?"

"That's the assumption. Most blondes can't throw black babies all by themselves." I rolled my eyes. "And you think we're prejudiced."

"Oh, I'm definitely prejudiced. But I have my reasons. I never met a blonde I liked."

"Well, then. I'll go red."

Moses's mouth split into a grin so wide I thought his face would split in two. It surprised me and it sure as hell surprised him, because he leaned over and braced his hands against his knees, laughing like he'd never laughed before. I grabbed the brush he'd taken from me and made a long red streak down the length of my braid. He wheezed, laughing even harder, but he shook his head no. Reaching out his hand, he demanded the brush.

"Don't do that, Georgia," he sputtered, laughing so hard he had tears in the corners of his eyes.

But I kept painting, and he lunged for me, trying to take the brush, but I spun, turning my body so that my back was pushing against him, creating a barrier between him and the brush in my hand. I held the brush as far out in front of me as I could, but Moses was taller, longer, and his arms easily wrapped me up and yanked the brush from my fingers. Now there was paint on my palms, and I turned and wiped them down his face, making him look like an Apache warrior. He yelped and immediately used the brush in his hand to repeat the motion down the side of my face. I leaned over and found the paint can, dipping my fingers in the silky red liquid. And I turned on him with a smirk.

"I'm just trying to obey the law, Moses. What was it? Thou shall paint?" I smiled an evil smile and Moses caught my wrist. I flicked my fingers and sent little droplets flying, covering his shirt in tiny red dots.

"Georgia, you better run." Moses was still smiling, but there was a gleam in his eye that made me weak in the knees. I smiled sweetly up into his face.

"Why would I do that, Moses? When I want you to catch me?"His grin cooled, but his eyes grew warmer. And then, still holding my wrist in one hand, he grabbed my braid, slick with paint, with the other and pulled me toward him.

And this time, he let me lead.

His lips were gentle, waiting for me to set the pace. I sucked at his mouth and pulled at his T-shirt, and generally wished there were no laws. No rules. That I could do what I wanted. That I could lay down in the shadowy interior of the barn and pull him down with me. That I could do the things my body wanted to do. That I could paint his body in red and he could use his body to paint mine in return, until there was no difference, no black or white, no now and then, no crime, no punishment. Just vivid red, like my vivid red longing.

But there are laws. There are rules. Laws of nature and laws of life. Laws of love and laws of death. And when you break them, there are consequences. And Moses and I, like a stream of fateful lovers who had gone before us and who would come after us, were subject to those laws, whether we kept them or not.

VII

MOSES

EVEN THE SMELL WAS HEADY. It made me dizzy and exacerbated the pounding in my head and the weight in my chest. Slashing red and yellow, swirls of silver, streaks of black. My arms flew, spraying and moving, climbing and blending. It was too dark to see whether I actually created what I saw in my head. But it didn't matter. Not to me. But it would matter to the girl. The girl needed someone to see her. So I would paint her picture, I would show the world her face. And then maybe she would go away.

I'd been seeing her off and on since mid-summer, since the night of the rodeo when I'd found Georgia tied up and taken her home. Ever since then, I'd started seeing Molly. She wrote her name in fat cursive letters and looped her Y in a long swirl. I saw that name on a math test. She showed me a math test, of all things. There was a crisp A at the top, and I suspected she was proud of it. Or she had been proud. Once. Before.

Molly looked a little like Georgia—blonde hair and laughing eyes. But she showed me things and places that meant nothing to me, like the math test. Sunflowers lining the sides of roads I'd never driven down, a turbulent sky, and rain drops against a window fringed by curtains with yellow stripes, a woman's hands, and an apple pie with an expertly woven pie crust, perfectly browned.

And then my painting was lit from behind, twin spotlights illuminating the underpass. I threw the can in my hand and slid down the slanted concrete wall, the spray-paint cans in my makeshift work belt slapping against my legs and clanking together like chains as I ran.

But the lights followed, trapping me between the beams, and I tripped, sprawling painfully, the cans digging into my abdomen and hips, the skin of my palms embedded with gravel. The car swerved and braked, and I was released temporarily from the glare as the lights shot over my head. I was on my feet again immediately, but there was something wrong with my right leg and I fell back down, crying out as the pain cut through my adrenaline.

"Moses?"

It wasn't the police. And it wasn't the girl's killer. I was pretty certain she had been killed. There was a certain solemnity and freshness to her colors that I only saw when the death was violent and unexpected. When the death was new.

"Moses?" There it was again. I turned, drawing my arm up to block out the light from the flashlight being leveled at me and find the voice on the other side.

"Georgia?" What the hell was she doing out at one a.m. on a school night? My mental monologue sounded like a parent and I stopped myself immediately. It was none of my business what she was doing, just like it wasn't any of her business what I was doing. It was like I'd spoken out loud, because she immediately asked:

"What are you doing?" Georgia sounded like a parent too, and I didn't answer her, as usual.

I struggled to my feet, wincing even as I realized there was something sticking out of my leg. Glass. There was a long shard of glass embedded in my knee where it had connected with the concrete.

"Why do you do that?" Her voice was sad. Not accusing. Not freaked out or wary. Just sad, like she didn't understand me and wanted to. "Why do you paint all over everyone's property?"

"It's public property. Nobody cares." It was a stupid thing to say, but I couldn't explain it to her. Just like I couldn't explain it to anyone. So I wouldn't.

"Charlotte Butters cared. Ms. Murray sure as hell cared."

"So you're just out tonight, keeping the community safe from paint?" I asked. The overpass was surrounded by nothing but fields of long golden wheat . . . or whatever it was they grew in Utah. A little cluster of businesses huddled around the exit ramp nearby, but they were a tiny island in the sea of gold.

"Nah. I saw you leave. I watched you head toward Nephi."

I stared at her blankly

"Your headlights hit my window when you left. I was still up."

That didn't make much sense. I'd been painting for at least an hour.

"I drove around until I found you; I saw your Jeep pulled off the side of the road," she finished quietly. Her honesty amazed me. She had no artifice. And when she tried to disguise her feelings I saw right through her. She was like glass—pure and clear and plain as day. And like glass, her honesty cut me.

I yanked at the shard in my knee, cursing as I did, and the diversionary tactic worked, because Georgia's eyes dropped to my wound. She moved her flashlight to get a better look and cursed right along with me when she saw the blood that was turning my pants black in the moonlight.

"It's not that big a deal." I shrugged. But it did hurt.

"Come on. I've got a first aid kit under the seat." She beckoned me with the flashlight, making a looping circle of light as she turned, expecting me to follow. Which I did.

She wrenched open the door, pulled out an orange plastic case from under the passenger seat and patted the seat expectantly.

"Can you climb up?"

I grunted. "It's just a scrape—you're not going to have to amputate or anything."

"Well, it's bleeding like crazy."

I eased my pant leg up and Georgia made herself busy playing doctor as I stared at the top of her pale blonde head and wondered for the millionth time why in the world she kept hanging around me. What was the appeal? The girl loved a challenge, that was easy to see. I'd watched her ride that black horse over fences and fields, flying like she belonged in the sky. I'd watched her coax and wheedle the stallion until he was so bewitched he now ran to her when she called him. But I wasn't an animal and I didn't want to be her next conquest, and I was pretty sure that's what I was.

The thought made me angry and as soon as she was done I pulled down my pant leg and stepped out of the cab, heading for my Jeep without a word. She trotted behind me.

"Go home Georgia. You're breaking another one of my laws. Thou shall not follow me."

"Those are your laws, Moses. I didn't agree to any of them."

I heard her trip behind me, and I paused in spite of myself. There was broken glass and and beer cans were everywhere. This underpass was a hangout on the weekends. More high school kids got drunk here than any other place in town, if the empty cans and bottles were any indication. I didn't want her to hurt herself. I walked back to her and took her hand, escorting her back to her truck.

"Go home, Georgia," I repeated, but this time I tried to say it a little more kindly. I opened the driver's side door to the rust bucket she had named Myrtle because it rhymed with turtle and that's about how fast it drove.

"Why did you paint that girl? On the overpass. Why did you do that? What does it mean?" Her voice was sad, almost like she felt betrayed. Betrayed by what, I couldn't guess.

"I saw her picture. So I painted her," I replied easily. It was mostly the truth. I really didn't see her picture, not the way I made it sound. Not on a flyer—though there was one on the post office bulletin board. I actually saw her in my head.

"You liked the way she looked?"

I shrugged dismissively. "She's pretty. It's sad. I like to draw." Truth. She was pretty. It was sad. I did like to draw.

"Did you know her?"

"No. I know she's dead."

86

Georgia looked horrified. Even in the moonlit darkness I could see how much I had upset her. I think I wanted to upset her. I wanted her to be afraid.

"How?"

"Because kids on flyers usually are. She's from around here, right?"

"Not really. She's from Sanpete. But it's a small town like this one. And it's weird that she just disappeared. She's the second girl to disappear like that in the last year. It's just . . . weird. Scary, you know?"

I nodded. The girl's name was Molly. And she was definitely dead. She kept showing me things. Not about her death. About her life. I hoped now she would leave me alone. This had been going on long enough. I had no idea why she'd come to me at all. Usually there had to be some connection. I'd never met Molly. But she would go now, I hoped. Paint them and they leave. It was the way I acknowledged them. And usually that was enough.

"So you being out here in the middle of the night, painting her . . . That's weird too," Georgia said bravely, her eyes holding mine.

I nodded again. "Are you afraid, Georgia?"

She just looked at me like she was trying to get in my head. My little horse whisperer, trying to whisper to me. I shook my head, trying to clear it. She wasn't my horse whisperer. She wasn't my anything.

"Yeah. I'm afraid. I'm afraid for you, Moses. Because everyone is going to see this. The police are going to see this. And people are going to think you did something to that girl."

"That's what they think everywhere I go, Georgia. I'm used to it."

"Do you always paint dead people?"

Her voice rang out like a whip, and I felt the truth slash across my face with all the crack and sting that secrets wield.

I stepped back, stunned that she had so easily unraveled this piece of me. I walked toward my Jeep, wanting nothing more than to run, run, run and keep running. Why couldn't I just keep running? I had seven months until the school year was up, but I was working on my GED and saving up all my money. Seven months. And then, as much as I loved Gi, as much as the thought of never seeing Georgia again hurt me, I was leaving this funny little town with all its nosy people with their suspicious minds, interfering hands, and busy mouths. And I would keep moving, painting as I went. I didn't know how I would survive, but I would, and I would be free. As free as I'd ever be.

Georgia trotted behind me, "You painted a picture of my grandpa on the side of our barn. He's been dead for twelve years. I was five when he died. You painted the lightning on Charlotte Butter's barn too. Her husband was killed in a lightning storm in that barn. You painted a man named Ray on Ms. Murray's whiteboard and I found out that Ms. Murray's fiancé was named Ray. He was killed in a freak accident two weeks before their wedding. You've been painting the walls inside the old mill. I saw those too. I don't recognize the faces you painted, but they're all dead too, aren't they?"

There was no way I could answer her without telling her everything. I wanted to tell her everything. But I knew better. So I just kept walking.

"Moses! Wait! Please, please, please don't keep walking away from me!" she cried in frustration, so close to tears I could almost hear them gathering behind her eyes. My heart ached and my will shattered. I did the only thing I knew would make her forget her questions, make her forget her doubt in me. Make us both forget.

I let her catch me.

And when she did, I turned to meet her and wrapped my arms around her so tightly that our hearts pressed together and found a similar rhythm. Mine pounded into her breasts and hers pushed right back against my chest, challenging me like she always did. I kissed her lips over and over, letting the color of her mouth drench my troubled mind, drowning out the pictures in my head, until there was only Georgia, only rose-colored kisses and moonlight, only heat. I touched her body and warmed my hands against her skin until her questions just floated away on the wind. And the girl I had painted on the concrete underpass kept her face lifted to the sky and left us alone.

GEORGIA

I DITCHED SCHOOL BEFORE the day ended and took Myrtle on a drive-by of the overpass so I could get a look at Moses's painting it in the daylight before they made him cover it up.

It was so beautiful. The girl laughed at an unknown admirer, her face tipped up as if toward the sun, and her hair flew around her shoulders. It almost made me jealous, and I was ashamed of my small feelings. But Moses had seen her like this. How that was possible, I didn't know. But he was the artist, and she was his muse, however briefly. And I didn't like that. I wanted to be his one and only. It was my face I wanted in his head.

I sat staring at the laughing girl, brought to life on a lonely underpass with spray paint and the genius of a modern-day Michelangelo. Or maybe Van Gogh. Hadn't Van Gogh been the crazy one? The girl Moses had painted was so full of life I was certain she couldn't be dead. But Moses thought she was. The thought made my stomach clench and my legs feel like cold jelly. Not because she was dead—that was horrible—but because Moses seemed to know. No one looking at it could possibly think Moses was mocking someone's grief or that his art was violent. But it was weird. And nobody knew what to do with him. He never denied any of it. But he didn't defend himself either.

And last night. Last night, I was scared and angry and confused. He had seemed so unattainable. So frustratingly distant! So when he turned on me suddenly and kissed me, holding me so tight that there was no distance at all . . . something inside me gave way. And when he tossed down his coat and we fell to the ground, hands and mouths and cumbersome clothing pushed and pulled aside to uncover the something beneath that kept us apart, I didn't protest and he didn't stop.

I grew up on a farm with horses. I had a very clear, graphic knowledge of the mechanics of the act. But nothing prepared me for the feelings, for the need, for the intense sensations, for the power, for the sweet agony. We occupied a space so primal and so ripe with the present that our heartbeats became a deafening metronome, denting time, marking the moment. I was so filled with wonder that I couldn't look away. I couldn't even close my eyes.

"Moses, Moses, Moses," my heart cried and my mouth echoed behind.

His eyes were as wide as mine must have been, his breaths as shallow, and when his lips weren't pressed to my lips, they were parted, panting as we clung to each other, hands clasped and eyes locked. Bodies moving in a rhythm as old as the ground we lay upon.

I knew myself enough to know that later on I wouldn't be proud of my lack of restraint. I wouldn't like the litter-strewn concrete edifice nearby and the weeds beneath my back. I knew I wouldn't be able to look my dad in the eyes for a while. But I also knew that the moment had been completely inevitable. I had been hurtling toward it from the second I laid eyes on Moses. My parents were religious people, spiritual people. I thought I was. I'd been raised going to church, week after week, counseled on the sins of the flesh. But nobody told me how it would feel. Nobody told me that resisting would feel like trying to breathe through a straw. Futile. Impossible. Unrealistic.

So I'd pulled the straw away and filled my lungs with air, filled my lungs with Moses, pulling him in with great big gulps, unable to slow down or focus on anything but the next breath.

Maybe I could have stayed away from him. Maybe I should have stayed away. But last night I couldn't. Last night I didn't. And by the light of day, sitting in the faded sunshine of an October afternoon, with another girl's face peering down at me, painted by my lover, by the boy who owned me body and soul, I wished that I had.

VIII

MOSES

THE POLICE QUESTIONED ME. It wasn't the first time I'd been questioned by the police over one of my drawings. I didn't offer anything. I didn't say much. There was nothing I could say, and they had nothing on me. The truth was, I didn't know anything. But I knew she wasn't alive. People who were alive didn't come visit me at odd hours and invade my thoughts. I just told them I'd heard about Molly missing and wanted to draw something for her. It was the truth. Kind of. The truth wasn't anything most people wanted to hear. People liked religion but they didn't want to have to exercise any faith. Religion was comforting with all its structure and its rules. It made people feel safe. But faith wasn't safe. Faith was hard and uncomfortable and forced people to step out on a limb. At least that's what Gigi said. And I believed Gi.

My grandma came rushing into the police station with frizzy grey curls flying and a look on her face that warned of trouble. Not trouble for me, luckily, but for the police officer who hadn't called her while I was being questioned. I was eighteen. They didn't have to call her, but they backed down pretty quickly under her wrath, and I was released within the hour, after agreeing to paint over my drawing. Hopefully Molly wouldn't come back when I did. It wasn't until we got home that Gigi unloaded on me.

"Why do you keep doing that? Painting walls and barns and drawing on white boards? You made Ms. Murray cry, got yourself arrested, and now this? Stop it! Or for hell's sake, ask permission first!"

"You know why, Gigi." And she did. It was the dirty little secret in my family. My hallucinations. My visions. The meds I'd been on most of my life made it a hundred times worse. They were meds made for people who had totally different problems, and when one medication didn't work, they would try something new. I'd spent my whole life in and out of doctor's offices—a ward of the state, an enemy of the state. Nothing had helped, and it wasn't until coming to live with Gigi that I had finally been free of the medication. No one ever considered that maybe they weren't hallucinations. They hadn't thought about the fact that maybe it was exactly like I said.

"I can't ask permission, Gigi. Because then I would have to explain. And people might tell me no. And then where would I be?" It was a legitimate argument as far as I was concerned. "Forgiveness is usually easier than permission."

"Only if you're five! Not when you're eighteen with a police record. You're going to end up in jail, Moses." My grandma was upset, and that made me feel like shit.

I shrugged helplessly. The threat wasn't new to me, and it didn't especially scare me. I didn't think it would be much worse than the way I lived now. There were a lot of concrete walls in prison, or so I heard. But Gigi wouldn't be there. And Georgia. I wouldn't ever be able to see Georgia again. She thought I was crazy though, so I didn't know why I cared.

But I did.

"It would be such a waste, Moses. Such a huge waste! Your art is awe-inspiring. It's wonderful. You could make a life for yourself with your gift. A good life. Just paint pictures for heaven's sake! Just paint quietly in a corner! That would be amazing! Why do you have to paint barns and bridges and walls and people's doors?" Gi threw up her hands and I wished I could explain.

"I can't. I can't stop. It's the only thing that makes it bearable."

"Makes what bearable?"

"The madness. Just . . . the madness in my head."

"Moses was a prophet," she began.

"I'm not a prophet! And you've told me this story before, Gi," I interrupted.

"But I don't think you understand it, Moses," she insisted.

I stared at my grandmother, at her round face, her adoring smile, her guileless eyes. She was the only person who had ever made me feel like I wasn't a burden. Or a psycho. If she wanted to tell me about baby Moses again, I would listen.

"Moses was a prophet. But he didn't start out that way. First he was a baby, an abandoned baby in a basket," Gigi started up again.

I sighed. I really hated the story of how I got my name. It was completely messed up. It wasn't cute or romantic. It wasn't a Bible story. It wasn't even Hollywood. But it was Gigi. So I stayed silent and let her do her thing.

"They were killing all the Hebrew baby boys. They were slaves and the Pharaoh was worried that if the Hebrew nation got too large they would rise up and turn against him. But Moses's mother couldn't allow him to be killed. So to save him, she had to let him go. She put him in a basket and let him go," Gi repeated with extra emphasis.

I waited. This wasn't the place she usually stopped.

"Just like you, sweetie."

"What? You mean I'm a basket case? Yeah, Gigi. I know."

"No. That's not what I mean. Your mother was a basket case, though. She made a mess of her life. She got so deep and so sick that there was no way she could take care of you. So she let you go."

"She left me in a laundromat."

"She saved you from herself."

I sighed again. Gigi had loved my mother, which made her more forgiving and compassionate. I didn't love my mother and I was neither compassionate nor forgiving.

"Don't mess up your life, Moses. You've got to find a way to save yourself now. Nobody can do it for you."

"I can't control it, Gigi. You act like I can control it." Even as I spoke, the heat started rising up my neck, and the tips of my fingers felt like they were pressed up against an ice-filled glass. It was a feeling I knew all too well and what came next would happen whether I wanted it to or not.

"They won't leave me alone, Gi. And it's going to drive me crazy. It *is* driving me crazy. I don't know how to live like this."

Gigi stood and wrapped her arms around my head, pulling my face into her chest like she could stand between me and everything that was already inside me. I kept my face pressed against her, my eyes closed tight, trying to think about Georgia, about last night, about how Georgia had refused to look away from me, and how my heart had felt like it was going to explode when I felt her come undone. But even Georgia wasn't enough. Molly was back. She wanted to show me pictures.

"Moses parted the waters of the Red Sea. You know that story too, right?" My grandmother spoke urgently, somehow understanding that I was fighting with something she couldn't see. "You know how he parted the waters so the people could walk across?"

I grunted in response as flashing images flipped through my head in rapid succession, like the girl who lingered nearby had opened a thousand page book in my head and made the pages turn at a dizzying speed. I groaned and Gigi held on tighter.

"Moses! You have to bring the waters back down, just like Moses did in the Bible. Moses parted the waters, just like you can do. You part the waters, and people cross over. But you can't let everyone cross whenever they want. You have to bring the waters back down. You can bring the waters back down and wash all the pictures away!"

"How?" I moaned, not even fighting anymore.

"What color is the water?" she insisted.

And I tried to imagine how that much water would look, rising up in enormous walls, held back by an invisible hand. Immediately the flipping images Molly was shoving into my skull slowed.

"Water is white," I bit out. "Water is white when it's angry." I was suddenly so angry my temples throbbed and my hands shook. I was so tired of never having a minute's peace.

"What else? Water isn't always angry," Gigi insisted. "What other colors?"

"Water is white when it's angry. It's red when the sun sets. It's blue when it's calm. It's black when it's night. It's clear when it falls." I was babbling, but it felt good. I was fighting back and my head felt clearer. Just like the water.

"So let the water fall. Let it come crashing down. Let it flow through your head and out your eyes. Water is clear when it washes the pain away, clear when it cleanses. Water has no color. Let it take the colors away."

I could almost feel it, the walls tumbling down, being spun up inside it, the way I'd been churned in the surf the time I'd gone to the ocean when I was twelve. I had gotten beat up by the waves. But there had been no pictures inside the waves. No people. There had been nothing but water and breathlessness and raw, natural power. And I had loved it.

"What does it sound like, Moses? What does the water sound like?"

Niagara. It sounded like the falls. I'd heard the sound of the waterfall in Hawaii as it fell around Ms. Murray and the man she loved. Ray. Ray had shown me the inside of the waterfall. It had been so loud that there was no other sound but the water. And it had roared in my head then. Now it roared again.

"It sounds like a lion. It sounds like a storm."

"So let the wall of sound fall down around you." Gigi was speaking directly into my ear, yet I could barely hear her, as if we, too, stood inside a waterfall that was so loud all other sound disappeared.

I let myself get lost in the sound. Lost in the best way. Freed from myself, from my head. From the pictures.

I saw those towering walls of water held back by the hand of a God who could do all things, a God who had done as one Moses asked, long before I lived. And I asked Him to do it again. I asked God to release the water. And Molly disappeared completely.

GEORGIA

MOSES STOPPED GOING to school for good after the cops pulled him out of class because of the painting he'd plastered under the overpass. I stayed away from him for four weeks. For almost a solid month, I kept my distance. And he never sought me out. I didn't know why I thought he would. But there were rules about this kind of thing, weren't there? You didn't have sex and then never call, never come by. You didn't take someone's virginity in the most epic, earthshattering way and go about your business. Or maybe he did.

But I knew he had felt what I felt that night. I knew he did. I couldn't be the only one. And those feelings were wearing me down. The desire, the overwhelming need to do it all over, to let him cover me and make me do all the things I had sworn I wouldn't do again was getting the best of me. I was absolutely miserable, and the Wednesday before Thanksgiving I couldn't stand it anymore. I drove to the old mill and found his jeep, parked up close to the old rear entrance. He had to be about done with the clean-up he'd been hired to do. But he was here now, and I scribbled a note on the back of a service check-up I found in the glove compartment of Myrtle and I wrote –

Moses,

Meet me at the barn when you're done.

~Georgia

I didn't want to sign my name, but I wasn't even confident enough to assume he would know it was me without my signature. Then I put the note under his windshield wipers, the words facing down so that if he missed it when he came out, he could almost read it right through the window, sitting in the driver's seat.

Then I scurried back to my house, made sure I smelled like roses with fresh breath and clean undies and I tried not to think about how pathetic I was, how disappointed I was in myself as I put a little mascara on my lashes, staring into my own eyes, purposely not seeing myself.

I waited in the barn for an hour. My dad came out once, and I almost gave myself away, turning with a huge grin only to see him instead of Moses. I was instantly filled with terror that my dad would know something was up and disappointment that Moses still hadn't come. There was a storm coming and as the weather turned colder, we often brought the horses in for the night. Lucky and Sackett, along with Dolly, Reba and Merle—the horses my parents used exclusively for equine therapy—were cozy in individual stalls, all of them brushed down and better groomed than they'd ever been. They gave me cover, and my dad fell for it. And I felt like a harlot when he headed back to the house, not a worry in his greying head, thinking his tomboy daughter was safe from the neighbor boy. Sadly, I probably was. But he wasn't safe from me. And yet, there was not enough shame to make me leave the barn.

He didn't come. I waited until midnight and finally wrapped myself in one of the blankets I'd spread over the straw, blankets I told myself we could sit on while we talked. And I fell asleep alone in the barn.

I awoke to the sound of rain against the tin roof, warm, comforted by the stirring of the horses and the smell of the clean straw beneath the blanket that had come loose while I slept. It wasn't especially cold. The barn was cozy and sturdily built, and I'd flipped on the space heater before I'd succumbed to sleep. The light above the door was just a bare bulb, and it threw a mellow light across the floor as I opened my heavy lids and considered staggering to the house and crawling in bed or just staying put. I'd slept in the barn before, many times. But those other times I'd brought a pillow and I wasn't wearing a lace bra that cut into my sides and jeans that were a little too tight to substitute for pajama bottoms.

It was when I sat up, shaking straw from my hair, that I saw Moses, just sitting in the far corner on a low stool my dad used for shoeing the horses. He was as far away from the horses as he could get, and thankfully, none of them seemed especially alarmed by his presence. But I was, just for a moment, and I let out a startled squawk.

He didn't apologize or laugh or even make small talk. He just eyed me warily, as if watching me sleep was what I had summoned him for.

"What time is it?" I whispered, my voice scratchy and my heart heavy. He just made me feel so damn heavy.

"Two."

"You just got home?"

"No. I went home. Showered. Went to bed."

"You're sleep walking, then?" I kept my voice light, soft.

"What do you want, Georgia? I kind of thought you were done with me." Ah. There it was. A flash of anger. Quiet, brief. But there. And I reveled in it. My mom always said negative attention is better than no attention at all. She was usually talking about foster kids who acted out. But apparently it also applied to seventeen-year-old girls who were in love with boys who didn't love them back. That thought made me angry.

"Do you love me, Moses?"

"No." His response was immediate. Defiant. But he stood and walked toward me anyway. And I watched him come, my eyes roving over him hungrily, my heart a huge, needy knot in my chest.

I didn't argue with him because I knew that's what he was going to say. And I had already decided that I wouldn't believe him.

He squatted down beside the square bales I'd turned into a love nest. But he said he didn't love me, so maybe my bed needed a different name. I laid back down and pulled the blanket around my shoulders, suddenly chilled and incredibly tired. But he followed me, hovering above me, his arms braced on either side of my head as he watched me watch him. And then he closed the distance and kissed my mouth chastely. Once, twice. And then again, not so chastely, with more pressure and more intent.

I breathed deeply and wrapped my hands around his neck, bringing him into me. I soaked in his scent, the sharp tang of paint mixed with soap and the red striped, candy mints his grandma kept in a bowl on the kitchen table. And something else too. Something I had no name for, and it was that unknown part of him that I wanted most of all. I kissed him until I could taste it in my mouth and when that wasn't enough, I pulled it through the palms of my hands and the brush of my skin against his as he moved his mouth to my neck and whispered in my ear.

"I'm not sure what you want from me, Georgia. But if this is it, I'm willing."

GEORGIA

WHEN THE SUN STARTED to push pink fingers against the little barn window that faced east, Moses rolled away from me and started pulling on his clothes, his eyes on the window and the dawn. It was November, and the sun rose sluggishly. It had to be after six. Time to go. My parents would be up and about soon, Mom probably already was. Thanksgiving dinner was a big job. Moses and I hadn't spoken much in the hours he'd stayed with me. I'd been surprised that he'd stayed at all, even sleeping for several hours before waking me again with kisses and warm hands, convincing me there was no way I could ever live without him. He had stayed silent throughout, and his silence now was almost more than I could take. I wondered how he'd learned to push the words away, to drown them, to not feel them pounding against his head and his heart, begging to be spoken. I told myself I could do it now. I could be as quiet as he was. At least until he left the barn. But as he walked toward the door, the words broke free.

"I think you do love me, Moses. And I love you back, though it would be easier not to," I said in a rush.

"Why would it be easier not to?" he shot back quietly, as if he hadn't told me he didn't love me without hesitation. He could say he didn't love me, but he didn't especially like being told he was unlovable.

"Because you think you don't love me. That's why."

"That's one of my laws, Georgia. Thou shall not love."

"That's not a law in Georgia."

"Not this again," he sighed.

"What would make you love me, Moses? What would make you move to Georgia?" I waggled my eyebrows as if it was all just a big, funny joke. "I've told you I would go red. I told you I would let you in my head. And I've given you everything else I have." I felt my voice catch all of a sudden and a flood of tears rushed toward my eyes like a dam had burst with those words. I turned away immediately and busied myself with folding the blanket that now smelled like him. I folded and straightened and then pulled on my boots while Moses stood frozen, six feet away. At least he hadn't left, though part of me wished he would.

"You're upset."

"Yeah. I guess I am."

"That's why I have that law," he whispered, almost gently. "If you don't love, then nobody gets hurt. It's easy to leave. It's easy to lose. It's easy to let go."

"Then maybe you should have had a few more laws, Moses."

I turned my head and smiled at him brightly, not sure if I was pulling it off. My nose stung and I was guessing my eyes were too bright. But I chattered on with forced cheer.

"Thou shall not kiss. Thou shall not touch. Thou shall not screw." But I didn't say screw. I called it like it was, as much as it felt like acid on my tongue. It wasn't that to me. It was love, not sex. Or maybe it was both. But at least it was both.

"You found me, Georgia. You chased me. You wanted me. Not the other way around," Moses said. He hadn't raised his voice. He didn't even sound upset. "I didn't break any of my rules. You broke yours. And you're mad at me because of it."

He was right. He was absolutely right. And I was so wrong.

"I'll see you later, okay?" I said quietly, not daring to look at him. "You and Kathleen are coming over for Thanksgiving, right? We eat early so we can eat all day." I was proud of myself for my composure. I despised myself for not kicking his ass.

"Yeah. Eleven, right?"

Small talk never felt so fake. I nodded and he waited, watching me. He started to say my name, and then he sighed and turned away. And without another word, he left the barn.

"Sunrise, the smell of straw, Thanksgiving dinner, a hot shower, a new day." I whispered my list of greats, trying not to let the tears fall, trying not to think about what came next and how I was going to get through the next few hours.

IX

MOSES

"**G**RANDMA!" She didn't move.

"Gigi!" I shook her and patted her cheek. But her head just lolled a little to the side and her eyes stayed closed. She lay on the kitchen floor, a heap of fragile limbs wrapped in her quilted robe. A broken glass lay at her side in three fat pieces, sharp islands in a large pool of blood tinged water. She'd hit her head when she fell, and the blood had merged with the water from her glass. It wasn't a lot of blood. It was as if she was dead before she hit the ground; the blood spilt looked insufficient, almost. Death should require more blood.

When I'd come home the night before, I'd gone straight up to the bathroom and then from there, straight to my room. I'd lain in bed trying to hold out on Georgia. She'd stayed scarce for a month. And now she wanted me? It made me angry. And yet I wanted to see her. I wanted to see her so bad. I finally gave in, threw on my jeans and a shirt and crept out of the house, not wanting to wake Gi.

What if she'd lain here all night?

I laid my head against her chest, and I waited, willing her heart to resume its beat against my ear. But she felt cold. And her heart stayed quiet. She was cold. Without realizing what I was doing, I ran for a blanket and covered her up, tucking the blanket around her body securely.

"Gigi!" I closed my eyes, needing her to tell me what to do. I could see people who were dead. I saw them all the time. I needed to see Gigi. I needed her to tell me what happened. I needed her to take me with her.

I got my brushes. Assembled my paints. And I sat next to her and waited for her to come back to me, however she could. And when she did I would fill her walls with all her pictures. I would paint each day of her life until this one—this last terrible day—and she would tell me what the hell I was supposed to do now. I opened myself up, wide open like a gaping canyon with sharp edges and steep cliffs. I parted the waters, and as I concentrated, the walls of water grew so high I couldn't see where they ended. Whatever wanted to cross could come. Everyone. Anybody. Just as long as they brought Gi back across.

But I didn't feel Gigi. I didn't see her. I saw my mother. I saw Georgia's grandfather, I saw the girl named Molly and the man named Mel Butters who died inside his barn. He had his horses with him and he was happy. His happiness mocked me now, and I raged at him as I ran past his images of long rides and summer sunsets. He drew away immediately. I felt Ray, the man who loved Ms. Murray. He was worried about her and that worry pulsed out of him in grey waves. She wasn't doing well. The picture we made for her didn't comfort her.

I felt all their lives and their memories and I pushed them aside, trying to find my grandmother. There were others too. People I'd felt, pictures I'd seen before, memories that weren't my own. These were people who had come to me over the years. People of all ages, of all colors. There was the Polynesian boy and his sister, Teo and Kalia, gang members who died in a turf war with the same gang I ran with for almost a year before being sent to live with Gigi. I'd resented losing that sense of belonging, though it had been a charade. I'd resented it like I resented all the other times I was uprooted. The brother and his sister tried to slow me down, to share their pictures of a younger sibling who was left behind, but I kept running, looking for Gigi.

As always, there were the lurkers, the gritty black smear that sat at the corner of my vision whenever I let myself get too deep. I never got too close or looked inside them. They stayed far away from the translucence that surrounded the people who showed me their lives. I wasn't sure, but I suspected the lurkers were the dead who couldn't let go, the dead who didn't believe in an afterlife, so refused to see the life after, even though it glowed like a sea of candles and beckoned them sweetly. Maybe they couldn't see it.

The sex, violence, and desperation of the kids in the gang, many who had abandoned all light, was a decadent cesspool for the lurkers. They were like a swarm around those kids. The longer I was in the gang, the better I could see them. Since coming to Levan, they'd stayed away.

And then there were people I didn't know, people I'd never touched, people who had never touched me. There were generations of them, standing back to back in a long endless line, and they smiled at me like I was home. But I couldn't find Gigi. And Gigi was home.

"Gigi!" I screamed, and my throat was so dry and sore that I stopped running through the world no one else seemed to be able to see. My head stopped spinning, but I was covered in paint. I had been painting the whole time I searched for my grandmother. The walls of Gigi's house were covered in images that morphed from one to another without rhyme or reason. I'd painted the man I was certain was my great-grandfather, Gigi's husband, a man I'd never met. I'd seen him in recent days. I'd seen him just beyond Gi's right shoulder, shimmering, as if he was waiting for her to join him. Now his face was there among the others.

And there were so many others. I'd painted lurkers swarming the four corners of the room with hollow eyes and mournful faces. And between the faces of those I recognized and those I did not were grasping hands, burning barns, crashing waves and lightning. My mother's face was there too, holding a basket, like she thought she needed to illustrate who she was. As if I didn't know. I'd seen her a thousand times in my head. There were gang signs on the walls too, as if Teo and Kalia were warning me away. Red swirled into black, black swirled into grey, grey swirled into white, until the images stopped where I now stood.

"Moses! Moses, where are you?"

Georgia. Georgia was in the house. Georgia was in the kitchen. I heard her breathless rush of words, calling first to me and then babbling into the phone, telling whoever she was talking to that Kathleen Wright was "lying on the kitchen floor."

"I think she's dead. I think she's been dead for a while. I can't tell what happened to her, but she's very, very cold," she cried.

I wondered how that was possible, when I'd just covered her with a blanket. I wanted to go to Georgia. She was afraid. She hadn't seen death before, not like me. But I was strangely numb, and my mind spun dizzily, still caught somewhere between the ground on which I stood and the Red Sea in my head.

But then she came to me, just like she always did. She found me. She wrapped her arms around me and started to cry. She pressed her face into my chest, ignoring the splotches of red, purple, and black that stained my shirt and smeared across her cheek.

"Oh, Moses. What happened? What happened here?"

But I couldn't cry with her. I couldn't move. I had to pull down the water. Gigi wasn't coming back with me. I couldn't find her, and I couldn't stay any longer, not on the far side of the bank where there were only colors and questions.

Georgia pulled away, her face streaked with paint and confusion. "What's wrong Moses? You've been painting. Why? Why, Moses? And you're so cold. How can you be so cold?" Her teeth chattered as if she was truly chilled by my presence.

I laughed helplessly. I wasn't cold. I was on fire. I wondered suddenly if Georgia had felt the ice in my hands, because that was the only place I was cold. I was hot. Burning. My neck and ears were on fire and my head was a raging inferno. So I concentrated on the walls of water, the towering sides of the channel in my mind, the channel that I needed to close. I didn't answer Georgia. I couldn't. I pushed away from her, blocking her out as I sought to block out the rest of them.

"Water is white when it's angry. Blue when it's calm. Red when the sun sets, black at midnight. And water is clear when it falls. Clear when it washes through my head and out my fingertips. Water is clear and it washes all the colors away, it washes all the pictures away." I didn't realize I was speaking until Georgia touched me. I pushed her away, needing to concentrate. I was pulling it down. The walls were starting to fall. I just needed to concentrate a little harder. Then I felt the ice start to spread from my hands up my arms and across my back, cooling my neck and calming my breath. And I was floating in it. The relief was so great my legs shook and finally, I reached out for Georgia. I could touch her now. I wanted nothing more than to hold onto her now. But just like the pictures in my head, Georgia was gone.

GEORGIA

WHEN I BURST THROUGH THE DOOR into the kitchen, the screen banging loudly, my mom whirled as if to reprimand me. But she must have seen something in my face. She set the bowl of potatoes down with a clatter.

"Martin!" She called for my dad as I stumbled toward her.

She'd been trying to keep everything warm on the stove. When Moses and Kathleen hadn't shown up at eleven, we wondered a little. Kathleen Wright wasn't the type to be late. At all. By 11:15 my mother was calling her house. But the phone just rang and rang, and Mom started to fret about cold turkey and mashed potatoes. So I volunteered to run over and see if Mrs. Wright needed help with anything and to hurry her and Moses along. She had insisted on bringing the pies for dessert even though my mom had resisted, saying they were our guests.

I hadn't wanted to go. I felt raw and tired, and I didn't need to see Moses any sooner than I had to. I already didn't know how we were going to sit across from each other without a scarlet letter appearing on my chest. Moses would handle it fine. He just wouldn't say anything. And I would sweat and squirm and not be able to taste anything I ate. Which made me angry and gave me courage as I flew out the door, the dusting of snow we'd gotten over night crunching beneath my boots. My Wranglers were stiff and clean, my best blouse pressed, and my hair carefully arranged in perfect waves. I even wore make-up. All dressed up for Thanksgiving and no one to see me. It was rude to be late for

Thanksgiving dinner, and I picked up my pace as I neared Kathleen's little, grey brick house and stomped up the front steps.

I knocked several times and then entered, calling out as I did.

"Mrs. Wright? It's Georgia."

The first thing I noticed was the smell. It smelled like turpentine. Paint. It smelled like paint. And it didn't smell like pies. It should have smelled like pies.

I stopped immediately. A little foyer lay beyond the front door, just big enough for a coat rack, a little bench, and a flight of stairs. To the left there was a tiny sitting room, to the right, the dining room, which sat off the kitchen. Along the back of the house was a big family room that Kathleen Wright's husband had added on forty years ago. It was accessible by walking through the kitchen or walking through the tiny sitting room. The first floor rooms made a sloppy, misshapen circle around the miniscule foyer with the staircase leading up to a bathroom and three small bedrooms on the second floor. I looked up the stairs, wondering if I dared go up them. The house was so quiet.

Then I heard a soft, swishing sort of sound. Swish, swish, swish. And then a foot fall. And one more. I placed the sound almost immediately. I'd listened with closed eyes to that sound several nights in a row as Moses painted my room.

"Moses?" I called, and I stepped through the door into the little dining room. Three steps and I saw her. Kathleen Wright was laying on the kitchen floor, covered in a lacy quilt that looked as if it had been dragged from her bed.

"Kathleen?" My voice squeaked as it rose in question. Maybe I should have run to her side. But it was so bizarre. I guess I didn't know what I was seeing. So I tip-toed, as if she were truly sleeping and I was intruding on her odd little nap.

I knelt by her side and pulled back the covers just a bit. Her grey curls were visible above the edge of the quilt, but I couldn't see her face.

"Mrs. Wright?" I said again, and then I knew. She wasn't sleeping. And this wasn't real. I must be the one sleeping.

"Kathleen?" I shrieked, falling back from my haunches. I caught myself instinctively, but felt a sharp slice, almost a tug, and yanked my hand away, scrambling and shrieking like death was biting and it was going to take me too. The seat of my freshly washed jeans were wet. I'd sat in some water and there was glass on the floor. It was just glass. Not death. But Kathleen Wright was dead and someone had covered her up, knowing she was dead.

I yanked a dish towel from the counter and realized I'd uncovered the pies—beautiful pies, all laid out on the counter. Four of them. There was a piece missing from the apple pie. I stared at the missing section for a second, wondering if Kathleen had sampled her baking before she died. It suddenly made the moment real and all the more tragic, and I turned away, wrapping my bleeding hand and clamoring for Kathleen's old phone on the wall. I had to step over her to get to it, and that's when I started to shake.

I dialed 911, just like we're all told to do in an emergency. It didn't take too many rings before an operator was there, an efficient-voiced woman, asking me all types of questions. I rattled off answers, even as my mind moved on to the horror I still hadn't faced. Where was Moses? I could smell paint. I could smell paint and I had heard someone. Paint meant Moses. I set the phone down, the operator still talking, asking me something that I'd already answered. Then I walked through the little door that led to the family room on wooden legs, my rear-end wet, my hand bleeding, my heart on pause.

He was covered in paint—head, arms and clothing streaked with blue and yellow, doused in red and orange, splattered with purple and black. He still wore the clothes he'd worn when he left me that morning, though nothing looked the same. The tail of his shirt was the only part that was untucked, strangely enough. But that wasn't the strangest thing. Not by far. The walls were covered in paint too, but there was nothing splattered or haphazard about the paint on the walls.

It was both manic and mesmerizing, it was controlled chaos and detailed dementia. Moses had painted right over the pictures and the windows too. The curtains were streaked with paint, incorporated into the pictures like he couldn't stop to pull them aside. From the amount of wall space he'd covered, he'd been at it for hours. There was graffiti and horses and people I'd never seen before. There were hallways and pathways and doorways and bridges, as if Moses was running from one place to the next, painting every inexplicable thing he saw. There was a woman's face over a laundry basket. Her long, blonde hair streamed out around her and the basket was full of babies. It was both beautiful and bizarre, one image becoming another and another, without rhyme or reason. And there Moses stood, staring at the wall in front of him, a section of white yet to be filled, his hands by his sides.

And then he looked at me, his eyes hollow and rimmed with circles so dark they made his burnished skin look pale in comparison. The streaks of paint across his face made him look like a weary warrior returning from battle, only to find devastation at his doorstep.

And I ran to him.

I've thought back on that moment so many times since then. Replayed it on a loop. The way I ran to him. The way I threw my arms around him, filled with compassion, completely unafraid. I held onto him as he stood there shivering, muttering something to himself. I think I asked him to tell me what happened. I don't remember exactly. I just remember he was freezing, icy to the touch, and I asked him if he was cold. And he laughed, just a brief, incredulous laugh. Then he shoved me away so hard that I fell back again, stumbling and then falling to the floor, my injured hand leaving a bloody smear across the pale carpet. There were slashes of paint everywhere, and my bloody handprint looked unremarkable. Completely unremarkable.

Moses wrapped his arms around his head, shielding his eyes, and repeated something about water, over and over. His lips were the only part of his face I could see and I watched them move around the words.

"Water is white when it's angry. Blue when it's calm. Red when the sun sets, black at midnight. And water is clear when it falls. Clear when it washes through my head and out my fingertips. Water is clear and it washes all the colors away, it washes all the pictures away."

I couldn't take anymore. The 911 operator had told me to wait. But I couldn't wait. I couldn't stay in that house for one more second.

And for the very first time, I ran away from him.

X

MOSES

I WOKE UP IN A PADDED ROOM. Not a cell. A room. But it might as well have been. When I came to they took my clothes, documented any wounds or marks on my skin, and gave me a pair of pale yellow scrubs to wear and socks to put on my feet. I was informed I could earn back my clothes as I followed the rules. Various people came to see me. Doctors, therapists, psychiatrists with little medical charts. They all tried to talk to me, but I was too numb to talk. And they all left eventually.

I was alone in my room for three days with meals brought in to me, some pencils to write with, and a lined notebook. Nobody wanted me to paint here. They wanted me to talk. To write in notebooks. To write and write. The more I wrote, the happier they were, until they read what I'd written and thought I was being uncooperative. But words were hard for me. If they let me paint, I could express myself. I was instructed to "journal" all my feelings. I was asked to explain what happened at my grandmother's house on Thanksgiving Day. Wasn't there a song about Grandma and Thanksgiving? I was sure there was and wrote it a few times in the notebook they provided.

"Over the river and through the woods, grandma has fallen down. The police save the day, and haul me away, from the shitty all-white town."

It made me sound cruel, writing about my grandma that way. But they weren't entitled to know about Gi. And I kept her to myself. If I had to be an asshole to keep them out, I would.

She was the only person who had been true and constant my entire life. The only one. And she was gone. And I couldn't find her. She wasn't with the others waiting on the other side for me to let them across. And I didn't know how I felt about that. For the first time, Gi had abandoned me.

The pencils I was supposed to write with were no longer than a couple inches; I could barely grip them between my index finger and my thumb, probably to make it harder to use them as weapons against myself or someone else. And they were dull. After my attempt at shocking them with my inappropriate levity, I didn't write anymore, but on the third day, I ended up drawing on the walls. When I'd worked my way through the pencils and had nothing left, I sat on the mattress in the corner and waited.

Dinner time came and an orderly named Chaz, a big, black man with a hint of Jamaica in his voice, was the usual suspect. I guessed they assigned him to me because he was bigger and blacker than I was. Always safer that way. Assign the black man to the black man. Typical white mentality. Especially in Utah where black men were outnumbered 1,000 to 1. Or something like that. I didn't actually have a clue how many black people lived in Utah. I just knew it wasn't very many.

Chaz stopped in amazement, and my dinner tray hit the floor.

GEORGIA

THEY PUT MOSES in a hospital far away. It was a two hour drive from Levan to Salt Lake. They took Moses and his grandmother in the same ambulance, and I was horrified for his sake, but then I realized he wasn't aware. They said he fought. They said it took three men to hold him down. And they stuck him with a tranquilizer.

I heard the word crazy. Psycho. Murderer. Yes, that one too. And they took Moses away.

Everybody said he killed his grandmother, ate a piece of Thanksgiving pie, and then painted the house. But even though I was afraid, afraid of what I'd seen and what I didn't understand, I didn't believe that.

They did a full investigation into her death, but nobody had told me anything.

Moses couldn't come to his grandmother's funeral. Her extended family did, and they all cried like they had killed her themselves. They sat on the pews in the Levan Chapel and there was no celebration, no joy of a life well-lived, even though Kathleen Wright deserved that. She'd outlived many of her friends, but not all. The whole town attended, though my angry mind accused many of wanting front row seats to the on-going drama that was Moses Wright. Mother and son, two peas in a pod. Moses would hate the comparison.

Josie Jensen played a piano solo, which is the only thing I remember well. *Ave Maria*, requested specifically by Kathleen. Josie was a bit of a celebrity in town because of her musical abilities. She was only three years older than me, and I looked up to her. She was everything I wasn't. Quiet, kind. Ladylike. Feminine. Musically gifted. But we had something in common now. We had both loved and lost, though nobody really knew it but me. Moses and I had been seen together, but nobody really knew how I felt.

People still talked about Josie too, though they did so with shakes of their head and sad eyes. Eighteen months ago, Josie Jensen had lost her fiancé in a car accident. Kind of like Ms. Murray, but Josie was engaged to a local boy and only eighteen when it happened. The town had gone crazy for a while. Some said Josie had even gone crazy for a while, though crazy is subjective. You can be crazed with grief and not crazy at all.

My mom had signed me up for piano lessons from Josie when I was thirteen, and I had tried, only to quickly come to the conclusion that we aren't all born with the same talents, and piano was never going to be mine. I wondered if Moses had painted Josie's fiancé's face somewhere in town. It made me sick to think about it.

A week after the funeral, Sheriff Dawson came by our house to officially tell me they had no idea who had tied me up the last night of the stampede. We weren't surprised. We were only surprised he'd actually stopped by to tell us. It had been months, they hadn't had any leads beyond Terrance Anderson, who had been cleared, and even though Sheriff Dawson couldn't prove it one way or another, he seemed confident it was just a prank gone wrong.

I didn't have the energy to care one way or the other. There was a new tragedy in my life, and that night at the stampede was insignificant compared to having Moses tranquilized and hauled away. It was small compared to Kathleen Wright, covered in lace, lying dead on her kitchen floor, Thanksgiving pies sitting innocently on the counter. It was meaningless compared to the turmoil I now found myself in.

It was then, with Sheriff Dawson sitting there in our kitchen just like he had the night of the stampede, that I found out Moses's grandmother had died from a stroke. Not murder. A stroke. My parents sat back in their chairs in relief, never even looking at me, not having any idea what those words meant to me. Natural causes. Moses hadn't hurt her. He had simply found her, like I had found her, and dealt with it in the way he dealt with death. He painted it.

"Will they let him go now?" I asked. My parents and Sheriff Dawson looked at me in surprise. It was like they had forgotten I was there.

"I don't know," Sheriff Dawson had hedged.

"Moses is my friend. I might be his only friend in the world. He didn't kill Kathleen. So why can't he come home?" The emotion was leaking out around my words and my parents mistook the emotion for post-traumatic stress. After all, I'd seen death up close.

"He doesn't really have a home to come back to. Though I heard Kathleen left him the house and everything in it. He's eighteen already, far as I know, so he can be on his own."

"He's not in the hospital anymore. He wasn't injured. So where is he?" I demanded.

112

"I don't know exactly . . ."

"Yes you do, Sheriff. Come on. Where is he?" I insisted.

"Georgia!" My mom patted my arm and told me to calm down.

Sheriff Dawson shoved his cowboy hat on his head and then took it off again. He seemed distressed and reluctant to tell me.

"Is he in jail?"

"No. No, he's not. They've taken him to another facility in Salt Lake City. He's in the psych ward."

I stared, not really understanding.

"It's a mental hospital, Georgia," my mom said gently.

My parents met my stunned gaze with sober faces and Sheriff Dawson stood abruptly, as if the whole thing had just gone beyond his pay grade. I found myself standing too, my legs shaking and my stomach swimming with nausea. I managed to make it to the bathroom without running, and was even able to lock the door behind me before I threw up the piece of pie mom had pressed upon me when she'd dished up a piece for Sheriff Dawson. Pie made me think of Kathleen Wright and tranquilizers.

MOSES

"CAN YOU TELL ME WHAT THE ARTWORK MEANS?"

I sighed heavily. The Asian doctor in the tan blazer, wearing the self-important spectacles she probably didn't need, considered me over her rims, her pencil poised to make notes of my mental deterioration.

"You need to talk to me, Moses. All of this will be so much easier for both of us."

"You wanted me to tell you what happened at my grandma's house. That's what happened." I tossed my hand toward the wall.

"Is she dead?" the doctor asked, staring at my grandmother's death scene.

"Yes."

"How did she die?"

"I don't know. She was laying on the kitchen floor when I came home that morning."

I should have known she was going to die. I had seen the signs. The nights leading up to her death I'd seen him hovering around her, the dead man who looked like the man in Gi's wedding photo. My great-grandfather. I'd seen him twice, standing just beyond her right shoulder while she slept in her chair. And I'd seen him again, just behind her as she'd rolled out her pie crusts Wednesday afternoon when I headed to the old mill to finish the demolition. He had been waiting for her.

But I didn't tell the doctor that. Maybe I should though. Then I could tell her someone stood behind her shoulder, waiting for her to die too. Maybe it would scare her to death and she would leave me alone. But there wasn't really anyone standing beyond her shoulder, so I held my tongue as she waited for me to speak.

She wrote in her notebook for a minute.

"How did that make you feel?"

I wanted to laugh. Was she serious? How did that make me feel?

"Sad," I said with a sorrowful frown, batting my eyes at her ridiculous, clichéd question.

"Sad," she repeated dryly.

"Very sad," I amended in the same tone.

"What went through your mind when you saw her?"

I stood up from my chair and walked to the wall and leaned against it, completely shielding my grandmother from her clinical gaze. I closed my eyes for a minute, reaching out just a little, parting the waters just a crack. I focused on the woman's shiny black head, her hair pulled back in a perfect, low ponytail.

She asked me several more questions, but I was concentrating on raising the water. I wanted to find something to make her run, screaming. Something true.

"Did you have a twin sister?" I asked suddenly, as an image of two little Asian girls in pigtails and matching dresses suddenly surfaced in my mind.

"Wh-what?" she asked, dumbfounded.

"Or maybe a cousin the same age. No. No. She's your sister. She died, right?" I folded my arms and waited, letting the images unfold.

The doctor pulled off her glasses and frowned at me. I had to give it to her. She didn't rattle easily.

"You had a visitor today. Georgia Shepherd was her name. She's not on your list. Do you want to talk about Georgia instead?" she parried, trying to derail me.

My heart shuddered when I heard her name. But I pushed Georgia away and thrust back.

"How did that make you feel, losing your sister like that?" I asked, not breaking eye-contact with the doctor. "Was she crazy like me? Is that why you wanted to work with crazy people?" I gave her a wild-eyed, Jack Nicholson smile. She stood abruptly and excused herself.

It was the first time I'd ever done something like that. It was strange and oddly wonderful. I had stopped caring if I was believed. If I never got out of the psych ward, I was fine with that. I was safe there at least. Gi was gone. Georgia was gone too. I'd made sure of that. It was the only thing I could do for Georgia now. She'd seen them put me in the ambulance. I'd fought. But as my eyes swam and the world spun, I'd seen her horrified, paint-streaked face. She was crying. And that was the last thing I saw before the world went dark.

Now I was here. And I didn't care anymore. It was all spilling out the cracks. Georgia teased me about my cracks, telling me I was cracked so the brilliance could spill out. And it was spilling out, brilliant and brutal.

And so it continued for the next few weeks. The hardest part was when the therapist or doctor hadn't lost anyone. There were people like that, and I had no one on the other side to use against them. To say I had the entire floor rattled would be putting it mildly. They tried to fix my cracks with medication, just like they'd done all my life, but the medication made the cracks wider, and short of putting me in a stupor, nothing they tried made me stop seeing the things I could see. And I started telling them all exactly what I could see. I didn't do it out of love or compassion. I did it because I didn't give a flying rat's ass anymore. I didn't break it to them gently either. I hit them over the head with it, Georgia style. In your face, tell you like it is.

GEORGIA

MY MOM HAD CONNECTIONS through her work with the foster system, and she found Moses for me. I don't think she wanted to find him. But for whatever reason—maybe out a lifelong compassion for troubled kids or out of respect for Kathleen Wright—she tracked him down. We had to be on a list in order to see him. The list was comprised of doctors, immediate family, and people Moses had been allowed to add.

My mom came with me the first time and we waited outside an official area while our names were relayed to another reception area on another floor. It was a building with different levels and pass codes and key pads. The reception area was as far as we got. We weren't related and Moses hadn't added any names to his list. I wondered if there had been any family to see him. I doubted it. My mom patted my hand and told me it was probably for the best. I nodded, but I knew it wasn't best for Moses. I would keep trying without her.

I skipped school and drove Myrtle to Salt Lake the next time I attempted a break in. Or a break out. I would take him away if he'd let me. It took me three hours to get there in that damn truck. I had to drive in the slow lane, pedal pressed all the way down, Myrtle shaking even worse than I was. I talked us both through it, patting Myrtle's dash and telling her there was nothing to be afraid of. We would take it slow. Cars and trucks flew by me in a swarm of horns and angry fists. But I made it. And I went again the next week and the next and every week for a month after that. Week after week, Myrtle never could get over her nerves and Moses never did let me in.

Finally, on my seventh week in a row, a woman came to the reception area and escorted me into a private meeting room. I'd noticed families being led to these rooms. My pulse sped up and my palms started to sweat in anticipation. I had high hopes that I would finally be able to see Moses. I needed to see him. I needed to talk to him.

"Georgia?" the lady looked down at her clipboard and smiled at me, though I could tell she wanted to get this over with. If she was a therapist or a psychologist, she needed to work on her poker face. She was impatient and had an irritated little wrinkle between her brows. Maybe it was because I was in cowboy boots and jeans, with my hair in a long, swinging braid. I probably looked easy to get rid of, easy to brush off and send away.

"Yes?" I responded.

"You aren't on Moses's list."

"Yes, ma'am. That's what they tell me."

"So why do you keep coming?" She smiled again, but she also looked at her watch.

"Because Moses is my friend."

"He doesn't seem to feel that way."

The hurt that was now a constant companion grew a size bigger in my chest. I looked at her for a long second. So prim in her little white coat. I bet she liked wearing that coat. It probably made her feel powerful. I wondered if she wanted to hurt me or if she was just the kind of doctor who was comfortable dispensing bad news.

"Georgia?" I guess she wanted me to respond to her statement. I fought the urge to rub my hands on my jeans, my nervous habit. The denim soothed me.

"He never has. He's always pushed me away. But he doesn't have anyone else." My voice didn't sound very strong, and that seemed to please her.

"He has us. We're taking very good care of him. He's making remarkable progress."

That was good. Remarkable progress was good. The ache in my chest eased a bit. "So what next?" I shrugged. "Where does he go from here?"

"That's up to Moses now." How wonderfully vague.

"Can I write him a letter? Could you give him a letter from me? Would that be okay?"

"No, Georgia. He's been granted phone privileges. He could have called you. He hasn't, has he?"

I shook my head. No. He hadn't.

"He is adamant. He doesn't want to see you or communicate with you. And we honor those wishes when we can. He has control over so little, and this is what he wants."

I wouldn't cry in front of this woman. I wouldn't. I took the letter I'd written Moses out of my purse, slapped it on the table in front of the doctor and stood. She could give it to Moses, throw it away, or read it to her monster babies for their bedtime story. They could all have a good chortle at my pain. Including Moses. Whatever the doctor decided, it was in her hands. I had done all I could do. I headed for the door.

"Georgia?" she called after me.

I slowed but didn't turn.

"He knows where to find you, doesn't he?"

I pulled the door open.

"Maybe he'll come to you. Maybe when he's released, he'll come to you."

But he didn't come. Not then. Not for a long, long time.

XI

MOSES

T HEY PUT ME IN A DIFFERENT ROOM without pads, which was nice, because then I didn't have to draw in the space above them. They told me to stop drawing, but short of tying my hands behind my back, which was apparently frowned upon since I wasn't "violent," I wasn't going to stop. They started bringing me blank paper and letting me draw instead of write, as long as I would talk to them about what I was drawing, and as long as I left the walls alone. I didn't like interpreting my drawings. But it was better than telling stories that were easier shared in pictures.

Eventually, they let me attend group sessions, and it was at my second or third one that Molly decided to come back. Suddenly she was there, flitting at the edges of my vision, someone I thought was gone. Someone I hadn't missed. Someone who made me think of Georgia. And it made me even testier than usual. I started looking for a way to get sent back to my room.

The group session was full of vulnerable people who I could terrorize. Adults of all ages, with all sorts of disorders and problems. Their pain and despair was a throbbing, inky black behind my eyes, with no color and light to create hope or escape. I was eighteen, and some eigh-teen-year-olds were apparently still treated as juveniles, depending on the opinion of the doctors. But when they'd brought me in, I was housed with the adults. Apparently the kids were a floor below. I was grateful I wasn't housed with them. Kids made it hard to be cruel.

Dr. Noah Andelin, a psychologist with a neatly groomed beard that he most likely wore to make himself look older, was conducting the group session. He stroked his beard when he was thinking, and it gave him a perpetually melancholy air. He was far too young to be a doctor, and way too young to be so serious. And sad. He had the saddest eyes I'd ever seen. He made me uncomfortable. He made it hard for me to be cruel too. And I needed to be cruel. To be left alone, I needed to be cruel. I picked on the therapists and techs when I could, and when I couldn't, I would pick on the patients that picked on everyone else. Sadly, they were usually the ones with the most loss. I usually ended up biting my tongue and pushing their dead away. I was an asshole. But I wasn't a bully.

I sat there, the bridge wide open, on the look-out for ammo when Molly stopped flitting and danced right in front of my eyes, blonde hair flowing, showing me all the same old things. I almost groaned out loud. This wasn't what I wanted. But then she started to hover around the edge of the circle, standing between two men across from me and star-ing back at me expectantly.

"Who knows a girl named Molly?" I blurted out, not thinking.

Dr. Andelin stopped mid-sentence. "Moses? Did you have some-thing you wanted to say?" His voice was gentle. Just like it always was. So gentle and kind. It made me want to pick him up by his lapels and toss him into the wall. I had a feeling there was some fire in him some-where. He tried to hide his physique beneath ridiculous tweed jackets with patches on the elbows, like a college professor from the 1940s. All he needed was a pipe. But he wasn't a weakling. I'd sized him up. It was something that came naturally to me. Who can hurt you? Who is a physical threat? And Noah Andelin, with his sad eyes and his neat little beard, could be both, I was convinced of it.

As soon as I spoke, I felt stupid. Molly didn't belong to anyone here. She was here because I was . . . though I had no idea why.

"What did you say?"

The question came from the man to the left of Molly, a man who looked about my age, barely old enough to be on the adult floor. His green eyes were sharp, though his posture was relaxed, his hands folded loosely in his lap. I could see a long jagged scar that ran from the bottom of his palm to the middle of his forearm. From the looks of it, he didn't want to live very badly.

"Molly. Do you know a girl named Molly? A dead girl named Molly?" I should have borrowed some of Dr. Andelin's kind and gentle approach. But I didn't. I just asked.

The boy leaped from his chair and flew across the circle to where I sat. I was so surprised I didn't have time to prepare before his hands were wrapped in my shirt, yanking me to my feet. I found myself nose to nose with a fire-breathing, green-eyed monster.

"You son of a bitch!" he spit in my face. "You better tell me how the hell you know anything about my sister!"

His sister? Molly was his sister? My head spun as he shoved me again, but this time he didn't want answers. He just wanted to knock me down, and we both fell back, upending my chair, and I forgot about Molly and enjoyed the way it felt to let go. We hit the ground with our fists flying and people screaming around us.

I almost laughed out loud as I caught him in the stomach and he immediately punched back, catching the grin as it crossed my lips and leaving blood in its wake. I had forgotten how much I liked fighting. Apparently Molly's brother enjoyed it as well, because it took Chaz and three other men to break it up. I made note of the fact that Noah Andelin hadn't hesitated about wading in and was the one sitting on my back, shoving my face into the floor to restrain me. The room was chaos, but between the upended chairs and the scrambling legs of the staff trying to get the other clients out of the room, I could see Molly's brother in the same position as I was, his head turned toward me, cheek against the grey speckled linoleum floor.

"How did you know?" he said, his eyes on mine. The din around us quieted slightly. "How did you know about my sister?"

"Tag. No more!" Dr. Andelin barked, sweetness and light all run out.

Tag? What kind of name was that?

"My sister's been missing for over a year, and this son-of-a-bitch acts like he knows something about it?" Tag ignored Dr. Andelin and raged on. "You think I'm gonna shut up? Think again, Doc!"

We were both pulled to our feet and Dr. Andelin instructed Chaz and another orderly I didn't recognize to stay. Everybody else he ordered out. A plump brunette therapist named Shelly stayed behind as well, and she hung back as if to document the meeting as Dr. Andelin righted three chairs in the center of the floor and instructed us to sit. Chaz stood behind Tag and the other orderly stood behind me. Noah Andelin sat equidistance between us, his shirt sleeves rolled up and a little blood on his lip. Looks like I clipped him on accident. Chaz handed him a tissue and Dr. Andelin took it and blotted at his lip before eyeing us both and straightening in his chair.

"Moses, do you want to explain to Tag what you meant when you asked if anyone knew a girl named Molly?"

"A dead girl named Molly!" Tag hissed. Chaz patted his shoulder, a reminder to calm down, and Tag swore violently.

"I don't know if she's his sister. I don't know him. But I've been seeing a girl named Molly off and on for almost five months."

They all stared at me.

"Seeing her? Do you mean you have a relationship with Molly?" Dr. Andelin asked.

"I mean, she's dead, and I know she's dead because for the last five months I've been able to see her," I repeated patiently.

Tag's face was almost comical in its fury.

"See her how?" Dr. Andelin's voice was flat and his eyes were cold.

I matched his tone and leveled my own flat gaze in his direction. "The same way I can see your dead wife, Doctor. She keeps showing me a car visor and snow and pebbles at the bottom of a river. I don't know why. But you can probably tell me."

Dr. Andelin's jaw went slack and his complexion greyed.

"What are you talking about?" he gasped. I'd been waiting to use this on him. Now was as good a time as any. Maybe his wife would go away and I could focus on getting rid of Molly once and for all.

"She follows you around the joint. You miss her too much. And she worries about you. She's fine . . . but you're not. I know she's your wife because she shows you waiting for her at the end of the aisle. Your wedding day. Your tuxedo is a little too short in the sleeves."

I tried to be flippant, to force him out of his role as psychologist. I dug around in his life to keep him from digging around in my head. But the savage grief that slammed across his face slowed me down and softened my voice. I couldn't maintain my attitude against his pain. I felt momentarily shamed and looked down at my hands. For several heartbeats, the room was as still as a morgue. Appropriately so. The dead were everywhere. Then Dr. Andelin spoke.

"My wife, Cora, was driving home from work. They think she was blinded—temporarily—by the sun reflecting off the snow. It's like that sometimes up here on the bench, you know. She drifted into the guard-rail. Her car landed upside down in the creek bed. She . . . drowned."

He supplied the information so matter-of-factly, but his hands shook as he stroked his beard.

Somewhere during the tragic recount, Tag lost his fury. He stared from me to Dr. Andelin in confusion and compassion. But Cora Andelin wasn't done—it was like she knew I had the doctor's attention and she wasn't wasting any time.

"Peanut butter, Downey fabric softener, Harry Connick, Jr., um-brellas . . ." I paused because the next image was so intimate. But then I said it anyway. "Your beard. She loved the way it felt, when you . . ." I had to stop. They were making love and I didn't want to see this man's wife naked. I didn't want to see *him* naked. And I could see him through her eyes. I stood up abruptly, needing desperately to move. Way too much information, Cora Andelin. Way too much.

The orderly got nervous and immediately shoved my shoulders, urging me to sit back down. I considered swinging on him and then sighed. The moment had passed, and no one wanted to tussle anymore. Not even Tag, who looked as though his brain had been wiped clean. He was looking at me with a dazed expression.

But Dr. Andelin was dialed in, his blue eyes intense and full of his own memories, and something else too. Gratitude. His eyes were full of gratitude.

"Those were some of her favorite things. She walked down the aisle on our wedding day to a Harry Connick song. And yeah. My tux was a smidge too short. She always laughed about that and said it was just like me. And her umbrella collection was out of control." His voice broke, and he looked down at his hands.

The room was so heavy with compassion and thick with intimacy, that if the five others present were able to see what I could see, they would have looked away to give the lovers a moment alone. But I was the only one to witness Noah Andelin's wife reach out and run a hand over her husband's bowed head before the soft lines of her inconsistent form melded into the flickering light of the fading afternoon. The room had windows that faced west, and though I had my complaints about Utah, the sunsets weren't one of them. Cora Andelin became part of the sunset. I didn't think I would see her again. And I hadn't even needed to draw.

"If you know all that—about Dr. Andelin's wife—then I want you to tell me about Molly," Tag whispered, straightening in his chair and swinging his gaze from Dr. Andelin back to me.

Noah Andelin rose to his feet. I didn't look at his face. I didn't want to see if I'd destroyed him. I'd disappointed myself a little. Where was the badass I had decided to be?

"Tag. I promise we'll revisit this. But not now. Not now." And with a nod to the orderlies, who seemed as shaken as he was, we were all ushered out of the room.

GEORGIA

IT WAS WEIRD, the things I missed. I missed his mouth and his green eyes and the way he could be sweet without knowing he was being sweet. I missed the smooth length of his throat, the place my nose would settle when I was close to him. I missed the paint brush twirling through his fingers and the way one side of his mouth curled slightly higher when he smiled. I missed the flash of white teeth and the sparkle of the "devil in his eye." That's what his grandmother had called it. And she was right. He had a naughty twinkle in his eyes when he was relaxed or laughing or teasing me back. I missed those things desperately.

The worst part was, I couldn't grieve for him. I had to hide all my feelings, which I'd never been good at. My family had a saying, "Georgia ain't happy, ain't nobody happy." And I wasn't happy. I was devastated. The whole town was still in shock over Kathleen's death, and even though Moses hadn't smothered her in her sleep or slashed her throat, the town still acted as if he had. My parents weren't much better. Moses had been weird. And weird was easily suspect. Weird was frightening and unforgiveable. But I found I missed that too—he was weird and wonderful and totally different from anyone I knew. From anyone I would ever know. And he was gone.

I got asked to my senior ball, which was held the last Saturday in January. Terrence Anderson asked me, of all people. I guess he'd decided he liked tall girls after all. Or maybe he just wanted to make Haylee jealous since they had broken up just after the school year started. I considered telling him no. Lord knows I had plenty of excuses. But Mom told me it was bad manners and that I should be grateful, after all that had happened, that people were moving on. I had laughed hysterically at that and Mom had sent me to my room, convinced I was sick. I cried myself to sleep and felt no better the following day.

I accepted Terrence's invitation to the dance, but I wore a black dress because I was in mourning, and the highest heels I could find just to make him feel stupid. If he was going to use me that was fine. But I wasn't going to make it easy for him. And that night, sitting on the bleachers in the high school gymnasium, watching couples dance and sitting beside a seething Terrence, I missed Moses most of all. It wasn't hard to imagine how he would look in a tux or a nice suit, I could have worn four inch heels and he would still be taller than me, and I had a feeling he would have liked my black dress and the way my body was changing.

Terrence just stared at my fuller chest with a sneer and I realized that my plan had backfired a little. The heels practically put my boobs at his eye level. I ended up taking them off and resigning myself to dancing in my bare feet and pretending Terrence Anderson was Kenny Chesney—Kenny was a little guy and a famous country singer, and he was plenty hot. Sadly, I found my tastes had changed dramatically, and cowboys and country singers, however hot, had taken a backseat to eccentric artists in mental institutions.

XII

MOSES

WE DIDN'T REVISIT it right away. Not with Dr. Andelin anyway. Tag and I were both put on isolation for three days due to the slug fest. Neither of us were allowed out of our rooms, and I was journaling with pictures once again, explaining "my thoughts and feelings" through my drawings. Dr. Andelin brought me a stack of sketch pads. Good ones. Not computer paper. And he brought grease pencils too. I don't think he asked permission. I think he was thanking me. I liked the non-verbal appreciation far better than anything he could have said, especially since I hadn't done it to make him happy. But I made sure to show my gratitude in my own way.

I drew and drew until my fingers cramped and my eyes wouldn't focus. And when I was done I had sheets and sheets of still life drawings and portraits. Umbrellas and pebbles in a stream and Noah Andelin in his neat little beard, laughing and looking up from the page at a woman who was gone but not forgotten. When I presented the pictures to the doctor on his next visit, he took them reverently and spent our entire session thumbing through them, not talking at all. It was the best session yet.

On the third day of isolation, Tag sprinted into my room and shut the door.

I stared at him balefully. I was kind of under the impression the door was locked. I hadn't even checked to see. I felt stupid for just sitting in a room for three days behind an unlocked door.

"They stroll the hall every few minutes. But that's all. That was ridiculously easy. I should have come sooner," he said, and sat down on my bed. "I'm David Taggert, by the way. But you can call me Tag." He didn't act like he wanted to engage in a brawl, which was a little disappointing.

If he didn't want to fight, I wanted him to leave. I immediately went back to the picture I was working on. I felt Molly there, just beyond the water, her image flickering through the falls, and I sighed heavily. I was weary of Molly. I was even wearier of her brother. Both were incredibly stubborn and obnoxious.

"You're a crazy son-of-a bitch," he stated without preamble.

I didn't even raise my head from the picture I was drawing with the nub of a grease pencil. I was trying to make my supplies last. I was going through them too fast.

"That's what people say, don't they? They say you're crazy. But I don't buy it, man. Not anymore. You're not crazy. You've got skills. Mad skills."

"Mad. Crazy. Don't they mean the same thing?" I murmured. Madness and genius were closely related. I wondered what skills he was talking about. He hadn't seen me paint.

"Nah, man," he said. "They aren't. Crazy people need to be in places like this. You don't belong here."

"I think I probably do."

He laughed, clearly surprised. "You think you're crazy?"

"I think I'm cracked." That's what Georgia said. But she hadn't seemed to mind. Not until the cracks had gotten so wide she'd fallen in one and gotten hurt.

Tag tilted his head quizzically, but when I didn't continue, he nodded. "Okay. Maybe we're all cracked. Or bent. I sure as hell am."

"Why?" I found myself asking. Molly was hovering again and I drew faster, helplessly filling the page with her face.

"My sister's gone. And it's my fault. And until I know what happened to her, I'm never gonna be able to get straight. I'll be bent forever." His voice was so soft I wasn't sure he meant for me to hear the last part.

"Is this your sister?" I asked reluctantly. I held up my sketch pad.

Tag stared. Then he stood. Then he sat down again. And then he nodded.

"Yeah," he choked. "That's my sister."

And he told me everything.

It turns out, David Taggert's father was a Texas oil man who'd always wanted to be a rancher. When Tag started getting in trouble and getting drunk every weekend, Tag's father had retired, sold some of his shares for millions and, among other things, purchased a fifty acre ranch in Sanpete County, Utah, where Tag's mother was from, and moved the family there. He was sure if he could get Tag and his older sister, Molly, away from their old scene, he would be able to clean them up. Tag's father thought it would be a good move for the whole family. Open space, lots of work to keep them busy, and good, wholesome people all around them. And there was plenty of money to grease the operation.

But the kids hadn't thrived. They'd rebelled. Tag's older sister, Molly, ran away and was never heard from again. The younger girls, twins, ended up following their mother back to Dallas when she filed for divorce. Turns out she liked Dallas better, too, and blamed her husband for her oldest daughter's disappearance. Then it was just Tag and his old man. And lots of money, space, and cattle. Tag struggled to stay sober, but when he wasn't drinking, he was drowning in guilt and eventually tried to kill himself. Several times. Which landed him in the psych ward with me.

"She took off. We don't really know why. She was doing better than anyone. I think she took some of my shit. I wasn't just drinking, you know. I had pills stashed everywhere. I don't know why she took it. Maybe her problem was worse than I thought. Maybe she just wanted to take it so I couldn't get it."

I waited, letting him talk. I didn't know how she died any more than he did. That wasn't what the dead wanted to share. They wanted to show me their lives. Not their deaths. Not ever.

"She's dead. Isn't she? You can see her so that means she's dead."

I nodded.

"I need you to tell me where she is, Moses. I need you to find out."

"It doesn't work that way. I don't see the whole picture. Just pieces. I don't always even know who the person belongs to. If I'm in a group, it could be anyone. They don't speak. At all. And if they do, I can't hear them. They show me things. And I don't always know why. In fact, I never know why. I just paint."

"You knew with Dr. Andelin!"

"His dead wife followed him around during the group session! And she showed them having sex, okay? It didn't take much to decipher that one!" I was getting agitated and Tag was moving in on me like he was getting ready to do battle.

"They show me pieces. Memories. And I don't always interpret them correctly. I don't interpret them at all, you know? I'm not Sherlock Holmes."

He shoved me and I resisted the urge to shove back. "So you're telling me that you've seen my sister before and you had no idea she was mine?"

"I saw Molly long before I ever met you!"

The truth of the statement suddenly slammed home.

I had seen Molly long before I'd ever met David Taggert.

And that didn't make any sense. It never happened like that. The dead that came through were always a result of my contact with the people close to them.

"She went away. I painted her face on an overpass and she went away." I'd seen her the night Gigi died. But that didn't count. That night, I'd seen every dead face that had haunted my life since the beginning. I just hadn't seen Gi.

"And she came back?"

"Yes. But I think she came back because of you."

"And what does she do?" Tag was yelling now, frustrated, his hands fisted in his dark hair, his green eyes blazing. I knew he wanted to start swinging. Not because he was actually angry at me, but because he had no idea what to do with his emotion. And I understood that.

"She shows me things. Just like they all do." I lowered my voice and kept my eyes level. It felt a little strange talking someone else down.

"Please. Please, Moses." Tag was suddenly battling back the tears, and I resisted the urge to start a fight, to push him down and pummel him just to get him back to the Tag that wanted to hit me and called me a crazy son-of-a bitch.

I turned away from him and sank down on my haunches, bracing myself against the wall, but my eyes found the picture of Molly staring up from my sketch book that I'd tossed to the floor. She smiled back at me, a heart-breaking illusion of happy-ever-after. There was no happy-ever-after. I closed my eyes and put my hands over my head, blocking out Tag and the smiling face of his dead sister. And I raised the water.

I focused on Molly Taggert, blonde hair flying just like Georgia's. I immediately lost concentration and felt the same old slice in my gut that I felt whenever I allowed her memory in. But with the thought of Georgia, the overpass I'd painted came into focus, the place where I'd taken Georgia's virginity and permanently lost a part of myself.

Immediately, I needed to paint, and I swore viciously, yelling at Tag to throw me the sketchbook and a pencil. It wasn't the same, but I had to have something. My hands got icy and my neck burned and in my mind I watched as the strip of land became pale and flat as the water split in half and was sucked into two towering walls, leaving not a single drop behind to moisten the ground.

They'd made me cover Molly's image on the overpass with paint. The Sheriff's Department had supplied me with a gallon of flat grey paint that covered the upsetting truth that children disappeared and the world was a scary place. But as I watched, the paint started to peel as if pulled by imaginary hands, revealing Molly once again in swirling lines and twinkling eyes and a smile that I could now see was identical to Tag's. We never saw what was obvious until we were hit over the head with it.

And then images started to flood my mind, the same images Molly always fed me.

"She always shows me that damn math test!" My arms were flying, and I drew the test with Molly's name in flowing script at the top.

The math test fluttered away as if Molly had whipped it out of my hands. I hadn't shown the proper appreciation for that red A circled at the top. Tag wasn't the only one in the family with a temper, apparently. The A in the circle became a star, just a simple golden star that morphed into a night sky with stars shooting and exploding, like she was staring up at a light show, so glorious and color-filled that I cursed the pencil in my hand and begged Tag to bring me something else.

Then Molly showed me fields, fields that looked just like the fields around the overpass and I tried not to curse in frustration. Instead, I drew the long golden strands of wheat in those fields, blending them with Molly's hair as she raced through my mind, until the wheat became weeds that brushed against the concrete overpass.

"Stop! Moses!" Tag was shaking my shoulders and slapping at my face. "What the hell, man! You're drawing on the walls!" Tag's voice faded off. "Actually, I don't give a shit if you draw on the walls."

But the connection was gone, and I was dazed. I was pissed too, and stepped back from the wild, star-filled sky, smudged and shaded and half-finished before me. If I would have had paint

I was breathing too hard, and so was Tag, as if he'd crossed to the other side with me and had run, chasing his sister through fields of wheat that led to nowhere and made absolutely no sense to me whatsoever.

He looked down at the images I'd tossed around the room and started picking them up, one at a time.

"A math test? With an A circled at the top?"

"It's red. The A is red." I hadn't been able to illustrate that with the pencil.

"And this overpass is in Nephi?"

I nodded.

"Nephi's only about an hour from Sanpete. You knew that, right?"

I nodded again. And Nephi was fifteen minutes north of Levan. All the kids from Levan were bussed to school in Nephi. It was practically the same town. And I wasn't going near either of them. Tag could beg and plead, and his angry green eyes could explode in his head, and I still wasn't going back.

"What's with the fields?"

"There are fields surrounding the overpass. There's a truck stop, a couple gas stations, a cheap motel and a burger joint a little farther down by the off-ramp, but that's all. It's fields and a freeway, and that's pretty much it."

"And what's this?" Tag pointed at the wall where my pencil had proven frustratingly insufficient at conveying the exploding colors and streaks of light.

I shrugged. "Fireworks?"

"It was Fourth of July weekend," Tag whispered.

I shrugged again. "I don't know, Tag. I don't know anything other than what she showed me."

"Why doesn't she just tell you where she is?"

"Because it doesn't work that way."

"Why?" Tag was getting frustrated again.

"That's like asking me why I can't live in the ocean. Or why I can't bench a thousand pounds or . . . why I can't fly, for hell's sake! I just can't. And no amount of focus or study or attention to detail is going to make those things possible. It is what it is!"

I picked up my sketch pad and realized I'd ripped every last page out, including the pictures that had nothing to do with Molly Taggert. Those pages were also tossed around the room. And there were no blank pages left. I started gathering them, despondent that I was going to be repainting walls again. Tag followed behind me, still clinging to the pages he'd picked up.

"She's got to be there," he said softly, and I stopped gathering and looked back at him. His eyes were bright and his shoulders were set.

"Maybe she is." I shrugged helplessly. I didn't want anything to do with any of it. "But can you imagine if they find her? Especially if I pointed them in that direction? They will throw my ass in jail. Do you understand that? They will think I did it." I didn't say killed her. It felt too cold to say it to his face, though we both knew what we were talking about.

Suddenly the door to my room swung open and Chaz barreled in, alarm marring his friendly face and robbing him of his ever-present white smile. Relief quickly replaced the alarm as he realized no blood had been spilled, and neither of us were incapacitated on the floor.

"Mr. Taggert. You are not supposed to be in here!" he huffed. Then he saw my grease painting and swore. "Not again, man! You were doin' so well."

I shrugged. "I ran out of paper."

Chaz ushered Tag out, and he didn't resist, but at the door he paused. "Thank you, Moses."

Chaz looked surprised at the exchange, but tugged on Tag, all the same.

"I'll take the blame for the drawing on the wall. I'm sure everyone will believe me." Tag winked, and Chaz and I both laughed.

XIII

MOSES

TAG WASN'T THE ONLY ONE who made a habit of sneaking
into my room for private sessions. Word started to get around
about what I could do. What I could see. What I could paint.

Carol, a psychiatrist in her fifties who never seemed fazed by anything and was married to her work, had lost a brother to suicide when
she was twelve. It was what had led her to work with the mentally ill.
That same brother started showing me roller skates and a scruffy stuffed
rabbit with a missing ear. So I told her what I saw. She hadn't believed
me at first, so I told her that her brother loved potato salad, the color
purple, Johnny Carson, and could only play one song on his ukulele,
which he played and sang to her each night before she went to sleep.
"Somewhere Over the Rainbow." That was the song. She had taken me
off the antipsychotics the next day.

Buffie Lucas was a no-nonsense psych tech who should have been
on Broadway. She sang as she worked and could do Aretha Franklin
better than Aretha Franklin could do Aretha Franklin. She'd lost her
parents within three months of each other. When I asked her if her mom
had given her a quilt made out of all her concert T-shirts before she died,

she had stopped mid-song. Then she smacked me and made me promise not to hold anything back.

People came, and they brought gifts. Paper and grease pencils, water colors and chalk, and about two months into my stay, Dr. June brought me a letter from Georgia. I'd done something that pleased Dr. June, and I suppose she was trying to reward me. I hadn't meant to please her. I didn't especially like Dr. June. But she'd seen a picture I'd drawn of Gigi. I'd meant to hide it and then hadn't been able to bring myself to put it away. It was a chalk drawing. Simple and beautiful, just like Gi always was. In the picture she was folded around a child, though I told myself the child wasn't me. June had stared at it, and then raised her eyes to mine.

"This is beautiful. Touching. Tell me about it."

I shook my head. "No."

"Okay. I'll tell you what I see," Dr. June said.

I shrugged.

"I see a child and a woman who love each other very much."

I shrugged again.

"Is this you?"

"Does it look like me?"

She looked down at the drawing and then back at me. "It looks like a child. You were a child once."

I didn't respond and she continued.

"Is this your grandmother?" she asked.

"I suppose it could be," I conceded.

"Did you love her?"

"I don't love anyone."

"Do you miss her?"

I sighed and asked a question of my own. "Do you miss your sister?"

"Yes I do." She nodded as she spoke. "And I think you miss your grandmother."

I nodded. "Okay. I miss my grandmother."

"That's healthy, Moses."

"Okay." Awesome. I was healed. Hallelujah.

"Is she the only one you miss?"

I stayed silent, unsure of where she was leading me.

"She keeps coming back, you know."

I waited.

"Georgia. Every week. She comes. And you don't want to see her?"

"No." I suddenly felt dizzy.

"Can you tell me why?"

"Georgia thinks she loves me." I winced at the admission, and Dr. June's eyes widened slightly. I'd just given her a meaty, dripping spoonful of psyche stew, and she was salivating over it.

"And you don't love her?" she said, trying not to drool.

"I don't love anyone," I responded immediately. Hadn't I already said that? I took a deep breath, trying to steady myself. It both pleased and bothered me that Georgia had been so persistent. And it bothered me that I was pleased. It bothered me that my pulse had quickened and that my palms were damp. It bothered me that at the mention of her name, I had immediately felt that rush of color behind my eyes, reminiscent of the kaleidoscope Georgia's kisses had always created in my head.

"I see. Why?" Dr. June asked.

"I just don't. I'm broken, I guess." Cracked.

She nodded, almost agreeing with me.

"Do you think you might love someone someday?"

"I don't plan on it."

She nodded again and persisted for a while, but finally her time was up, and she'd really only gotten that one spoonful, which made me happy.

"That's enough for today," she said, standing briskly, folder in hand.

She slid an envelope from the back of the file and set it carefully on the table in front of me.

"She wanted me to give this to you. Georgia did. I told her I wouldn't. I told her if you had wanted to contact her, you would have. I think that hurt her. But it's the truth, isn't it?" I felt a flash of anger that June had been rude to Georgia, and was bothered once again that I was bothered.

"But I decided to give it to you and let you choose whether or not you wanted to read it." She shrugged. "It's up to you."

I stared at the letter for a long time after Dr. June ended our session. I was sure that was what she had expected. She thought I would give in and read it, I was sure of that too. But she didn't understand my laws.

I tossed the letter in the trash and gathered up the drawings Dr. June had been flipping through. The one of Gi was there on top, and the intertwined figures made me pause. I pulled Georgia's letter back out of the trash, painstakingly unsealed it, and drew the single handwritten page from inside without letting myself focus on the curving letters and the swooping G at the bottom that began her name. Then I carefully folded the picture of Gi, the way Gi enfolded the child in the drawing. The child that wasn't me, not anymore at least. The child could be Georgia now, and Gi could look after her. Then I took the drawing and tucked it inside the envelope. I wrote Georgia's address on the outside and when Chaz brought me my dinner that night I asked him if he would make sure it got sent.

I slipped Georgia's letter beneath my mattress where I wouldn't have to see it, where I wouldn't have to feel it, where I wouldn't have to acknowledge it.

GEORGIA

HIS NAME WASN'T in the top left-hand corner but the envelope said Montlake and it was his handwriting that slashed across the envelope. Georgia Shepherd, PO Box 5, Levan Utah, 84639. Moses and I had had a discussion about Levan and her post office boxes, and apparently Moses hadn't forgotten it. The only mail boxes anyone had at their homes in Levan were for the Daily Herald, a newspaper most of Levan subscribed to, if only for the Sunday comics and the coupon inserts. The Daily Herald was delivered by paper boys or families and it was delivered door to door. But the actual mail was delivered to the little brick post office on the main drag and distributed to the keyed, ornate boxes inside. My family had one of the lower numbers because we'd inherited our box as it was passed down through the Shepherd line.

"So your family is Levan royalty, then?" Moses had teased.
"Yes. We Shepherds rule this town," I replied.
"Who has PO Box number 1?" he inquired immediately.
"God," I said, not missing a beat.
"And box number 2?" He was laughing as he asked.
"Pam Jackman."
"From down the street?"
"Yes. She's like one of the Kennedys."
"She drives the bus, right?" he asked.
"Yes. Bus driver is a highly lauded position in our community." I didn't even crack a smile.
"So boxes 3 and 4?"
"They are empty now. They are waiting for the heirs to come of age before they inherit their mailboxes. My son will someday inherit PO Box #5. It will be a proud day for all Shepherds."
"Your son? What if you have a daughter?" His eyes got that flinty look that made my stomach feel swishy. Talking about having children made me think about making babies. With Moses.
"She's going to be the first female bull-rider who wins the national title. She won't be living in Levan most of the time. Her brothers will have to look after the family name and the Shepherd line . . . and our post office box," I said, trying not to think about how much I would enjoy making little bull-riders with Moses.

When Mom delivered my letter, her eyes got tight and I could tell she wished she could just toss it and keep Moses away for good. But she didn't. She brought it to my room, set it softly on my dresser, and left without comment. The best part of opening any highly-anticipated letter or package is the moment before you know what it is. Or what it says. And I had been waiting for something from Moses for months, praying for something. I knew as soon as I opened it I would either be filled with hope or crushed beyond repair. And I was too worn out for either at the moment.

I ended up going for a long ride, taking the letter along, tucking it inside my coat so it wouldn't get wrinkled. It was February and we'd finally gotten a snow storm after a very cold, dry, couple of months. Rumor was that they'd found Molly Taggert's remains near the overpass where Moses had painted her picture. People were talking again and people were staring at me too, all the while trying to pretend they weren't staring. The lack of snow had made it possible for the dogs to work, to find her, but I was glad the dry spell was finally broken.

The empty white world was welcome, and when Sackett and I were far away from everything and everyone, I pulled the letter out and carefully opened it, as if I might inadvertently tear away something important. Maybe my own dry spell was finally broken. I pulled out a folded piece of thick drawing paper and carefully opened it, tucking the envelope back inside my coat. With shaking hands I studied the picture in my hands. I didn't know what to make of it.

It was beautiful, but more abstract than I would have hoped. I wanted concrete. I wanted words. I wanted him to tell me that he was coming back for me. That he couldn't stand being apart. But I didn't get concrete. I got a picture. How very Moses.

It was a woman, but she could be any woman. There was a child, and it could almost be any child. The woman was created from swirls and suggestions, breasts, hips, embracing arms and folded legs, all enclosing a small child with a brief sweep of dark hair. I looked at it for a long time, not knowing what to make of it.

Was it symbolic? Was it pointed? Was he making a statement about the loss of his grandmother? Was he trying to tell me he understood what I was going through? I didn't know how he could. And so I stared at the lovely, confusing bit of correspondence from the boy who had kept me guessing from the beginning. After a while, my hands grew cold and Sackett grew restless, and I headed back for home.

I framed the picture and hung it on my wall, determined to get some sense of peace from it, from the fact Moses had thought of me at all. But mostly I felt afraid and unequipped to tackle the days ahead, still unable to completely give up on Moses Wright. Mom had taken one look at the picture and turned away, and Dad just shook his head and sighed. And I settled in for a long wait.

MOSES

IN A SHALLOW GRAVE piled high with rocks and debris, fifty yards from where I'd painted her smiling face, the remains of Molly Taggert were uncovered. Tag said the truck stop nearby was called Circle A. The neon sign that marked the establishment was a red A inside a circle—just like at the top of Molly's math page. I'd never noticed it at all in my travels back and forth across the ridge between Levan and Nephi. I'd driven by that truck stop a hundred times and never made the connection. Too lost in my own head, definitely not Sherlock Holmes. The back of the truck stop butted up to a stretch of field that led into the little hills that rose into the mountain ridge that stretched along the east part of town and continued south for hundreds of miles. A golf course was wedged between those hills, and every year fireworks were launched from the first tee around the fourth of July. The red A and the fireworks were both easily visible from the overpass where I'd painted Molly's image, marking her resting place and not even knowing it.

Tag had cried when he told me. Big, wracking sobs that made his shoulders shake and my stomach tighten painfully, the way it had the night Georgia had told me she loved me. "I think you do love me, Moses," she'd said, tears coating her throat. "And I love you too." I didn't do well with tears. I didn't cry, so I didn't know why other people did. And Tag cried for his sister the way I imagined I should have cried for Gi. But I didn't cry, so I just waited until the storm passed, and Tag mopped up the tears on his cheeks and finished telling me the rest.

Tag had told his father about me. And for whatever reason—desperation, despondency, or maybe just a desire to placate his adamant son—David Taggert Sr. hired a man and his dogs to cover the area Tag had described. They'd caught her scent quickly, and they found her remains. Just like that. The police were called in and before too long, the police came to the loony bin, looking for me. I'd been questioned about

Molly Taggert before, but now they had a body. A body that was found eerily close to my dramatic display.

Sheriff Dawson came with another man, a round, pasty-faced, red-haired deputy that couldn't have been much older than me. The younger man sneered at me, clearly playing the part of the nasty sidekick on his favorite cop show. With his powdery complexion and his flaming hair, he reminded me of a scowling jelly donut.

Sheriff Dawson asked me all the same questions and a few new ones. He knew David Taggert was a patient at the institution where I was housed. He also knew what Tag had told his father and what his father had then relayed to the search team. And he knew it had all come from me. But when it was all said and done, Molly Taggert had been missing since July of 2005. In July of 2005, I'd been living in California with my uncle and his unhappy wife and their very spoiled children. In July of 2005, I served the entire month in a juvenile detention facility for gang related activities. And that was indisputable. As far as alibis go, mine was pretty airtight. Sheriff already knew that, from our conversation back in October, when I'd painted Molly's face on the overpass and got hauled in for questioning. But I had known it wouldn't stop him, or anyone else in law enforcement, from believing I was guilty of something. I'd told Tag as much.

"You had any further contact with Georgia Shepherd?" Sheriff Dawson asked as he closed his file and prepared to leave. The question felt a little strange at the tail end of all the questions about Molly Taggert.

"No," I said. The sheriff didn't meet my gaze but continued rifling through the thick pages in front of him. With his head tilted down and his hat removed, I could see his pink scalp through his pale hair.

"You and she were friends, if I remember right." He kept his head down and turned another page.

"Not really."

He glanced up. "No?"

"No."

Sheriff Dawson shot a look at the pudgy deputy. The deputy smirked. Heat rose in my chest, and I wanted to pop his fat face in. I didn't understand the look, but there was something ugly behind it.

"Hmm. But you were there the night she was attacked at the Stampede, right? You took her home, made sure she was all right."

I waited, the heat in my chest spreading to my ears. He already knew all this.

"We never really figured out what happened that night."

He paused again and suddenly slapped the file shut. "So you haven't had any visions about what might have happened there, have you? Maybe painted a mug shot or a finger print on the side of some barn? You know, something we can use to hunt the bastard down? We don't especially like people hurtin' our girls. So it sure would be nice to bring justice to whoever hurt Georgia."

I said nothing. I had hurt Georgia. I was sure that was what he was getting at. After all, she was the one who called the cops the morning Gi died. She was the one who stood outside and waited for the ambulance. She was the one who found out where I'd been committed and made a wasted effort to see me. But I didn't think that was what the sheriff was referring to. He obviously thought I'd tied her up too, psycho that I am.

But I hadn't tied her up. And I hadn't had any "visions" about who had. So I stayed silent and seated as he rose, along with Deputy Jelly Donut, and headed for the door.

"Moses?" The younger man exited, but Sheriff Dawson paused, his hand on the knob as he placed his cowboy hat back over his thinning hair. "I hear you're gonna be released in the next few days."

I nodded slightly, acknowledging that I was. He nodded too and pursed his lips, considering me.

"Well, good. That's good. Everybody deserves a fresh start. But I don't think you should come back to Levan, Moses," he said, stepping into the hall. "We're all out of fresh starts and second chances." He let the door fall closed between us as he walked away.

XIV

MOSES

THEY TOOK US BOTH OFF ISOLATION, and much to my surprise, Tag and I fell into a sort of friendship. Maybe it was our youth. Maybe it was Molly, maybe it was the fact that we were both in a psychiatric facility and neither of us especially wanted to leave—or as Tag put it, "rock bottom with no desire to climb higher"—or maybe it was just that Tag reminded me a little of Georgia with his twang and his humor and his cowboy persona. He was nothing like me, and they would have hit it off, I was sure of it. The thought made me strangely jealous, and I was struck again that she'd ever wanted me at all.

Tag was usually quick to smile, quick to anger, quick to forgive, quick to pull the trigger. He didn't do anything in half measures and I wondered sometimes if the facility wasn't the best place for him, just to keep him contained. But he had a maudlin side too. And one night after lights out, he came and found me, creeping down the hall undetected, the way he always did, seeking answers that none of the staff could give him, answers he thought I had.

Tag said I was aptly named. "Wasn't Moses a prophet or something?"

I just rolled my eyes. At least we weren't talking about the fact that I'd been found in a basket.

"MO-SES!" Tag said my name in a deep, echoing "God voice," reminiscent of the old Charlton Heston movie, *The Ten Commandments*. Gigi had loved Charlton Heston. I'd spent an Easter with her the year I was twelve and we'd had a Charlton Heston marathon that made me want to smear red paint above everybody's door and burn all the bushes in Levan. Come to think of it, I had smeared paint all over Levan, many times. It was all Charlton Heston's fault.

Tag laughed when I told him that. But the laughter faded, and he slumped back on my bed, staring up at the ceiling. Then he looked at me, measuring me. "If I die, what will happen to me?"

"Why do you think you're going to die?" I asked, sounding like Dr. Andelin.

"I'm here because I tried to kill myself several times, Moses."

"Yeah. I know." I pointed at the long scar on his arm. "And I'm here because I paint dead people and scare the livin' shit out of everyone I come in contact with."

He grinned. "Yeah. I know." But his smile faded immediately. "When I'm not drinking, life just grinds me down until I can't see straight. It wasn't always that way. But it is now. Life sucks pretty bad, Moses."

I nodded, but found myself smiling a little as I remembered how Georgia had lectured me every time I said something similar.

"Georgia's laugh, Georgia's hair, Georgia's kisses, Georgia's wit, Georgia's long, long legs," I murmured. I'd gotten comfortable with Tag and I repeated the list out loud, much to my embarrassment.

"What?"

I felt stupid but I answered him honestly. "Five greats. I was listing five greats. Just something someone used to do whenever I complained about how bad life was."

"Georgia?"

"Yeah."

146

"She your girl?" he asked.

"She wanted to be," I admitted, but wouldn't admit how I had wanted her.

"And you didn't want that? Not even with her hair, her kisses, and her long, long legs?" He smiled, and I liked him, in spite of myself. But I didn't say anything more about Georgia.

"You still want to die?" I asked, changing the subject.

"Depends. What comes next?" "More," I answered simply. "There's more. That's all I can tell you. It doesn't end."

"And you can see what comes next?"

"What do you mean?" I couldn't see the future, if that's what he meant.

"Can you see the other side?"

"No. I only see what they want me to see," I said.

"They? They who?"

"Whoever comes through." I shrugged.

"Do they whisper to you? Do they talk?" Tag was whispering too, as if the subject were sacred.

"No. They never say anything at all. They just show me things."

Tag shivered and rubbed the back of his neck, like he was trying to rub away the goose flesh that had crept up his back.

"So how do you know what they want?" he asked.

"They all want the same thing." And strangely, they did.

"What? What do they want?"

"They want to speak. They want to be heard." I hadn't ever put it into words, but the answer felt right.

"So they don't speak but they want to speak?"

I nodded once, affirming that Tag was correct.

"Why do they want to speak?" "Because that's what they used to do . . ." I hesitated.

"That's what they used to do, when they were alive?" Tag finished for me. "Yeah."

"So how do they communicate?" "Thoughts don't require flesh and bone."

"You hear their thoughts?" he asked, incredulous.

"No. I see their memories in my thoughts." I supposed that was even more bizarre, but it was the truth.

"You see their memories? All of them? Do you see everything? Their whole lives?"

"Sometimes it feels like that. It can be a flood of color and thought, and I can only pick up random things because it's coming at me so fast. And I can only really see what I understand. I'm sure they would like me to see more. But it isn't that easy. It's subjective. I usually see pieces and parts. Never the whole picture. But I've gotten better at filtering, and as I've gotten better, it feels more like remembering and less like being possessed." I smiled in spite of myself, and Tag shook his head in wonder.

"Are there any dead people here now?" Tag swiveled around looking right and left as if maybe, if he turned fast enough, he could catch a ghost unaware.

"Definitely," I lied. There was no one nearby, nothing to mar the quiet or the space except the branch outside my window that tapped and scratched against the glass and the squeak of rubber-soled shoes against the linoleum as someone hurried past my door.

Tag's brows shot up, and he waited for me to tell him more.

"Marilyn Monroe thinks you're hot. She's blowing in your ear right now."

Tag's finger immediately filled his ear canal as if a bug had flown in and was buzzing incessantly, trying to get out.

I laughed, surprising myself, surprising Tag. He was usually the one to tease, not me.

"You're shittin' me, right?" Tag laughed. "You are! Damn. I wouldn't mind it if Marilyn really did want to hang around."

"Yeah. It doesn't really work that way. I only see people who have a connection to someone I'm in contact with, or someone I've been in contact with. I don't see random dead people."

"So when you told Chaz that his grandfather had left something for him, did his grandfather show you the will?"

"He showed me a picture of his reflection, walking into the bank . . . the way he saw it as he approached. Then he showed me the safe deposit box." I liked Chaz. He was muscle around the place—unfailingly cheerful, always singing, and always dependable. He worked with some very violent people day in and day out and never seemed to lose his good will or his cool.

When his grandfather kept trying to come through, I'd resisted. I liked Chaz and didn't need ammo against him. I had no desire to hurt him. Since I'd been admitted, I'd gotten better at keeping the walls of water around me. I'd had nothing to do but practice and go to endless counseling sessions that didn't especially apply, although surprisingly, they hadn't hurt. But my constant contact with Chaz seemed to strengthen his grandfather's connection with me, and I could feel him on the other side, waiting to wade across. So I let him, just him, raising the walls just a bit, just enough.

Chaz's grandfather had loved him. So I told Chaz what I saw, what his grandfather kept showing me. And Chaz had listened, his eyes huge in his black face. The next day he didn't come to work. But the day after that he'd found me and thanked me. And he cried when he did. He was a big, black, mountain of a man, bigger than I was. Stronger than I was. But he wept like a child, and he hugged me so tightly I couldn't breathe. And I realized it didn't always have to be a weapon. What I could do didn't have to hurt people.

"Moses?" Tag pulled me from my thoughts.

"Yeah?"

"Don't take this the wrong way . . . but, if, you know, there's more, and it's not bad. It's not scary. It's not the zombie apocalypse. It's not fire and brimstone . . . at least, not as far as you can tell, then why do you stay?" His voice was so quiet and filled with emotion, I wasn't sure if anything I said would help him. And prophet or not, I wasn't sure I knew the answer. It took me a minute of thinking, but I finally had a response that felt true.

"Because I'll still be me," I answered. "And you'll still be you."

"What do you mean?"

"We can't escape ourselves, Tag. Here, there, half-way across the world, or in a psych ward in Salt Lake City. I'm Moses and you're Tag. And that part never changes. So either we figure it out here or we figure it out there. But we still gotta deal. And death won't change that."

MOSES

MOLLY TAGGERT'S REMAINS were taken back to Dallas for burial, David Taggert Sr. decided to put his ranch up for sale, and Tag and I were both scheduled for release from the Montlake Psychiatric Facility. I had some money and my clothing, though I hadn't needed either during my stay. My clothes had been boxed up and sent to Montlake when my grandmother's possessions were divvied among her children, at least the possessions she hadn't left to me.

A lawyer had been allowed in to see me about two weeks after I'd been admitted. He'd told me about my grandmother. Told me she had died of natural causes, a stroke. And then he told me she'd left me ten acres on the north end of town, her house, her car, and everything in her bank account, which wasn't much. I didn't want Gigi's house, not if she wasn't in it. Gigi wouldn't expect me to go back. The sheriff had made it clear that no one wanted me back. I asked the lawyer if I could sell it.

The lawyer didn't think anyone would buy it. The land would sell—he already had a buyer—but no one would want the house. Small towns and tragedy were like that. I asked him if he could have it boarded up for me, which he did. When it was all said and done, house boarded up, Gi's funeral paid for, my medical bills—the part not covered by the state—cleared, the land, my Jeep, and Gigi's old car sold, the lawyer brought me the key to her house and a check for five thousand dollars. It was more money than I expected, more money than I'd ever had, and not enough to get me very far.

I imagined my extended family liked me even less now than they had before, and I knew I wouldn't be welcomed into any of their homes, which was fine. I didn't want to be there, truthfully. But I didn't know where I would go either. So when Tag brought it up the night before we were both free to leave, I didn't have much to say.

"When you get out, where you gonna go?" Tag asked at dinner, his

150

eyes on his food, his arms on the table. He could eat almost as much as I could, and I was pretty sure Montlake's kitchen staff would enjoy a little reprieve when we left.

I didn't want to talk about this with Tag. I really didn't want to talk about it with anyone. So I fixed my gaze to the left of Tag's head, out the window, letting him know I was ready for the conversation to end. But Tag persisted.

"You're eighteen now. You are officially out of the system. So where you gonna go, Mo?" I don't know why he thought he could call me Mo. I hadn't given him permission. But he was like that. Worming his way into my space. Kind of like Georgia used to.

My eyes flickered back to Tag briefly, and then I shrugged as if it wasn't important.

I'd been here for months. Through Christmas, through New Year's, and into February. Three months in a mental institution. And I wished I could stay.

"Come with me," Tag said, tossing down his napkin and pushing his tray away.

I reared back, stunned. I remembered the sound of Tag crying, the wails that echoed down the hall as he was brought in to the psych ward the night he was admitted. He'd arrived almost a month after I did. I had lain in bed and listened to the attempts to subdue him. At the time, I hadn't realized it was him. I only put two and two together later, when he told me about what brought him to Montlake. I thought about the way he'd come at me with his fists flying, rage in his eyes, almost out of his head with pain in the session with Dr. Andelin. Tag interrupted my train of thought when he continued speaking.

"My family has money. We don't have much else. But we have tons of money. And you don't have shit." I held myself stiffly, waiting. It was true. I didn't have shit. Tag was my friend, the first real friend, other than Georgia, that I'd ever had. But I didn't want Tag's shit. The good shit or the bad, and Tag had plenty of both.

"I need someone to make sure I don't kill myself. I need someone who's big enough to restrain me if I decide I need to get shitfaced. I'll hire you to spend every waking minute with me until I figure out how to stay clean without wanting to slit my wrists."

I tipped my head to the side, confused. "You want me to restrain you?"

Tag laughed. "Yeah. Hit me in the face, throw me to the ground. Kick the shit out of me. Just make sure I stay clean and alive."

I wondered for a moment if I could do that to Tag. Hit him, throw him to the ground. Hold him down until the need for drink or death passed. I was big. Strong. But Tag wasn't exactly small. Surprisingly, the idea didn't really appeal anymore. My doubt must have shown on my face because Tag was talking again.

"You need someone who believes you. I do. It's got to get old always having people thinking you're psychotic. I know you're not. You need somewhere to go, and I need someone to come with me. It's not a bad trade. You wanted to travel. And I've got nothing better to do. The only thing I'm good at is fighting, and I can fight anywhere." He smiled and shrugged. "Honestly, I don't trust myself to be alone just yet. And if I go back home to Dallas I'll drink. Or I'll die. So I need you."

He said that so easily. "I need you." I wondered how it was possible that a tough kid like Tag, someone who fought for the fun of it, could admit that to anyone. Or believe it. I'd never needed anyone. Not really. And I'd never said those words to anyone. "I need you" felt like "I love you," and it scared me. It felt like breaking one of my laws. But at that moment, with the morning looming large, with freedom at my fingertips, I had to admit, I probably needed Tag too.

We would make an odd pair. A black artist and a white cowboy. It sounded like the start to one of those jokes about three men going into a bar. But it was just the two of us. And Tag was right. We were both stuck. Lost. With nothing to hold us down and no direction. I just wanted my freedom, and Tag didn't want to be alone. I needed his money, and he needed my company, sad as it usually was.

"We'll just keep running, Moses. How did you say it? Here, there, on the other side of the world? We can't escape ourselves. So we stick together until we find ourselves, all right? Until we figure out how to deal."

GEORGIA

I DIDN'T KNOW HOW to break the news, and I didn't know how to admit to my parents that they were right and I was wrong. I wasn't an adult. I was a helpless little girl, something I'd never wanted to be. Something I'd always laughed in the face of. I had been tough all my life. I had reveled in being tough, in being as strong as the boys. But I hadn't been as strong. I'd been weak. So damn weak.

I had been weak, and my weakness had created a child, a child who had no father. Maybe Moses hadn't abandoned me—how could he when he'd never belonged to me? I felt abandoned, though. Abandoned and so very alone. In his defense, maybe he was more alone, maybe he was the one who was truly abandoned, but I couldn't think about him, and when he didn't come back, it was easier to be angry.

Moses became a faceless man. It was the only way I could cope. I erased his image from my mind. And I refused to think about him. Unfortunately, the faceless man and I had created a faceless child that grew and grew inside of me until it was impossible to keep him hidden anymore. And I broke down in tears, something I'd been doing a lot more of, and told my mom what had happened between me and Moses. She sat on my bed, listening to me talk, the Georgia Shepherd I'd always been—tough, determined, and opinionated—turning into a waffling, quivering woman-child. When I finished, my mother was so still. Shocked. She didn't put her arms around me. When I dared look in her face she was just sitting, staring at the wall where Moses had painted a man transforming into a white horse. I wondered if I had just become something else before her eyes too.

Even with her shock and her cold reception to my confession, it was a relief to unburden myself. After months alone with my secret, months that had been the most terrible of my life, months of fear and despair, of worry for Moses, for myself, and mostly for a child I refused to give a face to, I laid it all at her feet and selfishly didn't care whether I was turning her world upside down. I just couldn't carry it anymore.

When we told my dad, he was the one who melted my mother's heart. He stood and walked over to me and pulled me up into his arms. And my mother cried. That's when I knew it was going to be all right and that's when I gave up on Moses coming back.

PART 2
AFTER

XV

GEORGIA

Seven years later…

ACROWD WAS GATHERED around the wall across from the elevators, making it hard to decipher who was waiting to go up and who was watching. A mural was being painted, and I couldn't see the artist at work, but the depth of the crowd made me think it might be something special to see if only I had the time or inclination to stand around in a hospital and watch paint dry. The elevator binged and the waiting crowd shifted a little, separating the waiters from the watchers and when the doors slid open I waited patiently for the elevator to empty so I could wedge myself inside and stand quietly with the others while I climbed the floors to my father's bedside.

Dad had been diagnosed with cancer the week before, and his doctors had moved aggressively. He'd had a large tumor removed from his stomach the day before, and his doctors were hopeful and gave him good odds of being cancer free. They'd gotten most of it, it hadn't spread, and they had started him on a chemo regimen to get the rest. But we were all scared. Mom was emotional, and I'd ended up spending the night with the two of them, even though I should have been home, keeping things going, and looking after the horses. I wasn't much help at the hospital, that was for sure. I'd slipped out earlier in the morning and gone back to the hotel room that Mom and I hadn't really needed, considering we both spent the night dozing in chairs in Dad's hospital room. But I'd needed a shower, a nap, and some room to breathe, and after I got all three, I was back, ready to spell my mother if I could convince her to step away and do the same.

Hospitals made me lightheaded and elevators did too, so I found a place at the back, called out my floor to a girl who was helpfully pushing buttons, and waited for the doors to close on the silent occupants. We were being entertained by an instrumental version of Garth Brook's "Friends in Low Places," which at one point in my life would have made me howl in outrage and loudly provide the lyrics to all the occupants of the elevator so that a truly great song would not be reduced to easy listening. But today it just made me sigh and wonder what the world was coming to.

The elevator doors began to slide toward each other and my eyes rose up to the lights that signaled the stops when a hand shot between the space and the elevator doors bounced back in affront. My boots made me tall—taller than my natural 5'9"—and I stood directly in the center of the car with my back pressed against the mirrored wall. People shifted immediately, making room for one more, but there was nothing blocking my view or my face when Moses Wright stepped onto the elevator. For a few seconds, maybe more, we stood five feet apart, face to face. The doors slid shut at his back, but he didn't look away. He seemed stunned, floored even. And I wondered if my face registered the same shock. I wished he would turn and face the door, the way normal people did. But he wasn't normal, never had been, and he remained motionless, staring at me, until I broke eye contact and fixed my eyes on the place where the ceiling and walls came together in the right-hand corner and focused on breathing so I wouldn't start screaming.

The elevator bounced lightly to a stop, and the doors opened again, allowing people to shuffle and shift. I stepped to my left as the space cleared, moving as far from Moses as I could get, putting a heavy-set man in a ball-cap between us. Moses maneuvered himself into the corner opposite mine, though I refused to turn and see if he was ignoring me as intently as I was ignoring him.

Floor after floor, the shuffling and rearranging continued as people came and went, and I wondered who Moses was there to see while I prayed we wouldn't get off on the same floor. When we reached the top floor and Moses still stood in the corner, with only two other occupants riding with us, I followed them out, my back so stiff I didn't know if I could walk, certain that Moses would be right behind me. But he wasn't.

When the elevator doors closed behind me, I sneaked a peek over my right shoulder, wondering if I had possibly missed his exit. But there was no one there but me as the down arrow chimed and the elevator whirred and began to descend. I wondered if he'd ridden to the top just to make me uncomfortable.

It had been almost seven years. A lifetime. Or two. Or three. His life, my life, our life. All three had been altered beyond recognition. But he hadn't changed that much. He was still Moses. A little taller, maybe. More muscular, possibly. Older, definitely. But twenty-five was too young to be described that way. He still wore his hair shaved in a barely-there crop, clean and tight, revealing the shape of his well-formed head. Very little had changed about his appearance—his eyes, the wide mouth, the angles of his face and jaw. All of it was exactly as I remembered. Exactly as I remembered, though I'd rarely allowed him time in my memories. Eventually I'd had to cut him loose. I'd had to make him as faceless as the people in the picture he'd sent me, the picture of the woman and the child that had become so precious to me, yet mocked me every time I looked at it.

He'd dropped off the face of the earth. Just disappeared. They whisked him away that terrible Thanksgiving morning, and beyond that picture, I never saw or heard from him again. He was just gone. And because of that, because it had been so long, maybe it should have taken me a minute to recognize him, to react. But it hadn't. I'd taken one look and my heart had sounded a deafening gong that was still reverberating loudly in my head and down my limbs, making me vibrate and shake and look around for a chair. But there was nothing but long hallways and rows of doors, and I slid down the wall until my butt hit the floor, pulling my long legs into my heaving chest so I had somewhere to rest my head. Moses Wright. I felt like I'd seen a ghost. And I didn't believe in ghosts.

MOSES

MY VISITOR WORE BATMAN pajamas and his feet were bare. He was small, but I didn't spend enough time with kids to know exactly how small—he could be anywhere from three to five, though I would guess younger rather than older. His hair was a mass of dark curls and his brown eyes were solemn and a little too big for his small face. He just stood there, at the foot of my bed, and as I eyed him wearily, he tilted his head and looked at me as if I were the reason he was there. I was always the reason they were there. The heat on my neck blazed and I reflexively moved my fingers, wishing I had a pencil, some chalk, something to get this over with as soon as possible. It had been a while. I had almost started believing my walls were impenetrable, unless I purposely lifted them.

I'd fallen asleep early, comforted by the rain that drummed softly against the tin roof and the wind that made the warehouse walls slightly shiver. I'd found the space almost two years ago, and it suited me. It was in downtown Salt Lake City, situated close to the old Grand Central Train station in a refurbished district that was still caught somewhere between restoration and dilapidation. There was a homeless shelter around the block to my right and a high-end day spa around the block to my left. Two blocks north there was a row of mansions built in the early 1900s, two blocks south there was a strip mall. The area was a conglomeration of everything, completely confused, and therefore, immediately comfortable. The warehouse had been partially converted to office space, but because of the residential area that butted up to the back, the owner was able to put an apartment on each floor.

I took the top floor apartment and all the open space that went with it, filling the exposed walls and beams with paintings that I had learned were easy to sell, especially when they were personalized. People came to see me from all over the world. I communed with their dead, painted what I saw, and those people went home with an original Moses Wright. And I made a killing doing it. No pun intended.

I'd built a reputation for myself. And I had a waiting list a mile long and a secretary to go with it. Tag had been my secretary in the early days. It had been his idea, after all. We'd been back-packing through Europe when disaster struck and we'd had our stuff stolen while we slept on a train. By the time we got off the train in Florence, I'd made a thousand Euros and Tag had enjoyed a romp with a rich Italian girl who had lost her mother the year before. The girl spoke fluent English, and she literally threw money at me as I rattled off a list of things there was no way I could possibly know unless her mother was showing me. Which she was, in colorful pictures and pastels, very similar to the landscape outside the train windows. The Italian girl cried all the way through our "session" and kissed my cheeks when I was done, but of course it was Tag who got laid, even though I'd sketched a quick drawing of the girl dancing in the surf, the way her mother remembered her best.

I'd been so afraid at first, reluctant to open the creative floodgates, especially when I felt like I had finally found a little space and a little control. I'd told Tag as much.

"I can finally block them out. Not all the time, but for the first time in my life, the dead aren't everywhere I look. I can block out their memories and their pictures and their desires. I've gotten so much better at it. And I feel in control for the first time in my life," I had said.

"But?"

"But it's harder for me to paint. With the channel closed, my mind closed off like that, I can't paint. See, when I pull down the wall, I turn off all the colors, I wash them away. And I need color to paint. I want to paint. I need to paint, Tag. I don't know what to do. It's a double-edged sword."

"So control it. Use it. When it's hot I turn on the air conditioner. When it's cold I turn it off. Can't it be like that? Let the colors in when you're painting. Turn it off when you're not." Tag shrugged as if it was the easiest thing in the world. It made me laugh. Maybe I could experiment.

"Yeah. Okay. But if I start painting pictures of things I shouldn't, and I get arrested for murder or robbery or some guy comes and hunts me down because I painted a picture of his dead wife having sex with someone else, I'll let you bail me out of jail . . . or the psych ward."

"Well, can't say we haven't done it before, right? Violence and art. It's a winning combination." Tag laughed, but I could see his wheels turning. Before long, we had jobs everywhere.

I painted a mural in Brussels, a chapel door in a little French hamlet, a portrait in Vienna, several still life paintings in Spain, and just for old time's sake, a barn in Amsterdam. They weren't all successes. We got run out of a few places, but most of the time, Tag would find someone who spoke English to interpret for me, I would paint, and people would marvel. And then they would tell their friends.

I ended up working my way through Europe, getting paid to create art by opening myself up to something that I'd always considered a curse. And even more importantly, for me, I got to see all the art I'd always dreamed of seeing. I loved filling my head with pictures, pictures that didn't have anything to do with me or with death. Until one day I realized that life imitates death, especially in artwork. The art of the past is all about death—the artists die and their art remains, a testament to the living and the dead. The realization was a powerful one. I didn't feel nearly as alone, or nearly as odd. I even wondered at times, gazing at something truly awe-inspiring, if all artists didn't commune with spirits.

We spent four years traveling and Tag and I split my earnings. I wouldn't have been able to do it without him. His charisma and comfort in every situation made people trust us. If it had been just me, painting pictures about the dead, I have no doubt I would have single-handedly brought back the inquisition and been burned at the stake as a witch, or been sent to a lunatic asylum. Images of Bedlam had danced through my mind more than once when we'd spent three months in England.

Tag's charisma drew people in, but his attention span needed honing. And Tag wasn't big on honing in on anything except the next job, the next gig, the next dollar. When we'd come back to the states we'd continued on just like we'd done in Europe, hitting big city after big city, painting for one wealthy benefactor after another. Tag had been a rich kid all his life, a rich Texan—which was a little different from a rich New Yorker—but a rich kid all the same, and he was comfortable everywhere, while I was comfortable nowhere. But to his credit, he made me as comfortable as I was ever going to be, and with his help, I became a rich kid too. We'd spent another year seeing state after state, landmark after landmark, grieving loved one after grieving loved one, until one day we decided it was time to let people come to us.

Tag was tired of playing manager to Moses Wright, and had his own dreams of blood and glory (literally), and I was tired of perpetual homelessness. I'd been a drifter all my life, and I found I was ready for something else. We'd landed in Salt Lake City, back where it had all begun, and for some reason it had felt right to stick around. I'd come back as a favor to Dr. Andelin, who had kept tabs on me and Tag as we'd trotted the globe and managed to stay alive and mostly out of trouble. I had agreed to paint a mural at Montlake, something hopeful and soothing that they could point to and say, "See? A crack baby painted this, and you can too!"

Noah Andelin was so happy to see us, and his genuine pleasure at our success, and our friendship, along with his gentle concern about our well-being, led to dinner and drinks later in the week, and it had been Dr. Andelin who had pointed us toward the warehouse apartments, thinking maybe it was something we would be interested in.

I'd worried about Tag staying put, because Tag needed to move like I needed to paint, and traveling for years had met each of our needs, keeping us both sane. But Tag rented the floor below mine, and instead of an art studio, he turned his open space into a gym and got involved with the local fight scene—mixed martial arts, boxing, wrestling. He did it all, and the activity kept him clean and focused. Before long he was talking about bouts, a fighter's clothing line called Tag Team, and collecting sponsors to open a new facility for local fighters to train to compete in the UFC. While I painted he pounded, while I raised the waters he raised the roof, and we settled into our respective floors and kept the monsters at bay. It was the closest we'd come to finding ourselves, and we were both learning how to deal.

And now, alone in my own bed, in my own space, with my own things and my own life, I had been awakened by Batman at the end of my bed, and I was irritated by the little trespasser. I turned over and concentrated on the water, on pulling it down on top of me so the boy, my little visitor, would go. I'd obviously picked up the straggler at the hospital today. Shaking hands and signing autographs and trying to paint while a crowd assembled around me was my least favorite kind of job.

I didn't like painting in hospitals. I saw things I didn't want to see. And I could always tell the people who weren't going to make it. Not because they looked any sicker than anyone else. Not because I saw their charts or overheard their nurses gossiping. It was easy to tell because their dead always hovered nearby. Without fail, the dying would have a companion at their shoulder. Just like Gi did before she died.

I'd painted a mural in the children's ward in a French hospital several years ago. A row of sick kids, cancer patients, had watched from their beds as I created a swirling carnival, complete with dancing bears and cartwheeling clowns and elephants in full regalia. But I'd seen the dead standing at the shoulders of three of the children. Not to drag them down to hell or anything sinister. It didn't frighten me. I understood why they were there. When the time came, and it would come soon, those children would have someone to meet them, to welcome them home. By the time I was done with the mural, the three children had died. It didn't scare me, but I didn't like it. And hospitals were filled with the dead and dying.

The mural I'd done for Dr. Andelin and the Montlake Psychiatric Facility had inspired several more around the valley. The cancer center came knocking about a month ago, applying a little pressure and doing a little hand-wringing, and I ended up agreeing to donate my time and talents to painting yet another hopeful, happy mural. It was good publicity. Publicity that I didn't want or need. But Tag was looking for sponsors for his club and when he told me one of the hospitals biggest patrons was on his list, I made sure the patron knew my price for the mural was a donation to Tag Team. But the mural had taken its toll on me.

I was tired. Incredibly so. And maybe the exhaustion was leaving me more vulnerable to small ghost boys and memories better left forgotten. Seeing Georgia had messed with my head and brought back the hopelessness of the old Moses. The Moses who couldn't control himself. The Moses who lost himself in paint. I didn't ever want to go back to Levan, or Georgia, or the time before. I had never wanted to go back, so over the years I had piled rocks on Georgia's memory, and I'd buried her at the bottom of the sea. But every time I parted the waters and let people's memories across, my memories of her would rise to the surface, and I would think about her, I would remember her. I would remember how I had wanted her and hated her and wished she would leave me alone and never let me go. And I would miss her.

And when I missed her, I would list the things that I hated. Five things I hated. She always had five greats, I had five hates. I hated her innocence and her easy life. I hated her small-town speech and small-town beliefs. I hated how she thought she loved me. That was the worst thing.

But there were things about her I didn't hate. So many things I couldn't hate. Her fire, her stubborn streak, the way her legs had felt wrapped around me, her eyes locked on mine, demanding that I give her everything as I tried to take her without falling in love with her. She had wanted all of it. Every last, private piece.

She was so beautiful still.

I pulled the pillow out from under my head and groaned into it, trying to smother the memory of her stunned face and her wide brown eyes, locked on mine. She was all grown up, with slightly fuller hips and breasts but a leanness to her face that made her cheekbones more prominent, as if youthful flesh had fled her face and settled in better places. She was a woman, straight-backed and steady-eyed. Even when she saw me and realized who I was, she hadn't shrunk or slunk away.

But seeing me had rocked her. Just like it rocked me. I saw it in the way her mouth tightened and her hands clenched. I saw it in the lift of her chin and the flash in her eyes. And then she'd looked away, dismissing me. When the elevator came to rest and the doors slid open, she stepped out without a second glance, long, jean-clad legs moving in a way that was both achingly familiar and totally new. And the doors shut without me getting off, even though we'd reached the top floor. I'd missed my floor. I hadn't wanted to get off and walk away. So I let her walk away instead. Little good that had done. I didn't know why she was there or what she was doing. And she hadn't smiled and given me a quick hug like old friends did when they ran into each other after many years.

I was glad. Her actual response was more telling. It mirrored my own. If she'd smiled and exchanged empty small talk, I would have had to make an appointment with Dr. Andelin. Several appointments. It might have wrecked me. Georgia had haunted me for more than six years, and from the look on her face when I'd stepped on the elevator, my memory hadn't left her alone either. There was solace in that. Miserable solace, but solace.

I lifted my pillow and peeked under my arm to see if he was gone. I breathed out gratefully. The little bat had flown. I bunched the pillow under my neck and switched sides.

I cursed and shot up from my bed, flinging the pillow wildly. He hadn't left. He'd just moved. He'd moved so close I could see the length of his lashes and the curve of his top lip and the way the Velcro on his black cape curled up at the edges.

He smiled, revealing a row of small white teeth and a dimple in his right cheek. I immediately regretted my string of curses and then swore again, the same words at the same volume.

I felt the butterfly wings of a visiting thought tickle the backs of my eyes and I threw up my hands in surrender.

"Fine. Show me your pictures. I'll paint a few and slap them on my fridge. I don't know who you are, so I can't exactly send them to your folks, but go right ahead. Let me see 'em."

The fluttering butterfly nudges became fully extended wings that spread through my mind and filled my head with a white horse whose hind quarters were dappled in black and brown, as if an artist had started to fill in the white space only to get distracted and leave the job undone.

The horse whinnied and galloped around a little enclosure and I felt the little boy's pleasure watching her toss her white mane and stamp her pretty feet.

Calico. I felt her name as he called out to her, the word wrapped around the memory in the only way I could hear it. The horse trotted around the enclosure and then drew close, so close that her long nose grew huge in my mind's eye. I felt her breath against my palm, and realized not only could I hear the little boy talking to her as he once must have done, but I could feel the stroke of his hand, as if it were my own as he drew it from the patch between her eyes to the snuffling nostrils that bumped at my chest. Not my chest. His chest. He shared the memory so clearly, so perfectly that I sat on the fence with him, and felt and heard the things he'd seen.

"The smartest fastest horse in all of Cactus County." Again I felt his voice in my head. Not spoken. Just heard. Just there, woven through the memory as if I'd caught not just a snapshot, but a video clip. The sound was muffled and muted, like a home video with the sound turned too far down. But it was there, part of the memory, a little voice narrating the scene.

And then the butterfly memory flitted up and away, and for a moment my mind was empty and blank like a broken TV screen.

Sometimes the dead showed me the strangest things—things that didn't make sense. Nickels or plants or a bowl of mashed potatoes. I rarely understood what they wanted to convey—only that they wanted to communicate something. Over time I'd come to the conclusion that the mundane wasn't mundane to them. The things they showed me always represented a memory or a moment that had somehow been meaningful. How, I didn't always know, but it had become clear that the simplest things were the most important things, and objects themselves weren't really important at all. The dead didn't care about land or money or the heirloom that had been passed down through the generations. But they cared desperately about the people they left behind. And it was the people that called them back. Not because the dead weren't adjusting, but because their loved ones weren't. The dead weren't angry or lost. They knew exactly what was up. It was the living that didn't have a clue. Most of the time, I myself didn't have a clue, and trying to figure out what the dead wanted from me was taxing, to say the least. And I didn't like dead kids.

The child stared, his deep brown eyes soulful and serious, waiting for something from me.

"No. I don't want any part of this. I don't want you here. Go away." I spoke firmly, and immediately another image pushed into my mind, clearly the child's response to my refusal. This time, I clamped my eyes closed and pushed back violently, picturing walls of water tumbling down, covering the exposed earth—the dry land, the channel that allowed people to cross from one side to the other. I had the power to part the waters. And I had the power to call them back again. Just like Gi told me, just like the Biblical Moses. When I opened my eyes the little boy was gone, washed away in the Red Sea. The Red, I-Don't-Want-to-See.

XVI

MOSES

BUT APPARENTLY ELI COULD FLOAT. That was his name. I saw it, written in wriggling, poorly-formed letters on a light-colored surface. *EL i*

Eli wasn't swallowed up in the waters I called down. He came back. Again. And then again. I even tried to take a trip, as if that had ever worked. Here, there, half-way across the world, there's no escaping yourself . . . or the dead, Tag reminded me when I complained, throwing my duffle in the back of my truck. The truck was new and smelled of leather and made me want to drive and drive and never stop. I rode with open windows and pounding music to reinforce my walls. But as I headed toward the Salt Flats west of the valley, Eli appeared in the middle of the road, his little black cape blowing in the wind as if he were truly standing there, a forlorn little bat boy in the middle of an empty highway. I ended up turning around and going home, seething at the intrusion, wondering how in the hell he was finding all my cracks.

He showed me a book with a worn cover and dog eared pages, a woman's voice faint and muffled, speaking the words to the story as Eli turned the pages. Eli sat in her lap, his head pressed up to her chest, and

I could feel her wrapped around him, as if I sat there too, in the well created by her crisscrossed legs. He showed me the horse, Calico, and the image of jean-clad legs walking past the table as if he sat beneath it in his own little fort. Random things that meant nothing to me and everything to him.

When he woke me at three a.m. with dreamy images of sunsets and horse rides, seated in front of a woman whose hair tickled his cheeks when he turned his face, I tossed back my covers and began to paint. I worked frantically, desperate to be rid of the child that wouldn't let me be. The picture in my head was one of my own making. Eli hadn't put it there, but I could see how they must have looked, the fair mother with her dark-headed son, his head tucked against her chest, seated in front of her on the horse with all the colors. The pair on the horse were moving away, moving toward the sunset spilling over the hills, the colors rich yet blurred, reminiscent of Monet, looking at beauty through a pane of wavy glass, discernable yet elusive. It was my way of keeping the viewer at a distance, allowing them to appreciate without intruding, observe without being a part. It reminded me of the way I'd come to see the dead and the images they shared with me. It was the way I coped. It was the way I kept myself intact.

When I was finished, I stepped back and dropped my hands. My shirt and jeans were splattered with paint, my shoulders impossibly tight, and my hands aching. When I turned, Eli looked on, staring at the brushstrokes that, one by one, created life. Still life, but life all the same. It had to be enough. It had always been enough before.

But when Eli looked back at me, his brow was furrowed and his countenance troubled. And he shook his head slowly.

He showed me the soft light of a lamp that looked like a cowboy boot, the way it tossed light on the wall. His eyes were trained on the wall and I could see a woman's shadow outlined in the light, and I watched as her shadow leaned in and kissed the child goodnight.

"Goodnight, Stewy Stinker!" she said, nuzzling the curve between his shoulder and his neck.

"Goodnight, Buzzard Bates!" he responded gleefully.

"Goodnight Skunk Skeeter!" she immediately shot back.
"Goodnight, Butch Bones!" Eli chortled.

I didn't understand the nicknames, but they made me smile. The affection dripped from the memory like water spilling from a downspout. But I still pushed it back, slamming the black doors down on the touching display.

"No, Eli. No. I can't give you that. I know you want your mother. But I can't give you that. I can't give her that. But I can give her this. You help me find her, and I'll give her this." I pointed at the drying picture I'd created for the persistent child. "I can give her your picture. You helped me make this. This is from you. I can give her this. You can give her this."

Eli stared at my offering for several long heartbeats. And without warning, he was gone.

MOSES

"IT'S BEAUTIFUL." Tag lifted his chin toward the canvas on my easel. "Different from what you usually do."

"Yeah. That's because it didn't come from his head. It came from mine."

"The kid?"

"Yeah." I rubbed my hands over the stubble on my head, anxious, and not sure why. Eli hadn't come back. Maybe painting had worked after all.

Tag had wandered up, unannounced, uninvited, just like in the early days, and I was grateful for the intrusion. He would come up when he needed a sparring partner or something from my fridge or a piece of art to temporarily place in a prominent position to impress whichever female he had over for the evening.

But he'd already worked out, apparently, and I wouldn't be taking any pent-up frustration out on him today. His hair was wet around the edges, curling and clinging to his neck and forehead, and sweat from his workout had soaked through his shirt and made it stick to his chest. Tag cleaned up well enough, slicking back his hair and donning an expensive suit when he was doing business, but he'd always been a little shaggy and rough-looking with a nose that had been broken a few too many times and hair that was always too long. I don't know how he could stand the heat of having hair on his head. I never could, it suffocated me. Maybe it was the fact that every encounter with the dead scorched my neck and made my head swim, and my body burned energy like a furnace.

Tag pulled off his shirt and mopped at his face while helping himself to a bowl of my cereal and a huge glass of my orange juice. He sat down at my kitchen table like we were an old married couple and dug in without further comment on the picture I'd spent half the night creating.

Tag was better at friendship than I was. I rarely went downstairs to his place. I never ate his food or threw my sweaty clothes on his floor. But I was grateful that he did. I was grateful he came to me, and I never complained about the missing food or paintings or the random dirty sock that wasn't mine. If it wasn't for Tag making himself at home in my life, we wouldn't be friends. I just didn't know how, and he seemed to understand.

I finished my own bowl of cereal and pushed it away, my gaze wandering back to the easel.

"Why is she blonde?" Tag asked.

I felt my brow furrow and I shrugged at Tag. "Why not?"

"Well, the boy . . . he's dark. I just wondered why you made her blonde," Tag said reasonably, shoving another huge spoonful into his mouth.

"I'm dark . . . and my mother was blonde," I responded matter-of-factly.

Tag stopped, his spoon paused in mid-air. I watched as a Cheerio made a desperate dive for freedom, plopping back in the bowl, safe for another few seconds.

"You never told me that."

"I didn't?"

"No. I know your mom left you in the laundromat. I know your life was shit growing up. I know you went and lived with your grandma before she died. I know her death messed you up pretty good, which is where I come in." He winked. "I know you've always been able to see stuff other people can't. And I know you can paint."

My life in a nutshell.

Tag continued. "But I didn't know your mom was blonde. Not that it matters. But you're so dark, so I just assumed . . ."

"Yeah."

"So . . . is the picture of you and your mom? Wasn't she a small-town girl?"

"No. I mean . . . yeah. She was a small-town girl. A small-town *white* girl." I emphasized white this time, just so we were clear. "But no. The picture is of Eli and his mother. But I don't think it's what he wanted."

"The hills. The sunset. It kind of reminds me of Sanpete. Sanpete was beautiful when I wasn't hung-over."

"Levan too."

I stared at the painting, the child and his mother on a horse named Calico, the woman tall and lean in the saddle, her blonde hair just a pale suggestion against the more vivid pinks and reds of the setting sun.

"She looks like Georgia," I mused. The woman in my painting looked like Georgia from the back. I felt a sudden sinking in my chest and I stood, walking toward the picture, a picture I'd created in desperation, setting a stage and filling it with characters from my own head. Not from Eli's head. It had nothing to do with Georgia. But my heart pounded and my breaths grew shallow.

"She looks like Georgia, Tag." I said it again, louder, and I heard the panic in my voice.

"Georgia. The girl you never got over?"

"What?"

"Oh, come on, man!" Tag groaned, half-laughing. "I've known you for a long time. And in that time you've never been interested in a single woman. Not one. If I didn't know better, I'd think you were in love with me."

"I saw her last Friday. I saw her at the hospital." I couldn't even argue with him. I felt sick, and my hands were shaking so much that I interlocked my fingers and hung them around my neck to hide the tremors.

Tag seemed as stunned as I had been. "Why didn't you say something?"

"I saw her. And she saw me. And . . . and now, I'm seeing this little kid." I took off running for my bedroom with Tag on my heels and terror thrumming through my veins like I'd just been injected with something toxic.

I pulled my old backpack down off my closet shelf and started ripping things out of it. My passport, a grease pencil, a stray peanut, a coin purse with random currencies that had never been cashed in.

"Where is it?" I raged, unzipping pockets and rifling through every compartment of the old bag, like an addict searching for a pill.

"What are you looking for?" Tag stood back and watched me tear my closet apart with equal parts fascination and concern.

"The letter. The letter! Georgia wrote me a letter when I was at Montlake. And I never opened it. But I kept it! It was here!"

"You put it in one of those tubes in Venice," Tag answered easily, and sat down on my bed, his elbows braced on his knees, watching me come unglued.

"How the hell do you know that?"

"Because you dragged that envelope around forever. You'll be lucky if it's still in one piece."

I was already digging deeper in my closet, pulling out tubes of rolled art that I'd picked up in my travels and then never took the time to frame or display. We'd sent stuff to Tag's father from all over the world, and he stuck it in a spare room. When we'd settled in, he'd brought it to us. Four years of travels and purchases, and the loot had filled the back of his horse trailer. We'd promptly deposited it all in a storage unit, not especially interested in going through it all. Fortunately, the tube Tag was referring to should still be somewhere in my closet, because he was right. I'd kept it with me, dragging it around like a prized locket that I never even opened. Maybe because it had never been opened, it never seemed right to set it aside.

"It was in a small—" Tag started.

"Did you read it?" I shouted, digging frantically.

"No. I didn't. But I wanted to. I thought about it."

I found the tube I was sure it was in and pulled off the lid with my teeth, sinking to my knees as I shook out the contents like a kid on Christmas. I had put the letter back in an envelope when I left Montlake to protect it, and it slid out agreeably and landed in my lap. And like that kid on Christmas, who has just opened something he can't decide if he likes, I just stared at it.

"It looks the same as it always has, every other time you've sat and stared at it," Tag drawled.

I nodded.

"Do you need me to read it?" he said, a little more kindly.

"I'm an asshole, Tag. You know that right? I was an asshole then, with Georgia, and I haven't changed a whole lot."

"You worried I won't love you anymore, after I read it?" There was a smile in his voice and it helped me breathe.

"Okay. Yeah. You read it. Because I can't."

I handed him the letter and fought the urge to stick my fingers in my ears.

He tore open the envelope, unfolded the sheet of paper filled with Georgia's words, and looked at it silently for a moment. Then he started to read.

Dear Moses,

I don't know what to say. I don't know how to feel. The only thing I know is that you're there and I'm here and I've never been so afraid in my life. I keep coming to visit, and I keep leaving without seeing you. I'm worried about you. I'm worried about me.

Will I ever see you again?

I'm afraid the answer's no. And if it's no, then you need to know how I feel. Maybe someday, you'll be able to do the same. I would really, really like to know how you feel, Moses.

So here goes. I love you. I do. You scare me and fascinate me and make me want to hurt you and heal you all at the same time. Is it weird that I want to hurt you? I want to hurt you like you've hurt me. Yet the thought of you being hurt makes me ache. Doesn't make much sense, does it?

Second, I miss you. I miss seeing you. I could watch you all day. Not just because you're beautiful to look at—which you are—not just because you can create beautiful things—which you do—but because there's something in you that pulls at me and convinces me that if you would just let me in, if you would just love me back, we could have a beautiful life. And I would really love for you to have a beautiful life. More than anything, I want that for you.

I don't know if you'll read this. And if you do, I don't know if you'll respond. But I needed you to know how I feel, even if it's in a crummy letter that smells like Myrtle because it's been in my jockey box for a month.

Even if you just listen and then you leave, I hope you'll let me tell you in person when you get out.

Please.
Georgia
P.S. My five greats? They haven't changed. Even with everything that has happened, I'm still grateful. Just thought you should know.

We sat in silence for several long seconds. I couldn't speak at all. The letter didn't tell me anything, not really. But Georgia was in the room with us now, her presence as real and warm as her brown eyes and the hot pink of her kiss. Her words practically leapt from the page, and they took me back like I'd been sucked through a worm hole and she was standing before me, waiting for me to give her a response. Amazingly enough, after all these years, I still didn't have one.

"Man," Tag whistled. "You really are an asshole."

"I'm going to Levan," I stated, surprising myself and making Tag rear back in amazement.

"Why? What's going on, man? Am I missing something?"

"It's nothing. I mean. I thought maybe . . ." I stopped. I didn't know what I was thinking. "Forget it." I shrugged it off. I took the letter from Tag's hand and folded it up. I kept folding it, tighter and tighter, until it was a fat little square. And then I held it in my palm and wrapped my fingers around it as if I could just toss it away, just toss away all the things that were bothering me. I could count them off on my fingers, just like Georgia's mom used to do with her foster kids, and I could toss them away.

"I may not be thinking clearly. I haven't slept very well in the last couple of days. And seeing Georgia . . ." My voice trailed off.

"So you're going to Levan. And I'm coming with you." Tag stood as if it was already decided.

"Tag . . ."

"Mo."

"I don't want you to come."

"This is the town you terrorized. Right?"

"I didn't terrorize anyone," I argued.

"When they talk about painting the town, I don't think you were quite what they had in mind, Moses."

I laughed, in spite of myself.

"I have to go with you to make sure they don't run you out with pitchforks."

"What if she won't talk to me?"

"Then you might have to settle in there for a while. Follow her around until she does. She was pretty persistent with you, it seems like. How many times did you turn her away? How many times did she keep coming back?"

"I still have my grandmother's house. It's not like I don't have any-where to go or any reason to be there. I've paid the property taxes on it all these years."

"You need some moral support. I'll pull a Rocky Balboa and train with tractor tires and chickens for a couple of days. If Levan is anything like Sanpete, they have plenty of both."

XVII

MOSES

W E PULLED OFF THE INTERSTATE just outside of Nephi and exited onto the old highway that connected Nephi to Levan. The Ridge is what it was called. Just a two lane stretch of nothing with fields stretching out on either side. We passed the Circle A with its big red sign sticking up high enough to be seen above the overpass and a mile down the freeway, telling truckers and weary drivers that there was relief in sight.

"Go back, Moses."

I shot him a questioning look.

"I want to see it. It was there, wasn't it?"

"Molly?"

"Yeah. Molly. I want to see the overpass."

I didn't argue, though I didn't know what there was to see. My picture was long gone, covered and forgotten. So was Molly. Long gone. Covered and forgotten. But Tag hadn't forgotten.

I turned around and found the dirt road that shimmied through the field, came out behind the overpass, and continued up into the hills. There were still broken beer bottles and fast food wrappers. A broken

CD player that had probably been there for a while, considering the make and model, lay abandoned on its side, wires protruding from the missing speaker. I didn't want glass in my tires and pulled off in the barrow pit a little ways off, just like I'd done that night so long ago. It was the same time of year and everything. It was the same kind of October—unseasonably warm, but predictably beautiful. The leaves were a hot riot on the lower hills and the sky was so blue I wanted to reach up and capture the color with my paint brush. But that night it had been dark. That night Georgia had followed me. That night I'd lost my head and maybe something else too.

Tag picked his way through the debris and just kept walking out into the field where the dogs must have canvased, noses to the ground. He stopped once and looked around, eyeing the hills, judging the distance to the freeway, measuring the length between the overpass and the back of the businesses that crowded the on and off ramps, trying to make sense of something that made no sense at all.

I turned away and walked to the cement walls that held the freeway on her shoulders. There were two sides, one slanting right, one slanting left, and I leaned back against the side still exposed to the sun, closed my eyes, and felt the warmth seep into my skin.

Wait! Please, please, please don't keep walking away from me!" *she cried in frustration. I could hear the tears in her voice and the fear too. She was afraid of me, but she still came after me. She still came after me. The thought made me stumble, it made me stop. And I turned, letting her catch me. And I caught her too, wrapping my arms around her so tight that the space between us became space around us, space above us, but not space inside us. I felt the drumming, the pounding beneath the softness of her breasts, and my heart raced to match it. I opened her mouth under mine, needing to see the colors, to feel them lick and climb up my throat and behind my eyes like flames from a signal flare. I kissed her lips over and over, until there were no secrets. Not hers, not mine. Not Molly's. There was just heat and light and color. And I couldn't stop. I didn't want to stop. Her skin was like silk and her sighs like satin, and I couldn't look away from the pleasure on her face or the pleas in her hands that urged me onward.*

Georgia's hair, Georgia's mouth, Georgia's skin, Georgia's eyes, Georgia's long, long legs.

Georgia's love, Georgia's trust, Georgia's faith, Georgia's cries, Georgia's long, long wait.

And then the cries of passion became something else. There was sorrow in the sound. And there were tears. Georgia was bent over with them, doubled over. And her hair streamed around her like the water falling from her eyes and wailing from her mouth, and her long, long legs were no longer around me but beneath her, kneeling, supplicating, and she cried, and cried, and cried...

I opened my eyes and sat upright, unsure of what had been my own memory or something else entirely. I felt sick and disoriented, almost like I'd dozed too long and gotten a touch of heat stroke. I rubbed at my neck with clammy hands. But it couldn't have been that long. Tag still wandered around in the field, looking for a sign that led to absolution or a road to reasons why. I winced at the setting sun and turned back toward the concrete wall to give him time to discover there was no such thing as either one.

Eli sat against the opposite wall, his stubby legs in Batman pajamas pulled up into his chest as if he too had settled in for a long, long wait. His hood covered his dark curls, and the small fabric points crafted to resemble bat ears gave him a devilish air totally at odds with his angel boy face.

I cursed loudly, louder than I'd intended, the sound echoing off the concrete walls and beckoning Tag to turn around. He did and raised his arms in question.

"Time to go, Tag. I can't be here anymore," I called, walking away from the little boy who was busily sharing images of the same galloping white horse with colors on her hind quarters. Then a fat rope spun in the air, making a perfect loop that dropped around the horse's neck and was pulled tight by some unknown hand. The horse tossed her pale mane, whinnied softly, and trotted around in my head unhappily. I didn't know how to set her free.

"He keeps showing me a white horse," I muttered, as Tag and I climbed back into my truck and pulled out onto the highway leading from one heartbreak and dropping us off at another. I didn't want to be here. I couldn't imagine Tag did either. "He keeps showing me a white horse with splotches of color on her rump. The same horse, over and over. Like the one in the picture I painted."

"A Paint."

"What?"

"It's called a Paint. That kind of horse. Her coloring. They call that a Paint."

"A Paint." I wondered suddenly if the horse was just symbolic. Maybe all the kid wanted me to do was paint. Maybe I just hadn't gotten it right.

MOSES

TAG WALKED BEHIND ME, trailing me through the front door and into a house that had been laid bare. There was no furniture, no dishes, no rugs on the floor. Nothing remained of my grandmother in the house. It didn't feel like her. It definitely didn't smell like her. It was dusty and dank and it needed a good airing out. It was just an empty house. I hesitated in the entryway, looking up the stairs, turning right and then left, testing the waters, until finally moving through the dining area into the kitchen, where nothing remained but the red-striped curtains that hung on the small window over the sink. The curtains in the family room remained as well. Nobody wanted those either. But I was guessing it had more to do with the fact that they were stiff with paint than with their outdated pattern.

Nobody had painted the walls.

I stopped abruptly and felt Tag at my back. I heard the way his breath caught in his throat and then the slow exhalation when he let it out on a stream of words even I wouldn't say.

I had found my grandmother at around 6:45. I only remember the time because she had a clock in the entryway that spat out a bird that cuckooed on the hour and sang on the half-hour. But on the quarter hours, the bird would stick his head out and tweet loudly, making you aware the time was passing. Warning you the hour was coming. I had walked through the front door that morning, half-dazed, longing for my bed where I could sleep off the lust and the love that were clinging to my skin, and that bird had squawked at me as if to say "Where have you been?"

I had jumped and then laughed at myself and stepped into the dining room and called her name.

"Gi!"

"Gi!" I said it again and heard my voice echo in the empty house.

I didn't mean to speak out loud, but Tag pushed past me and walked toward the walls filled with curling colors and twisted tendrils. It was like being on a spinning merry-go-round inside a circus tent, and everyone was a clown. The color was garish and grandiose, one color merging into the next, one face becoming another, like a photograph of a car in motion, nothing entirely captured, everything distorted by the perspective. I'd found Gigi at 6:45 in the morning. Georgia had found me at 11:30. I had painted for almost five straight hours and filled the walls with everything and nothing.

The clock had struck and the bird sang sweetly as I swept my aching arms up and down, finishing a face that had nothing to do with the face I wanted to see. And then Georgia had stepped into the house. Poor Georgia.

"That's Molly," Tag choked, his hand resting on the image of his sister looking back over her shoulder, beckoning me to follow. The gold paint of her hair spread out like a river and became the hair of several other girls, all running alongside her.

I could only nod. The whole thing was a blur. I didn't remember most of it. I didn't remember anything in detail. It felt like a dream, and I only had bits and pieces.

"Who are these other people?" Tag whispered, his eyes roving from one distorted drawing to the next.

I shrugged. "I know some of them. I remember some of them. But most, I don't really know."

"You like blondes.""Nah—I don't." I shook my head slowly, protesting.

Tag raised his eyebrows and looked pointedly at the girls surrounding Molly and at the painting of my mother a little ways off, the basket of babies in her arms.

I just shook my head. I couldn't explain the other side. I just painted what I saw.

"Mo?"

"Yeah?"

"This is freaky as shit. You know that, right?"

I nodded. "I didn't know it. Not really. Not then. I didn't even see it. I just lived it. But yeah."

We both stared a moment longer, until I just couldn't stand it anymore.

"So what would you think of a red couch in here?" I said. "'Cause that's what I'm thinkin'-"

Tag started to laugh, the loud bark of stunned mirth shaking out the cobwebs and the lingering sense of horror in the room. He shook his head at me like I was past saving. "You're sick, man. Really."

I laughed too, shoving him, needing the contact. He shoved me back and I stumbled backwards, grabbing at him as we each grappled to get the better position to land the other on his ass. We bounced into walls and ended up pulling down the paint covered curtains, letting the fading light pierce the color-drenched room. But it was the walls that would have to go. Not just the curtains. I wouldn't be sleeping in that house until the walls were white once more.

GEORGIA

THERE WAS A TRUCK PARKED at Kathleen Wright's old house. It had been there off and on for two days. The front door hung open, and a few cans of paint sat on the tail gate, along with ladders and drop cloths and a wide assortment of other things. The truck was black and shiny and brand new. When I peered through the window like the snoopy, small-town girl I was, I could see the creamy leather of the seats and a cowboy hat on the dash. The truck didn't look like anything Moses would drive. And I knew he'd never wear that hat.

But as far as I knew, Moses still owned the house. My stomach clenched nervously, but I refused to acknowledge it. He was probably there to clean it out and then he'd be gone. He probably wanted to sell it. That was all. Soon he would be gone again and I could go about my business. But my stomach didn't believe me, and I spent the days in a nervous frenzy, accomplishing everything on my to-do list and feeling no sense of satisfaction in any of it. Dad was back home from the hospital and other than a little residual weakness, was doing fine. Mom fussed, which made him irritable, and I just tried to stay out of the house.

But staying out of the house meant looking toward the rear windows of Kathleen's house every ten minutes. I'd noticed the windows were bare that morning when I'd taken Lucky for a turn around the west pasture that butted right up to Kathleen Wright's back yard. For years, those curtains had been tightly drawn. Now they were gone, and the windows were open as if someone were airing things out. I could hear music playing and as the day wore on, I thought I caught glimpses of Moses and someone else working inside. I was agitated and distracted, and the horses picked up on it, which was never a good thing, especially when working with a horse named Cuss.

I was breaking the horse for Dale Garrett, and Cuss was a big quarter horse with a bigger attitude. His name summed up his owner's opinion of him. Dean called my dad, and dad promptly turned Cuss over to me. Funny. The old boys in the county didn't want to call in a girl to break their horses—it rubbed against their manhood—and not in the way they enjoyed. Everybody knew when you called Doc Shepherd—my dad— to break your horse, you were really getting Georgia Shepherd, but it made the bitter pill easier to swallow. And I didn't care. Eventually, they would get over it. I would wear them down too. Just like old Cuss. I took inordinate pleasure in wearing down the ornery ones.

We were in the round corral and I was running Cuss, lunging him, no halter, just the two of us getting used to each other. I stood in the center of the corral with a rope in hand and swung it out, using it like a whip, never touching him, just making him change direction and respect my space. Every once in a while I'd step in front of him and make him turn around, making him run if he wanted to get away. Applying pressure. It was nothing new. I'd run him like this several times in the last week, and today I was ready to go to second base. Cuss let me approach, and I swung my rope in a lazy circle, just talking to him as I neared his shoulder. So far, so good.

Cuss was breathing hard and his eyes were trained on me, but he didn't shift. I laid the end of the rope against his neck gently, and then took it off again. I did it again, a little harder, and he trembled a little. I moved the rope to the other side, stroking his neck with it, getting him used to being touched, getting him used to the rope against his throat, desensitizing him. And then, carefully, slowly, I eased a loop up and over his neck, letting it hang loosely around his shoulders. I waited, holding the lead rope in my hands, waiting for him to tell me no.

"Before long, he'll be begging Georgia to tie him up," a voice said from somewhere behind me. Cuss skittered and whinnied, pulling his head away sharply and taking me with him, the rope searing my hands before I dropped it and let him go.

"I see some things haven't changed." I dusted off my smarting hands and turned toward him. I didn't have to see his face to know. It was almost a relief to get this over with.

Moses stood outside the corral, his hands hanging over the top plank, a foot resting on the bottom one. A man stood at his side, a toothpick in his mouth, his posture identical to Moses's. But that was where the similarities ended.

"Animals still don't like you very much, do they?" I said. My composure pleased me.

"It's not just animals. Moses has that effect on most people too." The stranger smiled and extended his hand over the fence. "In fact, I think I'm his only friend." I walked toward him, toward Moses, and took the proffered hand.

"Hi, Georgia. I'm Tag." There was Texas in his voice and he looked like he could handle Cuss handily if he wanted to. He brought to mind a good old country boy with a sprinkling of ex-convict thrown in, just to make you watch yourself. He was good looking in a rough sort of way, even with a nose that needed straightening and hair that needed a trim, but his smile was blinding and his handshake was firm. I wondered how in the world he'd ended up with Moses.

I met Moses's eyes then, the golden-green orbs that were all wrong, and still so wonderful, in his dark face. And much like it had a week ago on that crowded elevator, the earth beneath my feet shifted, just slightly, just enough to make me wonder if the ground was slanted or my perspective was just skewed. I probably stared too long, but he stared right back, tipping his head to the side, as if he too needed to readjust.

The man beside Moses cleared his throat uncomfortably and then laughed a little, saying something under his breath that I didn't catch.

"What's going on at Kathleen's? You sellin' the place?" I asked, ending the stand-off with Moses and turning away. Cuss still had my other rope looped around his neck, so I snagged another one from the fence post on the other side of Tag. Cuss was hugging the far side of the corral like he'd been sent to time-out.

"Maybe. Right now, we're just cleaning it up," Moses replied quietly.

"Why?" I challenged. "Why now?" I eyed him again without smiling, not willing to make small talk with a huge mistake. And that was what he was. A huge mistake. I wanted to know why he was here. And I wanted to know when he would be leaving. I circled toward Cuss, making him whinny and tremble, wanting to run, but apparently not wanting to run toward the strangers at the fence.

"It was time," Moses said simply, as if time held more sway than I ever did.

"I'd be interested in buying it, if you decide to sell." It would make sense. I'd thought about it for a long time, but I'd never wanted to track Moses down to make an offer. But he was back. And if he was selling, the house made sense for me, bordering my parents' property the way it did.

He didn't respond, and I shrugged like it didn't make any difference to me what he did with the house. I started moving toward Cuss, leaving the two unwelcome visitors to do what they wanted.

"Georgia?" I flinched when Moses said my name, and then Tag swore, a long, drawn-out shhhhiiiiiiit, that didn't make a whole lot of sense.

"Georgia? Does that horse belong to you?" Moses asked sharply.

"Who, Cuss? No. I'm just breaking him." I didn't look up at the question, but continued moving in on Cuss.

"No. Not that horse." Moses's voice sounded strange and I looked up, beyond the round corral and the small riding arena, out to the pasture where our horses grazed.

They were a ways off, a half a dozen horses or so, including Sackett and Lucky, who we used exclusively for equine therapy and nothing more. Lucky had turned out to be the sweetest, mildest old boy in the world. Completely house-broken, that one.

"The Paint. Is the Paint yours?" Tag asked, and his voice was equally strained.

"Calico? Yeah. She's ours." I nodded, finding the pretty horse with her white mane and bright colors and feeling the familiar lurch in my heart I always felt when I saw her.

Suddenly Moses was striding away from the corral, covering the ground between the back of his house and our property without a backwards glance or a "see you later."

Tag and I watched him go, and I turned baffled eyes on Moses's friend.

"I would ask you what the hell his problem is, but I stopped caring a long time ago." I reached Cuss and snagged the rope around his neck a little more firmly than I would have in other circumstances. He reared up and tossed his head, making me regret my hasty actions. I managed to free my rope from around his neck, but not without a little quick-footed hopping to avoid teeth and hooves.

"For his sake, I hope that's not true," Tag answered frankly, which baffled me even more. But he pushed off the fence as if to follow Moses. "It was nice to meet you, Georgia. You're nothing like I expected. And I'm glad."

I had no response but to watch him leave. He was twenty feet away when he called over his shoulder, "He's going to be tough to break. I'm not sure ol' Cuss wants to be ridden."

"Yeah, yeah, yeah. That's what they all say, until I'm ridin' 'em," I tossed back.

I heard him laughing as I started over with Cuss.

XVIII

MOSES

YOU WOULD THINK with a lifetime of seeing the dead, I would hate cemeteries. But I didn't. I liked them. They were quiet. They were peaceful. And the dead were tucked away in neat little rows beneath the soil. Tidy. Taken care of. At least their bodies were. The dead didn't roam cemeteries. That's not where their lives were. But they were drawn by their loved ones' grief. By their loved ones' misery. I'd seen the walking dead, trailing behind a wife or a daughter, a son or a father, many times before. But today, in the cemetery in Levan, there were no walking dead.

Today, I saw only one other person, and for a moment, my heart lurched as my eyes fell on her fair head and her slim figure crouched by a nearby grave. Then I realized it wasn't Georgia. It couldn't be Georgia. I'd seen the horse and heard Georgia say Calico, and I came straight here. Plus, the woman was a little smaller than Georgia, maybe a little older, and her blonde hair fell down in curls from a messy knot on her head. She left a little bouquet by a stone that said Janelle Pruitt Jensen in large letters and moved off toward a tall man waiting at the edge of the cemetery. When the woman reached him, he leaned down and kissed her, as if consoling her, which made me look away immediately. I hadn't meant to stare. But they were a striking couple—darkness and light, softness and strength. I could paint them, easily.

The man's skin was as dark as mine, but he didn't look black to me. Maybe Native, tall and lean with a way about him that made me think military. The woman was slim and girlish in a pale pink skirt, a white blouse, and sandals, and as they turned toward the exit and I got a look at her profile, I realized I knew her.

When I was a little kid, Gigi had made me go to church whenever I visited. One Sunday, when I was about nine, a girl had played the organ. She was maybe only thirteen or fourteen at the time, but the way she played was something else. Her name was Josie.

Her name came to me in my grandmother's voice and I smiled a little.

The music Josie had made was soul-stirring and beautiful. And best of all, it made me feel safe and calm. Gi picked up on that right away and we started walking to the church when Josie was practicing and we would listen in the back. Sometimes she would play the piano, often she would play the organ, but whatever it was, I would be still. I remembered Gi sighing and saying, "That Josie Jensen is a musical wonder."

And then Gi had told me I was a wonder too. She whispered in my ear, with Josie's music in the background, that I created music when I painted, just like Josie made music when she played. Both were gifts, both were special, and both should be cherished. I'd forgotten all about it. Until now. The woman's name was Josie Jensen and the grave she visited must be her mother.

I watched the couple walk away, lost in the memory of her music when, at the last minute, Josie stopped and turned. She said something to the man with her, who then glanced back at me and nodded.

Then she walked back toward me, picking her way around the tombstones until she stood a few feet in front of me. She smiled sweetly and extended her hand in greeting. I took it and held it briefly before letting go.

"It's Moses, right?"

"Yes. Josie Jensen, correct?" She smiled, obviously pleased that

I had recognized her too. "I'm Josie Yates now. My husband, Samuel, doesn't like cemeteries. It's a Navajo thing. He comes with me, but waits under the trees."

Navajo. I was right.

"I just wanted to tell you how much I liked your grandmother . . . your great grandmother, actually, yes?" I nodded as she continued. "Kathleen had a way about her that made you feel like everything was going to be okay. After my mom died when I was little, she was one of the ladies in the church who looked after my family, and she looked after me too, teaching me things and letting me hang out in her kitchen when I needed to figure out how to do this or that. She was wonderful." Josie's voice rang with sincerity and I nodded, agreeing.

"She was like that. She always made me feel that way too." I swallowed and looked away awkwardly, realizing I was having an intimate moment with a stranger. "Thank you," I said, meeting her eyes briefly. "That means a lot to me."

She nodded once, smiled a sad little smile, and turned away again. "Moses?"

"Yes?"

"Do you know who Edgar Allen Poe is?"

I raised my eyebrows, puzzled. I did. But it was an odd question. I nodded and she continued.

"He wrote something that I've never forgotten, and I love words. You can ask my husband. I buried him in words and music until he begged for mercy and married me." She winked. "Edgar Allen Poe said many beautiful things—and many disturbing things—but they often go together, you know."

I waited, wondering what this woman wanted me to hear.

"Poe said, 'There is no exquisite beauty without some strangeness in the proportion.'" Josie tipped her head to the side and looked back at her husband who hadn't moved at all. Then she murmured, "I think your work is strange and beautiful, Moses. Like a discordant melody that resolves itself as you listen. I just wanted you to know that."

I was a little speechless, wondering where and when she'd seen my work, flabbergasted that she knew of me at all, and still wasn't afraid to approach me. Of course, her husband stood fifty feet away, and I highly doubted anyone messed with Josie Jensen on his watch.

Then they were gone, and no one remained but me. Levan Cemetery had the feel of a well-maintained pioneer cemetery—not very big, but big enough and constantly getting bigger as the town grew and buried their dead. It faced west, sitting above the rest of the valley on a rise beneath Tuckaway Hill, looking out over farmland and pasture. From where I stood I could see the old highway, a long silver strip, cutting through fields as far as the eye could see. The view was serene and peaceful, and I liked that Gi's remains were here.

I walked down rows of stones, past Josie's mother, until I reached a long line of Wrights, generations of them, four at least. I stopped for a moment at Gigi's stone, laid a reverent hand on her name, but then moved on, searching for the reason I came. New stones, old stones, stones that were glossy, stones that were flat. Flowers and pinwheels and wreaths and candles decorated many graves. I wondered why people did that. Their dead didn't need crap covering their names. But like anything, that was mostly about the living. The living needed to prove to themselves and to others that they hadn't forgotten. And, in a small town like this there was always a little competition going on at the cemetery. It was a mentality that said, "I love the most, I'm suffering the most, and so I'm going to create a huge display every time I come so everyone knows and feels sorry for me." I knew I was a cynic. I was definitely a bastard. But I didn't like it. And I didn't especially think the dead needed it.

I found a long row of Shepherds and almost laughed at the name of one. Warlock Shepherd. What a name. Warlock Wright—maybe that's what they should have named me. I'd been called a witch before. I studied the stones, and I realized there were five generations of Shepherd grandfathers buried there as well, their wives buried at their sides. I found the first Georgia Shepherd and remembered the day I teased Georgia about her name. Georgie Porgie.

And then there it was, another generation, though it had skipped the one in between. A stone about two feet high and two feet wide, simple and well-tended, stood at the very end of the row, an empty patch of grass on either side, as if saving space for those who would cor

Eli Martin Shepherd. Born July 27, 2007, Died October 2͡5, ͡2͡0͡1͡1 was all it said.

A horse was etched in the stone, a horse that looked like his hind quarters were dappled in color. The Paint. A fat bouquet of wildflowers in a bright yellow vase sat beside the headstone and the song the woman had sung in Eli's memory, "*You are my sunshine . . .*" caught in my thoughts, and I found myself saying the words. Georgia's name wasn't printed on the stone, but I knew with a clarity both sick and shocking that she was Eli's mother. She had to be.

I counted backwards just to be sure. Nine months before July of 2007 would have been October of 2006.

Georgia was Eli's mother. And I was Eli's father. I had to be.

GEORGIA

I GAVE BIRTH TO ELI on July 27, 2007, a month before I turned eighteen. No one knew I was pregnant until I was three months along. I would have waited longer, but the snug Wranglers I wore every day wouldn't button and my flat stomach and trim hips were no longer flat enough or trim enough to wedge into tight, unforgiving denim. The horror of my predicament wasn't just the pregnancy. It was that Moses was the father, and Moses's name had become a hiss and a curse word everywhere I turned.

My parents and I talked about adoption, but I couldn't do it. I couldn't do that to Moses. It made what had been between us meaningless. And for me, it never had been and it never would be. Moses might never know about his child, and he might be forever alone in the world, but his child would not be. And even though I hated him sometimes, even though I'd made him the faceless man, even though I didn't know where he was or what he was doing now, I couldn't give his child away. I couldn't do it.

But the day Eli was born, it was no longer about me, or Moses, or about being strong or being weak. Suddenly it was all about Eli, a boy conceived in turmoil, a boy who looked so much like his father that when I gazed down into his tiny face, I loved him with a fervor that made the regret of his conception quake and crack and then crumble into dust—powerless to hurt us, paper against the flame of devotion that welled in my heart and set my child's precious face in stone, no longer faceless, no longer feared.

"What are you going to name him, Georgia?" my mom had whispered, tears streaming down her face as she watched her child become a mother. She'd aged in the months since I had unburdened myself on her. But with the sweetness of new life making the hospital room a sacred place, she looked serene. I wondered if the same serenity marked my own expression. We were going to be okay. It was going to be okay.

"Eli."

My mom smiled and shook her head. "Georgia Marie." She laughed. "As in Eli Jackson, the bull rider?"

"As in Eli Jackson. I want him to take life by the horns and ride it for all it's worth. And when he becomes the best bull rider that ever lived, better even than his namesake, everyone will chant Eli Shepherd instead." I'd planned out my response, and it sounded pretty damn good because I was sincere. But it wasn't for the bull rider that I named him Eli. That was just a lucky coincidence. I named him Eli for Moses. No one wanted to think about Moses. No one wanted to talk about him. Even me. But my child was his child. And I couldn't pretend otherwise. I couldn't completely blot him out.

I had thought long and hard about what I would name my baby. We got an ultrasound at twenty-one weeks and I knew it was a boy. I'd grown up reading Louis L'Amour and was convinced that I'd been born in the wrong time. If my child had been a girl I would have called her Annie. As in, Annie Oakley. As in, Annie get your damn gun. But it was a boy. And I couldn't name him Moses.

I dug through the bible until I found the verse in Exodus where Moses talked about his sons and their names. The oldest was named Gershom. I winced at that. It might have been a popular name in Moses's day—like Tyler or Ryan or Michael now—but I couldn't do that to my child. The second son's name was even worse. Eliezer. Moses said in the scripture that he was named Eliezer because, "The God of my father was my help, and delivered me from the sword of Pharaoh."

The baby book of names I bought and perused said Eliezer means "God of Help" or "God is my help." I liked that. Moses had been saved from the sword of Jennifer Wright, I supposed. Maybe he'd been saved so my son could come into the world. I was young, how would I know? But the name seemed fitting, because I had no doubt I was going to need all the help—from God and everyone else—I could get. So I named him Eli.

Eli Martin Shepherd. Eli because he was the son of Moses, Martin for my dad, Shepherd because he was mine.

I had finished my senior year heavy with pregnancy and graduated with my class. I never answered questions, never talked about Moses. I let people talk and let my middle finger answer for me when a response was demanded. Eventually, people just got over it. But they all knew. You only had to look at Eli to know.

Eli had brown eyes, just like mine, and my mom said he had my smile, but the rest was Moses. His hair was a mass of black curls, and I wondered if Moses's hair would have looked like that if he'd ever grown it out. It had always been cropped so short it was stubble. I wondered what Moses would think if he saw Eli, if he would recognize himself in our son. And then I would push those thoughts away and pretend I didn't care, making Moses faceless once more so I couldn't make comparisons.

But Eli was like me in other ways. He was full of energy and walked at ten months. I chased after him for the next three and a half years. He laughed and ran and would never hold still, except when he saw a horse, and then he'd be quiet and calm, just like I told him to do, and he would watch like there was nothing better in the world, nothing more beautiful, and no place he would rather be. Just like his mom. Other than the little kid drawings and the occasional food mess that he enjoyed smearing everywhere, he showed no inclination to paint.

I couldn't stay home and take care of him though, not all the time. My mom watched Eli three days a week while I drove an hour north for school at Utah Valley University, which had been my plan, even before Eli changed my priorities. Dreams of following the rodeo circuit and being the top barrel racer in the world were laid by the wayside. I decided to follow in my parents footsteps. Horses and therapy. It made sense. I was good with animals, horses especially. I would be doing what I loved and maybe I would learn something along the way that would help me come to terms with my relationship with Moses. I settled into my life in Levan. I had no plans to leave. It was a good place to raise Eli, among people who loved him. My parents had both been born there, and their parents, with one grandmother tugged over the ridge and into our valley from Fountain Green on the other side of the hill. In the cemetery, five generations of Shepherd grandfathers lay beside their wives. Five greats. And I was certain I would one day lie there too.

But Eli beat me to it.

XIX

MOSES

I DIDN'T STOP TO THINK. I didn't go back to Gi's and tell Tag what I had found in the cemetery. I was filled with a thundering outrage that I wore to mask the quiet horror of the truth. I drove straight to Georgia's and strode around the house to the corrals and outbuildings beyond. She wasn't in the round corral anymore. The horse she'd called Cuss was in the pasture, grazing near the fence and his ears perked up as I approached. He whinnied sharply and reared up, like I was a predator. I found Georgia filling the water trough, and like Cuss, her head came up, her back stiffened and she watched me approach with trepidation.

"What do you want, Moses?" She muscled a bale of hay nearer to the fence and reached for a pitchfork to divvy it up to the horses that watched me warily, unwilling to approach, even if dinner was served. Her voice was harsh, loud, but underneath I heard the panic. I was scaring her. I was big and I was male, and I was feared. But that wasn't it. That wasn't the reason she was afraid. She feared me because she had convinced herself she never knew me. I was the unknown. I was the kid who painted pictures while his grandmother lay dead on the kitchen floor. I was the psycho. Some even thought I had killed my grandmother. Some thought I'd killed many people. I really didn't know what Georgia thought. And at the moment, I didn't care.

"What do you want?" she repeated as I took the pitchfork from her hands and finished the job for her. I needed the distraction. Her hands fell helplessly to her sides and she took a step back, clearly unsure of the situation.

"You had a son." I continued to spear the bale of hay and shovel it over the fence in sections, not looking at her as I spoke. I never looked at the family members. I just kept talking until they interrupted me or screamed at me, or sobbed and begged me to continue. Usually, that was enough. The dead would leave me alone once I delivered the message. And I would be free until the next time one of them wouldn't leave me alone.

"You have a son and he keeps showing me pictures. Your son . . . Eli? I don't know what he wants exactly, but he won't leave me alone. He won't leave me alone so I'm here . . . and maybe that will be enough for him."

She hadn't interrupted me. She hadn't screamed at me. She hadn't run. She just stood with her arms wrapped around herself and her eyes fixed on my face. I met her gaze briefly and looked away again to a spot just above her head. The bale of hay was gone, so I leaned against the pitchfork. And I waited.

"My son is dead." Her voice sounded odd, as if her lips had turned to stone and could no longer easily form words. My eyes glanced off her face once more. She had, indeed, turned to stone. Her face was so still it resembled the sculptures in my books. In the muted light of the golden afternoon, her skin was smooth and pale, just like marble. Even her hair looked colorless, thick and white and spilling over her shoulder in that long braid that reminded me of the heavy rope that Eli kept showing me, rope that spun in the air and fell in a sinuous loop over the horse's head, the horse with colors on his back.

"I know he is," I said mildly, but the pressure in my head increased exponentially. The water was rising, pulsing, and my levies were close to bursting.

"So how can he show you anything?" Georgia challenged harshly.

I swallowed, trying to stem the tide and met her eyes again. "You know how, Georgia."

She shook her head briskly, adamantly denying that she knew any such thing. She took a step back and her eyes shot to the left, as if she was preparing to run. "You need to leave me alone."

I pushed the anger back. I shoved it hard so I wouldn't shove her. And I wanted to push her, wipe the denial off her pretty face, push her head into the dirt until her mouth was filled with mud. Then she could order me to go. Then I would deserve it. Instead, I did as she asked and turned away, ignoring the little boy who trotted after me, sending desperate images of his mother to my brain, trying to call me back without words.

"What does he look like?" She called after me, and the desperation in her voice was so at odds with her rejection that I stopped in my tracks. "I mean, if you can see him. What does he look like?"

Eli was suddenly in front of me, jumping up and down, smiling and pointing back toward Georgia. I turned, still angry, still defiant, but willing to go another round, and Eli was there in front of me again, standing between me and the horse corral. I looked at him and then back at Georgia.

"He's small. He has dark, curly hair. And brown eyes. His eyes are like yours." She winced and her hands rose to press against her chest as if to encourage her heart to continue beating.

"His hair is too long. It's curling in his eyes. He needs a haircut." The little boy brushed a droopy curl out of his eyes as if he understood what I was telling his mother.

"He hated haircuts," she said softly, and her lips tightened immediately as if she wished she hadn't contributed to the conversation.

"He was afraid of the clippers," I supplied, Eli's memory of the buzzing around his ears making my own heart quicken in sympathy. Eli's memories were shot with terror and the clippers were twice as big as his head. They resembled the gaping jaws of a Tyrannosaurus Rex, proving that memory wasn't always accurate. Then the image changed to something else. A birthday cake. It was chocolate with a plastic horse in the center, rearing up. Four candles flickered around it.

"He's four," I said, trusting that that was what Eli was trying to tell me. But I knew. I'd seen the dates on the grave.

"He would be six now." She shook her head defiantly. I waited. The child looked up at me expectantly and then looked back at his mother.

"He's still four," I said. "Kids wait."

Her lower lip trembled and she bit into it. She was starting to believe me. That, or she was starting to hate me. Or maybe she already did.

"Wait for what?" Her voice was so soft I barely caught the question.

"Wait for someone to raise them."

The pain on her face was so intense, I felt a flash of remorse that I'd cornered her like this. She wasn't prepared for me. But I hadn't been prepared either. It was aces as far as I was concerned.

"He would have been waiting a long time for you," she said softly, taking a few steps toward me and then stopping, her stance aggressive, her hands clenched. The grieving mother was gone. She was the wronged woman now. And I was the man who knocked her up and left town.

"That's how you want to play this?" I gasped hoarsely, all my anger back in full force, so angry I wanted to start ripping fence posts from the ground and flinging barbed wire.

"Play what, Moses?" she snapped. And I snapped too.

"The fact that you and I had a son. I had a son! We made a child together. And he's dead. And I never knew him. I never knew him, Georgia! I never knew a damn thing about him. And you're going to spit that shit at me? How did he die, Georgia? Huh? Tell me!" I knew. I was almost sure I knew. Eli kept showing me the truck. Georgia's old truck, Myrtle. Something happened to Eli in the truck.

Anger zinged in colorful zags and streaks behind my eyes. I felt the water start to part, separating, splitting, and the colors from the other side started to seep down the channel. I pressed my hands into my eyes, and maybe I looked as crazed as I felt, because when I pulled my hands away, Georgia had jumped the fence and began to run, her legs eating up the distance swiftly, as if she thought I would kill her too. And instead of making me pause, her flight just made me angrier. She was going to answer me. She was going to tell me. And she was going to do it now. I went after her, over the fence, arms and legs pumping, rage narrowed on her slim back and on her pale hair falling out of her braid, running away from me like I was a monster.

When I pulled her down, I wrapped myself around her and took her weight on mine. We hit hard, her head bouncing off my shoulder, my head bouncing off the ground, but it didn't slow her down any. She fought me, kicking and scratching like a wild animal, and I rolled on top of her, pinning her arms between us, pressing her legs down with my own.

"Georgia!" I roared, pressing my forehead into hers, controlling every part of her. I could feel her gasping for breath, crying, resisting me with all her strength.

"Stop it! You're going to talk to me. You're going to talk to me. Right. Now. What happened to him?" I felt the ice in my hands and flames at my neck, and I was reminded that Eli was there. I knew he was watching us, watching me restraining his mother. And I was ashamed. I didn't want to see him and I couldn't let her go. I needed her to tell me. I shifted so I wasn't crushing her, but I didn't lift my brow from where I pressed it into hers, controlling her head. *When a horse gives you her head, she's yours.* Georgia's words whispered in my memory. She wasn't giving me her head. But I was taking it.

"Talk."

GEORGIA

"MOM! I'M GOING!" I yelled as I strode through the kitchen and swiped my keys from atop the fridge.

"I wanna come too." Eli jumped up from the floor where he was carefully building a corral out of Lincoln logs and ran for the door, sending the little logs flying in all directions. I'd already bathed him and put on his favorite Batman pajamas, even attaching the little black cape so he could save Gotham between repairing corrals. I caught him up and swung him around, his little legs locking around my waist, his

arms around my neck.

"No, baby. Not this time. You're gonna stay with grandma and gramps, okay?" Eli's face crumpled and his eyes filled right on cue.

"I wanna come!" he protested tearfully.

"I know, but I won't be home until late and it won't be fun for you, buddy."

"It will be fun! I like to stay up late!" he squeezed his legs tighter and his arms were like a vise around my neck.

"Eli, stop," I laughed. "Grandpa said he would watch John Wayne and the cowboys with you. And I'll bet Grandma will make popcorn too. Okay?" Eli shook his head vehemently, and I could see he wasn't going to cooperate. I'd left him too often lately.

"MOM! Help!" I projected my voice so that my mom would hear, wherever she was.

"Go on, George! We've got him." My dad's voice came from the back of the house and I walked with Eli in my arms until I reached my parents' room. My dad was stretched out on the bed, remote in hand, boots off, his cowboy hat still perched on his head. He greeted us with a smile and patted the bed, coaxing Eli to join him.

"Come on, wild man. Sit by Grandpa. Let's see if we can find a good cowboy show."

Eli released my neck and slid from my body reluctantly, falling in a forlorn little heap on the bed. He hung his head to let me know he wasn't happy, but at least he was accepting. I kissed his head quickly and pulled back immediately so he couldn't grab me again. His arms could be like sticky tentacles.

"We're watching cowboy shows, Mommy. No mommies allowed." Eli pouted, excluding me like I was excluding him. Then he crossed his arms and sniffled, and I met my dad's gaze with a sigh.

"Thanks, Dad," I said softly and he winked at me.

"You heard him. No mommies allowed. Get out, girl," he repeated with a smile.

I flew through the house and out the back door, side-stepping chickens and my mom's two guinea hens, Dame and Edna, flipping back my hair and yanking open the door to Myrtle in a matter of seconds. When

206

the door closed, I turned the key, and the old truck roared to life, blaring Gordon Lightfoot's "If You Could Read My Mind" from the speakers. I loved the song and paused for a second, listening. This station always played country oldies. I felt like a country oldie myself sometimes. I was twenty-two years old, but lately I felt like I was forty-five. With a big sigh, I slumped forward and rested my head on the steering wheel, letting the song wash over me, just for a minute. I hated leaving Eli. It was always an ordeal. Right now, I just needed to catch my breath. There was no silence in my life. Ever. No time to breathe.

Tonight I just wanted to be young and beautiful and maybe dance with a couple of cute cowboys and pretend I had only myself to worry about, even pretend I was looking for a man like the other girls were. I wasn't. Eli was the only man in my life. But tonight, it would be nice to be held for a little while. Maybe the band would even play this song. I would request it.

Gordon finished wishing for a mind-reader and the next song in the line-up was about mommas not letting their babies grow up to be cowboys. I laughed a little. My baby was already a cowboy. Too late.

I sighed once more and raised my head from the wheel. I checked my rearview mirror, flipped down the visor and looked at my reflection, and finally slicked on some gloss and smacked my lips together. Then I put the truck in reverse and began to back out. Time to go. The girls would already be there, and I was running late, as usual.

It felt like hitting a curb. There was a thump and a bounce. Not even a very big bounce. Not even a very big thump. But something. I swore, and checked my rear-view again, wondering what in the world I'd run over.

I stepped out of the truck, and my eyes were instantly drawn to the tire. A black piece of something was wrapped up around it. A trash bag? Had I hit the trash can? I slammed the truck door and took one step. Just a single step. And suddenly I knew what it was. It was Eli's cape. Eli's Batman cape was wrapped around the tire.

Eli's cape. The cape Eli was wearing. But Eli was inside. Eli was sitting with my dad, watching the cowboys. I fell to my knees, scrambling, desperate, knowing I had to look. I couldn't look. I had to look . . .

MOSES

WHEN SHE FINISHED, I rolled off of her and sat up. She didn't move. She kept her arms crossed over her chest where I'd kept them pinned while she'd talked, her voice a harsh whisper in my ear. Her hair had come completely loose from her braid and was spread around her head in wild disarray. She looked like the painting I liked by Arthur Hughes. *The Lady of Shalott* – Georgia looked like the Lady of Shalott, hands folded, hair fanned out around her, eyes blank.

But her eyes weren't blank now. They were closed and tears dripped down the sides of her face. Her chest rose and fell like she'd just run a marathon. I put my hand on my own thundering heart and turned away from her, unable to climb to my feet. Unable to do anything but rest my head on my knees.

And then Eli showed me the rest.

Georgia's head lay against the wheel of an old pick-up truck and music poured out the windows. I was looking at her from an odd angle, as if I sat on the ground behind the rusted bumper. Georgia's hair was sleek and long, shiny and clean like she'd just blown it dry and was heading out for someplace special. She opened her eyes and popped down the visor to check the color on her lips. She rubbed them together and shot the visor back into place. My view changed as if the eyes through which I saw altered their position. I was staring at the back of the truck, at the tailgate that was hanging down. It was still so high. The picture bobbled as if I were attempting to climb. The engine roared and the view changed yet again, abruptly, awkwardly. Wheels, under-carriage.

And then Georgia's face, peering beneath the truck. The horror on her face transformed it. She looked hideous—gaping mouth and crazed eyes. She looked otherworldly, and she screamed, Eli, Eli, Eli . . ."

I felt her scream reverberate through me as the connection was suddenly severed and the feed in my brain went black. But Eli didn't leave. He just tipped his head to the side and waited. Then he smiled softly, sadly, like he knew what he'd shown me would hurt me.

And I put my face in my hands and cried.

GEORGIA

IT WAS ONE OF THE MOST terrible sounds I'd ever heard. Moses crying. His back shook in a parody of awful laughter, his head was cradled in his hands like he couldn't believe what I'd told him. Strangely enough, when he rolled away from me his expression was blank, frozen, like a granite wall. And then he tipped his head ever so slightly like he was listening to something . . . or thinking about something. And then he'd let out a horrible, wrenching cry, covered his eyes with his hands and lost it. I wasn't even certain why he cried. I meant nothing to him. Obviously.

He'd always been so remote and detached, able to pull away without the slightest indication that he was bothered by the separation. He didn't know Eli. He'd never known him. I had tried to tell him. I'd visited that damn facility week after week until they told me in no uncertain terms that I was not wanted. I'd written him a letter that no one would deliver. And then he'd just disappeared for almost seven years.

He'd never known Eli. He was right about that. But that should have made this news easier to bear. And from the way he cried into his hands, heartbroken, it wasn't easy at all.

I didn't dare comfort him. He wouldn't want my touch. I was the same as his mother. I hadn't taken care of my child, just like she hadn't taken care of Moses. I loathed myself almost as much as Moses loathed me, and I had felt that loathing coming off of him in waves. But that didn't stop me from crying with him.

I was always amazed that my tears kept coming. Day after day. There was a limitless supply. My grief was a deep, underground spring constantly bubbling up and spilling over and I cried with Moses, tears flowing, looking up at the true blue October sky above my head. It stretched endlessly and disappeared behind the mountains that ringed my town like silent sentries, keeping none of us safe. Beautiful mountains. Useless mountains. October had always been my favorite month. And then October took Eli. And I hated her. October gave me sunflowers—a peace offering, I suppose. I put them on his grave, and hated her again.

Now the sunflowers lined the grassy field where I lay beside my old lover, not moving, my eyes fixed on the empty blue of another empty day. Moses stayed bent beside me, mourning for a son he had never known. He grieved openly, desperately, and nothing he could have done would have surprised me more. His grief seeped through his hands and spilled into the ground beneath us, and his grief softened my heart. Eventually, he rolled to his back beside me, and though his lips trembled and his breath was harsh, his sobs quieted and no more tears fell.

"Why are you here, Moses?" I whispered. "Why did you come back?"

He rolled his head slightly and found my eyes. The anger was gone. Even the loathing, though I wasn't sure if it had simply been temporarily washed away. I met his gaze steadily and he must have seen the same thing in my face. No anger. Despair, acceptance, sorrow. But no anger.

"He brought me back, Georgia."

GEORGIA

I SPENT THE NIGHT STARING up at the ceiling in my old room, remembering the night Moses had lain on his back and painted until I'd fallen asleep with colors dancing behind my eyes and a white horse running through my dreams.

You're afraid of the truth, Georgia. And people who are afraid of the truth never find it.

That's what Moses had said, lying next to me, looking up at a blue sky that wasn't really blue. Color isn't real. I had a science teacher tell me that color is simply the way our eyes interpret the energies contained within a beam of light.

So did the blue sky lie by making me believe it was something that it wasn't? Did Moses lie when he told me Eli had brought him back? Was he trying to make me believe he was something he wasn't? He was right that I was afraid. But I didn't think I was afraid of the truth. I was afraid of believing something that would destroy me if it turned out to be a lie.

Sometime before dawn, I'd had that dream again, only this time, instead of the white horse, I saw Eli's paint, Calico, and when I stared into the horse's eyes I could see my son, as if he, like the blind man in the story, had been transformed into a horse that ran into the clouds, into a blue sky that wasn't really blue, never to return.

That morning, sitting at the breakfast table, I told my parents that Moses was back. Dad's face had paled and mom had reacted like I had just confessed that the reincarnated Ted Bundy was my new boyfriend. Despite my protests, she immediately called Sheriff Dawson who promised her he would stop by Kathleen Wright's old home and have a little friendly visit with the new homeowner. I doubted Sheriff Dawson would welcome Moses back to the community, even if his visit was temporary, as I had no doubt it was.

"Oh, George," my dad murmured as my mother chatted nervously with the sheriff. "You're gonna have to tell him. You're going to have to tell him about Eli."

The guilt and shame rose up inside me immediately, and I swallowed them down as I shredded my cold toast into pieces small enough to distribute meager rations to a legion of mice.

"I told him. Yesterday. I told him." I thought about the stormy confrontation of the day before and decided to leave it at that.

My dad stared at me, shock and disbelief all over his face. He wiped at his mouth and I shredded another piece of toast, and we listened to my mom worry about Moses Wright being back and the stress it was going to put on the entire community.

"How?" My dad protested. "How did he take it? I thought he was long gone. Suddenly he's back and he's all up to date?" My dad's voice rose and my mom looked over at him sharply.

"Martin. Calm down," she soothed, pulling the phone away from her mouth to spare Sheriff Dawson the sideline drama.

"Mauna. I had a little bit of cancer cut out. I didn't have my balls cut off, so quit treating me like a quivering invalid!" he shot back, and my mother's lips tightened.

He looked back at me and sighed. "I knew this day would come. I knew it. I wish you would have let me be with you when you told him. It couldn't have been an easy conversation." He swore and then laughed without mirth. "You are the toughest girl I know, George. The toughest girl I know. But that couldn't have been easy."

His compassion made me teary and I pushed my plate away, making the tower of bread teeter and topple. I didn't want to start crying so early in the day. If I started this early I would be laid out before noon, and I didn't have time for an emotional hangover.

"No. It wasn't. Not for me. And not for him."

My dad raised a brow derisively and sat back in his chair so he could meet my gaze. "I wasn't worried about Moses. You're the only one I care about in this discussion."

I nodded and headed for the door. My dad had a right to his anger. I guess we all did. I pushed through the screen door and paused on the porch to appreciate the cool bite in the air. It cleared my head immediately.

"How did he take it, George?" My dad had followed me to the door and was standing in the frame. "When you told him, how did he take it?" I could see that he was still angry, and he wasn't ready to stop fanning the flames. Anger was taxing, and whether or not I had a right to it, whether or not Dad had a right to it, suddenly I wasn't so sure it was a right I wanted to continue exercising.

I concentrated on filling my lungs once, twice, and then again before I answered him. "He cried." I stepped off the porch and headed for the barn. "He cried."

MOSES

"SO YOU'RE JUST GONNA GO," Tag said, throwing up his hands.

"Painting's done. Carpet's coming. I even have a buyer. No reason to stay." I stacked the unused gallons of paint in my truck and continued back inside, making a mental list of what still needed to be done before I could get the hell out of Dodge.

"You found out you had a son. With a girl you say you weren't in love with but who you can't get over. You also found out your son, her son, was killed in a terrible accident."

I ignored Tag and folded up the last of the drop cloths. Carpet would be here in an hour. Once that was installed, the woman I'd hired to come in and clean the place could start. In fact, I should call her and see if she could start on the kitchen and the bathrooms today, just to hurry the process along.

"You found all of this out yesterday. Today you're over it. Tomorrow you're leaving."

"I would leave today if I could," I replied firmly. I hadn't seen Eli in twenty-four hours. Not since he'd shown me how he died.

"Does Georgia know you're going?"

"She told me to leave her alone. Plus, she doesn't believe me."

That shut Tag up and his step faltered. He'd spent the night before coaxing details out of me, but that was one thing I'd failed to mention. I hadn't told him how we'd lain in the field, both of us emotionally drained, lying on our backs, looking at the sky because we couldn't look at each other. I hadn't told Tag what Georgia had said to me when I'd told her Eli had brought me back.

"The only thing that kept me from breaking when Eli died was the truth," she'd said.

And I stayed silent, not understanding, but waiting for her to make me see.

"People said things like, 'He's in a better place and you'll see him again. He's in heaven.' Stuff like that. But that just hurt me. That made me feel like I hadn't been good for him. Like he was better off without me. And it played on what I always suspected. I wasn't good for Eli. I was young and stupid and I wasn't careful enough with him. Obviously, I wasn't careful enough with him."

Her pain was so heavy it filled the air around us, and when I tried to breathe, it filled my lungs and made my throat close and my chest scream for oxygen. But she didn't stop.

"After the accident, the only truth I was sure of was that Eli was dead. I'd killed him. And that was something I was going to have to live with."

Georgia looked at me fiercely, her old fire lighting up her eyes as if expecting me to argue with her. But arguing was something I rarely did. I'd learned long ago that people were going to think what they thought, believe whatever they were going to believe, and speaking up wouldn't change their minds. So I met Georgia's gaze and waited.

"He's dead, Moses. That's the truth. I'm alive. That's also the truth. I didn't mean to kill him. Another truth. I would give him my life if I could. I would trade places if I could. I would do anything to have him back. Give anything. Sacrifice anything. Anyone. That's the truth too." Georgia stopped abruptly and inhaled deeply, her breath shuddering and skipping like her throat was too tight to draw it in all at once. She broke eye contact, turning her head as if my seeming acceptance of her truths rattled her a bit.

"So please don't lie to me, Moses. That's all I ask. Don't lie to me. And I won't lie to you. I'll tell you everything you want to know. But don't lie to me."

She thought I was lying. She thought I was doing the crazy thing with her. She didn't believe I could see Eli. She wanted me to tell her the truth, but when everyone called your truth a lie, what then?

"You're afraid of the truth, Georgia. People that are afraid of the truth never find it," I told her. But she didn't look at me, staring up at the sky once more, signaling that the conversation was over. I waited for several long minutes and finally rose to my feet, leaving her there, the Lady of Shalott, the Lady of the Lake, lying in a sea of grass. My legs were shaking and I felt drained all the way to my bones as I walked away.

"I did what I came to do," I told Tag. Although I had no idea if that was the truth, it sounded good. If that was what Eli needed me to do, to see, then it was done. Finished. All I knew was I wanted to leave, and the sooner the better.

"We're not done painting, though," Tag tried again.

I continued gathering supplies.

"There's another mural upstairs. Or did you forget about that one?" Tag asked.

"I didn't paint anything upstairs. I was pretty strung out. But I'm pretty sure I never went upstairs." I'd walked down those stairs and out of the house, straight to the barn where I found Georgia. And I'd never walked up them again.

"Come on. I'll show you." Tag climbed the stairs eagerly, and I followed decidedly less so. I was sick to death of seeing my handiwork. My stomach had been as knotted as a fisherman's net since I'd stepped inside G's house. And it hadn't eased yet. But when Tag pushed open the door to my old room and pointed at the wall, I realized that it wasn't my handiwork I'd forgotten about.

The stick-figure mural was still there.

"Maybe I'm wrong, but I'm thinking this is a Moses Wright knock off. Similar styling . . . but not quite there yet," Tag said, squinting his eyes and stroking his chin like he was actually studying a piece of art-work.

"It was Georgia."

"No shit?" Tag said in mock surprise, and I laughed, even though I was choking on the memory.

The last Saturday before school started, Georgia failed to show up on the fence line at lunch time like she'd done every other day. By the time I packed it in, I'd convinced myself that I was better off. Good riddance. I never wanted her anyway. I stomped up the stairs into the bathroom, showered with my teeth gritted and anger coming out my ears, only to walk into my room with a towel wrapped around my waist and halt in amazement.

Georgia had painted a mural on my bedroom wall.

It looked like a child's comic strip, complete with stick figures and speech bubbles.

The female stick figure had long blonde hair and cowboy boots and the male stick figure had bright green eyes, a paint brush, and no hair at all. The awkward stick people were holding hands in one frame, kissing in the next, and in the final frame, the girl stick figure—Georgia—was kicking the boy stick figure—me—in the head.

"What in the hell . . ." I breathed.

"Nice outfit!" Georgia chirped from where she was seated, cross legged, in the middle of my bed.

I shook my head in disbelief and pointed to the door. "Out."

She laughed. "I'll shut my eyes."

I grumbled and stomped to my dresser. With one hand I gathered up some clothes and stomped back out, slamming the bathroom door as if I was truly irritated. I wasn't. I was thrilled to see her.

I came back, fully dressed, with my arms folded, and I stood in the doorway and stared at her hideous drawing.

"Are you mad at me?" Her brow was wrinkled and her eyes were worried, and she wasn't smiling anymore. "I thought you would laugh." She shrugged. "I told Kathleen I was going to surprise you. And she said, 'Go right ahead!' So I did. I used your paints, but I put everything back."

"Why are you kicking me in the head?"

"It's our story. We meet. You save me. I kiss you. You kiss me back, but you keep acting like you don't like me even though I know you do. So I'm kicking some sense into you. And man, does it feel good." She grinned cheekily, and I looked back at her depiction. That was some kick to the head.

"It's a terrible mural." It was terrible. And funny. And very Georgia.

"Well, we can't all be Leonardo DiCaprio. You painted on my walls, I'm painting on yours. And you don't even have to pay me. I'm just trying to bond with you over art."

"Leonardo da Vinci, you mean?"

"Him too." She smiled again and laid back on my bed, patting the spot beside her.

"You could have at least given me some biceps. That doesn't look anything like me. And why am I saying, 'Don't hurt me, Georgia!'"

I plopped down on the bed and purposely landed partially on top of her. She wiggled and scooted breathlessly, trying to free herself from my intentional squishing.

"You're right. Maybe I should have written those words coming out of my mouth," she giggled. But there was a look in her dark eyes that had me ducking my head and burying my face in her neck so I wouldn't have to think about the inevitability of her pain.

She stroked my head and I breathed against her skin.
"Are we bonding over art?" she whispered in my ear.
"No. Let's bond over something you're actually good at," I mur-
mured back, and felt her chest vibrate with her laughter.

"She wanted to bond with me over art," I said, smiling a little.

Tag chuckled and crossed to the stick figures. He traced his finger over the heart Georgia had drawn over the kissing stick -figures. "I like her, Mo."

"She could always make me laugh. And she was right," I confessed.

"About what?"

"I was always acting like I didn't like her, even though I did."

"Imagine that," Tag said mildly. But his eyes found mine as he turned away and left my bedroom.

"Mo?" Tag called as he descended the stairs.

"Yeah?" I found I wasn't ready to part with this mural yet, and stood, soaking it in as if I'd discovered a ghostly Picasso, painting away in my old room.

"You've got company, man. But take your time. It's not the female variety."

When I came back outside, Tag was leaning against a white SUV with Juab County Sheriff's Department emblazoned on the side, talking to Sheriff Dawson like they were just a couple of cowboys shootin' the shit after a long day in the saddle. Sheriff Dawson hadn't changed much—maybe a few more lines around his blue eyes. He leveled them at me and they were decidedly cool. That hadn't changed either.

"Didn't you and my dad do some horse business a few years back?" Tag just continued talking, easy as you please, pretending not to notice the change in the temperature or the fact that the sheriff wasn't really listening anymore.

Sheriff Dawson shot Tag a look. "Uh, yeah. Yes, we did. But it's been more than a few years. I shoed some of his horses and sold him a couple Appaloosas he liked."

"That's right. You and I talked about rodeo a little bit. I used to do a little steer wrestling when I wasn't raising Cain. You did some team roping didn't you?"

"A little. I was a heeler. But I had more success in calf roping." The sheriff's voice was mild, but he wasn't distracted by Tag's good ol' boy conversation skills, and as I walked toward him, he ignored Tag completely.

"You sellin' the place?" he asked bluntly. He didn't extend his hand and I didn't offer mine.

I shrugged. I didn't owe him any explanations.

"Tag here says you've been painting. That's good. People might get the wrong idea if they see what you painted all over that house."

Tag shifted slightly, and a look crossed his face that I'd seen a few times before.

"You here for any purpose, Sheriff?" I asked calmly. I wondered if he had known Georgia was pregnant when he came to question me at Montlake about Molly Taggert. It was February, and Georgia would have been far enough along for someone to know. It shed some light on the snide comments and the little asides he had shared with his fat deputy. Sheriff Dawson was a close friend of Georgia's family. I had no doubt he knew all about Eli. For that matter, I had no doubt the whole town did. I wondered suddenly if my son had been treated with scorn or fear because of me, because of the things I had done. I wondered if Georgia had. The thought made my hands grow cold and my gut twist uncomfortably.

"I'm just here to find out what your plans are," he said plainly. Tag's face contorted again.

"Oh, yeah?" I shoved my hands in my pockets and tried not to think about how people might have treated Georgia when they discovered she had my baby in her belly. I tried not to think about how people might have looked at her and Eli when they were out and about in the community. I tried not to think about them whispering or watching closely to see if Eli was going to turn out like me.

"Georgia has suffered too much. Her family has suffered. They don't need you here adding to it, churning up a lot of talk and trouble all over again."

I couldn't argue with any of that, but it pissed me off that he was suddenly the family spokesperson.

"Georgia's a beautiful girl, isn't she?" Tag blurted out. "She seein' anyone? Hell, Sheriff. I don't see a ring on your finger. You ever think about givin' her a shoulder to cry on during all those troubled times? You've got twenty years on her, but some girls like older men, right?"

I had never wanted to pound my friend's face in more than I wanted to at that moment. And there had been several times in our travels when we'd come to blows. I wanted to slap the smirk right off Tag's face, and I wasn't the only one. Sheriff Dawson's ears were red and his concerned, public-servant face had slipped into something else.

"Seems a little weird to me, Sheriff. But I've seen stranger things. Small-town connections are like that. Hell, everybody's related to everybody. Everybody knows everybody. I'm not even from here, and I know way too much."

The sheriff's blue eyes were narrowed in on Tag's face, and though he kept a benign smile in place, I could see he wasn't overly pleased with Tag's two cents. Tag just sat slumped against the SUV, totally relaxed, completely unbothered by the enemy he had just made.

We all turned as a delivery truck rounded the corner and bounced along from pot hole to pot hole. The carpet had arrived. Sheriff Dawson slid into his SUV and pulled his door shut as the delivery truck pulled in with a jerk and a belch.

"If you paid half as much attention to those pot holes as you're payin' to Moses, the whole town would be happier, I'm thinkin'." Tag continued to talk, only stepping away from the SUV as Sheriff Dawson started it up, put it in reverse, and began backing out.

"You're right about one thing, Mr. Taggert," Sheriff Dawson called out his window. "Everybody knows everybody. And everybody knows all about Georgia and Eli. And Georgia deserves a whole helluva lot better." He met my gaze through his windshield, shook his head as if he couldn't believe I'd had the gall to return, and drove away.

XXI

MOSES

THE CLEANING LADY—who turned out to be a cleaning girl—couldn't come until the next day, though I tried to bribe her with more pay. She was seventeen, and her boyfriend had a football game she didn't want to miss. I'd torn her name from a flyer hanging on a bulletin board in the country mall, the little gas station that sat at the crossroads where the old highway forked, one road leading south to Gunnison, the other leading west to the old coal mine and a dozen other little spots on the map that could hardly be called towns anymore.

We threw our sleeping bags on the new carpet in anticipation of spending our first night in the house—and last night if things went as planned. We'd slept out on the grass the three previous nights, and it had been a little colder than either of us liked. Tag had made a teasing comment about us sleeping in Georgia's barn to keep warm, but the look I'd sent him had shut him up immediately. I'd told Tag about the morning my grandmother died. He knew I'd spent the night with Georgia in the barn that final night. He knew I'd come home and found my grandmother dead on the kitchen floor. The night in the barn had been the last moments of Before. They'd been my last moments with Georgia. Sleeping in the barn was no laughing matter.

It was after we'd eaten a couple cans of soup and almost a loaf of bread between us that the doorbell rang, clanging through the empty house and jarring us both. I almost expected Sheriff Dawson to be standing outside with assorted townspeople armed with torches, but Georgia stood on the doorstep, her face drawn with indecision, clutching a big book to her chest.

"I thought . . . thought . . ." she tripped over the words and stopped. Then she took a deep breath and met my eyes. She said each word crisply, not allowing herself to stumble again.

"I have pictures of Eli. I thought maybe you'd like to see them." She held out the big book, and I realized it was a photo album. It was at least five inches thick with the pages overflowing and the binding bulging around them. I stared at it, not taking the book, and her arms slowly lowered. Her jaw was tight and her eyes were hard when I finally lifted my eyes. She thought I was rejecting her. Again.

"I do. I would like to see them. But will you look at them with me?" I asked softly. "I want you to tell me about him. I want stories. I want details."

She nodded and took a hesitant step inside when I opened the door wider and ushered her in. Her eyes took in the bare walls and the new carpets and she visibly relaxed.

"I wanted her clock," she said.

"What?" I was staring at the smooth length of her hair and the way it fell from her shoulders, down her back and ended only a few inches above her waist.

"That cuckoo clock she always had in here. I loved it," she explained.

"Me too." I wondered where it had ended up. I hoped it wasn't in a box somewhere.

"Was there anything left in the house?"

I shook my head. "Just the paint." As soon as the words left my mouth, I wished I hadn't spoken them. I don't know what it was about Georgia, but she'd always had that effect on me. She breached my defenses and my truths started spilling out with all their warts and garish

222

colors.

Georgia just looked at me in that same frank way, as if trying to peel back my layers. But then she shrugged and let it go. We traipsed through the kitchen, and I apologized for the lack of furniture. We ended up sitting with our backs to the wall in the dining room, the book on our laps. Tag busied himself in the kitchen and greeted Georgia with a smile and a question about Cuss.

"You get thrown today, Georgia?"

"Nah. I rarely get thrown anymore. I've gotten better at waiting them out."

"It won't be long until he gives you his head," I murmured. Georgia looked at me sharply and I cursed myself silently once more.

"I'd like to watch you sometime. Moses and I have seen the world, but it's been too long since I've spent any real time with horses. Maybe you'll let me have a ride before we leave." Tag smiled and winked at her again before excusing himself and heading for the front door. I hadn't missed Georgia's flinch when he mentioned us leaving.

"I'm heading into Nephi for a little refreshment and possibly a game of pool. That honky-tonk is still on Main, isn't it?"

"Yeah. We don't call it a honky-tonk though, Texas. That's stretching it a little. We call it a bar. But there's a pool table in the back, and if you're lucky, someone to play with who can still stand," Georgia said dryly.

"Did ya hear that, Moses? She's already given me a nickname. Tag 1, Moses 0." He cackled and let himself out the front door before I could respond.

Georgia laughed, but I wanted to follow him out and throw his ass to the ground. Tag didn't always know when to shut his mouth.

But as soon as he was gone, I would have gladly welcomed him back.

The house was far too quiet without him, and Georgia and I were stuck in an empty room with everything and nothing to say. It felt oddly right and horribly wrong to be sitting beside her, our shoulders touching, our legs stretched out, side by side. With a deep breath and a shaking hand, Georgia opened the book and filled the silence with pictures.

There were pictures of a tired-looking Georgia with a messy braid and hollow eyes staring at the camera with a small smile, a black-eyed infant with a swollen face topped by a tiny blue hat in her arms. There were close-ups of wrinkly feet and miniature fists, of a naked behind and a mass of black hair. Everything documented down to the smallest detail, as if every detail had been noted and celebrated.

As we turned the pages, the time passed. The squalling infant with the bunched up face became a smiling baby with two teeth and drool on his chin. Two teeth became four, four teeth became six, and Eli celebrated his first birthday with a cake that was bigger than he was. In the next shot he had two fistfuls of icing and a bow on his head. In the next picture the bow was gone and there were globs of icing in its place.

"He was the messiest kid. I couldn't keep him clean. I finally just gave up and let him enjoy himself," Georgia whispered, looking down at the smiling child. "We gave him his first pair of boots that birthday. He wouldn't take them off. He would scream when I tried to remove them." She turned the page and pointed at a picture. Eli was asleep in his crib, his diapered rump in the air, his hands tucked beneath his chest. And he was wearing his boots. I laughed, but the laugh broke in my chest and I looked away quickly. I felt Georgia's eyes glance off my face, but she turned the page and continued on.

Christmases, Easter-egg hunts, and the Fourth of July. Pictures of Halloween and Eli holding a sack of candy wearing only a cape and a pair of underwear made me think about his Batman pajamas—the pajamas he had on whenever I saw him. "Did he like Batman?"

She looked at me sharply.

"Did he have a pair of Batman pajamas?"

"Yes. He did." She nodded. Her face was as white as the freshly painted walls behind us. But she turned the page without another word.

There were pictures of camp-outs and parades and the posed shots with slicked down hair and a clean shirt, which he rarely had in the candid shots. He was comfortable in front of the camera and his smile filled the pages.

"He looks happy, Georgia." It was a statement more than a question, but Georgia nodded, answering me.

"He was a happy kid. I don't know how much I had to do with it. He was full of mischief, full of laughter, full of all the best things, even though I didn't always appreciate it. Sometimes I just wanted him to hold still . . . you know?" Her voice rose plaintively, and she tried to smile but the smile wobbled and slipped and she shook her head, as if to underline her confession.

"I told you I wouldn't lie to you Moses. And the truth is, I wasn't the best mother in the world. I wished so many times that I could just have a second to breathe. I was tired a lot. I was trying to work and go to school and take care of Eli. And I just wished for silence. So many times I just wanted to sleep. I just wanted to be alone. You know how they say, be careful what you wish for?"

"Georgia . . . stop." I didn't understand why she was insisting on making sure I knew the "truth." It was like she felt unworthy of any credit at all. "It looks to me like you did just fine," I said softly. She swallowed and closed the book abruptly, shoving it off her lap and scrambling to her feet.

"Georgia," I protested, following her up.

"I can't look anymore. I thought I could. You'll have to finish alone." She wouldn't look at me, and I knew she was barely holding onto her composure. Her full mouth was taut and her hands were clenched as tightly as her jaw. So I nodded and didn't chase her when she ran for the door. Then I sank back down to the floor and held the book in my arms, clutching it tightly, but unable to open it. I couldn't look anymore either.

MOSES

AN IMAGE OF GEORGIA glimmered and grew—a laughing mouth and brown eyes, blonde hair flying as if she rode a horse that I couldn't see. But she wasn't riding a horse. She was bouncing on the bed. It was a bed covered in a denim quilt trimmed in rope and dotted with lassos. I watched her through Eli's eyes as she soared up and down once more, and then collapsed around him. Eli's giggles made my chest ache as if I were the one laughing, as if I were the one who couldn't catch my breath. Georgia smiled down at me as if to kiss me goodnight, as if I were staring up at her from the pillow that bunched up in my periphery. Then she was leaning in, kissing my face. Kissing Eli's face.

"Goodnight, Stewy Stinker!" she said, nuzzling the curve between his shoulder and his neck.

"Goodnight, Buzzard Bates!" he responded gleefully.

"Goodnight Diehard Dan!" she immediately shot back.

"Goodnight, Butch Bones!" Eli chortled.

I came awake shivering with a stiff neck and a wet cheek where I'd slobbered on the photo album Georgia had left. I'd fallen asleep clutching it, and it had ended up beneath my head on the floor. I wondered if it was my discomfort that had awoken me, or if it was the dream of Georgia kissing Eli goodnight, but I eased myself up and rose to my feet, only to feel the all-too familiar sensations of unwanted company. My fingers flexed and began to cool and I pushed back the overwhelming desire to fill the freshly painted walls with something else. Something alive. Or something that once had been.

I tested the waters carefully, resisting the call of creation, and I peeked through the shimmering falls, trying to get a glimpse of who it was that waited on the other side. I wanted to see Eli again. I was afraid he wasn't coming back.

At first I thought it was Molly. Her hair was similar, but as I let the waters thin, I could see that it wasn't. I let her cross, keeping my back to the wall, watching her curiously. She didn't show me anything. Didn't send images of loved ones or pieces of her life gone by. She just walked toward the longest wall in the family room, the wall Tag and I had covered in white paint. We'd covered all the walls, erasing everything. She laid her hand against it, almost in memorial. It reminded me of the way people traced the names of the soldiers on the Vietnam wall Tag and I had visited in Washington DC. That wall hummed with grief and memory, and it drew the dead when their loved ones visited.

The girl curled her fingers softly against the fresh paint and then looked back at me. That was all. And then she was gone.

My phone rang out in angry peeling, and I stumbled around until I found it. I checked the time before I answered the call, and knew immediately that it couldn't be good news.

"Moses?" his voice echoed like he stood in an empty hallway.

"Tag. It's three a.m. Where are you?'

"I'm in jail."

"Ah, Tag." I groaned and ran a hand down my face. I shouldn't have let him go. But Tag had been managing himself for a long time, and a beer hadn't derailed him in ages.

"In Nephi. I messed up, Mo. I was playing pool, nursing a beer, shootin' the shit with the local boys. Georgia was right, everybody was pretty plastered, but that just made it easier to win. Everything was just fine. Then these guys start talking about the missing girls. That got my attention and I asked him, 'What missing girls?' One of 'em brings me a flyer that's stuck to the wall. The girl that's missing is a little blonde girl, maybe seventeen. She was last seen in Fountain Green, just over the hill, on the Fourth of July. It made me think of Molly, Mo. They said rumors were she was kind of wild. People said the same thing about Molly, as if she was to blame for her own death." Tag's voice rose, and I could hear the same old pain rearing its ugly head.

"Then an old guy sitting at the bar perks up and mentions that you're back in the area. They all start speculating that you're the one that's been takin' all these girls all these years. They said there's been a few. They all remembered the picture on the overpass. One of 'em even knew that you were the one who told the police where to find Molly. I shouldn't have said anything, Mo. But that's not me. Ya know?"

Yeah. I knew. And I groaned, knowing what was coming. My face was hot and my breath short. I knew I was hated, but I didn't know the full extent of the reason why.

"Next thing I know, one of the old guys is swinging a pool stick at my head."

I groaned again. Tag loved a fight. I was pretty sure how it all ended.

"So, now I'm here, at the county jail. Sheriff Dawson was so glad to see me, he questioned me personally. In fact, I've spent the last two hours answering questions about where *I* was on the Fourth of July, as

if had something to do with the girl's disappearance. Then they started asking me questions about you. Did I know where *you* were on the
Fourth? Shit," Tag spat in disgust.

"I had a fight that night, remember? So luckily I was able to provide
them with a pretty clear timeline for both of us. I have to pay a fine, and
I'm sure the owner at the Hunky Monkey is gonna want me to pay for
damages. Which I will. But your truck is still there, parked on Main. So
you're gonna need to come get me in the morning."

"The Hunky Monkey?" My head was starting to hurt.

"Or whatever it's called. It might be the Honky Mama, but that
seems kind of derogatory," Tag mused before continuing on with his
narrative.

"It's all bogus. And they're gonna let me go. But not until tomorrow
morning. They're telling me I've had too much to drink and I will have
to sleep in a cell tonight. And I've been told not to leave the area for the
next 48 hours."

I could tell Tag wasn't the slightest bit drunk. I'd seen Tag drunk.
I'd pulled Tag from a bar before, swinging and cursing, only a few beers
in, and this wasn't even that.

"What do you want me to do?" I asked. "If my truck is sitting on
Main in Nephi, then how am I going to come get you?"

"I don't know, man. Go see if Georgia can help you out. I hope it's
still there. Sheriff Dawson made noises about impounding it, saying
something about a search."

"I didn't even own that truck in July. I bought it in August, remember? What in the hell do they think they'll find?"

"That's right. I forgot about that!" Tag cursed and I heard someone
telling him his time was up.

I said a few choice words that Tag heartily repeated and told him I
would figure something out and I would be there to pick him up in the
morning.

But morning found me with no solutions. I could go to Georgia, but
I decided I'd rather steal a bike and peddle home with Tag on my han-
dlebars than ask Georgia to help me bail my friend out of jail.

By the time the cleaning girl arrived in an old white van sporting a nervous smile, I was at my wits end. I took one look at her ride and offered her $500 to let me drive it in to Nephi. Her blue eyes got wide and she readily agreed, nodding her bleached-blonde head so vigorously her big pink bow slid over and fell in her eyes. I promised to have it back to her by the time she was finished in the house, and I headed out the door.

XXII

GEORGIA

I THOUGHT I SAW MOSES drive off in Lisa Kendrick's white van. He drove past our house with his head averted, as if he really wished I hadn't seen him. I had just come back from the post office and was stepping out of my little Ford pick-up when the van shot past. I never drove Myrtle again after Eli died. My dad had sold her to a friend in Fountain Green so I didn't have to see her anymore. Maybe it was melodramatic. But as my Dad had kindly said, there are some battles you have to fight in order to heal, and this isn't one of them. Just sell the truck, George. So I did.

I watched the van as it slowed at the corner, turned, and headed for the highway. He was headed north toward Nephi. Which could mean anything, but considering Tag had left the night before in Moses's truck, I had a pretty good idea that's where Moses was headed too. But in Lisa's van?

I slammed the door and headed for Moses's house, not caring if I was being a nosy neighbor. I wanted to get the photo album, and now I wouldn't have to face Moses again in order to do it. He'd asked me about Eli's pajamas . . . his Batman pajamas. I thought for a minute he was trying to wound me. But he couldn't have known Eli died in those pajamas. He couldn't have known. But it had shaken me, and I hadn't lasted very long after that. I wondered if Moses had continued turning pages after I'd gone.

The front door was unlocked and I called up the stairs as soon as I entered.

"Hello?" I thought I could hear water running. "Hello?"

The water shut off and a woman's voice shouted back down to me. "Just a minute!"

"Lisa? Is that you?"

Lisa Kendrick rounded the corner at the top of the stairs, wiping her hands on a rag, her hair frizzing out wildly from her head.

"Oh my gosh! Georgia, you scared me!" She fanned her face with the damp rag. "This whole house gives me the creeps."

"Did you let Moses take your van?" I asked, ignoring the comments about the house. The whole town needed to get over it already.

"Yes. I did . . . Should I have said no?" The teenager immediately started worrying her lip. "His friend took his truck, I guess. He just needed to get into Nephi, and he offered me $500 bucks. But my mom will kick my trash if anything happens to the van. But he said he'd bring it right back! I shouldn't have let him take it. He gives me the creeps too, actually. He's hot. But he's creepy. Kind of like Johnny Depp in *Pirates*? Totally hot, but way freaky." She was babbling and I was already bored.

"I'm sure it's fine. Don't let me get in your way. I just stopped by to grab something I left last night." Lisa's eyes widened, and I could see that she really wanted to know what I could possibly have left in the creepy house of a freaky hot guy, but she restrained herself and turned back to the bathroom, albeit slowly.

"I don't mind you sticking around. I don't like being here alone," she added. "My mom told me I couldn't take this job. But when I told her how much he was paying, she gave in. But I'm supposed to call her every half hour. What if she stops by and the van isn't here?" Lisa's voice rose in alarm. "I am going to be in so much trouble."

"I'm sure it will all be fine," I repeated, waving as I ducked through the arch and away from the girl. It amazed me that people were still talking about Moses Wright. Clearly, Lisa's mom hadn't shared the fact with her daughter that Moses and I had been involved at one point. I'd gotten my fair share of talk when Eli was born. People had quickly spread their conclusions about my baby's parentage. But maybe because I never talked, because I kept my head down and just lived, the talk had died and people stopped starring at Eli when we were out. I foolishly thought I would never have to talk about Moses. But then Eli had turned three, gone to pre-school, and suddenly, he had his own questions. And my son was as stubborn as I was.

"Is Grandpa my dad?" Eli had asked, spooning up mac 'n' cheese, and trying to get it in his mouth before the little noodles escaped. He refused to let me help him, and at the rate he was going, he was going to starve.

"No. Grandpa's my dad. He's your grandpa."

"Then who's my dad?" And there it was, the question that had never once come up before. Not in three years. And it hung in the air, waiting for my response. And no amount of head ducking or holding my tongue was going to make it go away.

I shut the fridge calmly and poured Eli a glass of milk, stalling, stalling.

"Mommy! Who's my dad?" Eli had given up on the spoon and had scooped up a handful of noodles. They were squishing out the sides of his little fist, but so far there were none in his mouth.

"Your dad is Moses," I answered at last.

"MO-SES!" Eli laughed forming each syllable with equal emphasis. "That's a funny name. Where is MO-SES?"

"I don't know where he is."

Eli stopped laughing. "How come? Is he lost?"

"Yes. He is." And that fact still made my heart ache.

Eli was quiet for several seconds, filling his hands with more pasta. I thought maybe he'd already lost interest in the discussion. I watched as he finally managed to press several orange noodles past his lips. He grinned, pleased with himself, chewed happily, and swallowed noisily before he spoke again.

"Maybe I can find him. Maybe I can find MO-SES. I'm a good finder."

He brought me back, Moses had said. Maybe Eli had found him after all. The thought made me stumble, and I shrugged the memory off as I walked through the kitchen and snagged the photo album from the counter. I paused for a moment, considering whether I should leave something for him. I knew there were duplicates, or pictures that were close enough that I could part with one of a similar shot. But I didn't want to start pulling my book apart. And I didn't want to leave the precious pictures in a stack on the counter for Lisa to see and for Tag to thumb through. I couldn't do that. And then I knew what I would do. I would make Moses a book too. I would make copies of the pictures I didn't have duplicates of, and I would write descriptions and dates and paste them alongside the photos so he would have the details he claimed he wanted.

Having reached a decision, I scooped the book up in my arms and turned back toward the front door. As I did, my eyes glanced off the living room walls, and my gaze stuttered and caught. In the middle of the back wall, about three-fourths of the way up, the paint was peeling. And it wasn't just a little bubble. It was a circle about the size of my palm, and the white edges were bubbled back, revealing dark swirls beneath.

I approached the spot and raised my hand to try to smooth it back, wondering what had happened. It reminded me of the time my mom had repainted the kitchen when I was ten. The original paint had been there since the seventies, and when she tried to put a fresh new coat of pale blue over the top, the paint had bubbled just like this. It had something to do with oil base and water base, though as a kid I didn't care. I'd just enjoyed peeling the long strips of paint from the wall as my mom had bemoaned all the time she'd wasted. They had ended up having to treat the walls with some kind of stripper and they'd even sanded them for good measure.

I tugged at one of the edges, unable to resist, and another section came off in my hand.

There was a face there.

The piece I'd pulled from the wall revealed an eye, a piece of a slim nose, and half of a smiling mouth. I peeled a little more, freeing the entire face. I remembered this picture. I'd only seen it once. I'd only seen it that terrible morning. I had never come back inside the house. Not until last night. And last night the wall had been perfect. Pristine.

It wasn't Molly. I don't know why that relieved me.

People had talked, especially when they'd found Molly Taggert's remains near the overpass. They said Moses had to be involved. They speculated that it was gang related, that he'd brought his violent affiliations with him. I'd just kept my head down. I'd just stayed silent. And I tried not to believe the things they said. I tried to focus on the life inside of me and the days in front of me. And in the back of my mind I kept the door open, waiting for him to come back.

Last night the wall had been perfect. Pristine. But now there was a face in a sea of white. I turned from the wall, scooped up my photo album and left the house.

MOSES

THE LITTLE CLEANING GIRL was sitting on the front steps when I finally made it back to Levan with Tag driving my truck, bringing up the rear. Luckily, my truck hadn't been towed and Tag had been released with some cash and a signature. She rose when I stepped out of her van and hurried down the walk toward me.

"Can I go now, Mr. Wright? I'm done."

I nodded and reached for my wallet, pulling out seven, one-hundred-dollar bills and I laid them in her shaking hand. With a nod and a tight grip on her windfall and her bucket of supplies, Lisa Kendrick ran for the van like she had dogs on her heels. She leaped inside and started it up, while Tag and I stared after her, a little surprised at her skittish behavior. She rolled down her window a few inches, and her words came out in a jumbled rush.

"Her name is Sylvie. Sylvie Kendrick. My cousin. She used to babysit me when I was little. She lived in Gunnison. She disappeared eight years ago," Lisa Kendrick said. "It was a long time ago. And I was only nine . . . but I'm pretty sure it's her."

I had no idea what she was talking about, and I started to question her, only to have her hit reverse and peel out of my driveway as if her nerve had finally failed her.

MOSES

"WE'RE GOING TO HAVE TO SAND IT DOWN OR SOMETHING."

Tag and I stood looking at the face that peered out of the white wall, a face that hadn't been there the day before. I was guessing, from what Lisa Kendrick had said as she'd rushed off, that the face belonged to Sylvie Kendrick.

"There's just something off in this house, Moses."

"It's not the house, Tag. It's me."

Tag shot me a look and shook his head.

"You seeing things that other people can't doesn't make you the problem, Mo. It just means there are fewer secrets. And that can be dangerous."

I walked toward the wall and pressed my hand over the face, the way the girl had done the night before. She'd touched the wall, demanding that I see her.

"I think we need to get out of here, Moses. We need to sand that down, slap another coat of paint on that wall, and we need to go. I have a bad feeling about all of this," Tag insisted.

I shook my head. "I can't go yet, Tag. I turned away from the wall and faced my friend.

"Yesterday you wanted to leave. You were lined out, ready to go," Tag argued.

"That girl knew her. Lisa, the girl who cleaned. She saw this face, she recognized it. And it freaked her out. She said it was her cousin. But she disappeared eight years ago. What does that have to do with me? What does that have to do with anything? I'm sure I saw her last night because of the connection with Lisa. That's how it works."

"But you painted her before last night," Tag argued.

"And I painted Molly before I met you," I responded, my eyes returning to the wall.

Tag waited for me to say more, and when I didn't, he sighed. "Molly and that girl," he pointed to the wall, "and now another one. Three dead girls in ten years isn't all that remarkable. Even in Utah. And you and I know it doesn't have a damn thing to do with you. You're just the unlucky son-of-a-bitch that sees dead people. But people here have already decided you had something to do with it. I heard those guys last night, and you saw that girl take off out of here like you were Jack the Ripper. You don't need that shit in your life, Mo. You don't deserve it, and you don't need it," he repeated.

"But I need Georgia." There. I said it. I'd known it since she'd shown up the night before with a photo album clutched to her chest. She'd opened the door just a crack and she'd stuck an olive branch through.

Tag couldn't have looked more surprised if I'd slapped him across the face with that olive branch. I felt like the wind had been knocked out of me too, and I found myself gasping for breath.

"It looks like the stick-figure kick to the head knocked some sense into you." Tag whistled. "Just seven years too late."

"I can't run this time, Tag. I've got to see it through. Whatever that means. Maybe I just end up making peace with my skeletons. Making peace with Georgia. Getting to know my son in the only way I have left." I couldn't think about Eli without feeling like I was caught in a downpour. But water had always been my friend, and I decided maybe it was time to let it rain.

"I can't stay, Mo. I'd like to stay, but I have a feeling if I hang around here too long with you, I'm going to be a liability. There's something about this place that isn't agreeing with me."

"I understand. And I don't expect you to. I may be here for a while.

The house could use more than just a little paint and some new carpet. It's been empty a long time. The bathroom is ancient, it needs a new roof, the yard looks like crap. So I'm going to fix it up. And then I'm giving it to Georgia. Maternity expenses, four years of child support, funeral costs, pain and suffering. Hell, the house probably isn't enough."

"Salt Lake is two hours away, less than that the way I drive. You'll call if you need me, won't you?"

I nodded.

"I know you, Mo. You won't call." Tag shot a hand through his mop and sighed.

"I'll call," I promised, but knew in my heart Tag was probably right. It was hard to need.

"You want my advice?" Tag asked.

"No," I answered. He just rolled his eyes.

"Good. Here it is. Don't go slow, Mo. Don't go easy. Go hard and go fast. Women like Georgia are used to holding the reins. But you broke her, Mo. And then you left her. I know you had your reasons. You know I get it. But she won't let you break her again. So you have to take her. Don't wait for her to say please. 'Cause it won't happen."

"We're not talking about a horse, Tag."

"The hell we aren't. That's her language, Mo. So you better learn it."

XXIII

MOSES

GEORGIA CAME BACK AGAIN that night, knocking on the door, carrying another offering, only this time it wasn't the photo album. I tried not to be disappointed. I wanted more, but when I'd arrived home that afternoon the book was no longer on the kitchen counter, and I had no doubt that Georgia had come and taken it away.

She shoved a pan of brownies in my chest and said in a rush, "I took the photo album."

I nodded, the brownies in my hands. "I saw."

"I just wanted you to know. I'll put together a book for you. I have so many pictures."

"I would like that. Even better than homemade brownies." I tried to smile but it felt forced and I told her to hold on as I set the brownies down on the kitchen counter and joined her on the front steps, wishing I knew what to say to make her stick around.

"I didn't make them. The brownies, I mean. I'm a terrible cook. The only time I tried to make brownies, Eli took one bite and spit it out. And he ate bugs. I was sure they couldn't be that bad, until I took a bite.

They were pretty terrible. We ended up calling them frownies instead of brownies, and we fed them to the goats. It's a wonder Eli survived." She stopped abruptly, a stricken look washing over her face. I wanted to wrap my arms around her and tell her it was okay. That everything was okay. But it wasn't okay. Because Eli hadn't survived.

Georgia stepped back off the steps and tried to pull herself back together, smiling brightly.

"But don't worry. I bought those brownies from Sweaty Betty. She makes the best baked goods in the state of Utah."

I didn't remember anyone named Sweaty Betty, and I had my doubts with a name like Sweaty Betty that they would taste any better than Georgia's frownies. In fact, I was pretty sure I would be letting Tag eat them all.

"You'll have to try again sometime," I suggested as she turned to leave. I was talking about her frownies, but I really wasn't. And maybe she knew that, because she just waved and she didn't pause.

"Goodnight, Stewy Stinker," I called after her.

"What did you say?" Her voice was sharp and she stopped walking, but she didn't turn around.

"I said goodnight, Stewy Stinker. Now you say, goodnight, Buzzard Bates."

I heard her gasp and then she turned toward me, her fingers pressed to her lips to hide their trembling.

"He keeps showing you kissing him goodnight. And it's always the same." I waited.

"He shows you . . . that?" she whispered brokenly.

I nodded.

"It's from his book. He . . . he loved this book. So much. I probably read it to him a thousand times. It was a book I loved when I was little called *Calico the Wonder Horse.*"

"He named his horse—"

"Calico. After the horse in the book, yes," Georgia finished. She looked like she was about to collapse. I walked to her, took her hand, and gently led her back to the steps. She let me, and she didn't pull away when I sat beside her.

"So, who's Stewy Stinker?" I pressed softly.

"Stewy Stinker, Buzzard Bates, Skunk Skeeter, Butch Bones, Snakeyes Pyezon . . . they were the Bad Men in Eli's book." Georgia said Pyezon like Popeye would say poison, and it made me smile. Georgia smiled too, but there was obviously too much grief in the memory to make it stay, and her smile slid away like the tide. "So if they were the bad guys, who were the good guys?" I asked, trying to coax it out again.

"They weren't the bad guys, they were the Bad Men. It was the name of their gang. Stewy Stinker and the Bad Men."

"No false advertising there."

Georgia giggled and the shell-shocked expression she'd worn since I called her Stewy Stinker faded slightly.

"Nope. Simple, straightforward. You know exactly what you're getting."

I wondered if there was hidden meaning in her statement and waited for her to clue me in.

"You're different, Moses," she whispered.

"So are you."

She flinched but then nodded. "I am. Sometimes I miss the old Georgia. But in order to get her back, I would have to erase Eli. And I wouldn't trade Eli for the old Georgia."

I could only nod, not willing to think about the old Georgia and the old Moses and the fiery way we had come together. The memories were burned in my head and coming back to Levan made me want to revisit them. I wanted to kiss Georgia until her lips were sore, I wanted to make love to her in the barn and swim with her in the water tower, and most of all, I wanted to take away the wave of grief that kept knocking her over.

"Georgia?"

She kept her eyes averted. "Yeah?"

"Do you want me to go? You said you wouldn't lie to me. Do you want me to go?"

"Yes." No hesitation.

I felt the word reverberate in my chest and was surprised at the pain that echoed behind it. Yes. Yes. Yes. The word taunted. It reminded me of how I had shunned her the same way that last night in the barn. *Do you love me, Moses? she'd asked. No, I'd told her. No. No. No.*

"Yes. I want you to go. And no. I don't want you to go," she amended in a rush of frustrated, pent-up breath. She stood abruptly, threw her hands in the air, and then folded them across her chest defensively. "If I'm telling the truth, then both are true," she added softly.

I stood too, bracing myself against the impulse to bolt, to run and paint, like I always did. But Tag said I was going to have to take her. He told me not to go slow. And I was going to heed his advice.

"I don't know what the truth is this time, Moses. I don't know," Georgia said, and I knew I couldn't run this time. I wouldn't run.

"You know the truth. You just don't like it." I never thought I'd see Georgia Shepherd afraid of anything. I was afraid too. But I was afraid that she really wanted me to go. And I didn't know if I could stay away. Not again.

"What about you, Moses? Do you want to leave?" Georgia threw my words back at me. I didn't answer. I just studied her trembling lips and troubled eyes and reached out a hand for the heavy braid that fell over her right shoulder. It was warm and thick against my palm and my fingers wrapped around it tightly, needing to cling to something. I was so glad she hadn't cut the braid. She had changed. But her hair had not.

My left hand was wrapped in her braid and my right hand snaked around her waist and urged her up against me. And I felt it, the same old charge that had been there from the beginning. That same pull that had wreaked havoc on our lives . . . her life even more than mine. It was there, and I knew she felt it too.

Her nostrils flared and her breath halted. Her back was taut against my fingers and I splayed them wide, trying to touch as much of her as I could without moving my hand. Her eyes were fixed on mine, fierce and unblinking. But she didn't resist.

And then I bent my head and caught her mouth before she could speak, before I could think, before she could run, before I could see. I didn't want to see. I wanted to feel. And hear. And taste. But her mouth filled my mind with color. Just like it always had. Pink. Her kiss was pink. Soft, sunset pink, streaked with gold. The rosy blush swirled behind my eyes, and I pressed my lips more firmly against hers, releasing her hair and her body to hold her face in my hands, to keep the colors in place, to keep them from fading. And then her lips parted beneath mine and the colors became leaping currents of red and gold, pulsing against my eyes as if the soft sweep of her tongue left fire in its wake.

The color popped like a needle to a balloon as Georgia suddenly wrenched herself away, almost violently. And without a word she turned and fled, along with the colors, leaving me panting and drenched in black.

"Careful, Moses," I said out loud to no one but my sorry self. "You're about to get thrown."

MOSES

WITH ONLY THE ONE VEHICLE BETWEEN US, I had to take Tag back to Salt Lake the next morning. I spent two days away, one day clearing my schedule for the next month, and for those who were insistent on keeping their appointments, making arrangements to have them come to me in Levan. If the people weren't talking already, I'm sure they would be when I started holding painting séances in my grand-mother's dining room.

I spent the next day shopping at a furniture store to outfit the house with the bare necessities. I wasn't sleeping on the floor and sitting against the walls indefinitely, so I bought a bed, a couch, a table and four chairs, a washer and dryer, and a chest of drawers. I spent enough money that the furniture store gave me free delivery, even to Levan, and I gladly accepted. In addition to the furniture, I gathered some clothing, some painting supplies and blank canvases, and the picture I'd painted for Eli before I'd even realized who Eli was. I was going to give it to Georgia. She had shared her pictures with me. I was going to share my pictures with her, if she would let me.

The trip back to Salt Lake had been fruitful in other ways too. Eli was back. I'd seen him for a second in my rear-view mirror as I'd driven away from Gigi's house. I had turned back immediately, slamming on my brakes and yanking on the wheel, turning my truck around and drawing questions from Tag that I couldn't answer. But Eli hadn't reappeared, and I finally gave up and headed out of town once more, hoping that I hadn't just seen him for the last time. I thought I caught a glimpse of him the next morning from the corner of my eye, watching me as I loaded some of my paintings in my truck. And then, last night he'd appeared at the foot of my bed, just like the first time, as if leaving Levan had forced an intervention.

He showed me Calico running in the fields and Georgia reading to him and tucking him in, just like before, but he showed me some new things too. He showed me chicken noodle soup, the noodles so fat there was hardly any broth. And he showed me his toes curling in the dirt, as if he liked the way it felt. I knew they were his toes because they were short and childlike, and as I watched, he made his name above his toes with one small finger, tracing the letters carefully in the dark earth. Then I watched as his hands built a colorful tower, struggling to snap the Lego pieces one on top of the other.

It was the oddest thing, little snippets and snapshots of the life of a little boy. But I watched them, with my eyes closed, letting him pour the pictures into my head. I picked through the images, trying to understand him better. I didn't want to miss something important, though it all felt important. It all felt absolutely vital, every little detail. I fell asleep dreaming I was helping him erect a wall made out of a million colorful plastic bricks. A wall that would keep him from leaving for good, the way Gi had left for good.

GEORGIA

AFTER I LOST ELI, I would come out to the horses, and without fail, the horse I was working with would end up lying down in the middle of the corral. Sackett, Lucky, or any of the other horses. It didn't matter. Whichever horse I was working with or interacting with would lie down like they were too tired to do anything but sleep. I knew they were reflecting what I was feeling. The first couple of times it happened, I just laid down too. I couldn't change the way I felt. Self-awareness wasn't enough. The grief was too heavy. But as I forced myself to get back up, the horse would get back up too.

Throughout the first year, there were days when I couldn't get Calico to budge. He would just stand there, perfectly still, his back to the wind. I thought he was depressed because he missed Eli. But over time, I realized he was mirroring me. I wasn't lying down anymore but I wasn't moving forward either. So I'd started working a few more jobs, taking care of myself a little better, and trying to take steps, even if they were small. Even if it was just so Calico would run again.

In the last few months, my horses had started to crowd me, to nip at me and nuzzle me. I supposed they felt my need to touch and be touched. Any mother could tell you that a child invades her space from the moment of conception. And for years after, space does not exist. It was one of the things I had missed. I'd even yearned for it. And then Eli died, and I had all the space I had thought I wanted. Not just a little space. Outer space. Galaxies. And I'd floated in it in agony, longing for the days when there had been no such thing.

Now the horses were crowding me, taking the space away, and I welcomed their heavy bodies and nudging noses, the way they tripped me up and followed too close. It healed me even as I pushed at them and begged for room to move. They knew better. Apparently, my body was saying one thing when my lips said another.

I had let Moses kiss me. And in that moment I was guessing my body and my lips had said the same thing. Sure, I had pulled away. But not right away. I'd let him kiss me first. I had opened my mouth to him and kissed him back. And today the horses were crowding around me again like I was sending out a homing beacon. They were swarming me and they were restless, mimicking the buzz I felt beneath my skin, mirroring my nervous energy. Sackett wouldn't meet my gaze and hung his head as if he was guilty of something. Looking at him, I realized then that I was ashamed of myself.

I'd let Moses kiss me. And he had no right to kiss me. He'd asked me if I wanted him to go. I shouldn't have waffled. I should have demanded that he go. Instead, I'd let him in. And he'd kissed me like I was still the girl who had no pride and no rules where he was concerned. Now he was gone, and Kathleen's house was locked up tight. He'd been gone for two days. No explanation. No goodbyes. For all I knew, I wouldn't see him again for seven more years. I realized my lips were trembling and there were tears in my eyes, and Sackett suddenly laid his head on my shoulder.

"Dammit, Sackett. Dammit all to hell. It is time to make some new, stricter laws in Georgia. From now on, anyone named Moses is not allowed in. No visits, no crossing boundary lines. Nothing. No one named Moses is allowed in Georgia."

I'd spent the night before on my laptop trying to dig up every last piece of information I could on Moses Wright. He wasn't on Facebook or Twitter. But neither was I. We had established a website and Facebook page as well as a Twitter handle for our Equine Therapy Sessions, and I haunted social media under that cover. But when I googled Moses Wright, I was amazed at what I found. The BBC had done a special on him, and there were videos all over YouTube of his painting sessions with clients, although the camera was usually trained on his canvas, as if Moses wanted to keep his face from the screen. There was a *Times* article about him and about his ability to "paint for the dead," and *People* magazine had done a small feature about the "other-worldly brilliance of Moses Wright."

I realized then that he had made an impressive name for himself and he was a bit of a star, though it seemed he did his best to keep the lowest profile possible. What had Tag said, just in passing, about them traveling all over the world? Judging from the volume of information coming from all corners of the globe, I had no doubt it was the truth. There were hundreds of pictures of his paintings but few of him, though I did find a couple of shots of him at some gala for a hospital. He stood between Tag and another man, a man the caption listed as Dr. Noah Andelin. I found myself wondering again how Moses and Tag had ended up together. Their connection was deep, it was easy to see. And I realized something else. I wasn't just ashamed. I was jealous.

"You still talk to your horses."

I jerked and Sackett shifted, not liking the spike of energy that shot through me or the fact that my fingers had yanked at his mane.

Moses stood silhouetted in the barn door, holding what looked to be a large canvas in his hand.

I hadn't realized I was still talking to Sackett, and I did a quick examination of what I'd just said. I believe I had just uttered an embarrassing rant on Moses not being allowed in Georgia. Oh, Lord, I prayed fervently, you can make the blind man see and the deaf man hear, so it shouldn't be too much to ask to make this man forget everything he's just seen and heard.

"What does Sackett think about those new, stricter laws in Georgia?"

I looked up at the rafters, "Hey, thanks for comin' through for me, Lord."

I loosened the cinch that secured the saddle around Sackett's middle and pulled the saddle from his back, hoisting it onto the saddle horse and removing the blanket beneath without looking at Moses. I was kind of surprised that he remembered Sackett's name.

Moses took a few steps inside the barn and I could see a small smile playing around his lips. I gave Sackett a firm pat on his rump signaling I was done, and he trotted off, clearly eager to go.

"You're back," I said, refusing to embarrass myself further by getting angry.

"I took Tag home. He had big plans to train for his next fight old school, like Rocky, but discovered that it's a little more appealing in the movies. Plus, I don't do a very good Apollo Creed."

"Tag's a fighter?"

"Yeah. Mixed martial arts stuff. He's pretty good."

"Huh." I didn't know what else to say. I didn't know anything about the sport. "Didn't Apollo Creed die in one of the movies?"

"Yeah. The black guy always dies at the hands of the white man."

I rolled my eyes, and he grinned, making me grin with him before I remembered that I was embarrassed and ticked off that he had kissed me and left town. It felt a little too much like the past. The grin slipped from my face and I turned away, busying myself shaking out the saddle blankets.

"So why did you come back?" I kept my eyes averted. He was quiet for a minute, and I bit my lips so I wouldn't start to babble into the awkward silence.

"The house needs more work," he replied at last. "And I'm thinking of changing my name."

My head shot up, and I met his smirk with confusion.

"Huh?"

"I heard there was this new law in Georgia. Nobody named Moses can even visit. So I'm thinking a name change is in order."

I just shook my head and laughed, both embarrassed and pleased at his underlying meaning. "Shut up, Apollo," I said, and it was his turn to laugh.

"Good choice. Apollo it is. There aren't any laws in Georgia about guys named Apollo, are there?"

"No," I said quietly, still smiling. I liked this Moses. It was a Moses I had liked before too, the Moses who teased and taunted and pushed and prodded, setting my teeth on edge while making me love him.

"I brought you something," he said, turning the canvas around and holding it in front of him so I could see.

I could only stare.

"Eli helped me," he said, quietly.

I couldn't look away even though his words repelled me. I didn't want this Moses. I wanted the Moses who smiled and teased. I didn't want the Moses who talked about the dead as if he were intimately acquainted with them.

"I started seeing him for the first time after I saw you in the elevator at the hospital. I didn't know who he was. I didn't put it together, not until I stepped back from the painting and saw you, riding a horse, holding Eli against you. And still . . . I didn't understand. I just knew I had to come here and find you." He stopped talking then. We both knew what had happened next.

"I want you to have it," he insisted gently.

When I didn't move to take it, he set it gently against a stall and left me alone with the gift from my son.

XXIV

GEORGIA

E ACH DAY THERE WAS ANOTHER PAINTING. One was left on the front seat of my unlocked truck. One was propped up on one of the tack shelves in the barn. And they were all of Eli. Eli sitting on the fence, his face so sweet and serious I could almost remember a moment just like it, as if Moses had taken a photo and turned it into art. But he had no photos. I'd taken them back. And there were no photos that even came close to what Moses created—the detail in the curls of Eli's bowed head at bedtime reading the worn yellow storybook, the depth of his brown eyes fixed on his horse, Eli's little feet in the dirt and his finger carving his name into the mud. The swirling brushstrokes and vivid color were signature Moses—even the mud looked decadent— and I couldn't decide if I loved the paintings or hated them.

There was one of me. In it, I smiled down into Eli's upturned face, and I was beautiful. Unrecognizably so. It was the Pieta starring Georgia Shepherd, and I was the loving mother, gazing at my son. My mother found that one when she went out to rake leaves. Moses had left it sitting on our doorstep. I was two steps behind her, but she found it first. And she held it for five minutes, staring down at it in agony and wonder, tears running down her face. When I tried to comfort her, she gently shook her head and went back inside, unable to speak.

Moses returning had been incredibly difficult for my parents, and I had no idea how to make it better. I had no idea if I could. Or if I should. And I didn't know if his art was helping. But Moses's pictures were like that, glorious and terrible. Glorious because they brought memory to life, terrible for the same reason. Time softens memories, sanding down the rough edges of death. But Moses's pictures dripped with life and reminded us of our loss.

I remembered how Moses had talked about art, about anguish, and I knew then what he meant. His pictures filled me with sweet anguish, an anguish so ripe and red that it threatened to turn bad if I looked away. So I found myself staring at the pictures constantly.

Other than the paintings, left where I wouldn't miss them, Moses kept to himself and watched me from a distance. I would see him across the pasture, standing at the fence that separated Kathleen's back yard from our property. He would always lift his hand, acknowledging me. I didn't wave back. We weren't friendly neighbors. But I appreciated the gesture all the same. I wondered at the brazen kiss with his hand around my braid and at his teasing in the barn, and hardened myself against further contact, though he made sure I saw him every day.

Most of the time, when I was running therapy sessions, Mom or Dad would join me as another set of eyes, watching the horse while I kept my gaze on the folks or vice versa. But Dad had another round of chemo scheduled, and Mom was going with him. They were going to stay in Salt Lake for a few days with my older sister and her kids before heading back. Mom didn't want to leave with Moses back in the neighborhood. I just had to bite my tongue and remind myself that I had made the bed I was now lying in. Literally. I'd lived at home too long. I'd relied on my parents through Eli's life and Eli's death, and now, at twenty-four, it was my own damn fault that they still treated me like I was seventeen.

Surprisingly enough, it was Dad that convinced Mom that I'd survived Moses once and I would survive him again. I didn't especially like his choice of words, but I held my tongue. Dad had been awfully quiet since our morning conversation the day after my very first run-in with Moses. Eli's death was in the air again, the anniversary approaching and making us all cringe and hold our breath, wishing for it to pass us by. Moses coming into town this month, of all months, felt like an omen. And not a particularly good one. Mom was jittery, Dad was pensive, and I was a wreck, if I was being honest with myself.

It was probably a good thing that I had a few days to myself, that it was only me in the corral. The horses were tuned into me, and they didn't like my mood at all. It took me a good hour, brushing them down, cleaning their hooves, getting my head straight and working out my own stress before I conducted a session with a small group I saw every week.

But my angst returned in full force when Moses wandered over at the end of my class. I didn't want to draw attention to him or to myself, and when I realized he wasn't going to talk or interrupt, I finished the session and bid the group goodbye as they loaded back into the treatment center van and drove off. I returned to the corral, hoping Moses had gone, but he remained, as if waiting for me. When he saw me coming, he climbed down from the fence and walked toward me. His brow was furrowed, and I tried not to give any credence to the way my breath caught and my hands shook when I watched him approach. He still appealed to me on a very primitive level. And I didn't want that. I was afraid of it. I despised myself for it.

"He keeps showing me random things," he said, shaking his head, not even pausing for a greeting or small talk. That was just like the old Moses, and I didn't want to question him. I didn't want to know what he was talking about.

"Eli keeps showing me random things," he repeated, and I felt myself soften even as my heart lurched wildly. I could not resist the lure of Eli, of hearing about him, even if it was all a fairytale told by a man who I really wanted to hate.

"Like what?" I whispered, not able to help myself.

"His toes in the dirt, chicken noodle soup, Legos, pine cones, and Calico. Always Calico." He shrugged and stuffed his hands into his pockets. "What do you think he's trying to tell me?"

I suddenly found myself smiling. It was the oddest thing. It was the oddest and most wonderful, horrible thing. I was smiling and my eyes were filling with tears. I turned away, needing a moment to decide whether or not I was going to accept a new truth.

"Georgia?"

Moses waited for me to take several long, steadying breaths while I found my voice.

"Those are his favorite things. He's telling you his greats." My voice cracked and my eyes sought his.

His face went blank for a second and then his jaw dropped slightly as if a gong had sounded in his brain. He looked stunned. Flabbergasted even.

"His favorite things. He's telling me his greats," he repeated, almost to himself. "I thought he was trying to communicate something. Maybe teach me something." Then Moses started to laugh.

"What? What's so funny?" His baffled amusement was hard to resist, and I found myself smiling even as I wiped my eyes.

"That's what they're all trying to tell me. I never understood it before. The random items. The everyday stuff. It's always driven me crazy." He choked on the words, trying to speak around the mirth. And it really wasn't that funny. In fact, maybe it wasn't funny at all.

I just shook my head, still smiling at his wheezing laughter. "I don't understand."

"Do you know how many times I've painted a still life of the most mundane thing? Mundane things that never made sense, but that people, the dead, seemed to care about. Buttons and cherries, red roses and cotton sheets on the clothes line. Once I painted a picture of a worn-out running shoe." He clasped his hands over his head, the laughter abating as the truth seemed to sink in. "And I always just assumed it had this great meaning that I just couldn't grasp. The families love that stuff. They come see me, I paint whatever their loved ones show me. They leave happy, I make money. But I never understood. I've always felt like I was missing something."

I wasn't smiling anymore. My chest hurt and I couldn't decide whether it was joy or pain that made it ache.

"And I *was* missing something, wasn't I?" Moses shook his head.

He turned in a circle, almost as if he couldn't believe he'd just solved the puzzle that wasn't ever really much of a mystery.

"They're telling me what they miss. They're telling me their greats. Just like Eli . . . aren't they, Georgia?"

MOSES

THE PAIN WAS A ROLLING, all-consuming wave inside of me. It had started small. Just an ache in my back and a weakness in my legs. I ignored it, pretending I still had time. It was early yet. But as the hours passed and darkness fell, the heat from the street found its way into my belly, and I was ripping at my clothes trying to escape the searing pain. I was being burned alive. I tried to run from it when it paused for breath, and it would abate as if it lost track of me for a few minutes. But it always found me again, and the wave of pressure and pain would roll me under.

But worse than the pain was the niggling fear in the back of my jumbled brain. I'd prayed so hard, just like I had been taught. I'd prayed for forgiveness and redemption, for strength and for a chance to start over. And mostly I prayed for cover. But I had a feeling my prayers didn't rise much farther than the simmering air above my head.

It hurt. It hurt so much. I just needed it to stop hurting.

So I begged for a pardon. Just something to take me away for a minute, something to help me hide. Just for a minute. Just something that would give me one last moment of peace, something to help me face what came next.

But there was no cover granted, and when the fog lifted and the fever broke, I looked down into his face and knew my scarlet sins would never be as white as snow.

I came awake with a start, breathing hard, the pain of the dream still gripping my stomach and curling my legs and arms into my chest.

"What the hell was that?" I groaned, sitting up in my bed and wiping the sweat from my forehead. It felt like the dream I'd had about Eli and Stewy Stinker, the dream that wasn't a dream. And then I'd woken up and seen the girl, the girl Lisa Kendrick said was her cousin. She'd walked through my house and touched the wall. And I'd made the connection.

But I didn't see the connection yet. Not this time. I stood from my bed and stumbled to the bathroom, washing my face and throat with cold water, trying to ease the heat on my skin that always came with episodes like this.

It hadn't been my pain—in the dream—it hadn't been my pain. It had been a woman. A girl . . . and she was having a baby. Her thoughts and her agony and then the child in her arms as she'd looked down into his squalling face all indicated child birth. His squalling face? I suppose that was right. She'd thought of the child as a boy.

Maybe it was Eli, showing me his birth, the way he'd shown me his bedtime ritual. But that didn't seem right either. It hadn't been Eli's eyes I'd looked through. It hadn't been Eli's thoughts in my head. But nothing with Eli had been like any other experience I'd ever had. The connection was different. More intense, more detailed. More everything. So maybe it was possible.

But it didn't feel right. Eli showed me images and perspectives relative and relevant to his understanding. As an infant, being born into the world, he would not have had that perspective. It was Georgia's perspective. It was as if I was looking through her eyes, feeling her emotions, her pain. Her despair. She had been filled with fear and despair. I hated that. I hated that she had felt so alone. Eli should have been celebrated. But in the dream, there was no joy or celebration. Just fear. Just pain.

And maybe it was just a dream.

That was possible too. Maybe I wanted to rewrite history so badly that my subconscious had re-created a moment that fed into my guilt and my regret, putting me there, in the room with Georgia as Eli had come into the world. I mopped at the water on my neck and walked down the stairs without turning on any lights, needing a glass of water or maybe something stronger.

I'd left the lamp on in the family room. I'd sanded down the entire wall where the girl had revealed her face. Last night I'd painted it again, covering Molly and Sylvie and the other, nameless, somewhat faceless girls beyond them with a thick coat of yellow. I wanted yellow in the room. No more plain white. I was tired of white. I got a beer from the fridge and held the can against my face, eyeing the cheerful, buttery wall, thankfully devoid of any dead faces. For now. I would paint the other walls when morning came.

My eyes skipped to the side as my thoughts mentally moved on to the next section of painting that needed to be done. The paint was bubbled on the far wall.

"Ah, shit." I'd been afraid of that, afraid that the other walls would need to be sanded down too. But it had been more than a week since the paint on the back wall had begun to peel. The other walls had shown no signs of bubbling or peeling. I walked to the adjacent wall and smoothed my hand across the ripples. And just like that, the paint came off like tissue paper being unwrapped and pushed aside.

My mother's face stared out at me with sad eyes and a slightly wistful smile. And I knew who sent me the dream. It hadn't been Georgia's perspective in the dream, it wasn't Georgia's memory. It was my mother's.

MOSES

IT WAS STRANGE. I'd been painting frantically since coming to Levan, though I'd controlled myself, resisting abandoned buildings and barns and cliff faces, and limiting myself to canvas. Every day it was another painting about Eli. I couldn't stop. Some of them I left for Georgia, wanting to share them with her the way she had shared her photos with me. I was almost afraid she would come storming over and throw them in my face and accuse me of mocking her pain. But she never did. I almost wished she would, just so I would have an excuse to fight with her. An excuse to see her.

I had kissed her and then doubted the wisdom of the move for days afterwards. That kiss was like a living, throbbing pulse of fuchsia in my head. Maybe that's why I felt compelled to paint. Eli came and went, showing me the same fleeting images and bits and pieces of his life with Georgia. But for the first time, my painting wasn't for the dead. The painting wasn't even for Eli. It was for me. I wanted to make him permanent. And I wanted to give permanence to Georgia.

But the dream of my mother shook me, as did the walls that wouldn't stay painted. For several days I just worked on the house and left my art alone. I didn't want to start channeling my mother in my paintings. I sanded down the entire living room once more, retreating all the walls with everything 4D's, the hardware store in Nephi, had in stock for pre-treating old walls. The new coats of yellow seemed to be holding, and I moved onto other projects, keeping myself busy with physical work, doing what I could on my own and hiring the rest out, watching Georgia from afar and wondering how I was ever going to bridge the gulf between us.

I had temporarily stopped painting, though Eli hadn't stopped sharing pictures with me. But he had started showing me new things. Flowers. Clouds. Cupcakes. Hearts. Drawings pinned to the fridge with chunky magnet letters. They were still things he loved, as far as I could tell. The images were fleeting and focused. Fat red hearts, cupcakes piled with white fluffy icing, and flowers that I wasn't sure even existed beyond a little boy's imagination. They were riotous and multi-colored, a garden of Dr. Seuss blooms. I didn't think these were his greats. This time I was pretty sure he really was trying to tell me something. I found myself talking to him, to the boy who danced in and out of my vision, never staying long, never making a whole lot of sense, but I talked to him anyway, hoping my limitations were not his.

I spent a Saturday removing the tub, toilet and sink in Gigi's old bathroom telling Eli about the first time I'd seen Georgia. I was little. Not as little as Eli. But young. Maybe nine or ten the first time I really remembered her. She had stared at me, just like the other kids at church. But her gaze had been different. She had watched me like she was dying to talk to me. Like she was wishing she could make me talk to her. And she smiled. I hadn't smiled back. But I had remembered that smile.

Eli answered with an image of Georgia, smiling, holding him in her arms, swinging him around and around until they both collapsed onto the grass and let the world spin above their heads. I took his memory to mean he hadn't forgotten her smile either.

So then I'd told Eli about the first time Georgia actually did talk to me. How Sackett had reared up in the barn and knocked her to the ground. How it had been all my fault. I told Eli I knew then that Georgia wasn't safe with me.

Eli's response baffled me. He showed me Georgia, crying his name, her face distorted with horror as she looked beneath the truck the day he died. It was the very last memory Eli had of his mother's face before he left the world.

"Eli? Don't do that!" I shoved my fists over my eyes and cried out, banging my head against the newly installed sink. I physically and mentally pushed back, not understanding why Eli would want me to see that again.

He stopped immediately, but I was shaken. I swore and paced for a minute rubbing my head, trying to ease the throb and clear the horrible image. And then my words came back to me.

I'd told him Georgia wasn't safe with me.

And Eli hadn't been safe. Even with the person who would have gladly died in his place. And she would have. Gladly. I knew that. And I think Eli knew that. I rubbed the back of my head, looking at the little boy in black and blue pajamas, standing so close I should be able to touch him, but couldn't. And he stared back, keeping his pictures to himself as I pondered the fact that maybe none of us are safe. Not truly. Not even from the people we love. Not even from the people who love us.

"So cupcakes . . . hearts . . . flowers. What's the deal, Eli?"

I saw Eli, his grubby hands gripping some ugly, half-bald dandelions, handing them to his mother, and Georgia, exclaiming over them like his arms were filled with roses. Then I saw a little, silver pie tin filled with mud, being presented with a happy giggle. And again, Georgia oohing and ahhing over the offering, even pretending to take a giant, muddy bite.

The pie tin dissolved into a new thought, and Eli was drawing hearts. Misshapen wobbly ones that looked more like upside down tri-angles with boobs than actual hearts. He was drawing them in every color on a white sheet of paper, signing his name in crooked letters, and handing it to Georgia, a declaration of his devotion.

The images switched off abruptly, and I was left staring at Eli, holding the wrench in my hand, still rubbing the back of my head. A huge goose egg was forming.

"Oh, I see." I grimaced, chuckling. "Flowers, cake, hearts. You're giving me advice. Very nice." I laughed again. "I gave her some pictures, but I'm guessing you think I should do more."

I saw myself, arms around Georgia, kissing her. My breath caught and I watched as if someone had caught us on film. Her hands clutched my arms as I took her mouth. I watched as my hands traveled up her back and framed her face. She didn't pull away, and for several long seconds, she didn't let go. In fact she kissed me back, her eyes closed, her head bent under mine.

"Eli . . ." I breathed, wondering how in the world I was ever going to kiss Georgia again if Eli had soaked it all up, every detail, without me even knowing he was there. When I'd kissed Georgia, I'd been afraid Eli would never return. But he had definitely seen me kiss Georgia.

And he'd seen Georgia run away from that kiss as I stood staring after her, dazed.

"Okay, buddy. That's enough."

I called down the waters on Eli's little demonstration, not especially wanting his romantic input, and as my mental walls went up, I lost him, finding myself alone in the old house, muttering to myself, considering how I was going to implement Eli's ideas . . . without him watching.

XXV

MOSES

THERE WASN'T MUCH TO DO IN LEVAN unless you rode horses. Or four wheelers. Or enjoyed the great outdoors. Or had friends. Since I didn't, on all accounts, I ended up watching Georgia more often than not. Sometimes I watched from an upstairs window, hoping she couldn't see me. Sometimes I watched from Gi's old deck as I sanded it down, giving me an excuse to surreptitiously track her as she worked with horses and people, day in and day out, usually in the big round corral. It seemed she'd picked up where her parents left off, doing the work they'd once done. And it suited her.

Her skin was tan and her hair bleached even blonder by the sun. Her body was long and lean—strong arms and legs and hands that were slim-fingered and firm on the reins. All of her was long . . . her hair, her legs, even her patience. She never seemed to lose her focus or her temper with the horses she worked with. She pushed and prodded and coaxed and wore them down. And she was wearing me down all over again. I couldn't take my eyes off her. She wasn't the kind of girl who should ever have appealed to me. She wasn't my type. It was the argument I'd had with myself when I'd come to Levan almost seven years ago and seen her, all grown up, laughing and riding and taunting me until I had to be close to her. She had focused in on me that summer, as if I was everything she had ever wanted. And that singular intensity had been my undoing.

Our son had that same quiet intensity. He often sat close by, perched on the fence, as if his spirit remembered the posture, though he had no physical form to make it necessary. He stared at his mother, at the horse she trained, and I wondered if Eli had come to visit his mother this way often. I wondered if the relationship between animal and woman, woman and child merged together in the quiet corral and created an oasis of comfort and peace that tamed all who entered there.

It was odd, seeing the woman and her child and knowing she was completely unaware that he was there with her, watching her, hovering over her like her own little guardian angel. I put down my tools and wandered over to watch her as she worked, wanting to be near her, to be near them, even if she would rather I stayed away.

When I climbed up on the fence near Eli, he didn't seem to be aware of me, as if he was caught between worlds. But Georgia was aware of me, and she stiffened slightly, as if she considered running away, and then she straightened her back, and I knew she was telling herself that it was her "damn property and Moses can go to hell." I could see it in the lift of her chin and the jerk of the rope in her hands. It made me smile. Luckily, she didn't tell me to go to hell. She didn't even tell me to leave.

So I sat, my eyes on the woman and the horse she wooed, but before too long, Eli's memories became so loud, I had no choice but to listen in.

"How do horses talk, mommy?"

"They don't talk, baby."

"Then how do you know what he wants?"

"He wants the same things you want. He wants to play. He wants loves. He wants to eat and sleep and run."

"And he doesn't want to do his chores?"

"No. He doesn't want to do his chores."

I saw her face as if I was looking down at her from atop the horse, and she smiled up at me sweetly, laughter in her voice, her hand on my leg. Not my leg. Eli's leg. Eli was showing me the memory. He must have been riding and Georgia must have been leading him around. The light was the same, sunset coloring the western hills, the corral bathed in a soft golden haze, the ground dappled with shadows and sunlight. I shook myself, trying to separate the scene in my head from the scene in front of me, but Eli wasn't finished.

"Does Calico love me?"

"Of course!" Georgia laughed, but Eli was very serious.

"I love her too. But how do I tell her if she doesn't talk?"

"You show her."

"How do I show her? Do I make a big heart with my arms?" Eli curved his small arms in a shape that slightly resembled a smashed heart. He teetered a little in the saddle and Georgia reprimanded him gently.

"Hold on, son. And no. I don't think Calico would understand if you made her a heart. You show her you love her by how you treat her. You take care of her. You spend time with her."

"Should I pet her a lot?"

"That would be good."

"Should I bring her apples to eat? She likes carrots too."

"Not too many. You don't want to make her love sick."

"Moses!"

Georgia stood below me, her hands clinging to my legs as if to keep me on the fence, and I was teetering the way Eli had when he raised his arms to make a heart. I gripped the nearby post and slid down inside the corral, my body brushing against Georgia as I did. We both jumped, but neither of us gave ground. The horse she was working with, Cuss, had strolled to the other side of the corral, and we were alone. Alone with the sunset and the horses and Eli's memories.

"Holy crap! Don't do that! I thought you were going down!" Her face was so close I could see the specks of gold in her brown eyes and the little groove between her brows that indicated her concern. I stared too long and watched as the groove of concern became a scowl.

"Moses?" she asked doubtfully.

I lifted my eyes from her face and saw Eli, still perched on the fence, his curls lifting in the soft breeze as if the wind knew he was there and welcomed him home.

"He's here, Georgia. And when he's near, I kind of get lost in him."

Georgia jumped back as if I'd produced a snake and offered it to her. But her eyes scanned the nearby area as if she couldn't quite help herself.

"Thank you for not letting me fall," I added softly. I felt disoriented, still feeling the dizzying effects of being in two places at once. Eli's memories carried me away completely, and returning to the present was jarring. It was unlike anything I'd ever experienced, the little windows into his life, so complete yet so insufficient. I wanted to stay in his head all day. I wondered suddenly if horses and girls spoke the same love language, and I knew instinctively that Eli was trying to help me with Georgia, telling me how to woo her.

"Is he still here?" Georgia asked, interrupting my thoughts.

She didn't have to tell me who 'he' was, but her question took me by surprise. I didn't know when she'd started believing me, but I wasn't going to argue about it. I looked back where Eli had been perched and discovered that he was gone. He had the attention span that was probably typical of a four-year-old, and he flitted in and out without warning. I shook my head.

"No."

Georgia almost looked disappointed. She gazed beyond me, past the corral to the hills that squatted west of Levan. And then she surprised the hell out of me.

"I wish I had your gift. Just for one day," she whispered. "You can see him. And I'll never see him again."

"A gift?" I choked. "I've never thought of it as a gift. Not ever," I protested. "Not once."

Georgia nodded, and I knew she hadn't considered it a gift either. Not until now. In fact, she hadn't ever known what to think. I'd guarded my secret and let her believe I was crazy. Deranged even. The fact that she now seemed to believe me, at least to some extent, made me giddy and nauseated all at once. And I owed her as much honesty as I could give her.

"For the first time in my life, I'm grateful that I can part the waters. That's what Gi called it, parting the waters. I'm grateful, because it's all I'm going to get. This is all Eli and I get. You got four years, Georgia, and this is all I get." I didn't say it angrily. I wasn't angry. But she wasn't the only one who was suffering, and sometimes there is comfort in the knowledge that you don't suffer alone, sad as that is.

Georgia bit her lip, flinching, and I knew what I was saying wasn't easy to hear.

"Do you remember that girl I painted on the underpass?" I said, trying to be as gentle as I could and still explain."Yeah." Georgia nodded. "Molly Taggert. She was just a few years older than I am. They found her, you know. Not long after you left town. Someone killed her."

I nodded too. "I know. She was Tag's sister."

Georgia's eyes widened, and she stiffened abruptly, as if she had suddenly put it all together. But I didn't want to talk about Molly. Not right now. And I needed her to listen. I reached out and tilted her chin toward me, making sure she heard. "But you know what? I don't see Molly anymore. She came . . . and she went. That's how it is every time. Nobody hangs around very long. And one day, Eli will go too."

Georgia flinched again, and her eyes filled with tears that she valiantly tried to hold back. We stood there, neither one speaking, each of us battling the emotion that had buffeted us from the moment our eyes met in a crowded elevator nearly a month before. Georgia was the first to give, and her voice shook as she gave me honesty in return.

"I cry every day. Do you know that? I cry every damn day. I never used to cry. Now, not a day goes by that I don't find myself in tears. Sometimes I hide in the closet so I can pretend it isn't happening again. One day, I'm going to have a day when I don't cry, and part of me thinks that will be the worst day of all. Because he will truly be slipping away."

"I never used to cry either."

She waited.

"In fact, that was the first time."

"The first time?"

"Out there, in the field. The first time I remember crying . . . over anything, ever." I'd pulled the waters down to make it all stop, to hide the image of Georgia's horrified face screaming Eli's name, and for the first time, the waters had spilled from my eyes.

Georgia gasped, and I looked away from her incredulous face, and felt the waters tremble and shift inside me and start to rise again. What was happening to me?

"You think your tears keep him close?" I whispered.

"My tears mean I'm thinking about him," she whispered back, still standing so close to me I could have leaned forward and kissed her without taking a single step.

"But all your memories can't be sad. None of his are. And you're the only thing he thinks about."

"I am?"

"Well, you and Calico. And Stewy Stinker." She laughed, a wet hiccup that she swallowed back. She stepped back abruptly, and I knew she was getting ready to pull away.

"So do what you used to do. When you need to cry, do what you used to do." There was a desperate note in my voice.

"What?" Georgia asked.

"Give me five greats, Georgia."

She winced. "Damn you, Moses."

"I've been thinking about it since you told me Eli was showing me his favorite things. You would be surprised how many times I caught myself making little lists of good things over the last seven years. And it was all your fault."

"I was such a pain in the ass, wasn't I?" She laughed again, but there wasn't much mirth in the short expulsion of air. "I drove you nuts. Buzzing around you like I had it all figured out. I didn't know anything. And you knew I didn't know anything. But you liked me anyway."

"Who says I liked you?"

She chuckled, remembering the conversation from the long ago day by the fence.

"Your eyes said you liked me," she answered bluntly, the way she would have once. And then she nervously tucked a loose strand of hair behind her ear like she couldn't believe she was flirting with me.

"Come on. Five greats."

"Okay. Um. Man, it's been a long time." She was silent for a minute. I could tell she was really searching. She rubbed her palms against her jeans, as if she was trying to wipe away the discomfort that was written all over her face, all over her body.

"Soap."

"Okay." I tried not to smile. It was such a random item. "Soap. What else?"

"Mountain Dew . . . with ice and a straw."

"This is pathetic," I teased softly, trying to goad her into a smile. She did smile a little, just a twist of her lips, but she stopped rubbing her hands.

"Socks. Cowboy boots without socks would suck," she announced, a little more confidently.

"I wouldn't know. But yeah. I can see that," I agreed, nodding.

"That's five," she said.

"We aren't counting ice and straws. They came with the Mountain Dew. Come on. Two more."

She didn't argue about the disqualification of two of her "Five Greats," but she was silent for a long time. I waited, wondering if she was done playing. Then she took a deep breath, looked at her hands, and whispered, "Forgiveness."

A burning ache rose in my throat that was both foreign and instantly familiar.

"Yours . . . or mine?" I asked, needing to know. I held my breath, trying to hold back my emotion and watched as she tucked her hands in her pockets and seemed to gather her courage.

"Both," she answered. With a deep inhale, she met my gaze. "Will you forgive me, Moses?"

Maybe she was seeking forgiveness for Eli because she hadn't yet forgiven herself. But I didn't blame her for Eli, I loved her for Eli, and I wanted to tell her there was nothing to forgive. But that wouldn't be the truth either, because I had other things to forgive. No one had ever wanted me, starting from the day I was born. But Georgia had wanted me. And because she had wanted me when no one else did, I had immediately been suspicious. I had immediately distrusted her. And I had always held it against her.

"I forgive you, Georgia. Can you forgive me?"

Georgia nodded, even before I finished asking. "I already have. I didn't realize it. But I've had a lot of time to think over these last couple of weeks. I think I forgave you the moment I saw Eli. The moment he was born. He was such a work of art. Such a little masterpiece. And you created him. We created him. How could I not love you, even just a little bit, when I saw him?"

I didn't trust myself to speak. So I nodded, accepting her forgiveness. And she smiled. I was too emotionally raw to smile back, afraid that parting my lips, even just a little bit, would re-open all my old cracks. So I touched her cheek, softly, gratefully, and let my hand fall back to my side.

"That's five greats then, Moses," she said. "Your forgiveness. And mine."

MOSES

I DIDN'T LET THAT FORGIVENESS go to waste. I brought flowers. I fixed dinner and bought cupcakes. And I kept drawing pictures. Not hearts, but pictures. I didn't think hearts were subtle enough. Georgia's parents were gone, which made it easier, and three evenings in a row, I found myself at her front door. And she always let me in. I didn't stay as long as I wanted. I didn't kiss her. But she let me in. And that was all I could ask for.

I'd gotten her permission to draw a mural in the indoor arena that had been added onto the barn. In the winter, all her therapy sessions and classes would be held there, and I wanted it done before the weather turned. The mural was similar to the mural on her bedroom walls. Georgia said her work was about transformation, and she thought the story of the blind man freeing himself through the use of the horse was perfect for what she and her parents did.

I was bent over, mixing paint when Georgia slid up behind me and thwacked my rear end, hard, causing me to lurch and sloshing paint on my shoe.

"Did you just slap my ass?" I rubbed at it, completely offended, more than a little surprised.

"It was in my way. And it's kinda hard not to look at."

"It is? Why?" My incredulous voice squeaked in a very unmanly way. Eli was watching us, his little shoulders hunched, his hand covering his mouth like he was laughing. I wished I could hear him. I wanted to slap Georgia's butt right back, but thought maybe this whole interplay wasn't really appropriate for my son to watch—and the thought made my heart turn in my chest.

"It's a great-looking ass. That's why," Georgia didn't sound particularly happy about it, honestly. But she sounded like herself, like the Georgia who was a little wild, more than a little blunt, and full of life.

"It is?"

"Don't sound so surprised. I love the way you look. I never could resist you. You were like crack to me."

"Your own little crack baby?" I grinned, thrilled that she couldn't resist me, and that she was admitting it.

I had a sudden image of Georgia tickling Eli as he howled with laughter, trying to get away from her. He managed to squirm free, but came right back and went on the attack, concentrating his little fingers on her rounded behind as she fled. She shrieked as loud as he had done, swatting at his pinching hands.

"Stop, you little stink! My butt is ticklish!"

Eli wrapped his arms around her waist and sank his teeth into her left butt cheek, which was right at eye level, and Georgia screamed and laughed, flopping onto her bed, yanking him up by his armpits, until she had him locked in her arms. His face was flushed with laughter, his curls floating with static electricity, as they giggled and tickled, each trying to gain the upper hand. Georgia tried to be serious once, saying, "You cannot bite my butt, Eli, it isn't appropriate," in a very stern voice, but they both collapsed back into snorts of laughter almost immediately.

"Moses? You're doing it again," Georgia said, mildly.

I looked back at her, the memory Eli had shared leaving a smile on my face.

"You're spacing off. Day dreaming again."

"I was thinking about your ass," I responded, truthfully. I walked toward her, ignoring my dancing angel boy who trotted along beside me.

She laughed right out loud, and I caught her around the waist with one arm and began to tickle her in earnest.

Eli had the best ideas.

We fell over in the straw piled against the wall separating the barn from the arena, and Georgia fought back, squealing, trying to tickle me too. But I wasn't especially ticklish, and before long I had her breathless and begging, shouting my name. It was the best sound in the world, and it definitely didn't make me feel like laughing.

"Please, stop!" she shouted, clinging to my hands. There was straw in her hair, straw in my hair, and we were flushed and untucked and generally looked like we'd been up to a lot more than tickling when her dad came strolling through the barn.

Well, shit.

The look on his face had me dropping my hands and stepping away, recognizing the fury stamped all over his features for exactly what it was. I was in trouble—even Eli fled in terror, there one minute, gone the next, the warm stream connecting us suddenly dried up. Georgia's back was to her father, and when my hands dropped she stumbled a little, grabbing at me. I gently set her aside, but I let her father come without protest or warning.

I didn't even lift my hands. I could have. I could have easily dodged the clumsy fist that connected with my jaw, but I took it. Because I deserved it.

"Dad!" Georgia shoved herself up between us. "Dad! Don't!"

He ignored her and stared into my eyes, his chest heaving, his mouth hard, his hand shaking as he pointed at me.

"Not again, Moses. We let you in. You ransacked the house. And worse, there were casualties. This isn't happening again."

He looked at Georgia then, and the look of disappointment he leveled at her was far worse than the anger he'd directed at me. "You're a woman, Georgia. Not a child. You can't act like this anymore."

She deflated right before my eyes.

"You hit me all you want, Mr. Shepherd. I had that coming. But don't talk to Georgia that way. Or I'll kick your ass."

"Moses!" Georgia's eyes flashed, and her spine was straight again. Good. She could be angry at me. Anger was better than defeat.

"You think you can come in here and get away with murder again? You think you can just get away with it?" Martin Shepherd said, outrage making his voice hoarse.

"None of us are the same people we used to be, Mr. Shepherd. I was one of those casualties, too. And I didn't get away with anything. Neither Georgia nor I got away with a damn thing. We've paid. Just like you've paid. And we'll all keep on paying."

He turned in disgust, but I saw his lips tremble, and I felt bad for the man. I wouldn't like me if I were him. But it was better that we air it out.

"Mr. Shepherd?" I said softly. He didn't stop. I thought about what Georgia had given me. I thought about the five greats. About forgiveness. And I passed it along.

"I'm sorry, Mr. Shepherd. I am. And I hope someday you can forgive me."

Georgia's dad missed a step, stumbled, and stopped. There was something powerful about that word.

"I hope you can forgive me. Because this is happening. Me and Georgia. This is happening."

XXVI

GEORGIA

I SPENT THE AFTERNOON in the small indoor arena conducting an equine therapy class with a group of kids with behavioral problems that were brought down from Provo, about an hour north of Levan. It was a smaller group than usual, maybe six people at the most, and all of them people I'd spent time with before. As I finished up the sun was starting to set and Moses was finishing up in the indoor arena. I'd followed my dad out of the barn after the awkward blow-up that morning. I'd needed to make sure he was okay and I'd needed to catch my breath.

"This is happening. Me and Georgia. It's happening," he'd said. And my heart had done a fat somersault and landed with a slosh in my churning stomach. It was happening. I believed him. And I was suddenly a little scared. So I'd left, following my poor dad out of the barn to help him come to grips with seeing his daughter engaging in tickle games and Moses being back in my life. But that was yesterday and now, here we were, alone in the quiet of the indoor arena. I'd just finished conducting a class and Moses was painting the long wall that connected the arena to the stable, and I wasn't sure what to say.

"You're good at that, you know. I heard some of it. You're impressive," he said easily, and I stared at him blankly, not sure what he was referring to. My brain was still stuck on tickling and the emotional conversation with my dad.

"The therapy. The kids. All of it. You're good," Moses explained with a small smile.

The praise pleased me, and I turned my face to hide my pleasure. I was way too easy. Too needy. I didn't like that about myself very much. But Moses seemed genuinely interested, asking me questions about this and that until I found myself talking freely about what I did while I removed the horses saddles and brushed them down.

"Horses reflect the energy of the people in the session. Did you see how down Joseph was? How quiet? Did you see how Sackett stuck his head in there and practically laid it on his shoulder? And did you see how aggressive Lori was? She gave Lucky a little push and he pushed her right back. Not hard. But then he stayed in her space. Did you see that? It's subjective, I get that. But there's something to be said for going head to head with a 1200 pound animal, moving it, leading it, riding it. It's incredibly empowering for people who have relinquished the power in their lives to drugs, alcohol, sex, illness, depression. Or in the case of kids . . . to those who have power over them, to those who control their lives. We work with autistic kids a lot. The horses unlock those kids. Everything that's bottled up seems to loosen up. Even the movement, the gentle rocking motion, connects with people on an elemental level. It's the same motion we feel when we walk. It's like we become one with something so powerful, so big, that for a moment we take on that sense of supremacy."

"I thought you were going to be a vet. Wasn't that the plan?" Moses asked quietly, cleaning his brushes as I finished up with the horses.

"I grew up watching my parents work with animals and work with people. And after Kathleen died and you left, I didn't want to do rodeo anymore. I didn't even want to be a vet. I wanted to figure out how to unlock you, just like I saw so many others be helped."

"Unlock me?" Moses looked shocked.

"Yes." I met his gaze frankly, but I couldn't hold it. Honesty was hard. And incredibly intimate. "So that's what I did. I got a degree in psychology. And then I got a master's degree on top of that." I shrugged. "Maybe one day you'll have to call me Dr. Georgia. But to tell you the truth, I'm not interested in doling out prescriptions. I'd rather just train horses and help people. I don't know how I would have survived the last two years without my work."

He was quiet for a minute, and I didn't dare look at him.

"Are horses really that smart?" he asked, and I gladly let him change the subject. I didn't especially want to talk about myself.

"I think smart is the wrong word, although they are intelligent. They are incredibly aware. They mimic, they react. And we only have to watch them to find clues about ourselves. And because of that, horses can be powerful tools. A horse will run a half mile out of blind fear. Nothing else. They aren't thinking while they run. They're just reacting. Dogs, cats, people— we're all predators. But horses are prey. Not predators. And because they're prey, they are instinct-based, emotion-based, fear-based. They are very in tune with heightened emotion, wherever it comes from. And they react accordingly."

Moses nodded, as if he was buying what I said. He walked toward me and the horses didn't react at all. He was calm. They were calm.

"Come here," I insisted, beckoning him closer. I suddenly wanted to show him.

"Georgia. You remember what happened last time," Moses protested, but he kept his voice soft.

"Hold my hand."

He reached forward and slipped his fingers through mine, palm to palm, and I took a step toward the horses.

"Are you afraid, Moses?" It made me think of that first time, when I'd taunted him to pet Sackett. But I wasn't taunting him. Not at all. I wanted to know how he was feeling.

"No. But I don't want them to be afraid." He looked at me. "I don't want you to be afraid."

"I'm not." I answered immediately. I heard Lucky whinny behind me and Sackett snorted as if he doubted the veracity of my claim.

"You are," he said.

"I am," I admitted on a sigh. "This is important to me. So I'm nervous." And as soon as I owned it, the fear left me. I reached for his other hand so that we stood facing each other, our hands locked.

"We're just going to stand right here, and you're going to hold my hands," I said.

Moses put his chin down on his chest and took a deep breath.

"What?" I asked softly.

"I feel like a child. I don't want to feel like a child with you."

"I don't see you that way." Truer words were never spoken. His hands engulfed mine and the contact was heady, almost to the point that I wanted to close my eyes so the room wouldn't spin.

"Okay. Then I don't want you to see me as someone you need to fix."

I shook my head, but I felt the swell and pull of grief expanding my chest and stinging my eyes and was grateful for the shadowed arena that we stood in the center of. The sun was almost down and light dappled the perimeter with soft squares of sunset gold, but the center where we stood was dark and I could feel the horses behind me waiting, patiently waiting, always waiting. Their soft huffs and knickers were a solace to me.

"I never wanted to fix you. Not ever. Not the way you mean."

"How then?"

"Back then, I just wanted you to be able to love me back."

"Cracks and all?"

"Don't say that," I protested, hurting the way I always did when I thought about the way his life began.

"It's the truth, Georgia. You have to come to terms with who I am. Just like I did." His voice was so low and soft that I watched his lips so I wouldn't miss anything.

Again, I felt the horses behind me. I felt them shift and then I felt a soft nudge at my back, and then again, stronger.

"Calico wants you to move closer," Moses breathed. I stepped closer. Calico nudged once more, until my body was separated from Moses by only a few inches. Calico brought her head past my shoulder and huffed softly, her breath lifting the loose hair around my face. Moses's eyes were wide, but his breath was steady and his hands stayed still and loose around my own. Then Calico moved around us and brought her body up flush against Moses's back. And she stood with her head down, her eyes half-closed and her body still. Moses could feel her there, but he couldn't see her. I felt the tremor in his hands and watched him swallow as his eyes moved past mine to where Sackett hovered nearby. And then Sackett was at my back, the side of his body pressing into me, supporting me, as if he and Calico had aligned themselves head to tail to keep the flies at bay. But Moses and I stood in between, sheltered by their massive bodies in the quiet shadows of the rapidly falling dusk.

"Can I ask you something?" I whispered, my heart pounding so hard I wondered if he could feel the vibrations in my hands.

"Sure." His voice was as soft as mine.

"Did you ever love me?" Maybe it was unfair to ask, with two 1200 pound truth detectors pinning us between them, but I couldn't hold the words back any more. "I loved you. I know deep down you don't really believe I did. You don't believe I could. But I loved you."

"Georgia." My name was almost a groan on his lips and I felt the tears spill over my eyes and hurry down my cheeks, eager to be free of the pressure that was building in my head. And then his arms were around me, drawing me up into him as if drawing strength from the Paint at his back.

"Why didn't you stay away from me?" he choked. "I told you so many times to go away. But you wouldn't. You wouldn't let me be. And I hurt you. I created this situation. I did. Do you know that I have lost every person I love? Everyone. And just when I started to hope, to think maybe things could be different with you, Gi died. And she proved me right. And I wasn't going to let you get anywhere near me. I was in a mental hospital, Georgia! A mental hospital. For three months. And I wasn't going to let that touch you. I wasn't trying to hurt you. I was trying to save you. I didn't come back because I was trying to save you . . . from me! Don't you get that?"

I shook my head fiercely, hiding my face in his chest, letting the soft cotton of his T-shirt mop up my tears. I hadn't understood that. I had thought he was rejecting me, pushing me away like he always did.

I hadn't understood. But now I did. And the knowledge swept up all my broken pieces and sealed them once again. There was healing in his words, and I wrapped my arms around him too, holding him as he held me, abandoning resistance. His body was hard against mine, firm, solid, welcome, and I let myself lean into him in a way I never had, comforted and confident that he wouldn't let me fall. The horses shifted, and I felt Sackett shudder as if he acknowledged my relief. Calico whinnied softly and brushed her soft nose across Moses's shoulder, and I realized then that I was not the only one trembling.

"Thou shall paint. Thou shall leave and never look back. Thou shall not love." Moses spoke against my hair. "Those were my laws. As soon as I was free, out of school, out of the system, I was gone. I wanted nothing more than to paint and run. Paint and run. Because those were the only two things that made life bearable. And then came you. You and Gi. And I started thinking about breaking a law or two." My heart was thundering against my chest as he forced the words out, and I pressed my lips together so the sob building in my throat would not break free at the wrong second and muffle the words I desperately wanted to hear.

"In the end, Georgia, I only broke one. I loved," he said simply, clearly, unequivocally.

He loved.

And just like that, Calico shifted and drifted away, lumbering toward the last rays of sunshine spilling through the far door that led out to the corral. Sackett followed behind her, moving slowly, his long nose snuffling along the ground as he moseyed, leaving me and Moses alone, wrapped in each other's arms as if their work here was done.

"Who are you, Moses? You aren't the same. I never thought there was any way I could love you again." There were tears streaming down my face, but I didn't wipe them away. "You didn't know how to love. I don't know what to do with this Moses."

"I knew how to love. I loved you then. I just didn't know how to show you."

"So what happened?" I asked.

"Eli. Eli happened. And he is showing me how," he answered softly. He didn't raise his head from my hair, and I was grateful. I needed a moment to find my response. I knew if I looked at him with pity or fear, or even disbelief, what we were building would crumble. And I knew then, if I was going to love him, really love him, not just want him or need him, I was going to have to come to terms with who he was.

So I pressed my lips against Moses's neck and I whispered. "Thank you, Eli."

I heard Moses's swift intake of breath and he held me tighter.

"I loved you then, Georgia. And I love you still."

I felt the words as they rumbled through his throat, and then I brought his mouth to mine so that I could savor their aftertaste. Nothing had ever tasted so sweet. He lifted me in his arms and I wrapped myself around him—arms, legs, old Georgia and new Georgia. And with one arm anchoring my hips and one arm banded across my back, Moses kissed me like he had all the time in the world and no place in heaven or hell he'd rather be. When he finally lifted his head and moved his lips from my mouth to my neck I heard him whisper,

"Georgia's eyes, Georgia's hair, Georgia's mouth, Georgia's love. And Georgia's long, long legs."

XXVII

GEORGIA

I WORKED OFF EXCESS ENERGY by running in the evenings, but when I went for my runs I didn't want to stop and make small talk, nor did I want people seeing my boobs bounce or making snide comments about my farmers tan in my running shorts. My arms and face were brown from working outside almost every day, but I wore Wranglers to work, and my legs weren't even close to the same shade. Maybe all small towns were like Levan, but people made note of the littlest things, people noticed and commented and talked and shared . . . so I avoided the town and ran down through the fields, past the water tower and up past the old mill when I couldn't sleep. And tonight I couldn't sleep.

With my parents home again and things changing rapidly between Moses and me, I was anxious and unsettled. I wanted to be with Moses. Simple as that. And I was pretty sure that's what he wanted too. But just like that summer seven years ago, Moses and I were hurtling forward at the speed of light, going from forgiveness to forever in days. And I couldn't do that again. My dad was right about that. I was a woman now, a mother—or I had been. And I couldn't act like that anymore. So I'd said goodnight to Moses and gone home early like a good little girl. But I wasn't happy about it. It was definitely time to be moving out of Mom and Dad's place.

I ran hard and I ran fast, the mini flashlights I carried in each hand streaking back and forth as my arms pumped a steady rhythm. My parents didn't like me running alone, but I was too old to be asking permission to exercise, and the only danger in the fields came from skunks and distant coyotes, and the occasional rattlesnake. I'd had to hurdle one once. It had been dead. But I hadn't known that until I'd seen it, still in the same spot, the next night. The skunks weren't deadly and the coyotes were scared of me, so other than the snakes, I wasn't too nervous.

The moon was so full my flashlights were unnecessary, and as I neared the old mill, heading into mile three of my five mile loop, the soft white sky backlit the old place and I studied it with new eyes. The old mill looked exactly the same. I wondered why Jeremiah Anderson had hired Moses to clean it out and pull down old partitions and demo interior walls if nothing was ever going to be done with it. The windows were still boarded up and the weeds were taller, but there wasn't seven years of growth and neglect around the place. Someone was keeping an eye on it.

Whenever I ran by, I remembered the desperation I'd felt the night before Thanksgiving seven years ago, the night I'd waited outside for Moses before chickening out and leaving him a note. But I always ran on by, ignoring the sense of loss, the old longing. But now, with Moses back and hope on my horizon, I found myself stopping for a minute to catch my breath instead of running past. Since seeing the face peeking out of the peeling paint on the wall in Kathleen's house weeks ago, I had been thinking about the walls at the old mill, about Moses's paintings. Something was niggling in the back of my brain. I didn't know if they were still there—brilliance hidden in a dark, dusty old building, boarded up where no one could see them. Someday, someone would want to see them. For me, someday was now. I picked my way through the old parking lot to the back door Moses had always used, sure that it would be locked up tight.

I checked the back service door and it was locked, just as I thought, just like it had been when I checked it that night. But when I checked above the door frame the key was exactly where Moses had always left it when he finished up each day. I fingered it, incredulous, and then slid the key into the deadbolt above the handle and turned it, still not believing it would actually open the door. But the door swung open with a screech of tired hinges, and without hesitation, I stepped inside. I don't know why I couldn't leave it alone. But I couldn't. Now I was here, I had my flashlights, and there was something I wanted to see.

Beyond the back door was a cluster of small offices and then a larger room that was probably a break room of some sort. It was much darker inside without the moonlight spilling over everything, and I held my flashlights extended like twin light sabers, at the ready to take out anything I might come across. The deeper inside I went, the more it changed. The interior was different. Moses had torn down all the smaller workstations in the warehouse portion, and I paused, swinging the lights in large circles, trying to get my bearings. The paintings had been along the back wall, in the corner farthest from the main door, as if Moses had tried to be discreet.

The thought made me chuckle a little. Moses had been anything but discreet. Moses's stint in Levan that six months in 2006 had been the equivalent of a never-ending fireworks display—all color, crash, the occasional small fire, and lots of smoky residue.

I kept my lights moving in big swaths, forward and out and back again, making sure I didn't miss anything. The light in my right hand shot past something huddled against the far wall and I jumped, dropping the light and then kicking it toward the shadowy figure as I scrambled for it. It rolled in an arc, the heavier end rotating around the lighter handle. When it stopped it sent a stream of light in the direction I was headed, illuminating nothing but the concrete floor and a pair of legs.

I shrieked, clutching at my remaining light and shooting it up and around so I could see what I was dealing with. Or who. The light touched on a face and I screamed again, making the light bobble and glance off yet another bowed head and then an upturned chin. The fear became giddy relief as the faces remained motionless and I realized I'd found Moses's paintings, complete with dancing forms and intertwined bodies spread across a ten by twenty foot section of wall. I stooped and picked up my flashlight, grateful that my clumsiness hadn't robbed me of the additional light.

It was almost whimsical, the painting. And it was much more cohesive than Moses's smeared, terror-filled depictions on Kathleen Wright's walls. The terror had been in Moses's hand, not in his subjects, if that made any sense. He had been terrified, and it showed in every brush stroke. This was different. It was a cornucopia of delights, full of oddities and wonder, little puzzles and pieces all interspersed throughout the nonsensical display. And it *was* nonsensical. It brought to mind our discussion of favorite things and well-loved memories, and I wondered if I was simply seeing the five greats, multiplied by a dozen contributors who were also depicted on the wall. I trained my light on each part, trying to connect it with the next, wondering if it was just the darkness and the difficulty of illuminating the entire thing all at once that made it seem so new. I remembered some of it. But he'd clearly added more after the fact. I had seen it in October. He'd left at the end of November. And in that time his painting had grown.

And then I found her. The face that had stuck in my mind and bothered me throughout the last two weeks.

I centered both of my lights above her face so I could see her better, and she gazed down at me reproachfully, light spilling down over her head like she wore a biblical halo. I felt a little sick and more than a little shaken as I realized I did know her. It was the same face I'd seen on the newly painted wall the day I'd gone to retrieve my photo album from Moses. Maybe it was the angle or the expression on her face, but where the image had seemed merely familiar on Kathleen Wright's wall, it was recognizable now. I had known her. Once.

The sound of old hinges being engaged ricocheted around the mostly empty space, and for a split second I couldn't place the sound. Then I realized the back door, the door I'd come through only minutes before was being opened. I'd left the key in the lock.

MOSES

THE LEVAN CHURCH was a cool old building with light colored brick, soaring steeple, and wide oak doors built in 1904. There had been some renovations done in the intervening years, and I thought it could use some stained glass, but I liked it. It always made me think of summers with Gi as a kid and the sound of the organ, peeling out over the community as I ran out the double doors and headed for home, eager for movement, desperate to be free of my tie and my shiny black church shoes.

I was restless. Anxious. I hadn't seen Georgia since the day before, and other than a quick text message, complete with my five greats for the day and her smiling emoticon for a response, we hadn't interacted.

I had a client come all the way to Levan for a session, and I'd spent the day painting a woman asleep at her desk, her hand clutching a pair of reading glasses, a messy pile of books nearby. Her mouth was slightly open, her hair gently curling against her cheek as she rested her pretty face on her slim arm and slept. The man who had commissioned me had told me how she often fell asleep that way, among her books, nodding off to dream land and never making it to their bed. His wife had died suddenly the previous spring, and he was lonely. Rich and lonely. The rich and lonely were my best clients, but I felt for him as we'd talked, and I hadn't been as brusque or as blunt as usual when I had communicated the things I could see.

"I didn't see the signs. All the warning signs were there . . . but I just didn't want to see them," he'd said. The woman had died of heart failure, and he was sure he could have prevented it if he'd been more proactive.

He'd left without his painting, which was the norm. I had some finishing touches to add and it needed a few days before it would be dry all the way through and I could send it to him. But he'd left happy. Satisfied, even. But I wasn't happy or satisfied, and I set off on a walk I didn't want to take in hopes of ridding myself of the excess energy that hummed beneath my skin. And I wanted to scout out Georgia's house and see if she was around. I shot her a message with no response and ended up swinging past the church, the dry leaves scurrying around my feet like a mouse battalion, racing across the road as the wind caught them and pushed them onward.

My client had talked about a snow storm coming. But the night wasn't especially cold, and it was still October. But Utah was like that. Snow one day, sunshine the next. The homes around the church were decorated for Halloween—ghosts twirling in the wind, fat pumpkins resting on porches, bats and spiders crawling up windows and hanging from trees. And when the organ started up, it was so Halloween appropriate I jumped a little and then cursed myself when I realized what I was hearing.

The lights were on at the church and a dark colored pick-up was parked close to the chapel doors. I stopped to listen and within a few bars knew exactly who was playing. I walked up the wide steps and pulled at the big oak door, hoping it was open, hoping I could sneak in the back and slide into a pew and listen to Josie play for a while. The door swung wide with a well-oiled sigh and I stepped into the rear foyer, my eyes immediately falling on the blonde at the organ and the man in the back row, closest to the foyer, listening to her play something so beautiful it made the hair rise on my arms and chills shiver down my spine.

I recognized him as the man in the cemetery, Josie's husband, and I slid into the end of the pew he was sitting on. He was sitting right in the center, his arms stretched out on either side, his booted foot crossed at the knee, his dark eyes on his wife. When I sat down he turned those eyes on me and nodded once, a barely perceptible movement, and I decided I liked him just fine. I didn't want to talk either. I wanted to listen.

The music was so beautiful, so sweet, that I wished Eli was here, just so I could look at him while I listened, but he'd kept his distance all day, and I found I missed him, and the music made me miss him even more. When Josie was done with the piece, she looked up from the keys and shaded her eyes a bit with her hands. Only the dais was lit, casting the rest of the chapel in shadows and she called out to me in her sunny way.

"Moses? Is that you? Welcome! Samuel, this is Moses Wright, the artist I told you about. Moses, my husband, Samuel Yates. Don't worry, Moses, Samuel won't bite."

Samuel leaned toward me, stretching out his right hand, and I stood and walked toward him until I could clasp it in my own. I sat back down a few feet from him, and Josie immediately started playing something new, leaving me and Samuel to make our own small talk, which neither of us seemed especially inclined to do. But he intrigued me, maybe because he seemed so comfortable with himself, so in love with his wife, and so at odds with this town we were both connected to. When he began to speak, I welcomed it.

"Are you here to paint?" he said simply. He had the slightest hint of something exotic in his voice. A cadence or a rhythm that made me think his native tongue was Navajo. Or maybe it was just his presence. The man definitely had a vibe going. I imagined he could be damn intimidating, but people had said the same thing about me.

"No. Just to listen."

"Good. I like the walls the way they are." There was a hint of humor there and I smiled, acknowledging it.

"Does she do this often?" I inclined my head toward the organ.

"No. We don't live here. My grandfather died a few weeks ago. We came back for his funeral and to help my Grandma Nettie with a few things. We're heading back to San Diego tomorrow. Josie does this for me. I fell in love with her in this building. Sitting right here, on this bench."

His candor surprised me.

"I fell in love with her here too," I said softly, and his eyes snapped to mine. I shook my head. "I was ten. Don't worry. Her music just made church a little more bearable. I had my eye on another little blonde, even back then."

"Georgia Shepherd is a damn fine horsewoman," he said. So Josie had told him about me and Georgia too.

"She is."

285

"My grandpa was a dyed-in-the-wool old-timer. Rodeo, ranching, women-belong-in-the-kitchen kind of man. But even he had to admit she was something else. Georgia rides like my Navajo grandma. Fearless. Beautiful. Like music." He nodded toward Josie and the music she coaxed from the keys. We sat, listening for several minutes before he spoke again.

"I'm sorry about your boy." His tone was simple, his voice hushed, and it was all I could do not to bow my head and weep. I met his eyes instead, and nodded.

"Thank you."

I found Samuel's simple condolence as overwhelming as it was welcome. Eli was my boy. And I'd lost him. His loss was fresh. His loss was recent. For me, he hadn't died two years ago. He'd died three weeks ago. For me, he'd died in the field behind Georgia's house as she told me about that terrible day, as I'd seen it all happen. And somehow, this man had given me the validation I didn't know I needed.

"You've come back to make things right." It was a statement not a question.

"Yes."

"You've come back to claim what's yours."

"Yes," I agreed again, softly.

"I had to do the same. I almost missed my chance with Josie. I almost lost her. I thought I had time. Don't make that mistake, Moses."

I nodded, not knowing their story, but wishing I did. I listened to the music for a moment longer and then stood, unable to sit still any longer, even with the beauty of the music and the quality of the company. I needed to see Georgia. I extended my hand once more toward Samuel, and he stood too, before he took it solemnly. He was tall like I was, and our eyes were level as I shared my own condolences.

"I'm sorry about your grandfather. You will miss him. But he's okay. You know that, don't you?"

Samuel tipped his head, considering me. I wished I'd left that last part off. But I could feel his grandfather's presence like a warm blanket, and I wanted to thank Samuel in the only way I knew how.

"Yes. I believe that. We are glad he's not suffering anymore. We knew it was coming and we were able to prepare."

My heart started to pound and my palms were sweating. I felt the anxiousness I'd felt all day flood my arms and legs as the words of Samuel and my client clanged in my head—*I almost lost her, I thought I had time. We knew it was coming. I didn't want to see the signs. All the warning signs were there.*

I ran out of the church, down the stairs, not caring whether Samuel and Josie Yates now thought I was as crazy as all the rumors claimed I was. I ran across the grass and sprinted toward home, trying not to consider what all the signs actually meant.

I thought Eli was there for me. I thought he was there to bring me back to Georgia. But I was back and Eli hadn't gone. Eli still hovered around. He still hovered around Georgia. Just like my great-grandfather had hovered around Gi in the days before she died. Just like the dead had hovered around the kids in the cancer unit. Just like that.

What if Eli had come for Georgia?

And then there was the girl. The blonde girl. All the blonde girls. All the dead blonde girls. Georgia was blonde. Even my mother, my mother had tried to warn me. All the signs . . . I'd seen them, and I hadn't wanted to see them. I should have known! This was my life, it had always been this way.

I ran, berating myself, terrified, until I reached Georgia's house. I flew past her little truck, up the walk, and pounded on her door like the mad man I was. When no one immediately came to the door, I ran around the side to the pair of windows I knew belonged to Georgia's bedroom. For all I knew, they'd remodeled the interior and I was going to get an eyeful of something unwelcome, but I was desperate. I pressed my face against the window and tapped, hoping someone, anyone, would hear. I could see through the slats on the blinds. The mural I'd painted so long ago leapt out at me in dizzying color and I wondered how Georgia had ever gotten a decent night's sleep in that room.

"Georgia!" I yelled, frantic. A small lamp on the bedside table was on but no one was in the room. I ran back around to the front yard, determined to go inside, whether the door was opened to me or not.

Georgia was staggering up the walk in a pair of running shorts and a sweatshirt, her long hair swept up in a messy ponytail.

"Moses?" The relief in her voice matched the relief in my limbs, and I crossed the grass in three strides and grabbed her, wrapping her in my arms and sinking my face in her tousled hair, not caring whether I was overreacting. I had never been so relieved to be wrong.

"I was so afraid—" we said in unison. I pulled back slightly and stared down at her.

"I was so afraid," she began again, and I moved one arm from around her back so I could smooth the hair from her face. She had a streak of something along one cheek, and her eyes were wide and her teeth were chattering. I realized she was shaking, and her arms were clamped around me as if she was trying to keep from falling.

"Georgia?" Mauna Shepherd stood in the doorway of her home with a rolling pin gripped tightly in her hands. I wondered briefly if she was baking or if she had actually grabbed it to defend herself against the man banging on her door.

"Are you okay, Georgia?" she asked, her eyes flying between us.

"Yeah, Mom. I am. But I'm going with Moses for a while. Don't wait up." Georgia's voice was steady, but her body continued to shake, and I was gripped by fear all over again. Something had happened. I hadn't been completely wrong.

Mauna Shepherd hesitated briefly and then nodded at Georgia.

"Okay. You know what you're doing, girl." She turned her attention my way. "Moses?"

"Yes ma'am?"

"I've had all the heartache I can take. Give me joy or go. Do you understand?"

"I understand."

"Good. And time would be good too. Give us all a little time. Especially Martin."

I nodded but didn't speak. But time was not something I was going to agree to. Time had never been my friend. And I didn't trust her.

XXVIII

GEORGIA

I LEFT MY ARMS AROUND MOSES as we walked and he didn't press me to speak, keeping his left arm tight around my shoulders, his lips pressing into my hair every few steps. Something had happened. Not just to me, but to Moses too, and I could not stop the tremors that kept rolling down my spine. We made it to the front porch and I suddenly couldn't face the inside of the house. I knew Moses had painted; I was sure he'd fixed the peeling section. He'd been working on the house since he'd arrived weeks ago. But I was afraid of the face on the wall.

"It's cold, babe," Moses said softly when I held back, urging me to go inside, and the endearment nibbled at my control.

"Let's just sit for a minute, okay?" I whispered, sinking down on the stoop. The wind was inconsistent, gusting up for a moment before it laid its head back down and decided to rest. It reminded me of trying to get Eli to go to sleep as a toddler. He never wanted to give up, and he would try desperately to keep moving, up until the last second, and then he'd take a little cat nap, only to revive himself enough to sit up and try to play once more. Tomorrow it would be two years since I'd lost him and the memory should hurt, but I found I loved the soft comfort of random reminders.

"I haven't cried today," I realized suddenly, and Moses gave in and sat down beside me, his size and heat making me curl against him and lean my head on his shoulder. He ran a big hand over my hair and left it cradled against my face. I turned my cheek and kissed his palm and felt him shudder. Then he wrapped both of his arms around me so I could bury my face in his chest and he could rest his head on my hair.

"If you keep being sweet I will break my new record," I whispered. "And I'll cry again."

"Crying from sweetness doesn't count," he whispered back, and I felt the moisture prick my eyes, just as I'd predicted. "Gi used to say happy tears watered our gratitude. She even had a cross-stitch that said as much. I thought it was stupid." I could hear the smile in his voice.

"Ah . . . so Gi was a believer in the five greats." I pressed my lips against his throat, wanting to get as close to him as I could.

"Gi was a believer in all good things," he rubbed his cheek softly against my hair, nuzzling me.

"Especially you."

"Even me," Moses said, lifting his hand to my chin. "What happened, Georgia? Why were you afraid?"

"I did something stupid. Got spooked. Ran home like a scared little girl."

"Tell me."

"Nah. It's nothing. But you were scared too. Why?"

Moses shook his head, as if he didn't quite know how to start.

"I feel like I'm missing something. Or losing something. Or maybe it's just the fear of never having it at all. I lost Eli before I even knew he was mine. And part of me is sure that history is going to repeat itself. There are patterns, Georgia, and . . ." he stopped as if he couldn't explain, and I could hear the note of desperation in his voice.

"This is happening, Moses," I whispered, reminding him of what he'd said. "You and me? It's happening."

He smiled a little and leaned his forehead against mine. "It's cold. Come in. Be with me for a while," he whispered, a note of urgency in his tone that made me shiver. And it wasn't from the chill in the air.

I wanted to. I needed to. But I couldn't get her face out of my head.

"The girl . . . the girl you painted on the wall in there?" I said, my voice as hushed as his was. I turned my head to stare at the front door, thinking about the walls beyond. "I recognized her."

"Molly?" he asked. I could tell I'd surprised him, baffled him even.

"No. Not Molly. The girl behind Molly."

Moses was quiet for a minute and then he stood, pulling me up with him. Holding my hand firmly in his, he pulled me behind him into the house. I let him, my legs shaking and my heart quivering. He pulled me through the house until we stood in the center of the room, looking at the walls that were in various stages of sanding and repainting. Her face was still slightly visible. Moses looked at it soberly and then tipped his chin so he was staring down at me. His green eyes were hooded. Worried. And I drank him in, unwilling to stare too long at the girl who looked out from the wall.

"Lisa Kendrick, the girl who cleaned my house, told me her name is Sylvie. Her cousin," Moses said. "She apparently disappeared the summer before I came to live with Gigi. She wasn't from around here, though. Lisa said she lived in Gunnison, I think."

I nodded, my heart sinking. "I didn't know her name, but . . . I remember her. She was in a therapy class my parents taught and then she stopped coming. I heard my parents talking about it, but I didn't realize it was because something happened to her. There's a 90 day program in Richfield for kids with substance abuse problems. She was one of those kids. I thought she looked familiar when I saw her face on the wall the day I came to get my photo album. And it bothered me."

Moses stiffened as if he knew I was gearing up for something else.

"I remembered your paintings at the old mill. I run by there all the time. You painted her there too, Moses. The paintings are all still there," I finished in a rush, and watched as his eyes widened. He looked past me, as if he was trying to pull old details from the recesses of his brain.

"I didn't even know the owner of the mill. Gi set the job up for me, arranged it all. And I just showed up and got paid, although I didn't actually get paid, come to think of it." He shrugged. "I meant to paint over the mural. I told myself I would. But . . . time ran out on me, I guess."

The thought seemed to make him anxious, and he frowned at me. "I can't believe they're still there. And I can't believe you went inside, all alone, in the dark."

"I didn't think it through. And it just kept nagging at me, you know? I thought the girl looked familiar. But I didn't know if it was because she was just a cute blonde like all the other girls have been."

"They've all been blonde?" Moses asked, but it sounded like he was seeking confirmation more than information.

"As far as I know. Yes."

"How many have there been?" Moses breathed, stunned. "I only drew three."

He'd drawn more than that . . . but the other girls didn't have faces.

"Mom and Dad were talking with Sheriff Dawson last July when the girl from Payson went missing. All told, there's been quite a few. Eight or nine. And that's over the last ten or twelve years. I don't know before that, and Sheriff Dawson seemed to think there could be more outside of Utah."

"And they think they are all connected?" Moses sounded resigned, like he knew what I was going to say.

"All blonde. All around the same age. All missing from small Utah towns. All disappeared during a two week span in July."

"You're blonde," Moses said grimly. Quietly.

I waited for him to continue. His lips were drawn into a hard line, and his eyes were glued to mine.

"Someone tried to take you, Georgia. That summer. July. Someone tried to take you. I think that person ran right past me. He bumped into me, Georgia. Your grandfather was the reason I came back to find you. I saw him standing on the side of the road. And he showed you falling. So I went back. And I saw him at the fairgrounds, just like I'd seen him in the barn and in the corner of your room while I painted."

"He was in the corner of my room?" I squealed in alarm.

"He showed me what to paint. The images on your bedroom walls are the way he saw the story. Haven't you ever noticed the man who becomes a horse resembles your grandpa? He saw himself in the story, the way we all see ourselves in the characters we love. It was his way

292

of watching over you. And I liked the idea. He had watched over you before."

I stared at him, oddly touched and more than a little freaked out. I couldn't decide what emotion to go with when I suddenly remembered what Moses had said about Tag being Molly Taggert's brother. It was so bizarre, that connection, that I couldn't believe I'd forgotten about it.

"Molly Taggert?" I prompted.

"Molly, the girl named Sylvie, and you! You fit the profile, Georgia," Moses stood abruptly and began to pace. "I got scared tonight. It all started coming together! I'm seeing her—Sylvie—I've seen her twice now. She won't let me cover her damn face! I've sanded that wall three times and it will be good for two or three days and then the paint puckers right there over her face! And I'm guessing it's because of Lisa. The thing is . . . Lisa didn't live here when I did. I didn't know Lisa. So I had no reason to paint Sylvie. I had no reason to paint Molly either, for that matter. I didn't meet Tag until after I left Levan! And I have no idea who the other girl is. Or was!" Moses was ranting and pacing, and my head was spinning.

"So what do you think it means?" I asked. He stopped pacing and scrubbed his hands over the stubble on his skull. I imagined it was soothing and wished I could hold him close and do the same, but he wouldn't hold still.

"The only thing I can think of is that I came in contact with the person who killed them. The connection is to the killer. Not to their family members. Their family members just bring them back . . . so to speak," Moses mused, and he looked at me desperately. "And that person wanted you."

"Maybe . . ."

Moses shook his head adamantly. "No. It's the only thing that makes any sense."

"Or maybe it was just Terrence Anderson," I finished flatly. Time for the rest of the story.

Moses stopped pacing and eyed me warily.

"I was at the mill tonight, back in the corner, looking at your paintings, feeling more than a little freaked out when I realized I knew that girl, when I heard the door open. The door I'd just come through. I squatted down, turned off my flashlights, and crawled along the wall toward the entrance, thinking I could kind of circle around." I looked down at my hands and realized how filthy they were. My knees too. In the soft lamplight, my legs looked like Eli's used to look every single night when I'd put him in the tub.

"Who was it?" Moses wasn't pacing anymore.

"Terrence." I shivered. And it had freaked me out until I had a chance to think it through. "His family owns that mill. They have for 100 years, actually. Terrence's dad inherited it from his father when Mr. Anderson Sr. died a few years back. From what I could tell, they are just using it for storage. They have a generator in there though, and when Terrence flipped a light on, one of those tall free-standing things they use at construction sites, I was completely exposed. But he was facing another direction and stacking stuff in the opposite corner and I crawled out while his back was turned. He left the door propped open and his pick-up running outside. His truck is one of those big diesel trucks, and it's loud. That, combined with the propped open door made it easy to walk right out without him hearing me. Otherwise the door would have given me away. It squeaked like the gates of hell."

Moses swore under his breath and squatted down in front of my dirty knees as if to inspect me for injuries. I was probably looking pretty scary now that we were inside and there was no moonlight to soften my edges.

"Do you think Terrence would have hurt you if he'd seen you?"

"No. I don't. I just didn't want him to catch me trespassing. And he still gives me the willies. Always has."

Suddenly Moses stood and scooped me up in his arms, making me squeal and wrap my arms around his neck as he strode through the kitchen and climbed the stairs exactly the way John Wayne scooped up Maureen O'Hara in *The Quiet Man*, my favorite movie of all time, and I protested just as loudly as she had.

"Moses!" I yelped, "What are you doing?"

"I'm going to run you a bath." He said simply, and plopped me down on the toilet seat as if I wasn't a 5'9", 140 pound woman, entirely capable of running my own bath. In my own house. He leaned over and started the water in what appeared to be a brand new tub. It was deep and free-standing with curving sides and big brass legs. The whole bathroom was new and decidedly feminine. It didn't look like what Moses would choose at all.

"That is a great tub," I blurted out, my eyes on the steam and the bubbles building beneath the heavy flow as Moses dribbled something in the water.

"I thought you'd like it," he answered simply. "It's yours, you know."

"What?"

"The whole house. It's yours. If you want it. If you don't, I'll sell it, and you can use the money to build something you like better."

I stared at him numbly. He stared back and then straightened from the tub, shaking the water from his hands and wiping them on his jeans. He gently began unwinding the elastic that held my hair off my face, though pieces were already falling free. My hair was heavy and the elastic was tight, so when he pulled it loose and ran his fingers through the strands, releasing the tangles and soothing my scalp, I sighed gratefully and closed my eyes.

"I want to take care of you, Georgia. I can't take care of Eli. But I can take care of you."

"I don't need that, Moses. I don't need someone to run my baths or carry me up the stairs, although I'm not complaining." I wasn't complaining at all. His hands in my hair and the steam rising up around us made me want to pull him into the brand new tub, fully clothed—or not—and fall fast asleep, warm and safe and more contented than I'd ever been.

"I don't want your house, Moses," I said softly.

His hands stilled in my hair.

"I thought you did."

I shook my head, and his hands tightened against my scalp. He was quiet for several seconds, but he didn't move away, and his fingers continued to sift through my hair, smoothing it down my back.

"There's nothing wrong with the house, Georgia," he said at last.

"Is that it? It's not haunted. Places aren't haunted. People are. I am." His tone was resigned, and I looked up at him with the same acceptance.

"Nah. That's not it, Moses. I don't want your house. I just want you."

XXIX

MOSES

I LEFT HER IN THE BATHROOM, heat and scent seeping beneath the closed door. I could hear the soft swish and lap of the water moving as she moved, and I found myself with a paint brush in my hand, staring out into the dark from the window in my old upstairs room, taking note of the light still shining from the windows at Georgia's house, hoping her parents weren't in a mild state of panic that she was here with me. A truck idled on the corner between our houses, a big diesel truck like the one Georgia had described Terrence Anderson driving. The thought sent the same sick dread curling in my stomach that I'd felt as she'd told me about crawling along the dirty floor so he wouldn't see her.

As I watched, the truck pulled away and ambled down the road, turning at the next block where my eyes couldn't follow. Even with the intrusion of Terrence Anderson, my mind continually tiptoed to Georgia on the other side of my wall. I could imagine upswept hair and long limbs spilling over the white porcelain of the tub, dark lashes on a smooth cheek, full lips softly parted, and I resisted the urge to start painting all the little details my mind readily supplied. If Vermeer could find beauty in cracks and stains, then I could only imagine what I could create from the pores of her skin.

If I only knew how to paint Georgia into my life, or how to paint myself into hers without overwhelming her, then maybe the trepidation I felt would melt away. I would never be easy to love. There were some colors that overpowered all the others, some colors that didn't blend.

But I wanted to try. I wanted to try so badly it made my hands shake and the brush fall from my fingers. I snatched it up and walked to the easel set up in the corner, the canvas calling to me, and I began to mix a little of this, a little of that. What had I told Georgia so long ago? What colors would I use to paint her? Peach, gold, pink, white . . . . there were fancy names written on the little tubes I bought in bulk, but I kept it simple in my head.

A sweeping brush stroke brought the line of her neck to life on the canvas in front of me. Then the little ridges along her slim spine, the pale curl on golden skin. But I gave her color too, a dapple here and there, pink and blue and coral, as if there were petals in her hair.

I felt her come up behind me, and I paused, breathing her in before I turned my head and looked down at her. She had donned her running shorts again, but had abandoned the dusty sweatshirt and wore a slim white tank top and nothing on her feet.

"I wanted to paint you," I said, by way of explanation.

"Why?"

"Because . . . because," I scrambled for a reason that didn't include her holding still and letting me stare at her for long periods of time. "Eli wants me to paint you." It wasn't exactly a lie.

"He does?" her voice was faint and she peeked at me almost shyly. It was strange to see her that way. Self-conscious in a way she'd never been.

"I seem to remember you wanting me to paint you. Before."

"I wanted a lot of things, Moses."

"I know." And I was determined to give them to her. Anything and everything within my power.

"Did Eli like to paint?" I'd never asked her if he was anything like me. I hoped not.

She began to shake her head and then she stopped and laughed. And just like that, I could see the memory of a forgotten moment, just a glimpse as if I had looked inside her head. But it wasn't coming from her. Eli sat cross-legged in the window seat and smiled like he had missed me. Missed us. And Georgia's eyes grew soft as she narrated the scene, without even realizing I could already see it in living color behind my eyes.

"It was late. I'd been up since dawn and hadn't stopped all day. Eli was crying, Mom and Dad were out, and it was way past bedtime. Eli still needed his dinner and a bath, and I was ready to cry with him. I warmed up some leftover spaghetti and opened a can of peaches, trying to soothe Eli who wanted chicken noodle soup for dinner.

"He wanted homemade soup with the fat noodles. But I told him we didn't have any more and that I'd make homemade soup on the weekend. Or Grandma would. Hers was better than mine. And I tried to make him happy with leftover spaghetti.

"But he didn't want it, and I wasn't very patient. I settled him at the table and made him a plate, trying to convince him it was exactly what he wanted every step of the way. I set a glass of milk in front of him and filled his favorite tractor plate with noodles and sauce on one side and sliced peaches on the other."

She stopped and her lips trembled a little. But she didn't cry. And Eli picked up where she left off. Eli showed me the moment he'd taken his plate and dumped it over his head, sauce and peaches pooling in his hair, sliding down his chubby cheeks and dripping down his neck. Georgia had just stared at him, stunned. Her face was almost comical she was so incensed. Then she sank to a puddle on the kitchen floor and started naming the things she was grateful for, the way some people count to ten to try to keep from exploding. Eli knew he was in trouble. His concern colored the memory in a hazy wash, as if his heartbeat had kicked up while he watched his mother try not to come unglued.

The view changed as he climbed down from his chair and trotted over to Georgia. He squatted down in front of her, and without missing a beat, rubbed his hand through the spaghetti sauce in his hair and wiped it on her cheek, very, very gently.

She reared back, sputtering, and he followed her, wiping his hand down the other cheek.

"Hold still, Mommy. I'm painting you," he demanded. "Like my dad."

Georgia froze and Eli continued rubbing his ruined dinner all over her face and arms as if he knew exactly what he was doing. She watched him silently, and her eyes slowly filled with tears that ran down her face and over the globs of spaghetti sauce and smeared peaches.

"He wanted to paint me," Georgia said, and I separated myself from Eli's memory so I could be with her in the moment. "He wanted to paint me. Just like you. He knew your name. He knew you painted the story on my wall, he knew you painted the picture I framed and hung in his room, the picture you sent me . . . after you went away. But that was the first time he did anything like that. Or said anything like that."

I didn't know what to say, the knowledge that Georgia hadn't withheld the knowledge of who I was from Eli left me speechless.

"That was right before he died. Right before. A day or two. Strange. I forgot all about it. He'd never shown any inclination to paint, yet he pulled that out of the blue. But I don't think I want you to paint me, Moses," Georgia whispered, her eyes on the graceful spine and the bowed head I'd just begun to create."No?" I didn't know if I could honor that request. With her so close, all I wanted to do was trace the lines of her figure and lose myself in her colors.

"No." She kept her eyes trained on the painting. "I don't want to be alone. I'd rather you paint us. Me and you." She lifted her gaze to mine. "Together."

I pulled her in front of me, her back against my chest so that she faced the canvas, and I began to draw, her head notched between my shoulder and my chin, my cheek resting against her forehead , my left arm wrapped across her chest, my right arm raised to the task at hand. Within minutes, I brought my profile into the picture, just my face and neck, bowed above hers. It was rudimentary, just outlines and suggestions, but it was still us, and my hand flew, filling in the details of the two of us together.

I forgot about Eli, sitting on my new bed, the bed I'd purchased to replace the narrow twin I'd slept in whenever I'd visited Gi, and lost myself in the sensation of Georgia close to me and the picture in front of me. And when Georgia turned in my arms and looked up at me with shining eyes, I forgot about the picture too.

I don't remember putting my paintbrush down or whether or not I screwed the lids back on my oils. I don't remember exactly how we got across the room, or how midnight became morning. I just remember how it felt to close the distance and bring my mouth to hers.

The kiss wasn't hard or fast. It didn't involve wandering hands or practiced seduction. But it was promise-laden. Heartfelt. And I didn't move to make it more.

I could have.

It shimmered there between us, the memory of how it had felt to fall headlong into the heat. But I didn't want more memories. I wanted a future, so I let the soft hue of hope wrap itself around us. I reveled in the sensation of mouths moving, lips touching, tongues tangling, the feel of Georgia's hands curled against my chest, the glide of color against my eyelids as the kiss deepened from lavender to purple, to midnight blue. And when it did, I lifted my head so that I wouldn't forget completely. Georgia's mouth stayed lifted as if she wasn't finished, her eyes like dark chocolate and her lids at half-mast. I wanted to dive back into those dark pools and pull the covers over us. But we weren't alone.

And as I looked beyond her rumpled hair and sweet mouth to the child who quietly observed, I sighed and bid him a soft farewell. Time for little boys to turn in. I tugged on my watery walls and whispered as I did.

"Goodnight Stewy Stinker."

Georgia stiffened in my arms.

"Goodnight, Buzzard Bates," I added gently.

"Goodnight, Diehard Dan," Georgia said quietly, and her lips trembled as her fingers twisted in my shirt, trying desperately to hold onto her composure. My arms tightened around her, acknowledging her faith and her effort.

"Goodnight, Eli," I said, and felt him slip away.

MOSES

I LAY IN THE DARK, listening to Georgia breathe beside me, and hoped Mauna and Martin Shepherd didn't lay awake across the way, worrying about their daughter who had loved and lost before. Give me joy or go, she'd said. And I really didn't want to go.

Georgia and I had talked for several hours, lying in the darkness of my room, watching the moonlight illuminate the stick figure story Georgia had drawn on my wall. Georgia seemed pleased that I didn't have the heart to cover it up and promised to draw the next chapter the following morning. With her head on my shoulder, touching but not tempting, kissing but not tasting, holding but not taking, we spent our first night together in seven years, and it was markedly different from the last. Maybe it was our desire to get it right or to not repeat the mistakes of the past. And maybe it was the knowledge that even if we couldn't see him, Eli was near. For me, he felt ever-present. For now, it was enough just to hold Georgia, and I kept the fires banked.

When I mentioned walking her home as midnight became one and then became two, Georgia wrapped her arms around my mid-section, laid her head against my chest and defiantly told me no. And I hadn't argued very hard. Instead I'd stroked her hair and felt her fall asleep against me, leaving me alone with my thoughts and the fears that had only deepened as the hours passed. I wondered if the way I was feeling was simply a byproduct of love. Now that I had it, now that I acknowledged I needed it, I was terrified of losing it.

At dawn, I crept from the bed and across the room, pulling on my boots and a jacket, not planning to go much farther than my back deck. It needed to be refinished and if snow really was on the horizon, I wanted it done soon. As I left the room I caught a glimpse of the painting I'd begun the night before, the picture of Georgia's graceful back and my head bent above her. I would do more. I would fill my walls with paintings of us, if only to convince myself that she was mine and I was hers.

Maybe then I would lose this sense of dread.

The morning was cold, colder than the day before, and I considered going back inside for gloves. I considered too long, though, and my hands were already two steps ahead of my brain. I dove in, working quickly to escape the chill, my breath puffing out around me as I got started on the deck, the smoothing out of all the rough spots strangely therapeutic. The sun rose without warmth, peering above the eastern hills, slinking over the shadowy valley and drawing my eyes from the deck to watch her slowly climb. A rooster crowed belatedly, and I laughed at the shoddy effort. I heard a horse whinny in response to the rooster and looked across the grassy field to see Georgia's horses gathered a little ways off. Calico separated herself from the others and whinnied again, tossing her head and stretching her legs, as if she knew I was watching her. She galloped across the field and then turned and galloped back, shaking her mane and kicking up her heels as if she was grateful for the sunrise. Sackett joined her, nipping at her, nudging her playfully, and I smiled again, remembering how I'd compared the Palomino to Georgia once upon a time. I watched them prance and play for several minutes when my eyes were drawn to something I hadn't noticed before. Maybe it was because my attention had always been riveted on Georgia when she worked with the horses, or maybe it was because the only time I'd gotten close to Calico she had stood at my back, but Calico had a brand on her hind quarters that was different from Sackett's.

I set down the bucket of stain, laid my brush across the opening, and made my way across Gi's backyard to get a closer look. Sackett and Calico watched me come, and though Calico tossed her head and trotted in a circle, neither of them ran from me. Progress. But when Calico drew up beside the fence between us, I stopped short. Calico had a circle A brand on her left flank—an uppercase A inside a circle. Like the circled A on Molly's math test. Like the Circle A truck stop that bordered the field where Molly's remains were found. I felt the hair rise on my neck and the knot in my stomach increase in size. Eli kept showing me Calico, right from the start. And I couldn't help but wonder if there was more to it than just his very real affection for the animal.

I considered going inside and waking Georgia up, but pulled my phone out of my pocket and tapped in Tag's number instead, hoping he would hear it ring at seven a.m. on a Tuesday morning and actually answer it. He was not always an early riser.

"Mo," he answered on the third ring, and I could tell he'd been up for a while. He had that amped up ring to his voice that he got after spending a couple of hours pounding on someone in his gym.

"Tag."

"Now that we got our names out of the way, what's up?"

"Calico, Eli's horse, has a brand on her butt that's different from Georgia's other horses. Why would that be?"

"They bought her from someone after she was branded," Tag said simply. And I nodded, though he couldn't see me doing it.

"Calico has a circle A brand, Tag. A circle with a big A inside it." I waited, trusting he would know the significance.

Tag was silent for several long heartbeats, but I let the silence stretch without filling it, knowing his wheels were turning.

"It could just be a coincidence," he said at last, but I knew he didn't believe it. In my experience there were no coincidences. And Tag had spent enough time with me to know that.

I swore, using one of Tag's favorite words, and I heard the fear and frustration echo the exclamation.

"What's going on, man?" Tag asked.

"I don't know, Tag. I've got my dead mother sending me freaky dreams, more dead girls popping up on my walls, a son trying to tell me something that I am clearly not understanding, and a woman in my bed that I'm terrified of losing." I scrubbed at my face, suddenly tired, wishing I'd just stayed in bed with Georgia. I couldn't lose her if I never left her side.

"What's Eli showing you? Besides the horse." I was grateful Tag didn't comment on the woman in my bed. I knew he wanted to. I could practically hear his restraint crackling across our connection.

"Everything. Anything." I sighed. "He shows me everything."

"But most of all, what is he showing you?"

"Calico, Georgia . . . freakin' Stewy Stinker and the Bad Men."

"Who's the bad man?" Tag shot back sharply.

"No. It's not that. It's a book Georgia would always read Eli." But even as I said it, I wasn't so sure. I walked as I spoke, making my way back across the yard. Georgia stood framed in the opening of the sliding glass door, a cup of coffee wrapped in one hand, trying to keep the quilt from my bed secured around her with the other. Her hair tumbled around her shoulders and her face was still soft from sleep. It was enough to make me weak in the knees and chase all the bad men from my mind.

"Gotta go, Tag. The woman in my bed is awake."

"Lucky son-of-a-bitch. Later, Mo. And don't forget to ask her where she got the horse."

GEORGIA

ELI NEVER HAD A FAVORITE COLOR. He could never decide. Every day it was something new. Orange, apple red, sky blue, John Deere green. He stuck with yellow for a whole week because it was the color of sunshine, only to change his mind and declare that brown was the best because Calico, Eli and I all had brown eyes, just like dirt, and he really loved dirt. Whenever someone asked what his favorite was, he said something different, until one day he answered "rainbow."

Last year, on the anniversary of his death, I bought fifty big balloons in as many colors as I could find, rented a helium tank so I wouldn't have to transport them, and let them loose out in the corral, in my own private little ceremony. I thought it would make me feel better, but as I released the balloons and watched them float up, up and away, I was overcome with grief, seeing the fragile little bubbles, all that joyful color, floating away beyond my reach, never to return.

This year I didn't know what I would do. I liked the idea of planting trees, but it was the wrong time of year. I liked the idea of donating to a charity in Eli's name, but I didn't have much extra to give. Moses had incorporated Eli into the mural in the barn—Eli rode the white horse as it climbed into the clouds, his head flung back, his little arms raised, his bare feet curled against the haunches of the magnificent creature. Moses was almost done, and it was spectacular. My parents hadn't said a word about it, but I'd caught my dad standing, looking at it in wonder, tears streaming down his cheeks. My dad still blamed himself for Eli's death. There was plenty of blame to go around. But the way he looked at that picture, smiling through his tears, made me think he was letting it go. And maybe that was enough. Maybe the fact that we were all moving forward, that Moses was back, maybe that was enough. Maybe we didn't need any grand gestures to telegraph our remembrance.

As I left Moses that morning, insisting that I could walk around the corner without an escort, he pulled me to him, kissed me softly, and told me he would miss me. And then he watched me walk away as if I were the balloon and he was the one wishing he hadn't let go.

"Georgia!" he called suddenly, and I turned with a smile.

"Yeah?"

"Where did you get Calico?"

It was such a random question, so at odds with his longing-filled gaze, that I stared at him for a couple of seconds, my thoughts temporarily tangled.

"We got her from Sheriff Dawson. Why?"

GEORGIA

THE HOUSE FELT UNUSUALLY still as I slipped in the door, padded down the hall to my room, and got ready for my day. The door to my parents' room was closed, and at 8:30 on a Tuesday morning, that was pretty unusual. But I didn't question my good fortune, not wanting to defend myself or the fact that I hadn't come home the night before.

The conversation would come, and there were decisions to make. But not yet.

I had a busy morning lined up. I had a two-hour session with my autistic kids from ten until noon and after that, an exploratory interview with some military higher-ups from Hill Air Force Base who were interested in using Equine Therapy for airmen and their families struggling with PTSD. Hill AFB was in Ogden, two and a half hours north of Levan, and I wasn't sure yet how I would make that work if they wanted me on base several days a week. But I was willing to explore it, and I was starting to think it might be a Godsend. Plus, Moses had a place in Salt Lake, which was only thirty minutes from Ogden, making the commute a few days a week much more doable, making life a whole lot easier for Moses if we wanted to be together. Levan was a great place to live, but not for Moses. I couldn't imagine him wanting to move into Kathleen's old house and spend the rest of his life here, painting pictures and watching me train horses and teach people. But maybe there was a way for us to do both.

At three o'clock, Dale Garrett was coming to get Cuss. The ornery animal was sufficiently house-broken and I was looking forward to showing Dale his improvements. But when three rolled around, my classes and meetings done for the day, Dale didn't want to talk about Cuss. In fact, he arrived in his pick-up, pulling his trailer, clearly prepared to take Cuss home, but then he sat in his cab on the phone for a good twenty minutes, making me wait and wonder. He held up a finger when I finally approached his truck, indicating for me to hold on, and so I stood with my arms folded, waiting for him to finish his call, more than a little irritated. When he climbed out and I greeted him, turning immediately back toward the barn where Cuss was waiting for his riding demonstration, Dale didn't waste any time letting me know what was on his mind.

"Did you hear about the Kendrick girl?"

I stiffened but kept walking, the conversation I'd had with Moses last night, running through my mind. We talked about a Kendrick, but somehow I didn't think she was who Dale was referring to.

"Lisa?"

"Yeah. That's her. The little blonde, seventeen or so?"

I cringed inwardly but kept my face neutral. "Yeah. And no. I didn't hear."

"They found the van she drives, door hanging open, pulled off the side of the road just north of town. She left her boyfriend's house in Nephi last night and never came home. Her parents realized this morning, called the boyfriend, called her friends, called all the neighbors, and eventually called the police. Whole town is in an uproar."

"Oh, no," I breathed.

"Yeah. Unbelievable." He looked at me steadily. "People are talking about you again, Georgia. And it's a damn shame. But your name is forever going to be linked with his."

I raised my eyebrows and pursed my lips. "What are you talking about, Dale?"

"Nobody's waitin' around on this one. Word is out that they already dusted the van for prints. Just preliminary stuff. And someone leaked out that Moses Wright's prints are all over that van."

MOSES

I FELL ASLEEP. That was all. I'd finished sanding the deck, my eyes straying to Georgia's corrals and outbuildings throughout the morning, catching a glimpse of her now and then, which helped me relax and eased the nagging worry I could not shake. When my back started to scream and my arms were sloppy with fatigue, I took a break, fixed myself some lunch, and climbed into the big brass tub Georgia had occupied last night, making me miss her and contemplate how I was going to get her there again as soon as possible. The heat and the lapping water soothed me, and I hadn't slept at all the night before. My eyes grew heavy and my thoughts slowed, and I finished my bath in a muggy stupor, sluggishly pulled on some jeans, and fell across my bed on my belly, my face sinking into the pillow Georgia had slept on the night before.

I was asleep instantly.

I woke up with a gun pointed at my head.

"THAT WAS TOO EASY. I didn't know how this was all going to go down. I thought I'd have to shoot you straight up when I came through the front door."

I wondered why he hadn't, and then decided shooting me in the back while I slept would be harder to explain. And he was going to have an explanation, I was convinced of that. He was dressed in his uniform, dark brown pants and dress shirt ironed and tidy, so official. And I had a feeling I was officially dead.

"You here to arrest me or kill me, Sheriff?" I asked conversationally, my hands in the air as he ushered me down the narrow stairs, his gun at my back. I didn't know where we were going, but my feet and upper body were bare and I wasn't dressed to leave the house. I wasn't dressed for the narrative he might have in mind.

We walked through the kitchen and stopped.

"Grab one of those knives. In fact, grab the whole block," he instructed, nodding toward the new, black handled set of knives I'd purchased for the house.

I stared at him, unmoving. I was not going to help him kill me.

He fired the gun, burying a bullet in the cupboard near my head. His eyes were flat and his shooting hand was steady.

"Take the knife!" he repeated, raising his voice, his finger on the trigger, just waiting for me to comply. I considered him for a moment, my heart racing, pulse pounding, adrenaline making me want to grab the knives, just like he said, and start hurling them toward him. I reached toward the block and drew out the longest, sharpest knife of the bunch and held it loosely in my hand. The sheriff obviously hadn't talked to his nephew about my appreciation for knives.

"You want me to throw this at you, Sheriff? Maybe cut you a little, so it all looks like you had to do it? You're just here to arrest me for something, I'm not entirely clear what, and I come at you with a knife, so you have to shoot me. Is that your plan? Shouldn't you be reading me my rights or telling me why I'm under arrest?"

"I'm here to question you in the disappearance of Lisa Kendrick," he said, finger on the trigger, eyes on my knife, waiting for me to make my move so he could make his. "When you're dead, I'm going to find her here. Tied up somewhere. Drugged. And no one will question me, no one will care if you're dead."

I didn't know if he was crazy or if I was just missing something again.

"You mean Sylvie Kendrick?" I asked, my head spinning.

"I mean Lisa. Such a lucky break for me, seeing her walking along the street last night. And I knew you drove her van when you came to the jail to get David Taggert. It was like a little miracle. Just for me."

"Did you kill my mother? Is that how this all started, Sheriff?" I asked softly, trying to put the pieces together as quickly as I could.

"I didn't kill her. I loved her. I loved her so much. And she was a whore. Do you know how it feels to be in love with a whore?" He laughed, but it sounded more like a sob and he stopped immediately, gritted his teeth and kept his hand steady. But I'd touched a nerve. I'd touched THE nerve.

"You don't look like me at all. I couldn't believe it when I saw you. Just a tiny little thing hooked up to a bunch of machines. I thought they must have made a mistake. I thought you were mine," he said, and slapped his chest with his left hand. "I thought you were mine, but I'm the wrong color, aren't I?" Another laugh that made me wince, inch for the door, and grip the knife in my hand. He took an aggressive step toward me, but he wasn't finished talking.

"You sure as hell aren't mine! I was so stupid. Jenny was sleeping around, obviously. I would have given her anything she wanted. It didn't make any sense to me. Does that make sense to you?" Jacob Dawson peered up at me in puzzlement, clearly wanting me to say something that he still hadn't come to terms with in twenty-five years.

"She was messed up. I thought I could fix her, but she couldn't leave the shit alone. She couldn't leave it alone. Just like Molly Taggert and Sylvie Kendrick. They reminded me of her. Pretty girls, but so messed up. Hurting their families. I did them a favor. They were heading the same direction as Jenny, taking drugs, running away from home, selfish bitches. I did them a favor. Saved them from themselves, saved their families from more hurt."

"How many others were there? How many others girls did you save?" I asked, trying to keep the sarcasm out of my voice. "And what about Georgia? That was you, right? At the stampede. You tried to take Georgia. She doesn't quite fit your profile, Sheriff. Neither does Lisa Kendrick."

"I didn't mean to take Georgia. Her back was turned to me, and I thought she was someone else. But then you came and I had to cut her loose. You actually did me a favor, you know. I would have hated to hurt Georgia. And Lisa will be fine. She won't remember anything. I shot her so full of shit she'll be lucky if she remembers her own name."

I didn't say anything. He wasn't very tall, wiry and lean, and much smaller than I was. I towered above him and probably outweighed him by sixty pounds. But he had a gun. And he was completely out of his mind.

Grief, guilt, twisted logic, and years of trying to keep his sins locked away, of trying to hide his face from the people who loved and trusted him had slowly eaten away at his humanity, at his reason, at the light that separated him from the darkness that waited for him. And here he was, standing in my grandmother's kitchen, on the spot where she left this life, showing me exactly who he was. It must be a relief. But he didn't do it for absolution. He didn't do it to gloat or to explain. He did it because he was going to kill me, if the inky smear clouding the edges of my vision were any indication. And they always were. The lurkers knew his intentions. And they were there, waiting for him to carry them out.

"I knew you were just messing with me all this time. You painted Molly Taggert's face on the overpass and I knew that somehow, some-way, you knew. I knew you must have seen me that night at the Stampede. But you never said anything. You acted like you didn't know.

"But then I saw the walls, after Kathleen died." His eyes bounced toward the living room, toward the wall that neither of us could see from where we faced off. "All those pictures on the walls. The girls. You painted the girls! And still . . . you never said anything. I didn't know what you wanted. I tried to stop. I wanted people to think it was you. But then I saw her. On the fourth, I saw her. The same day Jenny died. And she looked like Jenny. She smiled at me, just like Jenny used to. And she was strung out. Higher than a kite. I followed her home that night. And I took her."

I didn't know who he was talking about, but I guessed it was the girl who'd been missing since July, the girl Tag had seen on a flyer at the bar in Nephi.

"Then last night, I'm at the old mill with my nephew, he's dropping a few things off, I'm waiting in the truck, and I see Georgia Shepherd slink out of there and run like she's seen something that's scared her to death. I had Terrence drive by her house and I see her heading to your place, all wrapped around you. Does she know? Have you told her about me?"

I waited, not sure what he wanted, not sure if it mattered. But I wasn't in the mood for pillow talk.

"And why do girls always want the trash? Jennifer did. Georgia does. I don't get it."

I waited again, the irony that a murderer of countless women was calling me trash not entirely lost on me.

"I wanted to see what Georgia was up to. What you both were up to. So I went back to the mill after Terrence dropped me off. I haven't been inside since it shut down thirty years ago. Never had reason to. Imagine my surprise when I saw your painting on the wall. Molly, Sylvie, Jenny, others too, lots of others. I don't know how you figured it out, or what you want, but you came back to Levan when I told you to stay away. I gave you every opportunity to just go. And now you're back here, painting again." His voice rose on the last note, desperately, as if he truly thought I'd been playing with him all this time, a game of cat and mouse that finally made him break. He thought I'd come back to Levan for him. He thought the painting at the old mill was new, a new attempt to smoke him out. And it had pushed him over the edge.

I wasn't afraid. It was the strangest thing. My heart pounded and it was hard to breathe, but those were physical responses. In my head, in the part of me that saw things that nobody else did, I was okay. I was calm. People are afraid of the unknown. But it wasn't unknown to me. Death didn't scare me. But leaving Georgia at the mercy of Jacob Dawson did. If he thought she knew what he had done, he would kill her.

I might die, but Jacob Dawson had to die too. I couldn't let him live. Even if Eli saw me kill him.

And Eli would see.

He stood to my left, just beyond the length of my outstretched hand, standing there in his Batman pajamas, complete with hood and cape. He smiled at me a little, that same sad smile that made me wonder how much of the child remained. He didn't have a body anymore, a body that could grow, a body that indicated the passing of years and the gathering of experience. But he wasn't a four-year-old little boy waiting for someone to explain to him what was happening. He knew. And he'd been trying to tell me all along.

He'd been lingering to take me home.

XXXI

GEORGIA

IT SOUNDED LIKE AN ENGINE back-firing in the distance, muted, unthreatening. But Dale Garrett and I both turned toward it, our ears cocked, brows furrowed.

"That was a gun-shot," he mused, his eyes trained on the back of Kathleen Wright's home across the field. And I started to run.

"Georgia!" Dale Garrett cried. "Stop! Georgia! Son-of-a-bitch, girl!" I didn't know if he was behind me or if he was digging out his cell phone, but I hoped it was the latter. He was old and fat, and I didn't want him killing himself trying to chase me across the field.

I don't know how long it took me to get through the round corral, across the field, and over the fence into Kathleen's back yard, but it felt like years. Decades. When I reached the back deck and threw myself at the sliding glass door only to find it locked tight, I screamed in frustration and dread. Moses had been out on that deck for the greater part of the day, but he'd still locked the damn door when he was done. I ran around the house, fear making my thoughts pop like firecrackers, whizzing around uncontrolled in my head.

A white, Chevy Tahoe with Juab County Sheriff's Department written along the side in gold lettering was parked out front next to Moses's black pick-up and as I rounded the corner and ran toward the front door, a black Hummer swung in, gravel flying as it lurched to a halt. David 'Tag' Taggert shot out of the vehicle with a gun in his hand and murder on his face, and I almost collapsed in relief.

But that was before I heard the second gun shot.

"Stay here!" Tag roared, running for the front door. So I followed him. I had to. And when he burst through the front door without pausing, the first thing I noticed was the smell. But it didn't smell like paint this time. It didn't smell like pies either. It smelled like gun powder, and it smelled like blood. And then Tag roared again, and I felt his arm jerk as he fired his gun, and then fired again. Another shot rang out and a bullet hit the dining room window. Glass shattered as Tag stepped over something and then sank to his knees. At first I thought he was hit and I reached for him, my view of the rest of the room blocked by his big back. Then I realized Tag had stepped over Sheriff Dawson who was sprawled, staring up at the ceiling, a huge knife sticking out of his chest, a gunshot wound to his head.

And then I saw Moses.

He was lying on his side on the kitchen floor, blood growing in an ever-widening pool around his body, and Tag was turning him, trying to staunch the flow of blood, cursing Moses, cursing God, cursing himself.

And just like when Gigi died all those years ago, when Moses was covered in paint instead of blood, when death was on the walls instead of in his eyes, I ran to him. And just like before, I was helpless to do anything for him.

MOSES

IT WAS LIGHT, I FELT SAFE, and I was perfectly aware of who I was and where I was. Eli stood beside me, his hand in mine, and from a distance there were others too, coming toward me. If I had to paint it all, I doubt I could, but maybe paint could better capture it than words. Yet even with the soft effervescence and the unyielding light all around me, it was Eli who held my attention. He lifted his chin and contemplated me, searching my face. And then he smiled.

"You're my dad." His voice was clear and sweet, and I recognized it from the memories he'd shared with me, though it was easier to hear now, unfiltered, crystalline almost.

"Yes," I nodded, gazing down at him. "I am. And you're my son."

"I'm Eli. And you love me."

"I do."

"I love you too. And you love my mom."

"Yes," I whispered, wishing with all my soul that Georgia was here. "I hate that she's alone now."

"She won't be alone forever. It passes so fast," Eli said wisely, even gently.

"Do you think she knows how much I love her?"

"You gave her flowers and said you were sorry."

"I did."

"You kissed her."

I could only nod.

"You painted her pictures and hugged her when she cried."

"Yeah," I whispered.

"You laughed with her too."

I nodded again.

"Those are all the ways to say I love you."

"They are?"

Eli nodded emphatically. He was quiet for a moment as if he was mulling something over. And then he spoke again.

"Sometimes you can choose, you know."

"What?" I asked."Sometimes you can choose. Most people choose to stay. It's beautiful here."

"Did you choose to stay?"

Eli shook his head. "Sometimes you can choose. Sometimes you can't."

I waited, my eyes soaking him in. He was so clear, so sharp, so present and perfect that I wanted to take him in my arms and never let him go.

"Did someone come for you when you died, Eli?" I said, almost pleading, needing to know someone had.

"Yes. Gigi did. And Grandma too."

"Grandma?"

"Your mom, silly."

I grinned at him. He reminded me of Georgia, but I felt the grin fade almost immediately. "I didn't know if my mom would be here. She wasn't a very good person," I replied softly. It surprised me to hear him call her grandma as if she fulfilled that role as well as Gigi did.

"Some people mean to be bad. Some people don't. Grandma didn't mean to be bad." It was such a basic concept, said with such child-like wisdom and such a simple acceptance of good versus evil, that I had no response but one.

"Can I hold you, Eli?"

He smiled and was immediately in my arms, his own arms around my neck. And I buried my head in his curls and felt the silk of the dark strands tickle my nose. He smelled like baby powder, clean straw, and freshly laundered socks. I caught a hint of Georgia's perfume, as if she'd held him tightly just like this, right before he left her, and he'd carried her with him ever since. He was warm and wiggly and his cheek was smooth and soft as he pressed it against mine.

When we dream we don't know we dream. In our dreams our bodies are solid, we touch, we kiss, we run, we feel. Our thoughts somehow create reality. It was like that here too. I knew I didn't have a body and neither did Eli. And it didn't matter. Eli was solid and whole in my arms and I was holding my son. And I never wanted to let go.

Eli pulled away slightly and looked at me seriously, his brown eyes so like his mother's that I wanted to drown in them. Then he unlocked his arms from around my neck and held my face in his small hands.

"You have to choose, Dad."

GEORGIA

MOSES DIED ON THE WAY TO THE HOSPITAL. That's what they told me later. They wouldn't let us ride with him, so Tag and I jumped in his Hummer and followed the ambulance, breaking speed records and stumbling into the emergency room when we finally reached Nephi.

And then we waited, clinging to each other, while they tried to bring Moses back. Tag's face was white and his hands shook with horror as he told me that he believed Jacob Dawson had killed his sister, and probably all the other girls as well.

"Moses called me this morning, Georgia. He asked about the brand on Calico, about the circle A. And it nagged at me. I ended up calling my dad and asking him about it, just on the off-chance he knew something. And he told me the circle A was Jacob Dawson's brand. We bought a couple of horses from him the summer Molly disappeared. The horses we bought had that brand. My father even gave one of them to Molly."

"Anderson ranches," I supplied, numbly. "Jacob Dawson's mother was an Anderson. She inherited the ranch and her brother inherited the mill when their father died. She handed the ranch and all the livestock over to Sheriff Dawson when he turned twenty-one."

A slew of police came to the hospital—some of the officers were from the Sheriff's Department, some from Nephi city—and Tag was taken in for questioning. I was questioned as well, though I was questioned at the hospital and allowed to remain there. The sheriff had been killed, and it was Tag's bullet that had killed him, that and the knife in his chest that Moses had apparently wielded. I was afraid for Tag and for Moses, and I was worried that the truth might never come out.

Then my parents arrived and in hushed, disbelieving tones, they told me that Lisa Kendrick had been found bound and drugged in Jacob Dawson's SUV. And suddenly everyone wasn't quite as sure of the world as they once had been. Ironically, it was Jacob Dawson who had once told me, "You can never get too comfortable around animals. Just

321

when you think you've got 'em figured out, they'll do something completely unexpected." And he would know.

When I could no longer be brave, I found the little chapel, buried my face in my blood-stained hands and talked to Eli, whispering to him, telling him about Moses, about our story, about how he came to be, about how he was the best parts of both of us. And then I tearfully told him that I needed him to bring Moses back one more time if he could.

"Send him back, Eli," I begged. "If you have any pull in that place at all, send him back."

MOSES

I TOLD YOU RIGHT UP FRONT, right in the beginning that I lost him. The day I met Eli, he was already gone. I knew he was dead. I knew, and yet it still hurt. So much. I didn't lose him the way Georgia did. But I still lost him. I lost him before I knew him. And I wasn't prepared.

And each day, as I grew to love him more, as I watched him, as he showed me his short life and his huge love, it got harder, not easier. In truth—since I've decided that's all I have—I would gladly submit myself to anything else. Anything but that. But that is what was given to me. And I wasn't prepared.

I can't tell you how it felt to say goodbye. How it felt to choose. But in the end, mercifully, the choice was made for me, and I didn't have to do either. I held my little boy in my arms, and I heard his mother's voice from somewhere far off, telling him our story. A story about how Eli was born, how he died, and how, from beyond the grave he healed us. And Eli and I listened together.

The first few words of every story are always the hardest. It's almost as if pulling them out, speaking them into existence, commits you to seeing it all through. As if once you start, you are required to finish.

And we weren't finished. Georgia and I weren't finished. I knew that. And Eli knew it.

"You have to go now, Dad," he whispered.

"I know."

I felt myself slipping, almost falling, much like the way it felt when I called down the waters.

"Goodnight Stewy Stinker," I heard him say, a smile in his voice.

"Goodnight Buzzard Bates," I said, my tongue so heavy in my mouth I could barely form the words.

"See you soon, Diehard Dad."

"See you soon, little man," I whispered, and then he was gone.

GEORGIA

THEY SHARED HIS STORY on the 10:00 news—the little baby left in a basket at a dingy laundromat in a bad neighborhood in West Valley City, abandoned by a drug addict and expected to have all sorts of problems. And they shared his story again, twenty-five years later—the story of Moses Wright, the artist who communed with the dead and brought down a killer.

Both Tag and Moses were absolved of any wrong-doing in the death of Sheriff Jacob Dawson. And they were cleared quickly when Sylvie Kendrick's remains were found on his property, along with the remains of several, still unidentified girls. Lisa Kendrick made a full recovery, and though she doesn't remember Sheriff Dawson abducting her, she does remember walking along the road and having a vehicle pull up behind her, lights flashing.

Jacob Dawson is believed to have killed more than a dozen girls in Utah in a twenty-five year period, and may be responsible for similar disappearances of girls matching the same profile in surrounding states. Considering that he had inherited one hundred acres of land, including the land that bordered the truck stop and the highway overpass where Molly Taggert was found, there was still a lot of ground to cover, and, sadly, a lot of bodies to uncover.

The whole town of Levan followed the story, watching the reports, pretending like they had the inside scoop, and making up what they didn't know, just to feel important, just like the first time Levan made the news. It was a great story, and people love stories, just like they love babies.

And although people loved the story of baby Moses who grew up to be a seer of sorts, when the news cameras left and life returned to normal, it was a story that many people had a hard time believing and accepting. Like Moses said, if you're afraid of the truth you'll never find it. But that was okay. We didn't especially want to be found.

We let people believe what they wanted and accept what they would. We let the colors blur and the details fade. And in the end, people would tell the story and pretend that's all it was. It was a great story, after all.

A story of before and after, of new beginnings and never-endings. A story flawed and fractured, crazy and cracked, and most of all, a love story.

Our story.

EPILOGUE

GEORGIA

"**D**ON'T MOVE, I'M ALMOST DONE," Moses insisted, and I sighed and laid my head back down on my arm. He was obsessed with painting me. My pregnant body wasn't especially beautiful, but Moses disagreed, including my round belly as one of his daily five greats, along with my legs, my eyes, my blonde hair, and the fact that my breasts were a full size bigger.

Who needed a photographer when your husband was a world-famous artist? I just hoped that someday nude paintings of Georgia Wright wouldn't be hanging in some rich old man's bedroom, or worse, in a museum where thousands of eyes perused my greats, daily.

"Moses?" I said softly.

"Yeah?" His eyes lifted from the canvas briefly.

"There's a new law in Georgia."

"Does it directly contradict one of the laws of Moses?"

"Yes. Yes it does," I confessed.

"Hmm. Let's hear it." He set his brush down, wiped his hands on a cloth and approached the bed where I was positioned, draped in a sheet like a Rubenesque Madonna. I learned the term from him, and he seemed to think it was a good thing.

"Thou shall not paint," I commanded sternly. He leaned over me, one knee on the bed, his strong arms bracketing my head, and I turned slightly, looking up at him.

"Ever?" He smiled. I watched his head descend and his lips brushed mine. But his golden-green eyes stayed open, watching me as he kissed me. My toes curled and my eyes fluttered, the sensation of lips tasting lips pulling me under.

"No. Not ever, just sometimes," I sighed.

"Just when I'm in Georgia?" he whispered, his mouth curving against mine.

"Yes. And I need you here often. All the time. Frequently."

Moses kissed me deeply, stroking his hands up over the curve of my abdomen, and the baby kicked enthusiastically, making us pull apart abruptly and laugh in wonder.

"It's pretty crowded in there," he said soberly, but his eyes danced. He was happy, and my heart was so full I couldn't catch my breath.

"It's crowded in here too." I rested my hand on my heart, trying not to be an emotional pregnant lady and failing miserably. "I love you, Moses," I said, cradling his face.

"I love you too, Georgia," he said. "Before, after, always."

MOSES

I TRIED NOT TO HAVE ANY EXPECTATIONS. Life after death was one thing, life coming into the world was another. Georgia was calm. Beautiful. An old pro, as she put it. But I had missed the first time around, and I was afraid to blink for fear of missing something. And I was not calm.

Tag was not calm either. He had to wait outside. He was my best friend, but even best friends did not share some things. Plus, I didn't think Georgia could give birth and keep us both from passing out.

It was all I could do to hold Georgia's hand and stay at her bedside, praying to God, to Gi, to Eli, to anyone who would listen, to give me strength and self-control. Strength to be the man Georgia needed and self-control to resist covering the walls of Georgia's hospital room in a frenzied mural.

When our daughter came into the world, screaming like it was ending, I could only cry with her. I'd turned into a crier. After years of controlling the waters, they seemed to be controlling me. But how could I not cry? She was beautiful. Perfect. Healthy. And when they put her on Georgia's chest and Georgia smiled at me like we'd made a miracle, I could only nod and agree. We'd made two of them.

"Kathleen," she said.

"Kathleen," I agreed.

"I think she might have your eyes and your nose," Georgia said, comforting our daughter who most definitely did not have my nose. Or at least not yet. But she did have my eyes. They were my mother's eyes too. I could admit that now.

"Do you have your daddy's eyes?" Georgia cooed.

"She's going to have your coloring. Your hair," I contributed, looking at the pale fuzz on Kathleen's tiny head and the rosy hue of her skin. I was already wondering what colors I would use to match it.

"She's got Eli's mouth, Moses. Maybe she'll have his smile," Georgia's own smile slipped a notch and my heart stuttered in my chest. We missed him. We missed Eli. And his absence was the only shadow on this moment.

"I hope so. It was a great smile," I said. I leaned in and kissed Georgia's mouth, the mouth that was just like Eli's, just like little Kathleen's.

"My hair, your eyes, Eli's smile, her great-grandmother's name . . ."

"And Tag's charm. Let's hope she has Tag's charm." We laughed together.

Then Georgia spoke softly to our little daughter, stroking her downy cheek, cradling her in her arms. "Those are five greats for you, Kathleen. Five greats for today and for always."

Georgia and I grew silent for a moment, studying our baby girl. She'd stopped crying and was looking past us, her eyes wide, her little hand wrapped around my finger.

I turned my head, wondering what she could see.

And from the corner of my eye I saw him too. Just a glimpse. Just for a moment. And I caught a flash of that smile.

THE END

Want to go back to Levan? Read Samuel and Josie's story in *Running Barefoot*, available exclusively on Amazon.

Other books by Amy Harmon:

Making Faces
Infinity + One
A Different Blue
Running Barefoot
Slow Dance in Purgatory
Prom Night in Purgatory

Keep up to date with Amy Harmon via:

Newsletter
(http://eepurl.com/46ciz)

Website
http://www.authoramyharmon.com

Twitter
https://twitter.com/aharmon_author

Facebook
http://www.facebook.com/authoramyharmon

ACKNOWLEDGEMENTS

With every book there are so many people to thank that I dread writing the acknowledgments for fear that I will leave someone out.

First, my children. They reap the benefits of my book writing, but they also suffer with a blank-eyed, over-worked mommy sometimes. I am grateful for their love, humor, and patient eye rolls. For my husband, Travis, thank you for your enthusiastic, understanding support. We will get back to the gym together, I promise.

For my parents and in-laws, siblings and friends, thank you for thinking I'm awesome, or for at least telling me I am. I love you all and appreciate all you do for me and Travis and the kids.

For my assistant, Tamara Debbaut, bless you. Seriously. You keep my head attached. I'm not sure how I got so lucky, but I'm grateful every day.

For Dystel and Goderich, the whole team, thank you for having my back and making me believe that I'm a real writer.

For Mandy Lawler and Alpha Literary Services, thank you for your friendship and for all your work on this release. I feel fortunate to have snagged you before your life gets very, very busy.

For Karey White for your invaluable editing services, thank you.

For Cassy Roop of Pink Ink Designs, thank you for the formatting and for coming through for me in a pinch! It's great to make new friends. Also, Hang Le, for the incredible cover of *The Law of Moses*. People are floored by your work.

For EAGALA Equine Therapy and Allison and McKenna for letting me come observe your therapy session and answering so many questions. It was so incredibly eye-opening and touching. If you are interested in learning more about this fascinating approach to therapy, visit http://www.eagala.org/

For my fellow authors who are so supporting and gracious, to the bloggers who are so kindly enthusiastic about my work, and most of all, to the readers and friends, all of you who have me in grateful tears daily, thank you from the bottom of my heart. XXOO

Special Note:

Calico the Wonder Horse or *The Saga of Stewy Stinker* is a real story written by Virginia Lee Burton (1909 - 1968), who is the author of many classic children's books, including *Mike Mulligan and his Steam Shovel* and *Katy and the Big Snow*. *Calico the Wonder Horse* is published by HMH Books for Young Readers and no copyright infringement was intended.

Made in the USA
Lexington, KY
18 November 2015